Extract From a Diary

I am afraid the green darkness will come back. It was so long ago, when I was a child of five, that the nightmare really began.

I remember being very frightened. I was alone in a strange room staring at a picture on the wall. The scene was of mountains and a lake . . . so peaceful and cool and green. I knew that if I stared at it for long enough the lake would draw me in and I would sink into those calm waters, down and down into its quiet depths.

Forgetfulness is green. The colours of pain are orange, red and gold – the colours of autumn and of fire.

Sometimes now I am afraid. I fought so hard to escape, but my grief seems unbearable and the swirling mists are gathering in my mind, waiting to claim me. If I return to the time of the green darkness I am lost.

One

I shall tell my diary all the secret things of my heart, things I have never dared to whisper to anyone else. Where to start? Perhaps with the day I first came to live with Grandma, because that's when my memories begin . . . except that I cannot recall much of that time at all; it is the time of the green darkness . . . the green of cool forgetfulness, of mists that wrapped about me, and a dimly perceived pain.

It was December 1975, almost Christmas. I was five years old, and until that time I am told I was a lively, pretty child with soft, fair hair, blue eyes and an enchanting smile, but that was before . . . the green darkness.

There was a moment when I opened my eyes and saw her sitting on the edge of my bed, an old woman with a gentle, lined face and eyes that gazed at me with sympathy. She was smiling, and her eyelashes were wet, as if she had been crying.

"It's going to be all right, Annabel dear." Her voice was muffled as though she spoke from a distance, through the mists that still seemed to swirl about me. "I'm taking you to live with me. I shall look after you from now on. You mustn't be frightened anymore."

For a few moments I was confused. I could not think where I was or what had happened to me, then, as I gazed into those understanding eyes, I knew that she was my grandmother and I was safe, lying in a bed, the sheets cool and smelling of lavender.

Grandmother's hands were gentle as they stroked my hair, her voice and touch reassuring. I wanted to tell her so but I could not make the words come. Tears ran down my cheeks as I thought of my father – where was he? There was something at the back of my mind, behind that shroud of mist, something terrifying. I was aware of a swift, sharp pain in my heart and a deep longing for my father. Why was he

E

FLAME CHILD

Linda Sole

This first world edition published in Great Britain 1998 by
SEVERN HOUSE PUBLISHERS LTD of
9–15 High Street, Sutton, Surrey SM1 1DF.
This first world edition published in the U.S.A. 1999 by
SEVERN HOUSE PUBLISHERS INC of
595 Madison Avenue, New York, N.Y. 10022.

British Library Cataloguing in Publication Data

Sole, Linda
       Flame child
       I. Title
       823.9'14 [F]

       ISBN 0-7278-2248-9

Typeset by Palimpsest Book Production Ltd,
Polmont, Stirlingshire, Scotland.
Printed and bound in Great Britain by
MPG Books Ltd, Bodmin, Cornwall.

sending me to live with Grandmother? And why did he hate me?

"Don't cry, Annabel." Grandmother bent to kiss my forehead and I caught the dry odour of old skin mixed with lavender water. Her thin, blue-veined hands pushed my hair back from my forehead. "Sleep now and don't upset yourself. Daddy didn't mean to be angry with you. He's very unhappy. When he's had time to think things through, he'll come and see you, he'll realise he was wrong. Until then, just remember I love you. You'll be safe with me."

I closed my eyes as she left the room, trying not to cry. It was difficult because I was frightened and confused. Why did I feel so strange, and what had she meant when she spoke of my father having made a mistake?

He was angry with me; I could not remember what had been said or why he was cross, all I knew for sure was that he hated me.

When I was alone I lay staring up at the ceiling. Why was I here in this strange place? There was another place, a place I knew was warm and comforting. In that place there had been someone who used to kiss me. She had smelled of flowers and youth, a happy, dancing scent that made me feel good inside. I could still feel the softness of her arms and hear the musical sound of her laughter.

I thought she might have been my mother, but I could not be certain. Something was hiding from me, a thing so terrifying that I was afraid to reach for it. Much better to stay in that cool, green mist.

I transferred my gaze to the window, fascinated as I watched snowflakes make patterns on the glass. How lovely they were, like little floating stars; it was a shame they only lasted a few seconds before they melted. They were falling faster and faster, filling my vision with whiteness, shutting out the mist that still swirled about me as I drifted into sleep.

The next morning I was taken on a long journey in a car; the car was big and old-fashioned and it had a musty smell of leather and petrol fumes. Before long I began to feel sick. I stared out of the window, consumed by misery, seeing nothing but snow, falling faster and faster, enveloping the countryside in a cold, white blanket. The brightness hurt my eyes but I could not cry;

I was sealed into a padded chamber where nothing and no one could reach me.

The journey seemed to go on and on endlessly, past trees and fields, along narrow, winding country roads and isolated houses that seemed miles from anywhere. I did not think I had ever been this way before and the strangeness was all part of my waking nightmare. I was aware of the passing of time and yet I knew nothing but the dull ache around my heart.

After what felt like an eternity, the car finally came to a halt in a street and Grandmother told me to get out. I hesitated momentarily, then let my feet touch the ground, feeling the crunch of crisp snow beneath my shiny, black patent shoes.

"This will be your new home now, Annabel," she said.

I stared towards the house and my heart zoomed all the way down to my shoes. Beyond the small front garden was a three-storey, grey stone building that rose forbiddingly out of the thick cushioning of snow, its windows narrow and uninviting, veiled from curious eyes by yellowed net curtains.

My first impression of a dark ugliness was confirmed as we entered the narrow hall. The curtains blocked out the light, making it a place of shadows; forgotten by time, the cumbersome furniture musty with age.

Grandmother's name was Lily Cox. She had thin, white hair that she often wore dragged off her face and wound tightly into a bun at the nape of her neck. Her face was deeply lined and she had little hairs sprouting from her chin. She always wore a long, black dress with a white lace collar, and had been a widow for years and years before I was born. At the time of the green darkness I may not have been aware of these things; they came to me later, over the years.

That day I was aware only of a change in my life, a change that I saw as a punishment. I was not sure why I was being punished, but knew I must have done something wicked to make my father send me away from him. There had been a time when he loved me, but that was long ago.

That bleak, unwelcoming house was all a part of a continuing nightmare. I had a vague sense of unease; I felt cold, heat and light; I knew when it was morning and when it was night. I ate if food was put in front of me, washed when taken to a bowl of water, slept, urinated and breathed but felt nothing. Time passed and I became accustomed to my surroundings, to the routine that

4

my grandmother mapped out for us, but I was not living; it was a strange, passive existence.

Grandmother entertained her friends two or three times a week. Like her they were all widows, women who lived alone in their dark, silent houses, old, forgotten and dried-up as they waited for death. They spoke in hushed tones they thought I couldn't hear, mostly about the village and people they knew who had died – and then there were the times when they talked about me.

"It's such a shame," the women said as they saw me perched in my chair, hair brushed back and tied with a ribbon, pinafore dress neat and clean, a spotless blouse: a silent, lifeless doll staring blankly in front of her. "She's been like this ever since it happened, you say? Is there no improvement – no sign of her coming out of it?"

"Her father thought she was pretending at first." Grandmother looked at me with her sad old eyes and sighed. "I told him a child of Annabel's age couldn't fake something like this. Poor Philip was almost out of his mind with grief – but to accuse her! I know what he's going through, but I can't understand why he blames her."

"Poor little mite. As if she could possibly have had anything to do with it. Mind you, when you think of what he's lost . . . wife and baby . . ."

"Shush!" Grandmother put a finger to her lips. "We don't talk about the fire. It might upset the child. We can't be sure how much she remembers."

"She was there . . . actually in the room . . . wasn't she?"

"Philip found her standing outside the nursery. He carried her to safety then went back but it was too late."

Later, much later, when all the fragments of their gossip came back to haunt me, I would wonder what it all meant, but for the moment I listened and stored the pieces of the puzzle subconsciously.

I was for the time being cocooned in my cottonwool wrappings, within the green darkness, safe from the pain and guilt that was to lie so heavily on my mind for much of my life.

Grandmother carried in the Christmas tree; the sharp scent of pine stirred memories, bringing back a hazy picture of the woman who smelled of flowers and spring rain. Pain struck me to the heart, parting the layers of green-coloured mist to show me her face.

Grandmother glanced at me as I cried out. She began to talk of all the treats she was preparing for the festivities, chattering brightly, as if she sensed I was hurting.

"Come and help me dress the tree, Annabel," she invited, holding out her hand to me. "Shall we put the fairy on top?"

I nodded dumbly, watching as she took the pink and white doll in her hand and showed it to me. It was then that a picture flashed into my mind, bringing a memory so sharp, so bittersweet that the pain was unbearable. Reacting blindly in my misery, I snatched the fairy and threw it to the ground, stamping on its smiling face, crushing it beneath my feet.

"Annabel!" Grandmother cried. "Why did you do that? Now it's broken and it was so pretty."

She bent to gather the remains of the doll, then turned to me with a hurt expression in her eyes.

"Why?" she asked again. "Can't you tell me? Can't you speak to me, Annabel? Tell me what is hurting you so much that you haven't uttered a word for weeks . . ."

I shook my head, shrinking away in sudden fear as the lights began to flash behind my eyes. The haze was shimmering and the harsh colours were about to break through. It hurt too much. The pain was intense; I couldn't bear it. My mouth opened to scream but no sound came out.

"It doesn't matter, dearest," Grandmother said as she saw my distress. "It was only a doll . . . only a doll."

Her hand was reaching towards me. I retreated, my eyes drawn to something behind her . . . in the corner of the room. The brightness was leaping up in the shadows and the crackling noise filled my ears, beating at my brain, trying to force its way into my consciousness. I could smell the awful stench of burning, and fear coursed through me as I saw a shape in the middle of the brightness. The screaming started in my head. I put my hands to my ears as I tried to shut it out, but it went on and on, getting louder and louder until I could not bear it any longer.

"Annabel – what is it? Have you remembered something? Tell me – you must tell me, darling."

I shook my head and backed away from her, eyes darting in fear. I did not want to remember. I wanted to go back to the safe, cool world of my green darkness.

Whirling round, I ran from that room, from the terrifying brightness in the corner and reality.

"Annabel." Grandmother's soothing voice brought me back from that other place. "Daddy is here. He wants to see you, darling. He has a present for you." Taking her hand, I allowed her to lead me downstairs to the parlour. The Christmas tree blazed with tinsel and fairy lights; there was a silver star on top. My gaze was dragged unwillingly to the corner of the room but the brightness had gone and there was only a straggling fern in a brass pot.

My father was standing in front of the fireplace. For some reason I was reluctant to look at him, reluctant to meet the accusing expression in his eyes. Why was he staring at me like that, almost as if he hated me? He seemed so different from the father I had once known and loved.

This man looked tired and weary, his chin covered in a dark stubble. Somewhere in the deep recesses of my mind there was another man, a man who had smiled and kissed me with tenderness. But that was long before . . . before it all changed.

I wanted to hold on to my place of safety but this man was drawing me out; I could feel a sensation like pins and needles down my spine but I closed my mind to it; I was not going to give in to him.

"Hello, Annabel," he said. "How are you today?"

I stared at him. Why was he pretending to be kind? We both knew he didn't love me anymore. It was there in his eyes . . . the disgust and hatred. He could hardly bear to look at me. Once he had loved me; he had called me his darling and kissed me, tossing me into the air until I shrieked with pleasure . . . but that was before the green darkness.

"I've brought you a present," he said, holding out a parcel wrapped in shiny paper. "It's Christmas, Annabel. You know what Christmas is, don't you? You always loved it."

I made no response to his question, though I knew what he was saying as I knew so many other things, vaguely, without substance. The parcel was held out temptingly under my nose but I did not try to take it. So he unwrapped it for me, stripping away the glittery paper piece by piece as I watched in a silent, horrified fascination, sensing his intensity and knowing he was trying to punish me.

"It's a doll," he said and thrust it out for me to see. "A baby doll, Annabel. A baby you can hold . . . like the baby brother you . . ."

"No!" my grandmother cried suddenly. "No, Philip. Not in my house. Don't you dare to say such a terrible thing to her. I won't have it, do you hear? I won't let you blame her for what happened."

"No . . ." I whispered. "No, Daddy . . . No! No! No!" And then I screamed, loudly, piercingly and long . . . long after he had walked from the room. I went on screaming until the doctor came and gave me something that made me sleep.

It must have been after that day that the dream began to haunt me. At first it was not really a dream, that came more slowly over the years: at the start it was a vague sense of unease and . . . guilt.

From then on the memories are clearer. I remember waking up after the doctor's visit and feeling sick. My grandmother was sitting by my bed and she looked anxious; her eyes were watery and she seemed weary. I reached out to take her hand in mine, feeling the papery thinness of her skin. Her hand felt cold like ice.

"Are you ill, Grandma?" I asked and she shook her head, blinking as if struggling with some deep emotion that was painful to her. "Have I been naughty? Have I done something bad?"

"No, my darling, of course you haven't," she said and bent to kiss me, her lips dry against my damp cheeks. "I love you so much, Annabel. We shall manage together, you and me, you'll see."

There was something upsetting her, some deep grief she was trying to hide. My fingers tightened about hers and she squeezed them so hard it hurt, but I didn't cry out.

"What's wrong, Grandma? Why have you been crying?"

"Your father . . ." She blinked furiously and looked away from me, controlling the tears. "How much do you remember of what happened before you came here, Annabel?"

I screwed up my forehead, trying to remember but there was a strange blankness in my mind.

"You brought me here in a car," I said slowly. "It was Christmas and Daddy came. He was cross with me—" My hand

8

trembled in hers as for a moment I almost saw something that frightened me. "Why was he cross with me?"

"Don't you remember anything else, Annabel?"

I shook my head but it wasn't quite true; there was a curtain across that part of my mind people call memory. I could see shapes and pictures behind the veil of gauze, but at this time they made no sense. It was only later that I began to put together the pieces of the puzzle, to make the picture that would haunt me for so many years.

"Your father was upset," Grandmother said. "He didn't mean what he said, he didn't mean to accuse you of starting the fire. In his heart he knows it wasn't your fault. It couldn't be." This last more to herself than me. "It couldn't be—"

"The fire?"

The lights were hurting behind my eyes and I could hear the screaming . . . such terrible screams: a woman's screams.

"Just forget it." Grandmother patted my cheek and stood up. "If you can't remember anything that may be for the best. Just remember that I love you, that I'm going to take care of you." She gave me a loving smile. "And now I'm going to bring you something nice to eat."

Grandmother went away. I sat up in bed and wondered about what she had told me. What did she mean about my being blamed for starting a fire? I was never allowed near the fire in the nursery: there was a big wire guard right over it.

The nursery!

Where had that come from? It was a place where I had felt safe and warm. I could see it clearly in my mind, picture the large, old, velvet-covered sofa with its lumpy seat and pile of cushions, the dark blue and gold patterned carpet and the fluffy, white rug in front of the fireplace, my toys scattered about the floor . . . building bricks, dolls and a train. No, the train wasn't mine.

The lights were flashing behind my eyes again; it hurt and I didn't want to see the pictures they conjured up. I didn't want to remember, didn't want to smell that awful stench of burning; I didn't want to feel that mind numbing terror I had felt once before . . . before the green darkness. But I was not in that cool, green place now; I had come back and I knew I would not be able to escape to my other world again.

My grandmother returned with a tray containing a mug of

warm milk, biscuits and a chocolate cake, which she deposited on my lap.

"There you are," she said. "You deserve a treat after what happened yesterday."

"Was there a fire in the nursery, Grandma?"

She looked startled. "So you do remember?"

"I remember the nursery – but there was always a guard in front of the fire." My eyes went to her face and I saw a troubled expression there; it was as if she were confused, as if she were struggling against her own emotions. "There was a cot with white nylon frills . . ."

"Don't think about it, Annabel." She caught my hand and held it tightly. "It's all over now and best to let it rest. Don't try to remember. Just forget it all." She smiled and bent to kiss my cheek. "Eat up now. I made that cake specially for you."

Perhaps if Grandmother had told me the truth then I might have been spared so many years of uncertainty, of half-remembered dreams and the vague, unsettling sense of guilt.

Two

G randmother took me to the park today and we saw a squirrel eating acorns. It was so tame it let us get right up to it and I threw it a piece of my biscuit. Grandmother and I laughed as we watched the squirrel nibbling at the crunchy biscuit.

I love my grandmother, but she is so old. Sometimes I long for my mother. I do so wish I could remember her properly; I think she was pretty but I can't be certain. I am sure Grandmother has photographs of her but she has never shown them to me; she seems terrified of doing or saying anything that might remind me of . . . that other time.

All I know for certain is that my mother died when I was five and it made me ill. It was a long time before I could talk apparently.

I do remember my father – and the day he died.

It had been raining that day. I was in my room, reading the picture book Grandmother and I had borrowed from the library when I heard someone at the door. There were strange voices downstairs – one of them deep and – strong and I thought it might be my father: we had very few male visitors in Grandmother's house.

It had been so long since my father had come to see us – at least a year, for I was six and a half now. Suddenly, I was overcome with the desire to see him again and I went downstairs, pausing outside the open parlour door. I couldn't see who was inside but as the man spoke again, I knew it was not my father.

"He couldn't have suffered much," the voice said. "The road was greasy and the car went into a tree; hit it head on; must have been over in seconds."

"Had . . . had he been drinking?"

"Yes, I'm afraid so."

"It was the death of his wife and son," Grandmother said and there was a deep grief in her voice. "He went to pieces after it. Even blamed his own daughter for the fire, told me she had been playing with matches . . . but of course Annabel couldn't have

11

done it. I was afraid something like this would happen. I've felt
. . . that he simply didn't want to live."

"You don't believe it was suicide? It was an accident, Mrs
Cox, that's all – an accident."

"Perhaps." She sounded unconvinced. "All I know is that he
told me there was no reason for him to go on living now they
were dead."

"But his daughter—"

"I tried to make him think of his responsibility to Annabel but
he seemed to hate her. He wouldn't visit her, wouldn't have her
near him."

I crept away from the door and back up the stairs to my room, a
deep misery stirring inside me. My father hated me; he blamed me
for the deaths of my mother and baby brother; he believed that I had
set fire to the nursery with his matches. Had I? I still wasn't sure.

Sitting on the edge of my bed, rocking to and fro in my grief –
grief for the loss of my father as well as that of my mother and
brother – I tried to remember. There was a dream that haunted me
sometimes, a dream in which I saw myself in the nursery, a lighted
match in my hand. Perhaps I had dropped that match into the cot.

"No, Daddy," I whispered. "Please don't be cross with me. I
didn't do it . . . I didn't do it."

Was that true? The dream always ended with me waking up
in fright. I never saw beyond the moment the match was struck.
I did not know whether I was guilty or innocent, but I felt that I
must have done something wicked to make my father hate me
so much that he would rather die than see me again.

When we returned from the park that spring day almost five
years after my father's death, Grandmother had a funny turn.
She went a strange grey colour and couldn't breathe very well.
Watching her gasping and holding her chest as if she were in
terrible pain, I was very frightened. I did not know what to do
until she asked me to telephone for the doctor and I rushed
to obey.

The doctor came very quickly; he took her pulse, listened to
her heart, then said she ought to be in bed.

"It was nothing much," she replied, looking annoyed now that
she was feeling better. "I shouldn't have made a fuss. I'm all
right now – and I have to get Annabel's tea ready."

"I'm sure Annabel could get her own tea, couldn't you, my

12

dear?" The doctor was tall and thin and smiled down at me from a great height. "How old are you now?"

"Eleven, twelve soon," I said. "I could get tea for us both every day if Grandma would let me."

"There you are." He turned back to her. "It's time you let her do a few small tasks for you, or you could employ a housekeeper, someone to live in and look after the pair of you. It was a wonderful thing you did, taking Annabel in at your age, but you have to remember that you are over seventy now, Mrs Cox. Perhaps it's time to take things a little easier."

Grandmother tutted beneath her breath, but I could see that she was thinking about what he'd suggested. I wasn't sure then what was going through her mind, but it wasn't too long before I found out.

Grandmother was sending me away to school! I didn't want to go to boarding school, I would hate it. I knew I would hate it. When she told me I cried and cried, but although her mouth twisted with grief at my distress, she told me it couldn't be helped.

"You can come home in the holidays," she said. "I haven't stopped loving you, darling. This isn't a punishment because you've been naughty, you mustn't think that; it's just that I get so tired sometimes – and the doctor thinks it would be better for you to be with girls of your own age."

"But I don't want to go away," I cried, feeling desperate. How could she say she loved me when I was being banished? "Let me stay with you, please don't make me go to that hateful place. I've tried to be good . . . honestly I have."

"It isn't because you've done something wrong; I told you, darling. Please don't make such a fuss. I love you so much, and this is breaking my poor old heart."

Gazing up at her, I noticed the weariness in her face and was suddenly afraid. If she died I should be truly alone with no one to love me. To be loved was almost all that mattered to me.

"If it's best for you, I shall go," I said. "You mustn't be upset, you mustn't be ill because of me."

"If I'm ill it's because I'm old," she said and put her arms about me. "Never believe that you've been a burden to me, darling. I've enjoyed having you with me."

I swallowed my tears but said nothing.

13

"You'll be able to come home in the holidays and you're nearly twelve now . . . not a little girl any more."

I blinked back my tears. I hated the idea of boarding school, but my grandmother was right; it was too much trouble for her to have a child in the house all the time. She needed someone to look after her.

From the moment I arrived, I hated Rutledge Manor; I hated the teachers and the other girls, being forced to share a dormitory with five strangers, being away from home and being the new girl: all the others had started at the beginning of term. It made me different. But I was different anyway, there was something about me that made me an object of hostility from the start. I saw it in the way they looked at me and heard it in their laughter; they hated me as much as I hated them.

For the first few weeks I was utterly miserable. I wrote at least six letters to my grandmother begging her to take me home, but never posted any of them. She was old and not very well; I could never let her know how unhappy I was at this school; I would just have to bear it.

Then, when I had been at the Manor for just over a month, another girl arrived and things began to change. As soon as I noticed Mary Green standing in the assembly hall looking lost and unhappy, I knew exactly how she felt; the first day or so had been hell for me, too. One of the older girls had started to taunt her and she looked as if she wanted to cry.

"Leave her alone, Sally Barnes," I said, going up to poor Mary and putting my arm about her shoulders. "If you don't, I'll pull your plaits so hard you will have a headache for a week."

"You wouldn't dare," Sally said, her thin, spiteful face scowling at me. "I'm bigger than you are."

I looked at her and was suddenly angry; she was bigger than either Mary or I but I didn't care. "You might be bigger but you're stupid," I said. "If I see you upsetting Mary again, I'll make you sorry."

Just how I would achieve that was debatable, but like all bullies Sally was a coward at heart. She stared at me as if trying to make up her mind whether I really meant my threat, then went a funny putty colour and ran off with her friends. I knew then that neither Mary nor I would have any more trouble from that source.

14

"Oh, Annabel," Mary said gratefully. "Thank you for rescuing me." She offered a bag of sticky toffees wrapped in gold paper. "Take two or three, as many as you like. You're my best friend, Annabel. We'll do everything together, won't we?"

"Yes, if you like," I said, trying to sound offhand. "We can be friends."

Mary was a little plump, with a round, soft face, light brown hair and chocolate-coloured eyes; she seemed a bit of a baby, but she was still a lot better than most of the other girls. Mary told me her mother was dead and her father worked abroad for a construction company; that's why she'd had to come to boarding school. She didn't even have a grandmother to stay with in the holidays, so she wasn't as lucky as me.

I decided I would have to take her under my wing. Perhaps Grandmother would let me invite her to stay sometimes.

My birthday was on the twelfth of July and I was twelve at last. Grandmother bought me a new dress and shoes, then we went out to tea and to the park to feed the squirrels. I had wanted to ask Mary to stay for my birthday, but she had been taken to France for five weeks by her father. She invited me to go with them, but I preferred to be with Grandmother.

"It's a shame you couldn't have had your friend to stay," Grandmother said as we walked back to the house, enjoying the warm sunshine. "I'm glad you've found a friend at school. I've found a friend too, my dear. Her name is Miss Fisher and she's coming to live here and take care of me."

"Are you feeling worse?" I asked, studying her face. She was beginning to look very ancient and frail. I experienced a flicker of fear. I could not bear to lose her: she was all I had, the only one who loved me.

"No, I'm not worse, but the doctor was right, it is time I had someone in to look after me."

"When is she coming, this Miss Fisher?"

"Next week." Grandmother smiled and squeezed my hand. "I'm sure you will like her, Annabel."

I was determined to like the new housekeeper for her sake, and I did try, but from the moment she walked into the house, a mutual antipathy sprang up between us.

She was thin and sour, and she looked at me with dislike,

15

sniffing as Grandmother introduced us in a way that showed what she thought of me.

"You'll be going back to school soon," she said, clearly relishing the thought of my departure. "Your grandmother will get some peace then."

"Annabel is no trouble to me," Grandmother said, giving me a loving glance. "But I must admit I do tire easily these days."

Miss Fisher sniffed again but said no more. I knew she couldn't wait to get me out of the house.

She didn't have long to wait. All too soon it was time for me to return to boarding school. It was hard to leave Grandmother, but once I was back with Mary it wasn't so awful after all.

Mary was very brown. She was full of her holiday and told me all about it; I listened but I didn't envy her; it sounded as though she was left to amuse herself most of the time while her father attended business meetings. I had enjoyed myself with Grandmother. I wondered how she was and whether Miss Fisher was looking after her properly.

I might have gone on wondering, brooding about my home, except that something happened, something that was rather disturbing. If anyone had discovered what we'd done, I think we would have been expelled. I made Mary promise not to tell any of the other girls; she was frightened to death; she didn't want to do it, but I persuaded her.

It was our free afternoon and we went out into the gardens to enjoy that late summer sunshine. It was what they called an Indian summer, balmy days with soft breezes, and much warmer than usual for October.

There was a part of the school grounds that was out of bounds to the girls, though not to the teachers, who had their own private entrance, which they locked with a key – to keep us out, I suppose.

Mary and I used to sneak into the forbidden area through a gap in the hedge. We liked it in the forbidden zone, as we called it, because there were lots of trees to climb – another activity much frowned upon by our teachers – and because of the summer house.

Mary and I had been to the old summer house a few times; it was musty inside and the furniture was falling to bits. It had originally belonged to the family who owned the house before it was turned into a school, and looked as if it had been someone's favourite hideaway. There were sofas with cushions and little tables, books, an old gramophone with a handle but no records. We knew we ought not to go there, of course, but sometimes it's fun to do something you're not supposed to do and we had come to think of it as our special place.

Mary suggested we should go that particular afternoon. "We haven't been for ages," she said. "I've got some chocolate and a sherbert dip – let's go there and eat them."

Mary always seemed to have sweets and money in her pocket. Her father gave her a generous allowance to compensate for being away so often. It meant she ate far too many sweets and was miserable because she was fat.

"All right," I said. "Let's go to the summer house then, at least we shall be on our own."

We had to climb the garden wall to get into the forbidden territory. For some reason the gardener had recently mended the hole in our hedge, and the gate was locked. Miss Hadley had a key; I'd seen her using it only a day or so earlier.

Miss Hadley was our games mistress and one of the nicest teachers; she was younger than most of them, pretty and fun to be with. I liked her a lot.

The sun was so warm that afternoon. Mary and I played around a little, chasing each other and giggling as we experienced the release of being out of sight of the main building, taking our time about getting to the summer house.

Mary saw Miss Hadley first. She had entered through the gate, but because of the thick bushes where we had been playing, she did not see us as she passed. She went directly to the summer house, entered it, and closed the door behind her.

"Bother!" Mary looked disappointed. "We shan't be able to go there now. What does she want to go there for? It's our special place."

"Maybe she'll come out in a minute. We'll wait and see."

"I'll bet she's got a lover," Mary said and I stared at her in surprise.

"What do you mean? Miss Hadley? She must be nearly thirty," I scoffed in childish innocence. "Anyway, why would lovers want to meet here? There's nothing to do in there. I should have thought he would take her dancing or to the pictures."

I see now that I was immature for my age. Grandmother had told me nothing of what happens between a man and a woman,

17

and we seldom had a man in the house, unelss he came to clean the windows or repair a tap. Perhaps, because I had little contact with the other girls at school, I had been excluded from the whispering that went on in corners about sex and lovers. I knew about kissing, but that was the extent of my knowledge.

"Lovers do all sorts of things," Mary said importantly and then went bright red. "I saw something when I was in France this summer—"

"Tell me then," I demanded. "Come on, Mary – what did you see? What do lovers do except sloppy things like kissing and holding hands? I've always wanted to know."

Mary shook her head. "I can't—" she whispered. "It was awful." She looked as if she regretted having mentioned it at all.

I glanced consideringly towards the summer house. Was Miss Hadley doing something dreadful in there?

"I'm going to look through the window. Come on, Mary, you look too."

She shook her head, her face on fire. "I don't want to see."

"Well, you're jolly well going to," I cried and grabbed hold of her arm. She struggled and pulled back, but I wouldn't let go. "If you don't, you won't be my friend any more."

She looked upset, then nodded, giving in as she usually did when I insisted. "All right then, but I'm telling you – it's horrible."

Her declaration only made me more curious, and I was determined to see what was going on in there. We crept up to the small wooden building and peered through the windows. At first it was difficult to see anything through the layers of dirt and cobwebs that had built up over the years, then as my eyes became accustomed to the gloom inside, I saw them lying on the floor. At least I could see a man – a man with no clothes on – and he was on top of Miss Hadley, who was also undressed.

"See . . ." Mary hissed and averted her eyes in embarrassment. "I told you it was horrible. Let's go!"

"Shush!" I pressed a finger to my lips and turned back to the window, watching the man's bottom going up and down in an odd and rather frenzied way. Miss Hadley's legs were wrapped about him and she seemed to be wriggling about a lot underneath him.

I turned and grinned at Mary, thinking it was funny. She wasn't looking; her eyes were shut and her face was screwed up as if she felt sick. What a baby she was! I squinted through the window again. Now it looked as if the man with no clothes on was eating Miss Hadley's breasts. She was making strange noises, sort of screeching and moaning.

"Do you think he's hurting her?" Mary whispered. "When I saw it on holiday, the girl was screaming."

"Miss Hadley looks as if she's enjoying it . . . Oh, they've finished. I wonder why."

"Let's go," Mary begged, pulling at my arm. "Please, Annabel."

Mary looked so upset that I agreed, and we ran away. I was laughing, but Mary was quiet. When I asked what was wrong, she said everything was spoilt now and we must never go back to the summer house.

I agreed, but secretly I had other plans. If Mary didn't want to go, I would go alone. I was intrigued by what I had seen and wanted to learn more. From now on I would watch for Miss Hadley using her key to the gate and follow her.

I never did see her use that key, despite keeping a watchful eye on her in our free periods. About a year later, she was dismissed from her post at the school. I saw her leaving the headmistress's office in tears one morning after break and went up to her.

"Is something the matter?"

"It's that miserable old spinster in there," she muttered, blowing her nose and glancing back over her shoulder. "She's never had it and she hates to think anyone else should enjoy it . . ."

"Do you mean sex, Miss Hadley?"

She stared at me, her face slowly turning a brick red. "What do you know about sex, Annabel? You're far too young."

"I don't know anything, Miss Hadley." I gave her an innocent look. "I just wondered if that was what you meant."

"You may as well know," she said on a spurt of temper. "I've been dismissed for behaviour not fitting to my position here – in other words I've had a man. Well, I'm not ashamed of it and I don't care who knows."

I watched her walk away. I was sorry that she was leaving. I liked her and thought it unfair that she should be dismissed for doing something that looked like fun.

A lot of the girls felt the same way; I organised a collection and we bought her a leaving present. There was a lot of gossip and speculation, of course, but no one knew the real reason for her hasty departure. Mary might suspect it, but I didn't let her in on my secret.

I rather liked having a secret all of my own.

Miss Fisher had a secret, too. I discovered it when I went home for Christmas that year. She told me herself; I don't think she really meant to but it sort of slipped out.

Grandmother had sent me up to Miss Fisher's room to take her a letter that had arrived for her with the morning's post, and I walked straight in without knocking. She was sitting on the edge of the bed, looking at a pile of faded photographs and, as I went in, she jumped and spilled them all over the floor. I bent down and picked them up for her. They were all of a baby dressed in a knitted suit.

She snatched them from me with a scowl. "They're mine, give them here!"

"I was only trying to help," I said. "There's no need to look like that. It is a lovely baby – a boy, isn't it? Does he belong to a friend of yours?"

"That's none of your business," she muttered. "Coming in here, spying on me. I'm entitled to my private life same as anyone else." Her pale eyes were hostile as she glared at me. "You wouldn't like it if I pried into your secrets, miss!"

Why was she so angry? For a while it puzzled me, then the penny dropped. Miss Fisher had had a baby and she had never been married.

If anything it made me dislike her less knowing she wasn't as righteous as she had made out. I thought about Miss Fisher and her baby a lot after that and wondered what had happened to make her look sour all the time. Obviously, life had not been kind to her.

Was Miss Hadley going to have a baby? Was that the reason she'd had to leave the school?

Grandmother wouldn't tell me any more about Miss Fisher; she made me promise I wouldn't reveal what I had discovered to anyone else, and I didn't. It made our dour housekeeper a little more human; perhaps I should even get to like her in time.

At least she took good care of my grandmother and that was all that really mattered. Sometimes Grandmother seemed so frail now, and it upset me. I did not see how I should bear it if she died and left me completely alone.

20

Three

The wind was bitterly cold in the churchyard; it felt more like winter than June, and there was a dismal air about the moss-grown headstones, despite the valiant efforts of a thrush to cheer us with its song from the branches of a rowan tree. When they lowered Grandmother's coffin into the earth I felt the icy chills chase up and down my spine. She was dead; I would never see her face again, never see her smile or feel the gentle touch of her hands. How could I bear it? She had gone and I was alone; there was no one to care whether I lived or died. As I trickled a handful of earth into the chasm of her grave I felt that I too wanted to die.

The blessing was over; everyone was walking away, leaving her there. I stayed where I was, my feet seeming glued to the ground, unwilling to leave her there in that dark, cold place. I loved her. She was the one person who had ever really loved me. I felt it would be a betrayal of that love to desert her. I wanted her back, wanted to see her once more, to touch her, kiss her. Tears welled up in my eyes and slipped down my cheeks. If only this was India, then I could throw myself on her funeral pyre! I could die with her and then I would not feel this pain.

"Grandma . . . why did you leave me?"

"Come along, Annabel." Miss Fisher took my arm, pulling me back from the edge. "You can't do her any good now and she wouldn't want all this fuss."

Her voice rasped against my nerve ends, stinging me to a fierce response. I glanced at her, hating her at that moment.

"How do you know what she wants? She can't tell you, she's dead."

Edith Fisher was dressed in the severest black with a felt hat squashed down on her tightly permed hair. I thought she looked like a hooded crow with her long nose and sharp eyes. She was thin, ugly and bitter because of the way life had treated her; there was no sympathy in her face for me and I knew she disliked me. I wasn't very fond of her, but I was grateful for her devotion to my grandmother. If it had not been for Miss Fisher, Grandmother would have had to spend her last years in a nursing home. Instead, she had been able to stay at home, waited on with a tender patience by Edith until her final illness, which had been mercifully short.

"Are we going back to the house now?" I asked as she guided me from the churchyard, her fingers digging painfully into my arm. "What am I supposed to do? Should I ask people back for tea?"

"Mr Chambers will be coming," she said, sniffing in a way that showed her disapproval, both of the question and me. "Your grandmother's friends will expect to be asked. I prepared everything before we left."

Her attitude was huffy and told me I should have known she would be prepared: my lack of trust was not appreciated.

"Thank you, Edith. I wasn't sure."

Conscious of her disapproving gaze, I approached the little group of elderly ladies who had lingered outside the church, chattering like a flock of geriatric sparrows, and asked if they would care to come back to the house. It was expected and I wanted to do what was right, though I was dreading having to play hostess and hearing them talk about Grandmother the way I had heard them talk about so many others over the years. All I really wanted was to be alone with my grief.

A large, sleek, black car was waiting to take me home. I climbed into the back seat beside the considerable bulk of my grandmother's solicitor, breathing the various smells of leather and the musky body scent of the man mixed with Miss Fisher's rather sweet perfume.

"This is a sad occasion for you," Mr Chambers said, his heavy-jowled cheeks assuming a grief I knew was genuine: he had been a friend of Grandmother's for years and I had noticed him dabbing his eyes as we came out of church. "I'm sorry you were unable to see your grandmother before she died, my dear. She didn't want you upset, and the end came very suddenly."

I wanted to scream to him to stop, to block out what he was saying, but I battled my emotions and managed to appear calm as I said, "I spoke to the Sister at the nursing home. She promised me Grandma didn't have a lot of pain."

"That is something we must be thankful for," he murmured and patted my hand. "It is all very sad, but now we have to think of the future, Annabel. Lily would not want you to be unhappy. She was fond of you, as I'm sure you know."

"Yes, I do, thank you." I blinked rapidly as the tears pricked behind my eyes. I felt so terribly alone. "I . . . shall miss her."

"Yes, of course." He cleared his throat awkwardly. "In your situation . . ."

I glanced at him, recognising the kindness in his face. He was a comfortable looking man, not remarkable in any way except perhaps for his eyebrows, which were thick and bushy. His eyes were pale and rather weak as if he spent too much time reading the fine print of complicated legal documents, and his nose was too long.

"What is my situation, sir? Shall I be able to stay on at school another year and take my final exams?"

"Ah, here we are," he said in a hearty tone as the car halted at last outside the house.

The house looked even bleaker than usual with its blinds tightly drawn. Even the rose petals were turning black in the bud as if Grandmother's death had blighted their blooming. It was June, and in other gardens and other places summer was well on the way despite the cold winds, but in my heart it was winter. Mr Chambers's voice seemed to come from a long way off as he droned in my ear.

"I suggest we talk about all this later. Don't worry, Annabel, everything has been thought of. I shall be looking after your affairs until you are old enough to see to things for yourself."

There was an audible sniff from Miss Fisher, then she got out of the car and hurried up the path to the front door. Mr Chambers smiled at me reassuringly. My heart fluttering, I climbed out of the back of the car and followed the housekeeper into the house.

Mr Chambers talked to me alone in the front parlour after everyone but Miss Fisher had gone. She was in the kitchen, tackling the pile of dirty crockery, and the house seemed to echo with silence . . . the silence of the grave.

"You wanted to know about your future," he said gently. "I can tell you that your school fees have been provided for from your father's trust and will continue for your final years."

I had not even known there was a trust fund, but now I considered, I supposed his estate must have come to me after he died.

"And after that?"

"The fund will have served its purpose and can be wound up. It should provide you with a capital of perhaps five thousand pounds."

"I see. Thank you for explaining it to me. I was not sure if I could afford to continue my education."

"Then there is your grandmother's will," he went on. "She has left everything to you, apart from a small annuity to Miss Fisher."

"Grandmother wasn't rich, was she?"

"She was comfortable," he replied with a smile. "There's this house and its contents, which should bring in several thousand pounds, and after expenses I think perhaps another two thousand."

"So I shall have about seven thousand pounds without selling this house, that's quite a lot of money."

"It means you won't have to worry about your immediate future," he agreed. "But surely you will want to sell this house in time?" He glanced round the old-fashioned room with its high, dingy ceilings and ugly furniture, and I could tell what he was thinking. "You could sell all this and buy a nice little flat or a modern bungalow, Annabel. This house is rather gloomy, don't you think? More suitable for a large family who want to modernise it."

"I hated it when I was a child, but it's my home now. I don't know what I want to do yet. I haven't had time to think about it."

"No, of course not, but you couldn't live here alone. What about when you're at school? If you leave it empty it will get damp and become run-down. Much better to let me sell it now and invest the money until you're more sure of what you want to do."

"Miss Fisher could stay on, couldn't she? After all, it was her home, too. I could pay her a small amount from my income and she could live here as a sort of caretaker."

His pale eyes were thoughtful. "It's a possibility," he said at last. "Though I don't see why you should pay her. You could get rent for the house if you really want to keep it."

"But then someone else would live here. I would rather keep it as it is for a while." I gave him a wistful look. "Selling it would be like saying goodbye to Grandmother all over again."

"What a sentimental little puss you are," he said and patted my cheek with fatherly affection. "Very well, my dear. If it's what you want I'll talk to Miss Fisher."

Mr Chambers was surprised when Miss Fisher jumped at the chance to stay on at the house, but then, he did not know her as well as I did. She might not particularly like me, but she had loved Grandmother and she was used to the house and all its ways. She could coax the old Aga cooker to do just what she wanted and knew all about the creaks in the stairs and the way the wind whistled down the chimneys. She wasn't afraid of its dark corners or the old cellar with the dank, smelly well that had been boarded over years before.

It was the world outside she feared. I knew her secrets now. I knew she had been hurt many times, that she had been accused of theft – a theft she swore she had not committed – and I understood, for I knew what it felt like to be falsely accused. It would suit me if she stayed on to take care of the house.

After the lawyer had gone, I wandered upstairs to my grandmother's room. Miss Fisher had kept it ready just in case her employer returned from the nursing home and Grandmother's silver-backed brushes were spread on the dressing table; wisps of hair still clung to the ivory teeth of her comb. I could smell the lavender cologne she always wore and suddenly my grief rose up to overwhelm me.

"Why did you leave me?" I accused as tears began to slide down my cheeks. "Why did you desert me?"

I picked up the comb and began to drag it through my hair; its sharp teeth snagged in the tangles and I felt a tearing pain. Wild, unreasoned anger welled up inside me and I screamed aloud, throwing down the comb in my blind agony. Then I was snatching everything from the dressing table, dashing her precious trinkets to the ground in a fury of grief and guilt. She had no right to leave me! I hadn't done anything wrong. I didn't deserve to be punished. She had betrayed me, just as my father had all those years ago.

I was hysterical, out of my head with the force of my grief

as I crashed about the room, creating havoc in what had been a sanctuary of peace.

"Annabel!" Miss Fisher's shocked tones penetrated the wall of misery in my mind. "Now you just stop that. You stop that this minute!"

I stared at her wild-eyed. She grabbed me by the shoulders and gave me a little shake, then slapped my face. I drew a deep, shuddering breath as the hysteria faded.

"Why did you do this?"

I glanced round the room, shocked by the destruction I had wrought – Grandmother's beautiful things. In my distress I had smashed a glass pot with a silver top. I bent down to gather the fragments and felt the hopelessness wash over me. My fingers curled around a piece of glass but I did not feel the sharp sting as it cut into my flesh.

"Be careful," Miss Fisher warned. "Now you've cut yourself. Whatever next! You are a foolish, silly girl. Let me look – you're bleeding!"

"No! Leave me alone!"

I backed away from her, turned and ran from the room, down the stairs and out of the house. She followed to the end of the landing, calling to me to come back.

"It doesn't matter, Annabel. It was only a glass pot. Come back!"

I hardly heard her. Other voices were screaming in my head and I could see the bright lights flashing behind my eyes. I had to run . . . I had to escape from the pain.

Was it instinct that took me to the park that cold June day or something more – something that we call fate?

I have no idea how long I sat on the bench, staring at the squirrels playing beneath the trees without really seeing them. I was not consciously aware of people passing by or of them staring at me, though I must have looked an odd sight with my tear-streaked face and bloody hands, my hair blown into a tangle by the wind.

"Oh, Grandma . . ." I whispered, tears sliding down my cheeks. "I'm sorry. I didn't mean to do it."

"Surely it can't be that bad?"

The man's deep voice startled me. I glanced over my shoulder and saw him watching me, his expression a mixture of concern and amusement. He was tall and lean, in his early twenties perhaps, attractive rather than handsome, with grey eyes and a generous mouth that was beginning to smile at me.

"Is there anything I can do?"

He came round to my side of the bench, hesitated, then sat down beside me and reached for my hand. Turning it over, he looked at the cuts on my fingers; they were still bleeding and he shook his head, then took out a large white handkerchief and bound it around the wound.

"I should get a doctor to look at that if I were you."

"It's all right. I cut myself on a piece of broken glass, that's all."

"Is that what made you cry?"

"Yes, no! I broke something, a pot that belonged to my grandmother."

"Was it very valuable? Was she angry with you?"

"No." I fumbled for my hanky and blew my nose hard. "She's dead. We buried her today."

"I see," he said in a gentle voice that made me catch my breath. "I don't think she would mind about the pot really, do you?"

"No." I wiped my eyes. "She would be upset because I did it on purpose. I was angry with her for leaving me alone."

"Ah, I understand." He nodded to himself. "Now your anger has gone and you feel guilty because of what you've done?"

"It was wicked to damage her things. I wish I hadn't done it now."

"We all do things we shouldn't sometimes." His eyes were definitely reflecting amusement now. "I don't think it's a hanging offence, do you? I think in the circumstances your grandmother might understand."

"She loved me. She always loved me whatever I did. She looked after me when my parents died."

I gazed up into his face. Why was I telling him all this? I had never been able to talk to anyone about that time. Not even Mary.

"Then you were lucky to have her," he said. "Don't you feel that?"

"Yes, but I didn't want her to leave me."

"I don't suppose she wanted to leave you."

"No." I frowned. "I hadn't thought about it like that."

"I'm Lawrence Masters," he said, studying me thoughtfully. "Would you like to tell me your name?"

"Annabel . . . Annabel Wright."

"How old are you, Annabel?"

"Sixteen. Well, almost."

"You look younger. Maybe it's the dress."

I was wearing one of my school dresses because it was grey and suitable for the funeral. Realising how awful I must look, I blushed and pushed the hair back out of my eyes.

"I look a mess."

"No, just a bit wild and windblown," he said, mouth quirking at the corners. "Aren't you cold without a coat?"

"Yes. Yes, I am," I said and shivered as if to prove it. "I wasn't aware of until now, but it is cold, isn't it?"

He took off his leather jacket and placed it around my shoulders.

"Is that better?"

"Yes, but won't you be cold now?"

"I'll probably freeze to death," he said, teasing me. "So I suggest you let me take you home in my car while I'm still able."

I hesitated for a moment, remembering vague warnings about strange men, but this man wasn't strange at all. I felt safe with him, as if we had always known each other.

"All right." I stood up. "Where is it?"

"Just over there – see that rather decrepit-looking Rover, well, that's mine. At the moment, I'm a poor, struggling law student."

"Is that what you want to be – a lawyer?"

"I'm hoping to be a barrister." He gazed down at me as we walked together through the park to the street outside. "What about you?"

"I don't know. I haven't thought about it much yet; I've got another year or so at school. Probably a secretary or something."

He unlocked the car and opened the door for me, tucking my dress in so that it didn't get trapped by the door when he closed it, then climbed in beside me.

"So where do you live, Annabel?"

"Sixty-seven South Molton Street," I replied. When he showed no sign of recognition, I elaborated. "It's to your left at the end of the hill, then left again."

"I don't live here," he said. "I came to Cornwall to stay with a friend near Bodmin and I took a drive to see the countryside. This is where I ended up."

So he was a tourist. There were always a few at this time of year, even though our village wasn't one of the popular beauty spots.

"Do I have to go home straight away?"

He glanced at me, brows slightly raised. "Don't you want to?"

"Not yet. Could we just drive for a while? Please, Mr Masters?"

"Call me Lawrence." His eyes were thoughtful. "Why don't I take you out for some tea?"

"Would you really?"

"I don't have anything else to do," he said. "I'd be happy to do it if it would cheer you up a bit."

"Yes, please." I knew Edith Fisher would hold up her hands in horror at my trusting nature, but I didn't care. I liked this man. I pulled the sun visor down and glanced at myself in the mirror. "I look awful – do you have a comb?"

"You might find one in the glove compartment. A sticking plaster for your hand, too."

"Thanks." I glanced at him shyly. "You are very kind to bother with me."

I found the comb and a small box of plasters amongst the maps, sweet papers and various other bits and pieces. He shot me a speculative look.

"Don't you think you're worth bothering with?"

"I don't know . . . perhaps, when I'm good. But that's not often."

"You shouldn't put yourself down, Annabel. You're pretty and young, make the most of your life."

I unwound his handkerchief, taking my time before answering. I had never been paid compliments by a man before. Maybe the alarm bells should have been ringing; I wasn't completely naïve, but somehow I knew Lawrence wasn't going to harm me.

My hand had stopped bleeding. I stuck pink plasters over three deep cuts.

"I think your hanky is ruined."

"That's an understatement," he said ruefully. "Perhaps you should keep it in case it starts bleeding again."

29

"All right." I thrust it into my pocket. "It won't come out anyway, blood never does."

"I expect you're right. Now, where should we have tea? Is there somewhere nice near here?"

"The King's Head Hotel," I said. "I've never been, but they say it's very good: it's just the other side of the park."

"Maybe we should drive out of the village for a bit? I think I saw a nice old inn a few miles back up the road advertising real Cornish cream teas."

"All right," I agreed and settled into my seat with a sigh of relief.

It was nice being with him and, in any case, anything was better than going back to that house of shadows.

Is it possible to fall in love with someone at first sight? If it is, then it happened to me that day in the park. At the time I didn't think about it, I just knew I was happier than I had been for a long time.

Lawrence treated me as an equal, allowing me to talk, as if he knew I needed a release from my pain and grief. Encouraged by his willingness to listen, I just let it all pour out.

"You've had a rough time, Annabel," he said, when at last I stopped. "But things will come right, you'll see."

"Do they – always?"

"No, not always," he said, his smile warming me. "But I have a good feeling about you; I think you'll make it. You're much stronger than you realise, probably because of what you've been through." He glanced at his watch and looked startled. "Good grief! Is it half-past five already? I'm afraid I am going to have to take you home. I have to meet someone in an hour."

"The friend you are staying with?"

"No – someone else." He met my eyes for a moment. "She's my fiancée and she's coming down on the train. I have to meet her at the station."

"Oh, I see," I turned away so that he shouldn't see my face. "We'd better go then. You don't want to be late."

"You're right about that!" He sounded rueful, an odd expression in his eyes. "Vivien wouldn't be too pleased about being kept waiting."

I didn't answer. It was silly to feel this awful disappointment because he was engaged to be married. It wasn't as if I expected

30

him to sweep me up on a white charger and gallop off into the sunset. Life wasn't like that; it was sometimes painful, sometimes boring or frustrating, and occasionally wonderful. It had been wonderful for a few short hours.

I didn't wait for him to open the door when we stopped outside my house.

"Thanks very much for tea – and the hanky," I said, then jumped out quickly. "You'd better go. You don't want to keep your girlfriend waiting."

For a moment he sat looking at me through the open door, then he nodded. "No, I mustn't do that," he said. "It was a pleasure to meet you, Annabel. Take care of yourself – and don't go breaking any more pots."

I closed the door, stood back and waved as he drove off. A sharp sense of loss swept over me and briefly I wanted to cry again, but I told myself not to be a fool. Crying for Grandmother was one thing, but crying for a stranger I would never see again would be pathetic. He had been kind when I needed help, and I would remember him with gratitude, but it could never have been more than a short interlude. He was six or seven years older and I must have seemed a child to him. Besides, he already had someone special in his life.

Lifting my chin, I looked towards the house. Miss Fisher had pulled back the curtains and was watching me. I began to walk up the path: I meant to apologise for my behaviour. I hadn't liked Edith Fisher when she first came to the house, and she didn't like me much, but I was going to try and change that. After all, neither of us had anyone else. It made sense to be friends if we could.

Four

For the first time ever I was glad to go back to school. The house seemed so empty and filled with memories, most of them happy, but others I could not quite grasp haunted me now that I was alone for so much of the time . . . memories from that other time. Shadowy pictures, whispers that came to me out of the darkness, reminding me of things I would prefer to forget.

Back at school I began to feel better. I was young. Grandmother had been old. Her dying had been natural and not unexpected; it was silly for me to blame myself, to feel guilty, as if I had contributed to her death in some way. She had often told me I'd given her life meaning; she hadn't wanted to leave me; she hadn't betrayed me: it wasn't like when my father died. Understanding brought an easing of grief.

For a while I thought about Lawrence Masters; I wondered where he was and what he was doing. Eventually, I made a conscious effort to put him out of my mind. We would never meet again; it was an isolated incident, a part of the intricate tapestry that made life interesting and rich.

I threw myself into my life at school, joining in the end of term festivities with more enthusiasm than I'd shown before, and to my surprise I found I was enjoying them. I discovered I had more friends than I'd realised.

When I returned home at the beginning of the holidays, Miss Fisher had cleared Grandmother's room of all her personal things. I asked where they were and she told me she had packed them into a trunk in the attic.

"Why did you do that?" I asked. "I would rather have left things as they were when she was alive."

"Why? You ask, why?" She stared at me, then set her mouth primly. "If you don't know, Annabel, I'm sure I don't."

"I wouldn't have broken anything else," I said. "I was upset. You don't understand."

She gave a snort of disbelief and stalked off. I was upset by her attitude. What did she think I was, some kind of devil? She had never liked me, but she might have tried to be pleasant; it was only because of me that she was able to go on living in the house, hiding from the world.

Over the years I had discovered the truth about her bit by bit. The pictures I'd seen had been of her child. Her family threw her out when she became pregnant, and she'd been sent to a home for unmarried mothers, where she was persuaded to give up her child for adoption. After her bitter experience she had distrusted all men, becoming plain and sour. Then she'd been dismissed from her job for stealing money, something she rigorously denied.

'It was that foreign girl they took in to look after the children,' she'd told Grandmother. 'She stole it and put it in my coat pocket. We didn't get on because I'd told her off for being lazy.'

Grandmother believed her, though I was less sure; I thought she could have been lying; she might have taken the money because she was jealous of her employer's comfortable lifestyle.

She had been afraid of going to prison, protesting her innocence to save herself. She would naturally have lied to gain my grandmother's sympathy, but I was not afraid she would steal from me. She was safe in this house. If I let her, she would stay here for the rest of her life, and I had decided I wanted her to stay. I understood her. There was no love lost between us, but she was my one link with the past and in a strange way I needed her.

After she had gone that afternoon I went up to the attic; it was dark and dusty, so many cobwebbed boxes full of rubbish that it was difficult to find what I was seeking. When I finally discovered the trunk I was looking for, I took Grandmother's things back to my own room.

I stroked the silver handles of the brushes, laying them reverently on my dressing table.

"I'm sorry," I whispered. "I'll take good care of them in future. I promise."

"Annabel . . ." the voice was distant and yet close to my ear. "I love you. I'll always love you—"

Of course it was only in my mind, a product of my loneliness and longing, but it comforted me just the same.

It was towards the end of July when the letter came from Mr Chambers. I expected it would contain money for my allowance; the money was there, but the letter itself was a surprise. He had invited me to spend a few weeks of my summer holiday with him and his family at their holiday home in Polperro. I could tell by the tone of his letter that he felt sorry for me, having to stay in this gloomy house with only Miss Fisher for company.

At first it irritated me; I didn't need anyone's sympathy. My time was filled with books and solitary walks – often to the park – yet the days were so long, the nights so lonely, especially when my dreams came to haunt me. Sometimes I thought it might have been better to sell as Mr Chambers had suggested. Yet however full of shadows the house was, I thought of it as a refuge.

I read the letter several times and then decided to accept his invitation. I replied saying I would like to come, but once it was posted I began to have doubts. Mr Chambers was kind, but I hardly knew him, and I had never met any of his family. Supposing they did not like me?

It was too late to change my mind, the letter was on its way.

Mr Chambers came to fetch me himself in a big, black Rover – much smarter and newer than the one Lawrence Masters had been driving the day we met in the park.

It was a glorious morning, the sky blue and cloudless as we set out. Mr Chambers's family was already installed in the cottage in Polperro; there was just the two of us and I sat by his side throughout the drive. The village that was our destination was at the end of a great valley, which gradually deepened to a ravine: a place where time and motion seemed suspended; small, white houses clinging on to the steep slopes in defiance of gravity. Others lined the banks of the River Pol, running the whole length of the village, but it was to one of the cottages that seemed to rise out of the harbour itself that I was taken that day.

The building was oddly shaped, looking as though it had been squeezed in amongst the others. Many of the cottages were painted white, cream or pink, but this one was grey with flinty walls that gleamed wetly after a sudden shower which had blown up as we arrived. At the open windows pink curtains fluttered in the breeze as if inviting me in. Getting out of the car, I could smell the salty tang of the air and a faint aroma of fish.

Before I was taken to my room, I was introduced to Mrs Mary Chambers and her sons Steven and Mark. Steven was about thirteen, a sandy-haired boy with a gap in his front teeth and freckles. He was not often in the house, and after that day I seldom saw him, except at mealtimes. Mark was different. Almost nineteen, with dark hair, chocolatey eyes and a friendly smile, he was an attractive young man. I liked him at once and felt it was mutual. He shook hands with me, but winked as soon as his mother's back was turned.

"It's great to have you here, Annabel. I hope you like sailing?"

"I've never been. Do you sail?"

"We've got a small dinghy. I'll take you out later if you like."

"Plenty of time for that," Mrs Chambers said. "Is this all your luggage, Annabel?"

"Yes, just that case."

She smiled and nodded. Mrs Chambers was a thin, anxious-looking lady with a pinched nose and pale lips – very different from her comfortable husband.

"We'll get you settled in," she said and picked up my suitcase. "Come along. I'll show you your room. You'll be sharing it with Jacqui. She's Mark's twin, of course. She is out with her boyfriend at the moment; he's local and has taken her for a trip on his fishing boat."

"That's nice," I said but felt it was a touch unfriendly of Jacqui not to be there when I arrived. I suspected she had deliberately arranged to go out because she resented having me as a guest in her room.

The room was right at the top of the three-storied cottage and seemed to run the complete length of the top floor. The walls had been covered with woodchip paper and painted a uniform white. Its ceiling sloped at one end, giving it an old-fashioned charm, especially, I discovered later, at night when the bedside lamps were lit. There was plenty of space for the two beds, chest of drawers and wardrobes. Both beds had white candlewick covers, but there was an ancient teddy bear propped up on the one at the far end.

"Jacqui sleeps there," Mrs Chambers said. "And that's her

wardrobe and chest. You can use these, on this side. I think you'll find there is ample space for your clothes, Annabel."

She opened the wardrobe for me to look inside and I nodded dutifully. She was trying to be friendly and kind, though I thought she was rather puzzled by her husband's invitation to a girl none of them knew.

"More than enough, thank you. It was very kind of you to invite me here."

"Not at all. We're pleased to have you." She tucked a wisp of fine hair behind her ear. "I'll leave you to unpack. There'll be a nice cup of tea and sandwiches ready in about twenty minutes."

I thanked her again and she went out, leaving me to settle in. My first instinct was to look out of the window, from where I could see the harbour and the fishing boats that were moored there. The water looked grey and dirty, patches of oil lurking on the surface, but further out the sea was touched by sunlight and sparkled enticingly, silver and green, and tipped with white crests that moved relentlessly towards the shore. Overhead, the seagulls circled and wheeled, coasting on the warm currents then suddenly swooping upwards again, their cries echoing in the stillness.

I enjoyed watching them and all at once felt pleased to have come.

Turning away from the window, I unpacked my case, hanging the dresses, skirts and blouses neatly on the wardrobe rail. I set out my brushes and some tissues on the chest beside my bed and placed my underwear in the drawers. All that took no more than five minutes.

I hadn't been sure what to bring and now thought I had chosen all the wrong things. Grandmother had always liked me to be neat and tidy at home, but Steven and Mark had both been wearing scruffy jeans with the knees hanging out. I did not possess a pair of jeans: Grandmother hadn't approved of them. I wondered what kind of clothes Jacqui wore.

What I did next was wrong, of course, but tea would not be ready for twenty minutes, and I could not go down sooner in case I was in the way. Besides, I was conscious that my pleated skirt and long-sleeved blouse looked out of place in this cottage. It was my uncertainty and a desire to conform that made me open Jacqui's wardrobe and look at her clothes. Other people's things are always fascinating; like peeping through a keyhole into secret lives. As I'd suspected, Jacqui's clothes were very different from mine. She had only one smart dress hanging up, but several coloured cotton skirts and tops, also a denim skirt and jacket.

Grandmother had always thought that denim was a workman's cloth, but Jacqui's skirt looked stylish and it was much shorter than any of mine. Some of the girls at school had minis, of course, but my own skirts ended discreetly at the knee. In my grandmother's opinion, short skirts were indecent and at school our headmistress had enforced an almost puritanical dress code.

I was overwhelmed by the desire to try on the denim skirt, and without thinking what I was doing, I unzipped my own grey pleated one and pulled on Jacqui's. It fitted me perfectly. Staring at myself in the little mirror on the wall, I stretched this way and that in an effort to see how I looked. It was only possible to see about halfway down my legs whatever I did but I was pleased with the effect.

Perhaps it was my total absorption in my appearance that made me careless. If there were footsteps on the stairs I did not hear them, so when the door suddenly opened I swung round in alarm, my face a picture of guilt. Caught in the act, my cheeks flamed as I saw the girl in the doorway. Even if I had not known we were to share the room I should have recognised her at once; there was a distinct likeness to her twin. They both had the same dark hair – Jacqui's was shoulder-length and glossy – and the same dark eyes, but hers were not friendly as Mark's had been. She stared at me, then her eyes dropped to the skirt and her mouth tightened with temper.

"That's mine," she said. "How dare you! Who gave you permission to try on my things?"

"It was just curiosity," I mumbled, feeling hot and ashamed. "I'm sorry. I looked in your wardrobe by mistake and—"

"Don't lie," she said scornfully. "You were nosy, so you just went through my things." She walked to her chest of drawers and opened it as I hastily removed her skirt and hung it back in the wardrobe. Finding the rest of her things untouched, she turned on me accusingly. "What's the matter, didn't you have time to look in here? Why don't you do it now, while I'm here?"

"I only wanted to see what you would be wearing," I cried in desperation. "I didn't know what to bring – all my clothes are too smart for a holiday like this. All right, I shouldn't have tried on your skirt, but I've never worn a mini; I just wanted to see what it would look like."

Jacqui's eyes narrowed in suspicion, then homed in on my skirt and blouse. "Haven't you got any cotton skirts or T-shirts?"

"I've got a couple of school ones – and there's a red cotton skirt in my wardrobe."

She flicked her long, straight hair back impatiently. "Well, change into that then. You can buy a couple of T-shirts in the village tomorrow. You won't need what you're wearing, unless you want to dress up if we go somewhere special for dinner."

"Thank you . . . and I'm sorry."

Still feeling embarrassed, I changed into the cotton skirt and plain white gym shirt. Jacqui watched as I finished dressing, her eyes narrowed and critical. I sensed she was annoyed because I was intruding on her privacy.

"That's better," she said when I'd finished. "Don't touch my things again, Annabel. We have strict rules about that kind of thing in this house."

"I've said I'm sorry." I felt awful. She didn't need to keep going on about it. "I thought your skirt was smart. I couldn't help myself."

"You've got your allowance, haven't you?" She glanced at me with dislike. "Buy yourself some holiday clothes. My father is your guardian now; I'm sure he won't interfere with your choice."

"I suppose I could." There was no one else to tell me what to wear now. "Are there any shops here?"

"We go to a market in St Austell sometimes. You could buy whatever you need cheaply there. Ask my mother about it."

"Thank you." I glanced at my watch. "Do you think we should go down? Your mother said twenty minutes."

Her brows rose in surprise. "You don't have to wait up here until the last second. She only meant that tea would be ready then; you're free to come and go as you please. You can stay out all day if you like, as long as someone knows what you're doing."

Her tone was one of disbelief and she was looking at me as if I had come from outer space. Obviously she had been used to a freedom I had never known; my life had been governed by rules, both at school and at home.

"Grandmother always wanted to know where I was. I'm not used to being so – free."

"You poor thing," she said, slightly less hostile now. "You must have had an odd life. Look, we got off on the wrong foot. There's no need for anyone to know about the skirt – but you must promise not to do it again."

"Yes, of course," I agreed, relieved that she wasn't going to make me look a fool in front of everyone. "I am sorry, Jacqui."

"Forget it. Tell Mum I'll be down as soon as I've changed, will you? I've been out with Terry and my clothes stink of fish."

There was an air of satisfaction about her, as though she were hugging a delicious secret to herself.

"Is Terry your boyfriend?"

"Yes. I've known him for years, but this holiday we've started going around together. He's busy most of the time, either fishing or taking tourists out after the mackerel – that's what we were doing today."

"Do you have lots of boyfriends? I've never been out with anyone."

That wasn't quite true if you counted tea with Lawrence Masters, but he hadn't been a boyfriend, not in the way she meant. I still thought about him sometimes, making up stories in my head in which we met again and this time he fell madly in love with me. Nonsense, of course, but something to think about when I was lonely.

Jacqui saw the wistful expression in my eyes and frowned. "You sound as though you've been living in the dark ages. I suppose it's because you were brought up by your grandmother after your parents died. Being on your own so much must have been awful."

"I can't remember much about before my parents died," I said, my hackles rising at the note of condescension in her voice. "But living with Grandmother was all right. I loved her. Just because my clothes are all wrong, it doesn't mean I've been deprived."

"Prickly, aren't you?" She shrugged, her eyes going cold again. "I was trying to be friendly, but if you feel like that—"

She didn't want to be my friend. The expression in her eyes, her whole manner towards me, shouted resentment. I was a nuisance, an object of pity, someone she was forced to accept because her father had insisted.

"I don't need pity," I said. "If you'd wanted to be friends, you would've been here when I arrived."

"And ruin my whole day just for you – a stupid little girl my father feels sorry for! Now you're here I shall have to put up with you, but you're not my friend and never will be."

"I'll keep out of your way as much as possible. I'm going down now. I'll tell your mother you're changing."

How stupid I'd been to get caught trying on her skirt. It had spoilt any chance I might have had of making friends with her. She would never forget it and it made me feel guilty.

After half an hour in this house, I was wishing I had never come.

Over the next few days Jacqui and I were forced into each other's company more than either of us liked or wanted. Her parents assumed that because we were both girls of a similar age we would automatically share mutual interests. We did not, and I realised that even if she hadn't caught me at an awkward moment, she wouldn't have liked me; she had made up her mind before I arrived. For the sake of appearances we tried to be pleasant to each other, at least when anyone else was around, though alone in her room she made it plain she hated having me there.

I felt so miserable I might have wept into my pillow, except that I was determined not to let her see how I felt.

Jacqui's mother was altogether a much nicer person. A nervous woman, she did at least try to be kind. When she discovered I was short of holiday clothes she took me to the market, giving me time to browse, and helping me to choose.

"Very suitable," she approved as I purchased a pair of shorts and a couple of miniskirts. "Just right, Annabel. Jacqui wears hers too short, but yours will look pretty."

I also bought several short-sleeved tops and T-shirts in bright colours. I hesitated over a denim skirt, but imagining Jacqui's expression if I did, decided against it.

Mark had refused to come shopping with us, saying he didn't want to waste his holiday, but he had invited me to go sailing with him the following day.

*   *   *

40

I got up feeling excited and looking forward to the outing. Dressed in my new shorts and a pink shirt, I was relaxed for the first time since coming to Polperro.

The sun was warm when we left the house; its reflection on the water almost dazzled me and I shaded my eyes to look towards the horizon. I had never been in a sailing dinghy before and wasn't sure what to do, but Mark smiled reassuringly at me and gave me his hand to help me climb on board.

"Steady, that's it," he said, and his hand brushed my bare arm as he held me. "You'll soon get used to it, Annabel."

"Thanks," I murmured. "It's such a lovely day."

"You're lovely, too," he replied and made me blush.

I soon discovered that sailing was great fun. We seemed to skim over the waves and I tasted the salt spray on my lips. There was such a wonderful sense of freedom out there on the sea; I had a feeling of being truly alive as though I had woken from a deep sleep. I loved the motion of the dinghy and the coolness of the breeze in my hair, but more than anything else I enjoyed the way Mark's eyes followed my every movement. He made it clear he liked me a lot, which pleased me and made me feel good inside. So, when, as we were leaving the boat, he suddenly tried to kiss me, I let him. As he reached for me I closed my eyes and went limp, savouring the taste of his mouth, which was pepperminty and fresh, and discovering that kissing was a very pleasant sensation indeed.

I liked being kissed; it made me feel odd, sort of floaty and melty inside. Gazing up at Mark, I saw that he was enjoying it, too. His tongue was flicking against my lips; I opened them in a natural yet innocent response to his probing.

His arms closed about me, hugging me tightly against him. His kisses awakened something in me and I was aware of a sweet trembling sensation in my stomach. Pressing closer, I slid my arms about his neck and kissed him back with an eagerness that matched his own. We were both breathing hard when he released me and there was an excited look in his eyes.

"Boy, you're hot stuff," he said. "When you arrived you looked like a schoolgirl, but you're really sexy in those shorts."

"Sexy?" I tipped my head to one side, gazing up at him. "Am I? Do you like the way I look?"

"You know the answer to that," he said. "Don't pretend to be innocent with me, Annabel, not after that kiss."

I laughed, shaking my long hair back off my face. There was admiration in his eyes and something more – something that made me nervous yet excited me. He really liked me a lot. Instinctively, I knew he wanted something from me. More kisses and perhaps . . . perhaps what Miss Hadley had been doing in the summer house.

Although I'd watched her making love I had never thought about doing it myself; it was somehow apart from my safe, enclosed existence with Grandmother; wicked and fun to watch but nothing to do with me.

I had always been a little girl to my grandmother, and at school we were separated from the boys, except on parents' day. I knew that most of the other girls had experimented with French kissing, and some of them had gone further, allowing the boys they dated during their holidays to touch their breasts and their intimate parts. During the previous term there had been a great deal of excitement and a sense of shock in the dormitories when one of the older girls had been expelled for becoming pregnant.

Of course, since the sixties, society had become even more permissive, and women's magazines were forever telling us we were free to do as we wanted: the Pill was supposed to make that possible. Some of the girls at school whispered about it, but most were ignorant of how you actually came by it and I would never have dared to ask our doctor, even though in the eighties it was commonplace for young girls to do so. Besides, I hadn't even thought about it until now, when I had suddenly become aware of my own sensuality.

"Annabel." Mark was looking at me in a speculative way. "Would you like to go to a disco with me? There's one on in St Austell next Tuesday."

"I'll think about it," I said and giggled, then ran on ahead of him up the steep path and into the house. It wasn't difficult to guess what was in his mind. All at once I began to think this holiday might be fun, in spite of Jacqui.

I was still laughing as I burst into the front parlour, but my mirth died as I saw the man sitting in an armchair by the window. He was reading a newspaper, but looked up as I made my boisterous entry, his eyes going over me with unconcealed appreciation. Mesmerised, I stared back.

He was so good-looking it wasn't true. For a moment I thought

42

he must be a film or television star. Perhaps twenty-four or so, his hair was sun-bleached blond and his eyes an azure blue that set off his tan. He rose to his feet, towering above me. I noticed how large he was, with very broad shoulders. There was a tiny scar at the corner of his mouth which gave him a slightly satyric appearance, his smile seeming to mock me as his eyes travelled over me, dwelling for a moment on my bare legs before wandering leisurely up to my breasts and then my face. As our eyes met, he grinned at me in a friendly, but teasing way.

"You must be Annabel," he said. "I'm Terry Bradford."

"You're Jacqui's friend." I sat in the chair opposite and crossed my legs. "Are you waiting for her? Are you going out in your boat again?"

"Not today," he replied, eyes flicking to my tanned legs again. "We're taking a picnic to a little cove I know further up the coast." He paused for a moment, then arched his eyebrows. "Would you like to come with us?"

"Oh yes." My response was instinctive and immediate. "If Jacqui doesn't mind."

"If Jacqui doesn't mind what?"

The sound of her voice made me jump, my head swivelling round to see her standing in the doorway, hands on hips and a flash of annoyance in her eyes. My face must have been a picture of guilt as I met her angry glare. Clearly, she had heard Terry ask me to go with them and was very annoyed about it.

"I asked Annabel if she would like to come on the picnic," he said. He spoke in an easy, careless manner, seeming not to notice her annoyance. Then, as Mark followed her into the room, "Why don't we all go together? It would be fun."

"Go where?" Mark asked, and then as Terry explained, "If Annabel's going, count me in."

Meeting the cut and thrust of Jacqui's eyes, I tossed my head in defiance. "I should love to come," I said and looked invitingly at Terry. "It was sweet of you to ask me. Do you think I should change?"

His eyes went over me very slowly, almost as though he were tasting me, savouring the flavour, and bringing a flush to my cheeks. "No," he said at last. "You look perfect just the way you are."

"Thank you." Excitement went to my head, making me giggle. Mark's eyes flashed with jealousy and Jacqui was

43

staring at me hard: if looks could kill I would have been dead right then. Pride made me stick my head in the air. "Shall we go then?"

As we went out to the car, Jacqui caught my arm. Her fingers pinched my arm, making me wince.

"You think you're so clever, you little cat," she whispered in my ear. "Just leave Terry alone, or I'll make you sorry you were ever born."

She pinched me again, then let go of my arm and walked on to catch hold of Terry's hand, gazing up at him as if butter wouldn't melt in her mouth.

"You're so sweet to take all of us," she said, darting a backwards glance at me. "It's a real treat for poor Annabel. She's never been anywhere or done anything much. It was kind of you to take pity on her."

It was at that moment that I realised how spiteful she really was, and I decided that if I did try and take Terry away from her, it would be no more than she deserved.

Five

I don't suppose I would have done anything really if my chance hadn't come out of the blue a few days later. Jacqui had gone out with Mark in the dinghy and Steven had disappeared on business of his own, which usually meant chatting to the fishermen in the harbour. None of them had asked me what I wanted to do that day, and I was disappointed because I'd thought Mark was taking me sailing. For some reason I had slept late and Mrs Chambers was the only one in the house when I eventually went downstairs.

"So what are you going to do, Annabel?" she asked with that anxious look of hers. "It was thoughtless of everyone to go off and leave you alone."

"I don't mind. I think I'll explore the village. I haven't seen it all yet."

"That's a good idea," she said. "You are enjoying yourself, aren't you? Only we do want you to be happy."

"I'm having a lovely time, thank you."

"I have some chores to do this morning," she said, and I had the impression she felt it her duty to make up for the lack of consideration from her children. "But this afternoon I'll ask my husband to take us out for a drive somewhere – would you like that?"

"It sounds nice, thank you."

I left the house and set off into the village. The sun was very warm, and it was pleasant to be on my own for a while.

For more than an hour I wandered the streets of the old fishing village, absorbing the atmosphere. It had a special sleepy charm, which I liked. Much of it seemed untouched by the twentieth century. Some of the alleys were too narrow for cars to get down, and visitors had to explore on foot.

Polperro had always been popular with artists, who loved to paint its quaint cottages, which looked as if they had all been piled up on top of each other in a haphazard way. There were a few elegant Georgian houses; the oldest of all was sixteenth century and built near the Saxon bridge over the River Pol. Most of the cottages were typical fishermen's homes, though one of them was unusual in that it had been almost completely covered in intricate patterns of circles and whirls all made out of seashells.

I visited the Smugglers Museum, my imagination conjuring up vivid pictures of stormy seas and contraband being brought ashore at the dead of night – barrels of brandy and rolls of precious silk. How exciting those times must have been! It was there I bought a guidebook, telling stories of the old days. I could almost hear the roar of the Excise ship's cannon and see the frantic smugglers rushing to up anchor and escape to sea. Some of the stories in the book were so exciting that I was thoroughly absorbed as I read, leaning against a wall. When the shadow fell across my page, I was startled and my head shot up to discover who was blocking the sun, and I found myself gazing into a pair of mesmerising blue eyes.

"So we meet again," Terry Bradford said, mouth quirking at the corners. "All on your own then?"

"Everyone does what they want," I explained, not wanting him to know that I had been abandoned. "The others went sailing but I thought I would like to explore."

"What are you reading?"

"It's a guidebook, about the smugglers. I was thinking how exciting it must have been to live here in those days."

"More profitable than the fishing nowadays." He looked thoughtful. "Would you like to see a real smuggler's cave?"

Something in the way he regarded me made my toes tingle. For a moment I was silent, considering his offer, though in my heart I knew I was going to say yes.

"How would we get there?"

"In my boat." His eyes challenged me to accept. "Perhaps you just like to read about smugglers? I expect you would be frightened to be alone with one."

"*Are* you a smuggler, Terry?" I was beginning to be amused by the signals his eyes were sending out. It seemed to me it wouldn't be too difficult to take him away from Jacqui if I really wanted to; that pleased me, because it would serve her right for being so unpleasant to me.

46

"My great-grandfather was." Terry laughed, his teeth a white flash against the deep bronze of his skin. "I would be if I thought it worthwhile – not drugs, though. I don't hold with them. Tobacco and brandy like the old days, that's fair game, isn't it?"

"I don't believe you," I protested, enjoying our sparring. "You're making it all up."

"You won't find out unless you come with me, will you?"

"All right then." I felt a sudden surge of excitement. "I'll come – but I don't believe you're a smuggler."

"I shall have to convince you, shan't I?"

Terry's cave was a few miles along the coast. It took us about an hour to get there and then we anchored in deep water because he said the rocks were treacherous nearer the shore. The cliffs were quite sheer at one point, but there was a narrow inlet that hardly looked big enough to be called a cove.

"The caves are in there," he said, pointing towards the inlet. "At high tide you can't see the opening, and the first cave is flooded but they go inland for some way and then widen out."

"Where? I can't see anything."

Terry came to stand behind me. He placed his hands one each side of my head, tipping it so that I was looking in the right direction.

"Now look up," he said. "Follow that dark line like a fissure – see where it widens out slightly. That's it." His hand moved to the back of my neck, his fingers caressing the sensitive skin beneath my hair. A tingle of pleasure went down my spine. For a moment I lingered, allowing him to touch me, then moved out of reach: I was enjoying myself too much to give him his way just yet.

"It doesn't look big enough to be the entrance to a cave. You can hardly see it."

"That's precisely why it was chosen by the smugglers. It's difficult to find and even more difficult to enter from the sea." Terry laughed. "It wouldn't have been much good if the Excise men had been able to find it, would it? There's an easier way in from the cove itself."

"Will you show me?"

"I can't take the boat in; it's dangerous at low tide."

"How did the smugglers get in then?" I eyed him in suspicion.

47

"I don't believe there's cave up there at all. You made it up."

"The smugglers had men waiting in the cove," Terry said. "When the lantern was shown they would come out with their boats and row the cargo back to shore." He raised his brows at me. "We could get there on the raft if you're brave enough. I've been in from the sea."

He had an inflatable rubber raft stowed at one end of the boat for emergencies. I glanced at it and then down at the water; the sea boiled and frothed about treacherous spurs of black rock and I felt my stomach spasm with fear. It would be so easy to be dashed against those rocks and drowned.

Terry laughed as he saw the answer in my eyes.

"So what shall we do instead?" he asked. "Do you want to go back to Polperro? Or shall we stay here for a while? I can find us something to eat in the galley."

"Isn't there anywhere we could go ashore? A sandy cove where we could swim and sunbathe?"

As I turned to gaze up at him my breath caught. For a moment he seemed to hesitate, then he touched his lips to mine. At first it was the merest brush, teasing and gentle, deepening slowly to something more dangerous and exciting. His kiss made my pulses throb with a strange wildness, and I felt a strong, heady sensation flare up inside me. When Mark had kissed me I had thought it fun, but this was different. There was a power and a passion in this fisherman, an intensity that thrilled and yet frightened me. My eyes widened as I continued to look into his face and saw the hunger in him.

"I might be able to find somewhere," he murmured teasingly. "If you made it worth my trouble."

I sensed this was my chance. If I wanted to take him away from Jacqui, to pay her back for her unkindness to me, I could do it. But there would be no going back, no chance for second thoughts. My breath quickened and my heartbeat raced tumultuously. Why not? Why shouldn't I?

I smiled provocatively, teasing him as he had me. "You won't know unless you take me there, will you?"

Terry threw back his head and laughed with delight as he recognised the challenge. "No, I shan't, shall I?" he murmured and smoothed his thumb over my mouth. I could feel the hard

48

skin of his workman's hands and something stirred inside me. "I think it might just be worth finding out."

We swam naked in the cool water and afterwards lay on the sun-warmed sand. Terry had brought food from the boat and we cooked sausages over a fire he built on the beach from driftwood. Nothing I had eaten before had ever tasted that good. We fed each other and licked the fat from our fingers, laughing and kissing as we drank from beer bottles cooled in the ocean.

I was drunk on excitement, the strong beer and sheer joy. No one had ever paid me this much attention before; it made me feel as if I were suddenly important, as if he really cared about me.

He kissed me and teased me, and then we made love. Gloriously, wildly, with a fierce hunger that surprised us both.

I was hesitant at first when he started to do more than kiss me and struggled a little, but Terry held me down, kissing me and flicking at my breasts with his tongue until I discovered it was nice and began to squirm with pleasure. He talked to me softly, persuading me, gentling me as you might a nervous colt. I discovered that I wasn't really afraid, and after that first hesitation, went into his arms with a willingness born of my desperate need for affection. This was what I had been looking for all my life, someone who would love me, who would show their love freely, demonstratively.

There was such a well of love and passion in me waiting to be released, and Terry's loving had set that free. I was seized with the desire to laugh and shout my joy aloud. Nothing mattered to me but this wonderful feeling inside me. All I had ever heard or read about sex was nonsense; it wasn't painful, not enough to bother me, but perhaps I was lucky. For me love was like riding on the wind, as easy as breathing.

Terry was as eager as I. Like greedy children we snatched at forbidden fruit, gorging ourselves as if we might be cast out of Eden at any moment. We lay together on the blanket Terry had provided, in the sea with the shingle beneath us and the salt water in our mouths and eyes; we did it in the sand, rolling over and over until we were covered from head to toe and had to wash ourselves in the sea. We did it again on the deck of his boat, with me pressed up against the cabin wall and my legs wrapped around him. We were panting, desperate, hungry for the feast nature had so generously provided.

49

"Damn it, Annabel," Terry gasped as we lay entwined on the blanket. "You're insatiable. I knew you were a sexy little thing, but I had no idea you would be like this."

I bent over him. My hair was soaking wet and the water dripped on to his face. I shook myself like a puppy, making him recoil as it rained all over him, the salt stinging his eyes. He grabbed me, holding me pressed against his naked body so that I could not move.

"Too much for you, is it?" I teased, seized with a glorious new power, sure at that moment of his love. "I thought you came from a family of smugglers, that you were a real *man*—"

"You little bitch," he snarled and gnawed at my lips, then my breasts. "You certainly know what you want, don't you?"

He rolled me beneath him and began to thrust into me again, his hips grinding against me hard as if he were trying to punish or subdue me. I writhed and arched to meet him, losing all control as my nails gouged deeply into his back, and I screamed his name in ecstasy as he exploded inside me. It was an exquisite combination of pain and pleasure, almost like dying.

Finally, we were both exhausted. It was a long time before either of us could summon the energy to dress and by then the sun had already begun to dip over the horizon.

Terry seemed concerned as he realised how late it was. "It will be dark before you're back," he said as he weighed anchor. "What are you going to tell them?"

I shrugged carelessly. "Why should I tell them anything?" I didn't see that it was anyone else's business; I didn't even want to tell Jacqui now. What had started out as revenge had come to mean much more to me. I had wanted to hurt Jaqui because she had been unkind to me, but that desire had been washed away in the tide of pleasure making love had brought me. At that moment I was too happy to want to hurt anyone.

"Won't Mrs Chambers ask where you've been?"

"She might. I don't have to tell her." I glanced at him – almost shyly now that we were dressed and it was all over – wanting, needing reassurance. "When can we do this again, Terry?"

"I'm not sure we ought to do it again," he replied, an odd look in his eyes. "I had a free day today. Someone cancelled a fishing trip at the last moment, but I'm booked up most days this month. Besides, there's Jacqui to think of—"

"What about Jacqui?" The guilt in his eyes was beginning to

make me angry. He didn't really care about me; I had just been a bit of fun to fill a few hours. Suddenly my feeling of elation drained away and I felt used and dirty. I said resentfully, "You can't love her or you wouldn't have done all that with me."

"That was different," he muttered, uneasy now. "You're the kind of girl men lose their heads over, Annabel. Any man would want an experience like that if they got the chance, but—"

"But what?" All my happiness was gone. I felt as if he had slapped me and I wanted to hit him, to hurt him in some way. I was hurt, bewildered that he could just dismiss what had happened between us as a mere experience. This had been the most wonderful day of my life. How could he prefer that cold cat Jacqui to me? I wanted to shout and scream at him, but I was too proud to let him see how much he had upset me. "Come on, admit it, Terry – you can't pretend you didn't enjoy what we did."

"No," he said quickly, too quickly, as if he had sensed my anger. "It was great. Fantastic, but I like Jacqui. I'm fond of her, I wouldn't want to hurt her."

He was trying to persuade me again, but I wasn't going to fall for that soft talk a second time.

"She doesn't have to know," I said, feeling desperate. He couldn't just ditch me. He couldn't! I'd thought he cared for me . . . loved me. All my pent up longing and need had poured out in an eagerness to be loved and now he was telling me it meant nothing to him! I was stunned, shocked, unable to understand what had happened to me. How I could have been such a fool? "We can still see each other—"

"I'm not sure." His eyes avoided mine. "Maybe we could meet next week if I can get a day off."

He didn't want to see me anymore, that was coming over loud and clear. He was already regretting it had happened. He cared for Jacqui more than he did me and that stung. It hurt me so much that I moved away from him, staring out across the water as I fought to keep the tears inside me.

I could blackmail him, threaten to tell Jacqui, but that would reveal how much he had hurt me. It would make me feel even more foolish, more used and humiliated than I was already.

"All right," I said, my back towards him. "If that's the way you want it—"

They were waiting for me when I walked into the cottage. Mr

51

Chambers, Mary, Steven, Mark and Jacqui, all sitting there staring at me: judge, jury and executioner. I felt their accusing eyes absorbing every detail of my dishevelled appearance; my clothes were crumpled and my hair was stiff with salt, but even more damning were the marks on my throat and my swollen lips. Jacqui's eyes widened as if she guessed how I'd got them.

"Where have you been?" Mr Chambers cried. "We've been worried to death! I was about to send for the police."

The euphoria of those hours on the beach evaporated, leaving me empty and afraid. I looked into the faintly accusing eyes and the enormity of what I'd done hit me like a douche of cold water. What would they say when they knew what had happened – what would they think?

They would think I was cheap, a dirty little slut who had given herself to the first man who asked, and I had! How could I have been such a fool? What had seemed so beautiful to me there on the beach now seemed sordid and nasty. Shame washed over me, making me feel sick. I covered my face with my hands and began to sob. At once Mrs Chambers was on her feet, hastening to put her arms about me, holding me as I wept.

"What happened?" she asked in a different tone. "Oh, my dear, look at the state of you. Annabel, tell me what happened, please?"

"I can't," I mumbled. "It's too awful. I feel so ashamed." I sobbed louder and clung to her. I was frightened, close to hysteria, my mind whirling in confusion. What had I done? What had I done? Everyone would hate me. "Please don't make me. I'm sorry I was late. I'm sorry you were worried. I didn't mean to upset everyone."

She stroked my hair, murmuring gentle forgiving words. "Come along now. We'll go upstairs and then you can tell me when we're on our own."

"Please don't make me," I begged.

She drew me trembling and fearful from the room. I buried my head against her bony breast and sobbed bitterly. Even when we were alone in the bedroom I shared with Jacqui I held out for several minutes; then in answer to her patient coaxing, I whispered the first words of shame.

"It was Terry," I mumbled between sobs. "He took me out in his boat. We . . . went to a cove and then—" I hung my head. "I didn't understand . . . what he wanted to do." I gazed up at

52

her, an appeal for understanding in my eyes. "It was my fault. I shouldn't have gone. I shouldn't have let him—"

"What did he do to you, Annabel?" She looked stern. "I know this is upsetting for you, but I have to ask – did he kiss you?"

"I let him kiss me. It was fun but then . . . he started touching me and he—" Her cold expression terrified me. I started to stumble over my words, to become incoherent. "I did say no but he . . . he . . . I don't know, I can't . . . I didn't mean to—"

"He raped you, that's what you're trying to say. Terry Bradford raped you."

Her face had gone a ghastly putty colour and she looked as if she felt sick. I was so ashamed, so terrified by what I had done that I could not answer her, could not tell her that I had been a willing partner.

"We trusted him and he did that to you – a child. An innocent child!"

Disgust and horror mingled in her eyes; her face was so white I thought she might faint.

She was blaming him for the whole thing, exonerating me. I should have told her then; I should have made it clear that it was my fault but I was confused and ashamed – afraid that she would look at me with that same disgust if I confessed.

"I'm so sorry that this should have happened while you were our guest. I feel it's my fault for having neglected you."

"It was my own fault," I whispered, eyes downcast. "I should never have gone with him. I shouldn't have let him—"

"You mustn't blame yourself. You were perhaps naïve to let a man you hardly know kiss you, but you believed yourself safe because he was Jacqui's friend." A shudder of revulsion went through her. "It could have been her. My own daughter! When I think of the way we've welcomed him into this house. But no more! That young man has to pay for what he has done."

"What do you mean?" I stared at her, my eyes opening wider. Now I was really scared. What had I done?

"You get into bed, Annabel. I'm going to ask a doctor to examine you, then my husband will go to the police. Terry has to be punished. Otherwise, he might do it again to some other unsuspecting girl." She shook her head sorrowfully. "Who would have thought it? He seemed such a decent young man."

"Please don't," I cried. I had to stop this; it was all snowballing out of control. She mustn't go to the police! I couldn't bear all the questions, the shame of being interrogated, of having to confess that I had lied. "Please don't tell them. Everyone will talk about me, say it was my fault for going with him; they will think I'm wicked. Please don't go to the police, don't make me talk to them." My hysteria was rising and I had begun to shriek in my distress.

Mrs Chambers put her arms about me, rocking me to and fro as I sobbed. I felt the touch of her hand on my hair and wept all the more. I was so ashamed, so guilty.

"Get into bed now," she said. "We must have a doctor to make sure you're not badly hurt, then we'll see. I'll talk to my husband, hear what he has to say about this."

"Must you tell him?" I stared at her miserably. "I'm so ashamed. I feel dirty—"

"There's no reason for you to feel that way," she said and touched a bruise on my neck. "I sensed as soon as you came in that something bad had happened; it was there in your eyes. No one will blame you, Annabel, you can rely on me for that: it's obvious you put up a struggle."

"You–you're not cross with me?"

"Not with you, no. But I'm furious with Terry. He's old enough to know better." She kissed my forehead. "Get undressed and try to relax. I'm going to ring the doctor and then I shall come and sit with you."

Left alone I took off all my clothes and went over to the mirror. Bruises were beginning to show on my breasts, arms and throat. I was aware of a stinging soreness between my legs that really hurt and when I looked down I saw there was blood on my inner thighs. Terry had been rough that last time, and I thought it quite likely the doctor would find evidence of physical abuse.

I bore the examination with fortitude, weeping only when he covered me with the sheet and patted my hand in a kindly manner. Doctor Andrews was an elderly man, perhaps sixty-five, white-haired and a little vague. He was shocked and distressed by the bruising all over my body.

"There is no doubt in my mind that she has suffered a serious assault," he said to Mary Chambers. "It is most unpleasant to see a young girl abused in this way."

"Should we go to the police, doctor?"

"In my opinion she has suffered rape whether she gave partial consent or not. I would be willing to give evidence on her behalf, but the police will want their own doctors to examine her . . . and these cases are not always straightforward. They can be extremely stressful for the victim."

Mrs Chambers looked at me, her expression troubled, then nodded as if reaching a decision. "Would you like Dr Andrews to give you something to sleep?"

"Yes, please," I whispered.

He took a syringe from his bag and filled it from a little bottle, then smiled reassuringly and injected the fluid into my arm.

"That's right, my dear," he said. "You just relax and everything will seem better in the morning."

"If I could be sure we've done the right thing," Mrs Chambers said. "All that really matters now is Annabel. She's had a terrible time . . ."

My eyes were closed and I was drifting away as I heard the doctor reply.

"Your husband told me a little of her history. She suffered a trauma when she was five. As I understand it, her father blamed her for a fire in which her mother and baby brother were killed. Of course she was too young to understand what had happened, but she knew she was being held responsible in some way. If it were to happen again it could have disastrous consequences for her mentally."

Everyone was kind to me the next day – except Jacqui, who ignored me completely. Steven offered to lend me his kite and Mark brought me a box of chocolates. There was an odd, hurt expression in his eyes as if he didn't understand what was going on.

"I shouldn't have gone off with Jacqui," he apologised in a choked voice. "She wanted us to be on our own, but if we'd waited for you it wouldn't have—"

"You mustn't blame yourself, Mark," I replied in a subdued tone and glanced away. "It wasn't your fault. It wasn't anyone's fault but mine."

"I could kill him for what he did to you!" he declared, then rushed from the room without looking at me again.

I felt sorry that I had hurt him. Somehow it had all gone wrong. If I'd gone with Mark to the disco and we'd made love it would have been natural and innocent, but now I felt soiled, guilty. I could hardly bear to look at myself in the mirror.

Mrs Chambers fussed over me. She understood that I preferred to sit quietly in the house and she shooed her sons out into the sunshine.

"Annabel wants to rest today and be quiet," she said. "She's had an upset, let her be on her own for a while."

Jacqui came in later, her eyes red-rimmed and accusing. I sensed her hostility and I guessed her mother had forbidden her to meet Terry.

"I'm going out," she said as her mother followed her into the room. "I shan't be long."

"Remember what I told you. I won't have you talking to that man, Jacqui. You are never to be alone with him again."

"You don't have to go on about it." Jacqui was resentful. "I've finished with him anyway, but I still think it's unfair to condemn him without a hearing."

"He will deny it," her mother said, grim-faced. "What else would you expect?"

"I'm going for a walk," Jacqui said. "Don't panic if I'm not back in half an hour. Don't forget I've been alone with Terry plenty of times and nothing happened to me."

Mrs Chambers shook her head and apologised as Jacqui went out. "I'm sorry, Annabel. This whole thing has been a shock for her. I think she was quite fond of him."

"It's all my fault. If I hadn't gone with him . . ."

"It might have been Jacqui one day," she said. "Men like that are a menace to society. I still think we ought—" She stopped as I flinched and her face softened. "Doctor Andrews thinks it's better this way. He says you should have professional counselling – would you object if Mr Chambers arranged for you to see someone? I think it might make it easier for you to accept what happened."

I dropped my gaze, blushing. "If you really think I should. I don't want to cause more trouble."

"It's no trouble at all," she said. "I'll take you myself and no one else need ever know, except my husband."

"You're so kind." My eyes watered. "I feel so ashamed."

"You're very young, Annabel. Whatever happened it wasn't your fault. Terry is older; he should have known better. Just try to put it all out of your mind."

"I'll try," I whispered.

*　　*　　*

56

I was alone in the bedroom later that afternoon when Jacqui came in. Mrs Chambers had given me some magazines to read and I was lying on the bed, munching the chocolates Mark had brought me. Jacqui threw off her jacket and stood glaring down at me, her eyes blazing with temper.

"You lying little bitch," she said. "I've seen Terry. He told me everything. He's ashamed of what he did but he says you practically begged for it. You've been making eyes at him ever since you met him."

I sat up, drawing my knees against my chest and hugging them. "That's not true," I said defensively. "He . . . he kept looking at me, flirting with me. Anyway, I only went with him because you were so mean to me."

"I knew it was all your fault!" She looked as if she hated me. "I told Terry to go to the police and sort it out with them."

"What did he say?" I felt sick inside. Supposing he took her advice – would I be in trouble for lying?

"He said no one would believe him." There was doubt in her eyes now. "He said everyone would take your side because you are so young."

"Perhaps I'm telling the truth," I retorted. "He might not have raped me, Jacqui, but he was very rough with me. He hurt me. Do you want to see my bruises?"

Her cheeks flushed and she turned away. She wanted to blame me, but there was a tiny seed of doubt in her mind.

"If he really cared about you he wouldn't have asked me to go with him," I said. "I admit I wanted to take him away from you; I wanted to hurt you, but having sex was all his idea. I'd never done it before."

She whirled round then, her eyelashes wet. "You spiteful little cat!" she cried. "I hate you. I wish you had never come here. I loved Terry and now you've ruined everything."

She turned and ran from the room in tears. When she had gone I felt sorry. I wished we had been friends and that the rest of it had never happened, but it was too late for regrets.

All that was left now was the guilt.

That evening I told Mr Chambers that I was going home. He looked at me in concern, his weak eyes filled with pity.

"If that's what you want," he said. "I am sorry your holiday should have turned out so badly, Annabel. Mary and I feel responsible."

"You mustn't blame yourselves," I said. "It was my fault."

"I've been in touch with a psychiatrist. I think he might be able to help you get over this feeling of guilt," he said, looking anxious. "You'll have to travel into Exeter to see him, but I think you should go."

"Yes, I will," I agreed. "I'll feel better when I'm home."

"When do you want to leave?"

"Tomorrow – if it's no trouble?"

"I'll drive you home myself," he said. "Mary is willing to come to the doctor with you."

"I think I would rather go alone, if you don't mind?"

"Of course." He patted my hand, looking awkward. "You're a brave girl, Annabel."

I turned away so that he should not see my tears. I did not feel brave; I felt wretched, plagued with guilt and contrition.

Jacqui was already in bed with her back towards me. I said goodnight to her but she didn't answer.

I didn't blame her. I was sorry for what I'd done, but there was no way I could change anything.

I went to see Dr Mills a week after my return home. He was a tall, spare man with intelligent eyes and a probing manner. At our third session he talked to me for a while, then asked if I thought I might be pregnant.

"No." I blushed. "It's all right."

"Well, that's a good thing. If you had needed an abortion that would have complicated things, as it is—"

I glanced up, hearing a different note in his voice.

"You've convinced yourself that you were wholly to blame," he said. "Just as you did when you were five years old. You feel guilty because Jacqui was hurt and in your mind you've made yourself responsible – you did the same when your father was killed."

"But Terry didn't rape me," I repeated the words no one seemed to believe. "He may have been a little forceful, over-persuasive . . . but I encouraged him so it was my fault."

"And I suppose you made your father's car run off the road?" His quiet voice cut through the protective layers I had built around my memories.

"I . . . don't know." I stared at him, beginning to feel sick inside. "He didn't want to live because they were dead. He loved them more than me."

"Tell me about it, Annabel." He leaned towards me, his eyes so intense that I felt as if he could see into my very soul. "Do you believe you set fire to the baby's cot?"

"No!" I was trembling and the screaming had started in my head. "No, it wasn't my fault. It wasn't—"

I shrank back, pressing my hand to my temples as the pain struck. The colours were burning behind my eyes: red, orange, gold and a clear cold blue – so bright and fierce that they hurt.

"But you believed it because your father said it. That's true, isn't it? That's why you have this rage inside you, this guilt . . . because you were accused of a crime you did not commit."

He was pushing me to the limit, making me remember all the grief I had buried deep inside me. I was sweating and the screaming in my head was getting so bad I could hardly bear it. My mouth went dry; I was shaking all over as I ran my tongue over my lips.

"Yes," I whispered. "I must have done it. My . . . father hated me because I killed them."

"No!" Dr Mills said sternly. "You were made to believe you were guilty, Annabel. You were in shock; your father accused you because he was out of his mind with grief; he transferred his own guilt for not rescuing them to you, and you accepted the blame because you loved him. Then he died before his time and once again you were consumed with guilt."

"Yes." I closed my eyes, the tears squeezing from beneath my lashes. "Daddy died because I had robbed him of everything he loved."

"I don't think that's true." Dr Mills studied my face. "Let's face the worse case scenario, Annabel. Supposing you did set fire to that cot . . . it must have been an accident. You were a child; you couldn't have known what would happen when you struck that match, even if you did. You were not responsible."

"I feel responsible."

"I should like to try hypnosis," he said, leaning towards me with that intent look. "I think it might be possible to reach down into your subconscious, to take the dream on from where you habitually wake up." He paused and made an arch of his hands, fingertips to fingertips. "Would you be willing to let me try, Annabel?"

"I don't know," I whispered. "I have to go back to school. Perhaps next time I'm home on holiday."

"I can't force you. It wouldn't work if you weren't willing, but I really think we should try."

"I'll think about it," I promised. "I'll make another appointment when I come back from school."

His eyes probed into mine, seeing too much. I shrank back, reluctant to expose my inner self. My guilt was too raw, too painful.

"The fire was an accident: your father's death was an accident. You have to stop blaming yourself, Annabel. You must stop feeling guilty every time something goes wrong in your life. We all make mistakes and sometimes we hurt others, but that doesn't necessarily make us bad people."

But I was bad, my father had said so. He had driven his car off the road because I had destroyed all he loved. I heard the words of absolvement Dr Mills said over me as if they were a prayer, but the guilt was too deeply entrenched for me to believe him.

If I was not evil why had I tried to take Jacqui's boyfriend from her? Why had I lied afterwards?

Because you were lonely and scared, a little voice whispered in my head but I shut it out.

"Are you listening to me, Annabel?" Dr Mills smiled at me kindly. "I'm telling you it's time to let go of the past, time to be a happy, normal girl."

"Thank you," I whispered. "I'll try not to . . . I will try."

"Good. Now don't forget to make that next appointment."

"No, I won't," I promised.

I left his consulting room certain I would never go back. He was getting too close to the truth, probing too deeply into that time of the green darkness. I was afraid to go on with the dream, to discover what had happened after I struck the match.

I was convinced I had somehow started the fire and that if it was confirmed beyond all doubt, I would not be able to bear it.

Six

M ary had fallen in love. She was full of it when we returned to school, talking endlessly about her boyfriend's virtues, and about the way he had made love to her while they were in France.

"Jonathan is so wonderful, exciting but tender, and considerate as well," she told me over and over again. "He was staying at the camp-site up the road and we met when my bike got a puncture. It was love at first sight, Annabel. I know that sounds silly, but that's what happened." She looked at me and blushed. "You won't tell anyone, will you? We were careful, so it's all right, but I don't want anyone else to know that I . . ."

I noticed how much slimmer she was and older, her babyish ways suddenly gone. It seemed that falling in love had made her grow up.

"I thought you didn't like sex, Mary? You said it was awful when we watched Miss Hadley in the summer house."

"Well, we shouldn't have watched," she said. "That was rotten of us. Making love is special and private. I ought not to have told you really, but we've always shared all our secrets and I wanted you to know. I'm so happy. We can't get married for ages, but Jonathan says we'll get engaged on my next birthday." She eyed me curiously. "So what did you do on your holiday then?"

"Nothing much," I replied with a shrug. "I went away for a few days but it was boring. Nothing worth telling happened."

I had so many secrets I could not share, even with Mary. I listened to her enviously, wishing that my first experience of sex had been as wholesome and simple as hers. As it might have been if it had been with Mark instead of Jacqui's boyfriend.

I thought about that meeting with Lawrence Masters in the park and my foolish dreams about him and wished with all my heart that I could go back to that day, when I was still an innocent.

61

Lawrence I was sure would have been a gentle considerate lover. It wasn't as if I'd liked Terry much when you thought about it; I'd been envious of Jacqui because I wanted someone special of my own.

It was a long time before I could stop feeling guilty about her, but then about ten months later I received a letter from her out of the blue. My surprise was absolute and I was nervous as I opened the envelope, expecting another tirade, but what she had written was pleasing as well as surprising.

'Dear Annabel,' she began. 'I am writing to tell you that I have just become engaged. No, not to Terry, someone much nicer who really loves me. It took me a while to get over Terry but not as long as I thought it might. I have realised you were right. If he had loved me he wouldn't have asked you out on the boat – and he wouldn't have done whatever it was he did do to you. I've thought it all through and decided it was partly my fault. If I had been kinder to you it might never have happened. So I want to say I'm sorry, and that I have forgiven you. I hope you can forgive me. Yours truly, Jacqui Chambers.'

I sent her a pretty card congratulating her on her engagement. I was glad she had found someone else; it eased my sense of guilt but there was still a nasty taste in my mouth, a lingering bitterness because of what I'd done.

Most of the girls at school were having affairs or getting engaged but my first experience had put me off casual encounters. I wasn't interested in dating any of the men I met – mostly brothers of the girls in my school – though Mark did write and ask me if I would meet him in Exeter one holiday. I told him I was busy.

In a way I regretted turning him down, but I knew it wouldn't work. With him I would always be reminded of that summer in Polperro, and that was something I wanted to forget. And I was beginning to forget. I was doing very well in school, passing all my exams and learning to put the past behind me.

One thing I found amusing was Edith Fisher's increasing devotion to me. I wasn't sure how it had happened, but gradually over the months and years she had attached herself to me, almost as if she were my blood relation.

"You've always got me, Annabel," she had started to say. "Whatever you decide to do with your life, I'm always here for you. You know you can rely on me."

"Thank you, Edith," I said. "You know I shall be going away, probably to London, when I leave school, but of course I want you to stay on here, take care of the house – just in case I need it."

"Yes, I thought you would," she said and smiled at me oddly. "We need each other, don't we?"

She was a little strange sometimes, but who wouldn't be living in that house all alone? I let her think what she liked; she took care of the house and cooked for me when I went home. Without her I should have had to sell the house and I still wasn't ready to let it go. It was my only link with the past.

When I was twenty I found myself a one-bedroomed flat in London. I had applied for a job at the headquarters of a small charity and was taken on as a kind of girl friday, doing all the odd jobs plus helping out on the reception desk.

The senior receptionist was Jane Sparrow, a plump, pretty girl with mousy brown hair and greenish eyes. Her clothes for work were usually rather dowdy dresses or suits, which she wore with clumpy shoes and plain blouses. After work she lived in jeans and sweatshirts, most of them printed with political statements. Not that she cared much about politics; she thought it was the thing to do and her boyfriend was an activist in some rights group or other.

Despite the differences between us we got on quite well and we went out together in the evenings sometimes, making up a foursome with her boyfriend and her brother Ken. We frequented the trendy coffee bars or went to discos or the pictures, but we weren't close friends – not the way Mary and I had been for years.

Mary was about to get married. She had written to tell me the news and invite me to the wedding, and I was telling Jane about it that morning as we were checking through the appointments list for the day.

"What will you wear?"

"I'm not sure. There's a dress I like in . . ."

I broke off mid-sentence as I saw the man. Something caught my attention, making me look at him more closely. He wasn't exactly handsome; his face was too thin and pale and there was a suggestion of ill health about him. In his late thirties perhaps, well-dressed and with an air of prosperity, he should have been just another face amongst all the others. So why my eyes followed him as he crossed the reception hall I had no idea. Perhaps it was instinct or a premonition, but I was almost prepared for it when he suddenly put out his hand and stumbled.

I had reached him before anyone else had even noticed anything was wrong. I grabbed his arm, steering him towards a small settee in the corner of the reception hall. He leaned on me heavily, obviously ill.

"Thank you," he said in a slurred voice, sinking down on the settee. "It's so stupid. I just need some sugar." He fumbled at his waistcoat pocket, his hand shaking so badly that when he managed to extract the silver box he could not open it. His eyes looked very strange, almost owlish. "Please . . ." He handed me the box. "I feel such a fool."

I opened the lid and offered it to him. He took two of the sugar lumps from inside and popped them into his mouth. He looked so ill that I was really concerned.

"Is there anything else I can do, sir? Would you like me to ring for a doctor?"

"It isn't necessary." He put another sugar lump into his mouth. "I shall be better in a moment. I'm a diabetic and I missed my mid-morning snack. It was a stupid thing to do. I'm prone to hypos if I don't stick to the rules. It's my own fault."

"It must be difficult for you," I sympathised. "I knew someone at school who suffered with diabetes. She had these attacks after sports sometimes."

"That must be why you were so quick to help," he said, giving me a grateful smile. The shaking had nearly stopped. His eyes were focusing on me now. "People often think diabetics are drunk when they're having a hypo. If the attack goes too far we start talking rubbish." He gave me a wry look. "Much as I'm doing now."

"Not at all," I assured him. "You have an unfortunate illness. I'm sure most people understand."

"Some do." His speech was already crisper and he was back in command of his actions. "Perhaps you could help me again, Miss . . . ?"

"Annabel Wright," I supplied. "I'm a sort of girl friday: messenger, receptionist and tea-maker."

Amusement tugged at the corners of his mouth. He had a

pleasant smile and was rather attractive. Now that his eyes were back to normal I saw they were a deep velvet brown.

"I'm Sir Charles Cheshire," he said. "I have an appointment with Mrs Winterly. Perhaps you could let her know I've arrived?"

"Of course, Sir Charles." I watched anxiously as he got to his feet but he seemed steady enough. "I'll ring through to Mrs Winterly's office and someone will come down."

"How very kind," he murmured. "Thank you."

I returned to the reception desk and made the call. A few minutes later Mrs Winterly – the charity's financial director – came down to meet him. As they moved towards the lift, Sir Charles threw me a parting smile.

"What was wrong then?" Jane Sparrow asked as they disappeared from sight.

"He just felt a little unwell, that's all," I said. There was no need to tell her of Sir Charles's illness.

"Oh," she said, losing interest. "Why don't you take your lunch break now, Annabel. I'll see to things here."

I nodded, collected my raincoat and went out into the busy London streets. It was raining again and the pavements were wet and slippery beneath my feet. When the weather was fine I liked to eat sandwiches in the park, but today I would have to settle for one of the crowded coffee bars.

Sir Charles must have completed his business and departed before I returned to the reception desk, because I didn't see him again that afternoon. I was sorry I'd missed him and wondered if he was feeling better. However, the next morning a bouquet of yellow roses was delivered to me at work. A card was attached; it read, 'Thank you. Perhaps we could have lunch sometime? Charles Cheshire.'

"You must have made quite an impression on someone," Jane said, a flicker of envy in her eyes. "Those roses are gorgeous. Who sent them?"

I showed her the card. "You remember, the man who felt unwell. He had an appointment with Mrs Winterly."

"Yes." She looked thoughtful as she returned the card. "I've heard the name before, though I hadn't seen him until yesterday. He's quite a VIP, I think, does a lot of charity appearances, opening fêtes and bazaars, and he sits on the board of an arts council as well as running his own business. Printing, I think. Pots of money, naturally, and not married." Her eyes gleamed wickedly. "You've struck oil, Annabel. He probably fancies you."

"Jane! You shouldn't say things like that, of course he doesn't. The poor man was simply grateful because I was concerned enough to help him, that's all."

Her mouth formed a glossy red O as she pouted at me. "With your looks? He isn't exactly Mr Adonis, is he? You've bowled him over and he's madly in love with you."

"And you've been reading too many romantic novels. You've got it all wrong, Jane. I doubt if I shall ever see him again."

I turned away to help someone at the reception desk, then took some notes into the office and made a start on the typing, my gaze straying every now and then to the window to look out at the grey skies. London could be depressing on a wet day.

As it turned out, I was wrong to assume that the message on Sir Charles's card was merely an impulse that would soon be forgotten. I received a phone call later that afternoon, just as Jane had brought in two mugs of tea. I answered automatically, giving the name of the charity.

"May I speak to Miss Annabel Wright?" the voice said.

"Speaking. How may I help you?"

"It's Charles Cheshire," he said. "I just wanted to thank you again for helping me yesterday."

"But I didn't do anything," I replied, flushing as Jane arched her pencilled brows at me. "Besides, your flowers were more than adequate. They are lovely; everyone has been admiring them all day."

"I'm glad you liked them," he said. "You may think that what you did was nothing, but you saved me from making a fool of myself in public and that is important to me."

"I was very glad to be of help, Sir Charles."

Jane was pulling faces at me. I shook my head at her but she was incorrigible and I had to turn away or I should have laughed at her antics.

"Just Charles, please." He paused, then, "I wondered if you would consider having lunch with me . . . perhaps on your day off?"

"I should like that," I said, feeling a mild excitement. I wasn't often invited out by an attractive man and a knight at that. "It's Tuesday next week."

"Would Claridges suit you? Or would you prefer something more trendy?"

"I've never been. I should enjoy the experience, thank you."

"Twelve thirty then. Good afternoon, Annabel. I shall look forward to our lunch."

"So shall I. Thank you for inviting me."

As I put the phone down Jane winked then turned away to direct someone looking for the ladies cloakroom. We had a little flurry of activity as people arrived for appointments, and it wasn't until nearly an hour later when we were preparing to leave for the day that she returned to the subject of Sir Charles.

"There you are," she teased. "I told you he was interested. Lunch at Claridges, lucky you! You'll be marrying him next."

"Jane, you are an idiot," I said and laughed. "A man like that wouldn't be interested in me."

Her fine brows went up in surprise. "I should have thought it was you who wouldn't be interested," she said. "I was just pulling your leg, Annabel. He's much too old for you, besides you know Ken is mad about you."

"That's nonsense too," I said and shook my head as she tried to insist. "We're just friends, that's all." I picked up my jacket and slipped it on. "How old do you think Sir Charles is?"

"Forty if he's a day," she said. "Too old, Annabel. Forget it. After a few years of marriage you'd be a nursemaid rather than a wife."

"That's a bit unfair," I replied. "I quite like him. Anyway, I don't suppose he's in the least interested in me, so it won't happen, will it?"

"Ken has got tickets for a show next week, it's Elton John, I like him, don't you?" Jane was obviously trying to change the subject. "I said you would come – you will, won't you?"

"We'll see," I said and smiled. "It all depends on how many other admirers I've got queuing up to take me out."

She stared at me in concern for a moment, then laughed. "Oh you! I never know when you're joking, Annabel. Shall I tell Ken it's all right then?"

"Yes, if you like," I said. If I didn't go out with Jane and the others I should probably spend the evening on my own in the flat. "Yes, of course I'll come, thanks."

As Jane fetched her coat I looked at the vase of yellow roses and wondered. Was it possible that Jane was right, that Sir Charles was seriously interested in me?

* * *

I rang Mary that evening and asked what she wanted for a wedding gift.

"Oh, anything," she said. "Some cut glasses or a tea set, the usual thing."

"You haven't made a list then?"

"Well, we did but we've got most of it already. All I really want is to see you there," she said. "It seems ages since we met. When we're married you'll have to come and stay."

"Yes, I should like that," I said. "I'm looking forward to the wedding."

"So am I." She giggled. "What have you been doing recently? Met anyone nice?"

"Well yes, I have," I said. "He's older than I am and there's nothing serious in it, of course, but he's asked me out for lunch next week."

"I'm so pleased," she said. "Jonathan sends his love."

"Give him mine. I'd better ring off now, Mary. I want to wash my hair this evening. I'm going down to Cornwall tomorrow to see Edith."

"You haven't sold the house then? I thought you might, now you're living in London."

"No, I couldn't do that. Edith wouldn't know what to do if she had to leave."

"Well, you know best. Bye for now."

"Bye—"

I was thoughtful as I replaced the receiver. I had thought of selling the place once or twice recently, but it wouldn't be fair to Edith. I visited her occasionally, and she wrote to me if anything needed doing at the house. Otherwise we seldom communicated. I supposed she must have come to think of the house as her own.

I drove down on the Friday afternoon. It was late when I arrived and there were no lights showing at the front of the house, so I let myself in with my key.

"Edith . . . Edith," I called. "Are you here?"

I heard the sound of a door opening upstairs, and the shuffle of slippered feet, then she appeared at the top of the stairs, dressed in black, her hair as tightly frizzed as ever and carrying a lighted candle in an old-fashioned chamber-stick.

68

"What's the matter?" I asked. "The electricity hasn't been cut off, has it?"

"I wasn't expecting you," she said. "You didn't say you were coming down, Annabel."

"I thought I would surprise you," I replied and switched on the hall light. "That's better. Why didn't you put the upstairs light on, Edith?"

"I like candlelight," she said. "It's softer, more gentle on the eyes."

She was walking down the stairs to meet me. "Is there something the matter with your eyes? Have you been to the doctor?"

"I'm perfectly all right," she replied and blew out the candle. "It saves on electricity and I prefer it when I'm alone." She turned her bright gaze on me. "You look well. It's a long time since you came down."

"Yes, I know. I'm sorry, there never seems to be time."

"How long are you staying?"

"Just tonight and tomorrow morning," I said. "I'll drive back after lunch."

"Have you eaten? There isn't much in the house, just some cheese and eggs."

"I'll make us some cheese omelettes," I offered.

"You go into the sitting room and put a match to the fire. I'll get supper; it's my job, remember? I'm here to look after you when you need me. I'm always here when you want me, Annabel."

"Yes, I know. Thank you, Edith."

The house felt very cold and damp, as if no one lived there. I wondered if Edith was taking proper care of herself.

In the sitting room the materials for a fire were laid in the grate as if waiting for my visit. I bent down and struck a match, shivering as I blew on the paper to make it flare into life. It took a while, because the paper and wood were a little damp.

Once I had the fire going properly, I set the guard in front of the grate and went into the hall and down the passage to the kitchen. The house seemed even more gloomy than I remembered, and full of shadows.

Edith was busy beating eggs and mixing in a pile of grated cheese. I glanced in the pantry and the cupboards; there was hardly any tinned food and no fruit, vegetables or staples.

"Are you finding it difficult to manage?" I asked. "Shall I ask Mr Chambers to increase your allowance?"

"I've enough for what I want," she said, giving me a reproachful look. "If I'd known you were coming I would have been prepared."

"Shall we take the omelettes into the sitting room? It'll be warmer there."

"You can take yours on a tray," she said. "I'll have mine here. I'm used to it."

"Wouldn't it be nicer if we ate together?"

"I know my place, Annabel. I'll eat here."

We'd had this conversation before. I gave up and went back to the sitting room, making up my mind that I would go on a major shopping trip the next morning. At least I could make sure there was some food in the house before I returned to London.

I stocked the pantry and bought a large joint of beef for our lunch the next day. Edith cooked us a traditional lunch and I managed to persuade her to let me eat in the kitchen with her. She seemed better, more like her old self, and I was happier about things as I drove back to London. If she was becoming a little odd, it was probably because she lived alone in that terrible old house.

Perhaps I would ask Mr Chambers what he thought I ought to do about it; he had once suggested I sell and buy something more modern: a bungalow would be far more sensible, and I no longer needed to hold on to the past. The dreams had stopped coming long ago and my childhood seemed far behind me now. I was happy enough living and working in London, though sometimes I found the routine dull. I was looking forward to my lunch with Sir Charles Cheshire, which would be quite an adventure.

On the Tuesday morning, back in London, I dressed with care, choosing a pretty blue wool dress with a navy jacket and shoes, and styling my hair off my face to show large gold stud earrings. I had dabbed a little of my favourite perfume behind my ears and was wearing a pale peach lipstick. Despite looking forward to the outing, I was a little nervous as I left to keep my appointment. Was I dressed suitably or would I look out of place at the exclusive hotel?

My nerves disappeared soon after Sir Charles greeted me with a warm smile of approval and we were conducted to our table by a deferential head waiter. The rich, slightly austere charm of the famous restaurant folded around me, in the background a discreet murmur of voices mingled with the tinkling of glass and the aroma of expensive perfumes and cologne. It was a world away from the noisy coffee bars where I usually lunched, with their neon lighting, cigarette smoke, and the blare of popular music usually making conversation impossible. I felt much more at home in the civilised atmosphere of this dining-room.

"More wine, Annabel?" Sir Charles refilled my glass with the Chateau Leoville-Poyferre he had chosen. "I hope this is to your taste?"

"It's very good, Sir . . . Charles. Sorry, I keep forgetting."

"You'll get used to it," he said. "At least, if as I hope you intend to consider my offer?"

I toyed with the smoked salmon in front of me, not answering immediately. He had offered me a job as his personal assistant, which as he'd already explained with the little boy smile I was beginning to find very appealing, was really just a fancy title for a glorified girl friday.

"You gave me the idea when you described yourself that way," he said. "I already have secretaries and assistants for the business side of my life, but I've begun to realise that I also need someone to look after me personally. Remind me of appointments, go through my letters, make sure I take my insulin and eat when I should. I'm becoming forgetful about these things, which isn't good for my health."

I thought privately that it sounded as though he needed a wife, but of course I didn't say so. He was offering me a job that I would be mad to turn down, but the speed at which he moved had left me breathless and I hesitated: a job like that would require a great deal of commitment.

"Well, Annabel, have you made up your mind? Or are you trying to think of a polite way to refuse?" His eyes quizzed me: this man was no fool.

I had already taken too long over my answer and he looked a little offended. I let caution slide. I wasn't going anywhere much in my present job, which was often monotonous.

"I think I should enjoy the opportunity of travelling with you," I said. "I was just wondering why you should want me. I can type and I have a good memory, but I can't take shorthand and I'm not a linguist. Oh, I have a smattering of schoolgirl French, but you could find someone with better qualifications than mine."

"I speak fluent French and German myself," he replied. "You

have the qualifications I require. For me a pleasant smile and a caring personality are more important than shorthand. I'm not the easiest of men to work for, Annabel. And when I say I need looking after, I mean it. You could be on call up to eighteen hours a day, and you won't get many days off." His thick brows arched mockingly. "Have I frightened you off now?"

"No, no, you haven't." I laughed as the look of satisfaction entered his eyes. "Do you always get everything you want?"

"Not always," he replied, a shadow passing over his face. "But quite often."

I was beginning to be intrigued by this man. At first glance he was not handsome but there was strength of character in his face despite the signs of ill health. He was an intelligent man, cultured and sophisticated, and in some vague way he reminded me of someone I had met long ago in a park. Lawrence Masters had been much younger, of course, but they were the same kind of men – men a little like my father, I thought, though my memory of him was so hazy I could not really picture him any more. There was a lot to be learned from association with Sir Charles; through him I should have the chance to travel and see people and places not available to me in my present position.

Charles began to speak again as I sipped my wine.

"You would have to live in, naturally. I'm not given to walking in my sleep so you won't need to lock your bedroom door at night, though you will find there's a key. I shan't abuse your trust, but I shall expect absolute loyalty."

I had made up my mind; I should be crazy to turn down such a wonderful opportunity. Besides, I liked him, and I found him attractive.

"When do you want me to start? I suppose I ought to give my employers two weeks' notice."

"Is that really necessary? I was rather hoping you could fly with me to France this weekend."

"I'm entitled to a week's holiday. I suppose I could offer that in lieu of notice."

"I would be happy to reimburse you for any financial loss."

"That won't be necessary. I think I'm going to be very happy working for you, Charles."

"I certainly hope it will be a good arrangement for us both," he replied and lifted his glass in salute. "To my new girl friday . . ."

Seven

"Well, I think you're mad," Jane said when I told her the next morning that I was leaving at the end of the week. "I don't care what he's paying you, it's not enough. You'll be waiting on him hand and foot; it's almost slavery."

"That's nonsense," I said, thinking that some of her protestations might be due to a touch of jealousy. "I'm going to enjoy myself. All I've got to do is make sure he remembers his appointments and do a little typing. Booking travel arrangements and checking a few letters isn't exactly slavery, is it?"

"But you'll never be free to see your friends and relations."

"I don't have any relations, unless you count Edith, of course, and she isn't really. Besides, I'm sure I'll be able to come out with you occasionally, and Mary's getting married." I thought that being Charles' assistant was going to fill a lot of gaps in my life, which had admittedly been lonely at times.

"I still think it's a mistake," Jane insisted. "But if you've made up your mind . . ."

"He is such a gentleman," I told her, excitement lending sparkle to my voice. "I feel so comfortable with him, Jane. I think it's going to be very interesting travelling with him and learning what he does . . . just being involved."

"It wouldn't be my idea of heaven," she admitted. "But you've always had your own ideas. I suppose he goes to the opera and concerts, you like that sort of thing, don't you?"

"Yes, I do." I smiled as Jane pulled a wry face. Anything that could be labelled highbrow was anathema to her. "But I also enjoy coming out with you sometimes. That doesn't have to stop because I'm leaving. We can still be friends."

"Why don't we go for a meal this evening?" she suggested. "I'll give Mike and Ken a buzz and fix it, if you like. We ought to celebrate your new job. If it is a cause for celebration?"

"That sounds good," I said. "Let's go to a Chinese restaurant. My treat, as I'm getting a pay rise."

"You're on," she said. "Though I doubt Ken will let you pay for everything, you know how he is."

"Well, I'll pay for the food anyway," I compromised. "He can do the wine if he insists." I glanced at myself in the mirror. "If we're going out this evening I think I'll have my hair done."

Ken Sparrow was the manager of a supermarket owned by one of the big chains. He was twenty-six, tall and good-looking in a rather flashy way, with long, brown hair and dark eyes. His hair was thick and glossy and he spent a lot of time in front of mirrors combing it into place.

When we met that evening he was wearing white jeans, a black roll neck sweater and a black leather jacket, the revers edged with silver studs. His boots had built up heels and he wore a heavy silver identity bracelet on his wrist. Sometimes I couldn't help being amused because he was so preoccupied with his own appearance, but he was cheerful and generous, and I hadn't met anyone else I preferred who had shown an interest in me.

He let out an embarrassing wolf whistle when he saw me. I was wearing a black and white mini dress with a series of eye catching stripes. To compliment it I had on barely black tights and leather boots that reached almost to my knees. I'd had my hair cut in a new style that lunch-time and I was feeling good.

"You look fantastic in that dress, Annabel," Ken said, his eyes raking over me. "Very, very sexy."

"Then perhaps I shouldn't have bought it," I said. "I thought it was different but now I'm not sure it's really me."

"It's you all right," he murmured with a cheeky grin and slipped his arm about my waist, his teeth nibbling at my ear. "You smell great."

I pushed him away with a smile to soften the action. Ken never missed an opportunity to touch me, but although he made his aspirations of going to bed with me pretty obvious, he seemed satisfied with the kisses I allowed him in the back of Mike's car – so far.

I knew Jane was sleeping with her boyfriend but they had been a couple for almost a year now. Ken had hinted a few times that it might be a good idea if I went on the Pill, but when I ignored his suggestion he hadn't gone on about it and I was grateful. It was convenient to go around in a foursome, but I wasn't sure I wanted to go to bed with him. I had let the relationship drift on because the alternative was to spend my evenings at home with a book.

The restaurant we'd chosen was small and intimately lit with Chinese pen and wash drawings on the wall and pretty sunshades hanging from the ceiling. It was frequented mainly by young people and the tables were occupied by groups of between four and eight, not always in mixed couples. There was a lot of chatter and noise and I couldn't help contrasting it with the meal I'd shared with Sir Charles.

The dishes of food were brought to the table in rapid succession, smelling fragrant and deliciously piquant. We gorged ourselves on barbecued spare ribs, Peking duck and spicy pancakes, prawns with sweet and sour sauce, rice, mixed vegetables and beef with beansprouts, followed by lychees and washed down by several bottles of cheap red plonk.

We mellowed considerably as the evening wore on, discussing everything from the worrying effects of the AIDS virus to the scientists' theory of the greenhouse effect, which was receiving a lot of newspaper coverage, and a football match the men had watched on TV the previous evening.

I was feeling very relaxed when Ken looked at me across the table.

"Have you ever smoked pot?" he asked, and when I shook my head. "Do you want to try it?"

"I'm not sure." I thought for a moment. "No, I don't think I do."

"It's not dangerous," he coaxed. "Not like popping barbiturates or injecting heroin."

"Have you got some grass?" Jane asked, and giggled when he put a finger to his lips. "Great! That stuff really turns me on." She gave Mike a coy look. "Shall we go back to our place?"

The warning bells sounded in my head and I said I ought to be getting home, but everyone shouted me down. Somehow, as the bill was paid and we all went outside and piled into Mike's car, I let myself be carried along with the others. It wasn't the first time we had all gone back to Mike's flat, but we usually just sat around, sipped a little wine and played records. This evening there was an air of suppressed excitement about the others that rubbed off on me. I would have to live on another planet not to know that my friends sometimes took drugs, but

75

so far I'd steered clear of them. I hadn't been to any wild parties so this was the first time I'd been made to face up to the drug scene. I suppose I was curious. Most people said smoking pot was harmless, a little like drinking too much wine: it wasn't like taking one of the hard drugs.

I had half convinced myself by the time we got to Mike's flat. He let us in and switched on some subtle lighting and soft music, creating a dreamy atmosphere. We all sat on cushions on the floor and looked expectantly at Ken. He took the stuff from his jacket pocket and rolled four cigarettes, which he handed round. Jane snatched hers eagerly, moving her eyes heavenward in an expression of bliss as she took the first few puffs; the smoke curled around her, its scent strangely compelling.

For a moment I watched the others, then put the reefer to my mouth and drew on it gingerly. Jane was already beginning to giggle. She snuggled up to Mike, who began to caress her breasts through her thin shirt. As I felt the smoke curl over my tongue I was still tense and uncertain, nervous of letting go of my inhibitions. Experience had taught me that it was better to be in control, but maybe because my friends were enjoying themselves, or because the wine had already relaxed me, I went on smoking.

The effect on me was gradual, however after a while I started to relax. Nothing seemed to matter anymore and I wondered why I'd been so worried. I was drifting on a cloud but didn't feel crazy or reckless, just happy and at ease. When Ken leaned over to kiss me there was nothing more natural than that I should kiss him back, my mouth responding to his probing tongue. It seemed more fun than when we'd kissed in the back of Mike's car and I made no objection as his hand covered my breast, squeezing and moulding it with a firm, gentle touch.

"That feels good," I murmured, nestling against him. Then, as he moved his hand away, "Don't stop. I like it."

"It would be better without this," he murmured against my ear and pulled at my dress. "How do we get this off?"

Laughing, I turned so that he could tug the back zip down the length of the dress. Somehow I wriggled out of it and went back to his arms wearing my bra, panties and boots. Ken unhooked my bra and slipped the straps off my shoulders. His hands caressed my breasts, then his mouth was covering the nipples, warm and teasing as he sucked and nibbled at me. Giggling, I pressed against him as he began to push my tights down over my hips, his fingers moving to investigate the warm silkiness between my thighs.

I made a faint murmur of protest as he rubbed feverishly at my clitoris. We were not alone in the room and that didn't feel right to me, but the drug was taking over and I was becoming very aroused; the warm honey was running and Ken was moaning. A part of my mind was aware that Mike and Jane were making love at the other side of the room, but it no longer seemed to matter. Their cries of excitement only made my own desire stronger and I was giggling helplessly as Ken tugged at my boots. They were tight fitting and he was impatient, but at last they came off, followed swiftly by the rest of my clothing, then he was on top of me, thrusting into me with savage haste as if he were afraid that I would change my mind.

It was all over so quickly that I hardly knew it had happened. My head was swimming and I lay beneath him, floating in a drug-induced haze.

When I woke the next morning on the settee with my clothes strewn all over the place and Ken still sleeping on the floor beside me, I was overcome with revulsion. Although the events of the previous evening seemed to have an unreal quality I could remember what had happened before I passed out and felt cheated. At least with Terry on that sunlit beach I had known what was going on; it made me angry that Ken had felt it necessary to get me high on drugs before he made his move.

Feeling dirty and used, I picked up my things and went into the bathroom, where I was sick into the toilet. So much for the harmless effects of pot! It certainly didn't agree with me, my tongue tasted of ashes and my head ached. I showered and dressed, scrubbing my mouth with tooth-paste and a finger. When I returned to the sitting room, which smelled of stale bodies and marijuana, the others were beginning to stir. Ken yawned and looked at me, then grinned.

"Some night, wasn't it?" he said, looking pleased with himself.

"Not that I noticed," I muttered. "I'm leaving, Jane. If you don't watch it, you'll be late for work."

"Hey, Annabel!" Ken clawed up. "Don't go like that. It was good between us last night."

My eyes raked him scornfully. "For you perhaps," I said. "If you need drugs to get you going I'm not surprised you're a rotten lover. It wasn't an experience I would want to repeat, so I shan't be seeing you again."

He was still standing there with his mouth open when I slammed the door behind me. There was a finality in the harsh sound of it and I knew I was closing that particular door for good.

Outside in the cold I shivered as I hailed a taxi, still conscious of the bad taste in my mouth and wondering what it was about me that seemed to attract the wrong kind of men. Why couldn't I find someone decent and loving who would ask me to marry him?

Maybe it was something in me . . . something unlovable. Maybe deep down inside I was evil . . . because once long ago I had done something that was so terrible, so wicked and unspeakable that I still had to be punished for it.

It surprised me just how much my new employer was capable of packing into a day. We flew to Paris that weekend and he went straight from the taxi into a meeting at Le Crillon in the Place de la Concorde with someone from the board of a French arts council.

"I shall be at least an hour," he said. "You had better stay in the hotel, Annabel, because I shall want to leave as soon as my meeting is over. Have a coffee and read a magazine." He glanced at his watch. "Remind me I must eat something before we go on to the next appointment."

"Yes, of course. I hadn't forgotten."

Sir Charles had briefed me the previous evening when I moved my things into his flat. He had given me the routine of insulin injections, snacks and main meals that he must stick to if he wanted to avoid the sort of accidents he found so embarrassing.

I ordered a pot of coffee in the lounge and took out my book, but my thoughts wandered and after a while I put it away and amused myself by watching people come and go. The hotel was one of the finest in Paris and the women were very smart, their clothes simple but chic. I listened to the clink of cups and glasses, the tinkle of the women's laughter and thought that it should be easy to cultivate a similar style for myself.

One dress I would never wear again was the black and white mini: I'd thrown it away as soon as I got home that morning.

Jane apologised when she turned up for work an hour late. She looked at me sheepishly and tried to make excuses for her brother's behaviour.

"Ken is really sorry, Annabel," she said. "You didn't mean it when you said you wouldn't be seeing him again, did you?"

Jane was unaware of my true reasons for finishing with Ken. She imagined me to be upset over the loss of my virginity; she didn't know it was lost long before on a sunlit beach.

"You'll feel differently about things when you've had time to think it over," she said. "After all, it had to happen sometime."

Now that I had cooled down I wasn't angry with Ken anymore; it had been my own fault for smoking pot, for losing control of the situation. Even so, I didn't want to see him again. I imagined that his love-making would be much the same whether he was high or not and I wasn't interested in being anybody's quick lay. I had come to the conclusion that Ken was too young for me; I thought I might prefer an older man, someone caring who would treat me with respect. Someone who would love me; someone I could trust.

My heart lifted as I saw Charles coming towards me. He smiled and I felt warmed. I got up and went to meet him.

"Would you like some fruit and coffee before we leave?" I asked. "Or would you prefer a snack in the car?"

He glanced at the slim gold watch on his wrist. "I think we have time for coffee," he said. "Not getting bored, Annabel?"

"I've been people watching. I never get bored with that."

"Good girl." He looked at me with approval. "I have another appointment before lunch, then a meeting over lunch. You can take a couple of hours off then and meet me at three sharp. We shall be driving out of Paris for my four o'clock appointment, then we're back to the hotel for six o'clock drinks with the Minister. Dinner will be just you and me, then there's a reception at the Embassy this evening . . ."

"Yes, I've got all that. You do want me to accompany you to the reception?"

"Yes, I may need you. One has to drink because it looks odd if one sticks to mineral water all the time, and I confess I like to indulge even if I shouldn't – but watch me if I have more than a couple because I could get a reaction."

He had told me that only a month prior to our first meeting he had been rushed to hospital in a diabetic coma. The dietician had given him a very strict diet to follow and he was finding it difficult to balance: too much carbohydrate meant his tests came up high, which could result in another coma; too little sugar in his blood and he could go into a sudden hypo.

"Fine," I said and smiled. "I'm looking forward to it."

"Do you know," he replied, "I suddenly find that I am too."

I spent the two free hours exploring Paris, or the small part of it that was within walking distance of the hotel. It was sunny but very cold, so I didn't sit at one of the pavement cafes. Instead, I walked along the smart part of the Champs Elysées. This beautiful wide avenue with its chestnut trees had always been a favourite haunt for the devotee of fashionable life, but one end of it was beginning to become rather tatty, thanks to the proliferation of tourists shops and cheap restaurants, so I strolled up the Rue de Berri to the Rue du Faubourg St-Honore.

This was much more to my liking, with its exclusive boutiques. Here one could browse amongst the antique shops with their tempting displays of magnificent bronzes, silver platters, marble statues and *objets d'art,* besides all the glorious gilt wood furniture. I lingered outside an expensive patisserie with its mouth-watering display of chocolates, cakes and petits fours, but resisted temptation.

There were several exclusive designer dress shops in the vicinity, and I gazed into the windows wistfully. Venturing inside a boutique with a pretty peach and white decor, I surveyed the wonderful clothes hanging on the rails.

"May I help you, *mademoiselle?*"

The sales assistant's approach flustered me. I shook my head. Everything was so expensive. The prices took my breath away. I was about to leave when I saw it. It looked as if it had been made for me: a pale, grey silk dress that seemed to speak to me. The assistant noticed my hesitation and smiled knowingly.

"This would be perfect for you," she said, taking down the hanger to display it temptingly. "You have the colouring for it."

It was strapless with a knee-length flaring skirt and came

with an embroidered scarf to drape around the shoulders. The price was far more than I had ever paid for a dress, but calculating quickly in my head, I reckoned I could just afford it now that I was working for Sir Charles.

On impulse I tried on the grey dress, and as soon as I saw myself in the mirror I knew I had to have it. It would empty my current account, but it was worth it. I wanted to look my best for the reception that evening.

Leaving the shop with my extravagant purchase, I felt light-headed, reckless. My present employer was paying me a generous wage, but who knew how long the job would last? For all I knew, he was in the habit of hiring and firing on impulse.

It had started to drizzle with rain. I returned to Le Crillon and made myself tidy, then took a taxi to the Place Vendome to meet my employer. He emerged from the Ritz Hotel with another man and stood talking for a moment, then shook hands and came to me as I stood waiting on the pavement a few feet away.

"Right on time," he said as he glanced at his watch. "Do you have anything with you, Annabel? I shall probably need something before we get there."

"In here," I said, indicating my large shoulder bag. "Sugar, an apple, chocolate and a small packet of savoury biscuits."

His mouth quirked at the corners. "Very efficient. I shan't need to worry with you around, shall I?"

"That's what I'm here for, isn't it?"

"Yes, I suppose it is," he said, but somehow his voice lacked conviction.

The reception at the Embassy that night was my first taste of another kind of life. The people, the clothes and jewels they wore fascinated me. It was a glittering occasion, something to be remembered when I was back in my own flat doing a nine to five job on a less than adequate salary. I had to hang on to reality and remember it could happen at any time. But for that evening at least I was going to make the most of what was offered, and I rather enjoyed mixing with members of the French Government, a couple of British lords and some visiting American film stars, who were being treated rather like royalty.

I was glad I had invested in my dress, especially as Charles had had a corsage from the famous flower shop Lachaume delivered to me before dinner. Lachaume was the most exclusive florist in

Paris, and to receive a floral tribute from them was a tremendous thrill. I was complimented several times on the corsage and my dress.

My one glass of champagne lasted all evening. I wanted to keep a clear head so as to watch over Charles and take everything in. The conversation was fascinating – at least as much as I could understand of it. Most people conversed in French, apart from the English aristocrats and the visiting Americans, but I was able to catch a few phrases and quite a few of the French speakers switched to English for my benefit when they realised I wasn't fluent in their language.

I decided to make a point of brushing up on my French before we came to Paris again. As I heard people discussing the ballet and various artists and sculptors it made me aware of gaps in my education and upbringing. Amongst this cultured society I was an ignoramus, and felt ashamed of my ignorance. I had gathered a smattering of knowledge at school; I knew of course about Renoir, Modigliani, Picasso and all the great masters one was taught to appreciate in art class, but I couldn't air an opinion on their techniques with any degree of authority, nor did I know many of the modern artists being discussed. It fired me with the desire to learn, to improve myself.

The evening passed off without any disasters, perhaps because Sir Charles was being ultra-careful. He seemed very well as we returned to the hotel in our taxi and he was in a cheerful mood as we said goodnight.

"I thought we might take a trip on the river in the morning," he said. "It's the best way to see Paris, Annabel. You get a wonderful view of Notre-Dame from the Bateaux Mouches."

We were sharing a suite of rooms, which consisted of two bathrooms, two bedrooms and a sitting room. I undressed, took a shower, slipping on a thin nightie and a wrap, then, just as I was about to retire, I remembered I'd left my book in the sitting room and went to fetch it. Having recovered it, I was about to return to my bedroom when I heard a crash from Sir Charles' room. For a moment I hesitated, not liking to intrude, then I remembered why I was here. I went to his door and knocked.

"Are you all right? Do you need anything?"

There was no reply so I opened the door and went in. Charles was in the act of removing his shirt and turned in surprise. From the bathroom came the sound of running water, which explained why he hadn't heard my knock.

"I heard something fall," I said, blushing. His skin looked smooth and firm, and his stomach was flat. Despite his bouts of ill-health he had a good body. "I thought you might be unwell. I did knock but you didn't hear me. Sorry."

For a moment his eyes narrowed and he seemed to hesitate, then he nodded. "I'm fine. My test was normal so there's no need for you to worry, Annabel, but thank you for making sure."

"Good night then." I closed the door softly as I went out.

As I went into my own room I was breathing hard. Seeing Charles like that had aroused desires I'd thought left behind on a sunlit Cornish beach. Since that crazy afternoon with Terry no other man had come close to exciting me until now. I'd let my defences down under the influence of the reefer I'd smoked in Mike's flat with predictable consequences, but this ache inside me was different. All at once I was yearning to be in the arms of the man I had just left.

I wondered if I would be embarrassed when I saw Charles the next morning, but I wasn't. He greeted me with a smile and our itinerary for the day.

"I have another meeting this morning, then we fly back this evening," he said. "From now on I want you to follow a routine, Annabel. If you put out my insulin bottles and syringe each morning and then replace them in the fridge I shan't forget to do it. That's my main worry. I just can't seem to remember whether or not I've done it these days."

"Don't worry. From now on I'll check the levels myself and remind you if you forget."

"After lunch I'll take you on the river. We both deserve a little treat before we go home."

"I'll look forward to it," I said, my cheeks flushing.

I had to turn away so that he shouldn't see my expression. He was a very attractive man when you got to know him, and I was beginning to like him a lot.

After lunch together, Charles took me on one of the boats that made regular trips up and down the river; it was still quite cold but the sun was pleasant on our faces. I hugged my coat collar around my neck and listened in fascination as Charles gave me a running commentary, pointing out all the beautiful buildings, the ancient bridges and the park, an oasis of green in the middle of the city; and of course, the great cathedral. But it was Charles himself who held my attention, with his quiet voice and his air of authority; he seemed to know so much and I felt myself falling more and more under his spell.

I was sorry when we had to leave Paris and fly home, yet I was caught up in the fascination of my new life. I liked the idea that Charles relied on me, that I was important to his welfare, and I was determined to make a success of my job.

The next morning at the flat everything was ready for him. Charles did his injection as I prepared breakfast for us both, then I checked that he had used the correct amount of insulin and replaced the bottles in the fridge. I made a note in a little book I had bought for the purpose. It was a routine that was to become second nature.

"We'll go through the mail now," he said, as we finished eating. "You can make notes on the letters I want you to answer for me."

The mail consisted mostly of requests from charities asking him to contribute or open some fête or other. Some were refused, others set aside for further consideration, but most were accepted. Despite his hectic routine he had time for the less fortunate in life.

After he'd left for his office, I tidied the flat, typed up the letters, answered two phone calls and arranged flowers. We had agreed that I should ring his office at a quarter to one to remind him to take the second injection of the day before he went out to lunch.

"Yes, Annabel," he said when he answered my call. "I did remember today, thank you."

But there had been many times in the past when he'd forgotten; such lapses had resulted in his emergency admission into hospital on more than one occasion. Charles had almost died the last time, but it wasn't so much a fear of death as of public embarrassment that had made him decide to employ a watchdog.

I thought he was too sensitive, but it troubled him, and of course he did have a high profile; it would be damaging to his image if someone were to think he was drunk when he was in fact ill. At home or in the office small lapses could easily be rectified, but the real danger was when he was travelling on his business from his office in London to the printing works in Northhampton.

"I could come with you," I offered when he mentioned the problem. "I can drive. I learned when I was eighteen."

"You are going to be of even more use to me than I thought," he said as we drove into the country to meet a client one afternoon, soon after our return from France. "The insurance companies make it so difficult for someone like me to drive myself. If you are going to stay with me I might not bother with driving at all." He arched his brows. "Or am I being too hopeful?"

"I'm not thinking of leaving if you're satisfied with me. I don't think I've ever been as happy as I am working for you, Charles."

"You don't find it irksome being with an invalid all the time?"

"That's nonsense," I said, "and you know it. You're a fit man, providing you follow the rules."

"Yes." He smiled ruefully. "I'm feeling better than I did a couple of weeks ago, and that's because you're a dragon. You certainly keep me in line. I'm very grateful. In fact I don't know what I should do without you now."

His praise warmed and thrilled me. What he really needed was a wife to look after him, of course; I wondered why he had never married. He was attractive if not wildly handsome, and obviously wealthy – surely his single state must be from choice? Many women would have jumped at the chance to be his wife.

Could he perhaps have homosexual tendencies? It was a possibility, of course, but somehow I didn't think so. There was at times a certain chemistry between us that would not be there if he were indifferent to women. Although always correct in his manner towards me, I had a feeling Charles liked me more than a little, and was becoming more aware of me in a physical sense. I had seen him look at me with an oddly wistful expression in his eyes, as if he thought I was an elusive butterfly, fluttering just beyond his reach.

As the weeks went by, I realised that he was too much of a gentleman to presume on our relationship. He had given me his assurance that he would not abuse his position and, despite the growing attraction that I was sure was mutual, he would not step over the line he had drawn between us.

It was clear to me that if I wanted the relationship to develop into something deeper, I should have to take the initiative.

Eight

C harles had given me time off for Mary's wedding. I apologised for having to leave him for the whole weekend but he said it wasn't important.

"I have a private visit of my own this weekend as it happens," he said. "I shall be in Scotland. You won't be able to contact me but don't worry, Annabel. I shan't be alone."

After all he had said about my being indispensable to him, that left me feeling a bit miffed. I wondered why he was being secretive about his plans, but he wasn't telling and I couldn't demand to know, could I?

Once I arrived at Mary's home my feeling of pique soon faded. She was so happy that I was swept up in the general mood of excitement. I had bought her a pretty crystal glass bowl and she loved it, placing it on the table with all the other gifts she'd received. I noticed a similar bowl further down the table.

"Great minds," I said with a laugh and glanced at the card. "To Jonathan and Mary with best wishes from Lawrence," I read aloud. "Who is Lawrence?"

"Jonathan's cousin." She pulled a face. "He isn't coming to the wedding. I'm glad in a way because—"

"Mary!" Her stepmother called to us from the doorway. "I'm sorry to interrupt, but it's time you left for the hair-dresser, Mary."

After she had gone, I helped Mrs Green to arrange flowers, then when Mary got back, went to change into my clothes for the wedding. From then on we all moved into overdrive and soon it was time for the cars to take us to church.

Mary looked lovely. I know everyone always says that about a bride, but this time it was true. Watching her walk down the aisle to stand by Jonathan's side, I remembered the first day I'd seen her at school, plump and shy and looking miserable. Well, she was radiant today, her happiness shining out like a beacon of light; I felt a little pang of envy when I saw the way she looked up at her new husband.

Briefly, I recalled the man I'd met in the park on the day of Grandmother's funeral. It was a long time since I'd thought about Lawrence Masters and I wasn't sure why he was in my mind that day. Except that I had been attracted to him at the time.

The memory faded as Mary turned to walk back down the aisle. Then we were all outside and the photographer was doing his stuff just as a wintry sun decided to make its first appearance of the day.

We shivered in the cold wind, then piled into the cars hired to take us to the reception. Here we found a sumptuous buffet waiting, an enormous three-tier cake with replica bride and groom and masses of champagne. The reception itself was a merry occasion with witty speeches by the bride's father and the groom. Mary laughed a lot, her eyes sparkling with excitement when she stood up to cut the cake with Jonathan; then he kissed her lingeringly and we all cheered and clapped.

When it was all over everyone went outside to see the happy couple off in their car. Just before she bent her head to get into the back seat, Mary turned and tossed her bouquet in my direction. I caught it as she intended and she laughed.

"Don't forget to invite me to *your* wedding," she called.

I promised I wouldn't and waved until the car was out of sight.

Sir Charles was back at the flat before I got in on Sunday afternoon. He was working at his desk when I went through to the sitting room and looked tired. He laid down his pen and smiled as he saw me.

"Did you have a good time at your friend's wedding?"

"Yes. Mary looked lovely, and I caught the bouquet."

"I hope that doesn't mean you're thinking of getting married soon?"

"I don't have a boyfriend." I glanced away. "How was your weekend?"

"It was a little tiring . . . and cold," he replied. "I'm glad to be back in London."

"So am I."

Our eyes met in shared understanding.

*   *   *

During the first five weeks I spent as Charles's girl friday, we made four trips abroad, travelling twice to Paris, once to Germany and once to New York. It was the American trip which was to prove significant.

He was combining a business trip with setting up a cultural exchange for the arts council, and the hectic pace of the huge, sprawling city was too much, as we rushed from one place to another like frantic ants. And the food was all wrong for Charles. Everyone was so hospitable, offering wonderful meals at all hours of the day, most of them high in carbohydrates that played havoc with Charles's diet. To balance the effect of all these starchy foods, he took extra doses of insulin. Disaster struck the evening before we were due to fly home.

Our hotel was close to Central Park and we had taken a taxi from a party, which had been held at the home of an influential financier. I noticed Charles was quiet during the drive but assumed that he was just tired. He had packed an awful lot into the past few days. I spoke to him as we took the lift up to our suite but he only grunted in reply. Since I had found the party exhausting myself I wasn't surprised he wasn't in the mood for conversation.

We had been in our apartment for only a few minutes and I was about to say good night when I realised something was wrong. Charles had slumped down on the settee, his head lolling as if he had passed out. I'd watched him at the party so I knew he had eaten nothing all evening and he had been drinking. I had noticed that every time he put his glass down it was assiduously replaced by a full one even if he hadn't finished the original drink; it would have been impossible for him to judge how much alcohol he was consuming.

"Do you need sugar?" I asked, bending over him in concern. He was sweating and shaking, his eyes glazed, and in no condition to answer. For a moment I panicked. Supposing I gave him sugar and he already had too much in his blood? Yet the signs of a hypo were all there. Calling a doctor might waste precious time. I had to follow my instincts and act now.

I found the special glucose drink he kept for emergencies in the bedroom. Mixing it in a glass, I took it back to him. His eyes were closed and he seemed only semi-conscious. Kneeling beside him, I supported his neck and pressed the glass to his mouth. He muttered something unintelligible and tried to push me away, but I forced his mouth open with the rim of the glass and poured the mixture into him. It wasn't easy because he had begun to fight me, and some of the glucose ran down his chin and on to his white dress shirt.

All the time I was praying that I wasn't making a mistake. If I had guessed wrongly, I could be giving him the equivalent of poison. Most of the glucose had gone down his throat and I shouldn't have long to wait for a reaction. I sat beside him, letting his head fall on to my shoulder and stroking his hair. The traffic outside was a muted growl, otherwise all around was silent, somehow emphasising my fear and anguish; if I had made the wrong decision and he died I should never forgive myself.

"Please don't die," I whispered, tears slipping down my cheeks. "I want you to live . . . I want you to live."

"Thank you for that kind sentiment," the voice was barely a whisper but it made the tears run faster. "I'll be all right in a minute or so. Don't worry. You did the right thing, Annabel." His fingers exerted a gentle pressure on my arm, then he sat up and passed a hand across his damp forehead. "That was a bad one; it has given me a headache."

"Would you like a cup of tea?" I asked, getting to my feet and gazing at him anxiously. He was still pale but his eyes were returning to normal.

"Would you make one?" he said, giving me a smile. "I think I'll take an aspirin or something then have a bath and go to bed."

I was thankful for the hotel's complimentary tea making service, which was quicker and more convenient than sending down for room service at this hour. The kettle was soon boiled and by the time Charles had taken his pill he was looking better.

"It was lucky for me you were here," he said. "At the very least that little episode would have resulted in a stay in hospital. I can't thank you enough for acting so promptly, Annabel, and for not sending for the doctor."

"You don't have to thank me. That's why I'm here."

"Yes . . ." He hesitated and something passed between us. It was brief but tangible and I knew the events of that evening had broken down barriers. "Well, good night, Annabel."

I watched as he walked unsteadily into the bathroom.

Although had recovered from the hypo he was far from well. Now was not the time to take our relationship further, but I believed it was coming closer.

The morning after we returned to England, Charles told me I could take the day off. I paused in the act of buttering my toast and stared in surprise.

"There's someone I have to see," he said. "I shan't be needing you so you're free to do whatever you like."

"What about this evening?"

"I may not be in until very late. Feel free to stay out as late as you like. After all, you haven't had much time off since you've been with me."

It was like the time he went to Scotland. I was a little piqued by his air of secrecy, but he obviously had no intention of telling me where he was going or who he was going to meet. I felt at a loss, suddenly having the whole day to myself, and after he left I decided to phone Jane.

"I can't manage lunch," she said. "Why don't you come over this evening? We'll get fish and chips and have a good natter. Mike won't be home; he's going out with his darts team."

"I'll look forward to it. Bye, Jane."

The flat seemed empty. It had been thoroughly cleaned while we were away by a woman who came in once a week, and everything sparkled and gleamed. There was nothing much for me to do. Restless and bored, I plumped up a few cushions, running my hand over the soft leather of the chesterfield sofa, then let my eyes travel round the room. The mellow shine of wood that had been faithfully polished over the centuries; the fine, antique porcelain figurines Charles collected, and the gleam of old silver all contributed to the feeling of luxury.

It irritated me that I was so restless because Charles had gone off on some mysterious errand of his own. Yet I knew it was not really my affair. Maybe I was becoming a little too attached to my employer; I should remember my place. I was the hired help and I had no right to feel the way I did.

For most of the morning I mooched about, reading magazines and listening to Charles's collection of Maria Callas records, then I flicked through his books, noting which ones were well thumbed and had obviously been read over and over again. Thackery and Dickens were there, along with Shakespeare and

Keats, but there was also Joyce, Dylan Thomas, Graham Green and a much loved copy of John Buchan's *The Thirty Nine Steps*. Charles had diverse tastes and interests, and was beginning to intrigue me more and more.

Who was he really? I had noticed a certain melancholy in him at times – was it because of his illness? Or was there another reason for those shadows in his eyes?

He talked to me occasionally of his parents, who were both dead, and of his childhood home, but there was still much I didn't know, and so much I wanted to know. Despite his busy life, innumerable friends and acquaintances, I sensed an inner loneliness that made me wonder about the real man.

Driven from his flat by a sense of frustration, I spent the afternoon visiting the National Gallery. There I whiled away several hours in contemplation of the glories of Rubens and Renoir amongst many others, then I had tea in the gallery cafe and went back to the flat.

I was early for my visit with Jane and had to stamp my feet in the cold until she arrived with a parcel of fish and chips. She was apologetic and rushed about getting things ready.

After we had eaten, I helped to wash up and then we took our coffee into the sitting room. We talked and made an effort to be easy with one another, but it didn't work very well and by eight thirty I was ready to leave.

"Must you go already?" she asked. "Ken said he might pop over about nine. He had to work late or he would've been here sooner."

"I don't want to see him," I said, annoyed as I realised she must have phoned and told him I would be there. "You know that, Jane."

"But he's been so miserable since that night. He wants a chance to apologise. He says you wouldn't let him explain. He wants to marry you, Annabel."

"I'm not angry but I don't want to see him," I cried and got to my feet. "If you must know, I'm in love with Charles."

"Oh . . ." She looked stunned. "Well, that's that then, isn't it?"

"Yes." I gave her an appeasing smile. "We can still be friends though, can't we?"

"Of course," she replied, but there was a chill in her eyes. "If you want to."

We had never really been close friends and our worlds had drifted apart. This evening had been a mistake. I couldn't wait to get back to the flat and see if Charles was home.

"I'll ring you," I promised, picking up my jacket. "I must go now. Charles might be back and need something."

Outside in the street I hailed a taxi. I hadn't realised myself until I said the words to Jane, but I really was in love with Charles. Was it so surprising? He was sophisticated, intelligent and very much a man of the world, and yet he was also vulnerable. When he was wrapped up in his work he forgot to take care of himself and he needed me. It was because of that need that I loved him: no one had ever needed me before.

There was a spring in my step as I ignored the lift and ran up the stairs to the apartment. I couldn't wait to be home.

I was surprised but pleased to find Charles in his favourite chair reading a newspaper when I walked in. He had eaten something on a tray and looked as if he'd been back for a while.

"I thought you would still be out. Is there anything I can do for you?"

"No, nothing." A weary smile played over his lips. "My plans changed, that's all. Did you have a good evening?"

"It was all right."

I picked up the tray and took it back to the kitchen. My heart was racing. Now that I was fully aware of my feelings for Charles I was impatient to deepen our relationship. I wanted to put my arms around him and feel the warmth of his body next to mine, but I was nervous. If I threw myself at him and he was embarrassed it would mean that I would have to leave. Yet his strong sense of honour would prevent him from making the first move. Besides, I'd made up my mind it was time Charles got what he needed – the loving companionship of a woman who cared for him.

Alone in my bedroom I undressed, went into my bathroom and took a shower, then slipped on a satin wrap and tied it loosely about my waist. I combed my hair, dabbed perfume behind my ears, between my breasts and at my wrists. My skin was tingling from the shower, making me feel cool and deliciously sensuous. Dispensing with make-up, I smoothed some lotion into my skin, enjoying the silkiness of my own flesh and imagining the touch of Charles's hands.

I went barefoot into the sitting room. Charles looked up, eyes widening in surprise as he saw the way I was dressed.

"Is something wrong, Annabel? You're not feeling ill?"

"I've never felt better," I said, my voice husky with desire. "I came to see if there was anything you wanted before I go to bed."

"No, I don't think so," he replied but the look in his eyes belied his words. The loneliness in him that night was a tangible thing.

Glowing with the warmth of my new-found love, I walked over to his chair, and knelt down on the soft, thick carpet beside him. My wrap fell open revealing the deep valley between my breasts and the scent of my body lotion wafted gently upwards, seductive and tempting. Charles caught his breath and a nerve flicked in his throat. I touched his cheeks and felt him shudder, then I leaned across and brushed my lips over his. More than anything I wanted to give him the pleasure I knew he would find in possessing my body; I wanted to serve and fulfil him, to give him happiness.

"Are you quite sure there's nothing you want, Charles?" I whispered.

He stared at me, an expression of disbelief in his face. Then a glow started deep down in his eyes and his hand trembled as he reached out to take a strand of my hair in his fingertips, letting it slide between them with a kind of wonder. I had not been mistaken; he wanted me badly.

"Are you certain about this?" he asked. "I'm almost twice your age, and you know my health isn't what it might be."

He was warning me about giving too much and yet his eyes beseeched me to ignore his words. I saw the raw longing in him and my heart leaped with joy.

"I think I may be in love with you," I said. "I don't really know much about love, Charles, but I do know I've never felt this way about anyone else. I want to be with you all the time. When you're not here I miss you, and I want to make love with you very much."

He reached for me then, his fingers trailing down my throat in trembling adoration of the young, sweet flesh I offered so willingly.

"Bless you for this, my darling," he murmured. "You can't know how much it means to me, especially tonight."

I had no idea what he meant nor did I care as he drew me onto his lap and held me close to his heart. For a long time we just sat there, Charles stroking my hair, his mouth whispering against my throat and ear. Then I stood up and he rose with me, taking my outstretched hand as we walked into my bedroom together.

Charles taught me about tenderness that night. I had never experienced anything like the sweetness and gentleness of his loving. There was passion in him as he possessed me, but the warmth that gradually suffused my body and made me ache with delight was like nothing I'd ever known before.

In its way it was more pleasurable than the multiple climaxes I'd reached during that wild afternoon with Terry on the beach. There was a gentle satisfaction in being lavished with love and gratitude, for I sensed a part of it for him was gratitude. In my arms he had found warmth and love . . . and youth. For a while he was as he might have been had he never known the debilitating illness that had dragged him down, sapping his energy and spoiling his life.

For me there was the joy of feeling I was loved. Charles had given me something no man had ever offered me before and I worshipped him for it. I kissed his face, cupping it between my hands, tasting his lips with my tongue. I kissed and caressed his body, delighting in the pleasure I gave him as he moaned and closed his eyes in ecstasy. At that moment I wanted nothing more of life than the privilege of ministering to his needs.

"Thank you," he whispered. "Thank you, Annabel. You've made me feel whole again. You've given me more than you realise."

Because I had not been in a sexual relationship for a long time – other than that brief, unsatisfactory episode with Ken, which had certainly not been planned – I had not been taking the Pill, and it did not occur to me that I was running a risk until afterwards. Neither of my previous relationships had resulted in a pregnancy and if I thought of taking precautions at all, it was in a vague way as something I ought to get around to sooner or later. Besides, I was too happy to worry about it, and perhaps subconsciously there was another reason for my neglect: a desire to bind Charles to me by giving him something I was sure he wanted very badly.

*   *   *

Charles was not a demanding lover. Two weeks passed before we made love for the second time, but it wasn't important. There was a quiet understanding between us, a feeling of belonging together. That was all I needed. Charles had told me that I was necessary to him.

"You've become indispensable, Annabel," he said. "Before you came into my life it was empty. You've made me feel young and whole again. I don't think I could contemplate life without you now."

I believed then that he would ask me to marry him, it was just a question of time.

Three weeks after we had become lovers, he again told me that he would not be in until late in the evening.

"I think we'll go to Paris at the weekend," he said as he left that morning. "I have some appointments but there will be time for sightseeing and some shopping. How would you like to buy a new wardrobe in Paris?"

"You don't have to buy me things."

"But I want to. I'm sorry about this afternoon, but there is something I want . . . need to finish."

I was curious about his plans but not anxious. Charles cared for me deeply, nothing else mattered.

After Charles had gone I rang Jane and told her I was going to my old flat. I had decided to give up the tenancy and there were a few things I thought she might like.

"I'm taking a taxi there now. If you can take an hour off you can have those Elton John records Ken gave me."

"Thanks, I should like to have them," she said. "I'll see if I can get there."

The flat felt cold and alien. Remembering how many evenings I had spent there alone, a girl with few friends and painful memories, I rejoiced in my new life. With Charles I had entered a different world, a world I much preferred to my old one.

As I was about to start packing the doorbell rang. I went to open it.

"Jane . . ." The words died on my lips as I saw Ken standing there. "What do you want? How did you know I was here?"

"Jane rang me. She knew I had the day off and asked me to collect some records for her."

"You'd better come in then." I moved back to allow him to enter. "I've sorted them out; they're in that cardboard box on the table."

Ken glanced at the box and then at me. He took a hesitant step towards me. "Annabel, you've never let me explain about that night at Mike's flat. I didn't mean to upset you . . ."

"I think you knew exactly what you were doing." My eyes flicked over him scornfully. "You didn't have to get me stoned to have sex with me, Ken."

"I'm really sorry." He gave me one of his flashy smiles. "Won't you give me another chance, Annabel?"

"Please take the records and go." I wanted nothing to do with him. His presence in my flat made me uncomfortable; he was a reminder of a night I wanted to forget.

He suddenly grabbed my arm and pulled me hard against him. I pushed him off but he tangled his fingers in my hair, forcing my head back. His teeth scraped against mine, his knee went between my legs and he rammed himself up against me. I could feel the hardness of his erection through the thin material of my dress.

"You were willing enough," he muttered. "You're a bloody prick teaser, that's what you are. What you need is a seeing to."

"And you're going to give me one, I suppose?" I laughed in derision. "You're a one second wonder, Ken. You wouldn't know a female orgasm if it looked you in the face."

"You bloody bitch!" he cried, enraged. For a moment he looked stunned, then he struck me across the face.

I brought my knee up sharply and he gave a cry of pain, staggering back as he clutched himself between the legs. The respite was only momentary. He was preparing to launch himself at me again, but before he had recovered his breath I picked up a sharp kitchen knife that had been lying next to the box of records and held it poised to strike.

"Come near me again and I'll use this on you," I threatened. "I'll mark you, Ken. I mean it! You won't look so pretty when I've finished."

"You wouldn't dare . . ." He advanced a couple of steps, then stopped and seemed hesitant.

"Just try me," I said, a smile fluttering about my mouth as I saw the uncertainty in his eyes. "This knife would make a mess of your looks, believe me."

"Crazy bitch," he said and swore. "You loved it that night, no matter what you say. You're like an iceberg one minute then a bloody whore the next."

"Crazy or not, I'll give you something to remember me by if you touch me again." I backed away from the table. "Take those records and get out."

"I'm going," he snarled. "I must have been mad to think I was in love with you. You're weird, Annabel."

"Get out or I'll . . ."

He gave a squeak of fright as I raised my arm, made a dive for the box and retreated to the door; there he turned to glance back at me before going out and slamming it behind him.

I rushed to bolt it after him, feeling sick. My knees were about to give way and I was feeling faint. I didn't know whether I could have actually carried out my threat or not, though for a moment I had felt so angry that I just might . . . I just might?

And if I could have used that knife on Ken in my anger, it was possible that as a child I just might have dropped that lighted match into the cot. Turning, I made a dash for the bathroom, retching again and again as I was sick into the toilet . . .

Nine

W e had a wonderful time in Paris. Charles had planned the trip so that we had time to explore the magical city together. We visited several galleries, including the Louvre, wandering through its vastness for hours to gaze spellbound at the magnificent paintings. Charles knew so much more about these things than I did, and he began to teach me little things about the way certain brush strokes could be more of a signature than the artist's name itself.

"See the way the paint is applied, Annabel," he said. "And those frantic brush stokes; that's typical of Van Gogh's later work after he was taken to the asylum. Now compare the vivid colours with those pictures we saw of Van Goyen; the smudgy greys and browns and the way he relies on atmosphere rather than detail. Then think about Van Meegeren . . . said to have been one of the best forgers ever. His picture *The Supper at Emmaus* was widely accepted as being by Vermeer because it had the visual signatures, but scientific tests later proved it a forgery. Remember that lesson and learn that even experts can be fooled."

"What do you think she is saying?" I asked, gazing up at the Mona Lisa. "That secret smile of hers fascinates everyone who sees it, but I always wonder what she was thinking."

"Probably that she was hungry and wished the artist would get a move on," Charles said with a laugh. "Speaking of which, I think it's time we ate, don't you?"

We had lunch at a cafe near the river, eating leisurely as we watched people strolling by in the early summer sunshine. It was much warmer now than when we had first visited Paris together and the chestnut trees were in full bloom. Even the air seemed to taste like wine to me as I nursed my secret hopes and let them nurture and grow inside me.

After lunch we walked by the river and I had my portrait drawn by one of the artists on the Left Bank. Charles said that it was very like me and asked if he could have it. Of course, I said yes, and hugged his arm, feeling happier than I could ever remember being before. We went back to the hotel and made love.

Our bodies entwined in a warm, languorous sensuality, fitting together so naturally that it was as if we had been made for each other. Pleasure washed over us in little wavelets rather than a great rushing tide, leaving us both satiated and at peace.

"Tonight I'm taking you to the opera, but tomorrow I shall be in a meeting all day," Charles said as he watched me dressing afterwards. "I want you to use the time to buy yourself those new clothes. We're going out together more often in the evenings from now on, and that means you're going to need evening gowns and some good suits or dresses, Annabel. Just choose whatever you like and have the bill sent to me, spend as much as you need."

"If that's what you want." I bent to kiss him. My will was subservient to his. He was my lover, my mentor, my father and my god. Never had a woman been a more willing slave to her man than I. "Thank you, Charles."

"I want you to be happy. You've given me so much, Annabel. I'm very grateful."

His words made my heart sing. I was young and in love and it seemed that everything I had ever wanted was within my grasp, the torment and guilt of my childhood long behind me. Happiness was there, just waiting for me to reach out and take it.

We flew back to London the next day and I went to the doctor as soon as Charles had left for his office. When I left I knew for certain that I was carrying my lover's child and I was filled with an overwhelming sense of joy.

Charles was thinking about asking me to marry him; I sensed that he had been on the verge once or twice, hesitating only because he felt that he was too old for me, and because of his illness. An affair was one thing but he had been reluctant to ask too much of me. Marriage would mean that I was tied to a man much older than myself, a man with uncertain health who might become more of an invalid as the years went on. In my own mind the pleasures of being married to Charles, a man I both loved and respected, far outweighed the disadvantages, but he was too unselfish to ask for what he would consider a sacrifice of my youth and beauty. My pregnancy would change all that. It would make him see how right it was that we should be together.

I decided to tell him that evening. Charles had no engagements for once and I cooked for him myself. Cooking was one of my accomplishments, something I had excelled in at school, and I put a great deal of effort into producing a meal that Charles could enjoy but which would not destroy his diet. He was impressed and told me that it was as good as anything he had ever eaten in a restaurant. I glowed as I basked in his praise.

Charles made me feel so good about myself. When I lay in his arms all the painful memories were banished to a far corner of my mind where they could not hurt me. How could he imagine that I would not gain as much from our marriage as he? It was what I wanted more than anything else in the world; there was nothing that would give me more pleasure than to be his wife, look after his home . . . and bear his children.

We had coffee and liqueurs, then I told him. He stared at me in blank disbelief for several seconds before he spoke. "This is a shock. I never dreamed—"

"You aren't angry with me, Charles?" I felt a prickling sensation at the nape of my neck. What was wrong? I had been so sure he would be pleased, so sure that my instincts were right, that he must want a son of his own. He had so much to give a child.

Charles raised his head and there were tears in his eyes. I knelt at his feet, gazing up at him. He reached out to stroke my hair, his fingers playing in its silkiness.

"You are quite sure, Annabel?"

"I went to the doctor today while you were at the office. I . . . I thought you would be pleased, but you're not, are you?"

"You mustn't think that," he said quickly. "It was a shock. I didn't ask if you were on the Pill because I thought it didn't matter – that my illness had made me incapable of having a child, as I've been told it sometimes does."

"It is your child, Charles. I swear it."

He saw the hurt in my face and shook his head. "I don't doubt you," he said. "Don't be upset, Annabel. I'm delighted, believe me. If I've caused you to think otherwise, forgive me. I had given up all hope of becoming a father." Suddenly

100

the delight was in his eyes. "You've given me so much and now this—"

"I love you, Charles," I said, gazing up at him earnestly. "All I want is to make you happy."

"Bless you, my darling." He leant forward to kiss me. "I shall always be grateful to you." His hand caressed my head. "Of course this means we shall be married as soon as possible."

"Oh, Charles," I whispered.

I felt safe and warm. At last I had found the sheltered harbour I had been looking for since I was a child of five. Charles loved me. He would look after me and care for me and I would no longer be alone. I would never need to go back to that place of green mists that hovered somewhere in the buried regions of my mind.

Charles and I were married in London at a registry office. He thought that it would look slightly ridiculous for a man of his age to have a white wedding with all the fuss and publicity that would attract.

It didn't matter to me, all I wanted was to be his wife.

Mary and her husband came to our wedding. She was visibly pregnant and very pleased with herself. I hugged her and congratulated them both, but I kept my own secret to myself.

The ceremony was brief and our friends had been asked not to shower us with confetti as it made such a mess on the pavements outside. It all seemed to be over quickly and the reception was quite small, very different to Mary's. I had so few friends I wanted to invite and Charles asked only a cousin and his wife.

"We don't want to get involved with all that just yet," he said. "When we come back from Venice, I'll take you down to Larkspur, and we'll give a big party, introduce you to everyone."

I sent a card to Edith Fisher, telling her I was getting married, but I didn't invite her to the wedding. I doubted whether she would have wanted to travel all the way up to town. Besides, she was not really my family and I wanted no reminders of the past on my special day.

The next morning we flew off to Venice for our honeymoon.

We spent two glorious weeks together in that wonderful place, walking in St Mark's Square, watching the pigeons and taking gondolas along the intricate waterways, beneath golden arches and ancient bridges of indescribable beauty. The sun shone the whole time, bathing us in a soft warmth that had a magic all of its own.

"I wish we could stay here for ever," I said to Charles as I stood on the balcony of our hotel and let the mellowed charm of Venice sink deep into my soul. There was something so heartbreaking about its ancient palaces and the sound of the water lapping against the walls that I wanted to cry. "It's so beautiful, Charles."

"You are beautiful," he said and came to put his arms around me. "But Venice is special, I must admit. We shall come again, Annabel. There's so much I want to show you, a whole world that I want to share with you."

I turned in his arms, lifting my face for his kiss. I knew that a part of my charm for Charles was that I was so innocent of the world and so eager to learn. He enjoyed teaching me, seeing my innocent pleasure in all the new sights and sounds he was able to spread out before me. It had given a new meaning to his life, an outlet for the wealth he had amassed over the years which meant so little to him in itself, and there was the child growing inside me.

"Besides, I want to take you to Larkspur," he said. "It's time you saw the house where I was born."

"Shall I like it?" I asked, gazing up at him. "Larkspur . . . it's a pretty name."

"It's all right as a house, I suppose," he said grudgingly. "It has been in the family for years, but I prefer to live in London. I don't suppose we'll use it all that much. But it might be more peaceful for you when the time comes . . ." His hands caressed my slightly rounded belly. "And the country is better for children."

"I shan't want to be away from you, Charles."

"We'll work something out," he said. "We can go down at weekends or I can commute."

I felt the first flicker of doubt and I wasn't sure I wanted to visit Larkspur if it meant that Charles and I might be separated.

"We're nearly there." Charles turned to me with a smile. "Tired, Annabel?"

"No, not at all." I shook my head and glanced out of the window.

We were in the village now. Barrington was a few miles south of Cambridge and had an open, picturesque aspect despite the rather ugly chimneys of the cement works which spoiled the skyline at one end. There were broad greens on either side of the through road, an old inn with white plastered walls, and several thatched cottages.

Larkspur House was situated outside the village. It stood back off the road, protected from prying eyes by a crumbling brick wall and a tangled mass of overgrown trees. A stranger might drive by and not know it was there at all. It was even more isolated, Charles told me, in winter when the mist drifted over the low lying road.

I sat forward as we came to a halt outside, looking at the faded rose bricks and the long, leaded windows with a sense of wonder. How could Charles prefer to live in London when he had this wonderful house?

I was enchanted with it and I couldn't wait to go inside; there was something so timeless and peaceful about it, and I felt that it had sat there slumbering in the sunshine just waiting for me.

"Look at the conservatory," I said as we got out of the car. "All that lovely white ironwork supporting the dome . . . it's so beautiful, Charles. I love it."

He gave me an amused look and unlocked the front door. As we entered I could see that someone had been in to clean but it still had an unloved, unlived-in air. There was a surface shine to the furniture and fresh flowers had been placed in a vase in the hall, but it was obvious that the house had been neglected for a while. I thought that I would enjoy making it come back to life.

"May I explore?" I asked eagerly. "Please, Charles, I want to see everything."

"Do as you like," he said with an indulgent smile. "It's your home now, Annabel. You'll find me in the small sitting room opposite the kitchen when you've finished. I'll put the kettle on."

I hardly heard him as I drifted away, opening doors and peeping into rooms, most of which were closed and cold, the furniture still covered with white sheets. I found a room with dark leather settees and chairs and an impressive mahogany desk, which had been prepared for use and which I guessed was

Charles's study. There was a large dining room, a library with long windows that opened out onto the terrace and neglected flowerbeds, two drawing rooms and the smaller back parlour Charles preferred. Upstairs there were several bedrooms and bathrooms, one of which still had an original Victorian porcelain bath and washbasin, but the master bedroom had an en suite shower, bath, vanity unit and all the modern conveniences necessary for comfort.

Charles had just carried a tray of tea into the small sitting room when I rejoined him.

"Well, what do you think?" he asked. "Could you be happy here?"

"I love it," I replied. "That fireplace in the large drawing room is gorgeous and the friezes . . ." I breathed a sigh of reverence.

"The fireplace is genuine Adam," he said. "Quite a lot of the house is original Queen Anne, but the friezes and fireplace were put in later when one of the restorations was done."

"It could be made into a real home, Charles. With some thought and a little time."

"You must do as you like. It will give you something to think about when you come here for the birth of our son."

"So sure it's going to be a boy?" I asked with a teasing look. "Supposing we have a girl?"

He came to put his arms around me, looking down at me as if I were some kind of a goddess.

"I shall be happy whatever we have," he said. "Just as long as the child is well and strong."

"It will be," I promised, knowing that the anxious look in his eyes was because he could not quite shake off the fear that our child would inherit his illness.

"Sit down and have a cup of tea," he said. "I want you to take care of yourself from now on, Annabel."

"I shall, don't worry, darling."

Charles was being so protective of me. He was like a child who had been given a fabulous toy and still couldn't quite believe it. I felt that if I asked for the moon he would reach up and snatch it from the sky to place it at my feet. I had no need to ask for anything; he gave me everything that any woman could possibly want.

*　　　*　　　*

104

Charles went back to London on Monday, leaving me at Lark-spur to prepare for our first dinner party. I was a little worried about him being alone at the flat but he promised to telephone every morning.

"I'm so much better now than I was," he said, "and you can ring me every day at the office to remind me to take my insulin as usual. It's only for a few days."

"It's just that I shall miss you."

"I'll miss you too," he said and kissed me.

I drove him to the station at Foxton, then went straight back to Larkspur. As I let myself in I could feel the house opening itself to embrace me, welcoming me home.

Charles had insisted that I ask the woman who came in every now and then to oversee things to help me clean the house right through. I telephoned her at once and she readily agreed to give me the extra time.

"I really appreciate you coming so quickly," I said when she arrived later that day.

Mrs Robson was a pleasant, motherly woman with iron-grey hair and a cheerful smile. I liked her immediately.

"It's about time this place was opened up," she said, looking round with satisfaction. "I've always felt it was a pity that Sir Charles didn't come down more often."

"We shall be here more in future. To be honest, Mrs Robson, I've fallen in love with the house."

She gave me a look of approval. "That's nice, Lady Cheshire. You're different from what I expected. I can tell you that the announcement of your marriage caused quite a stir round here."

"What do you mean?"

Her dark eyes sparkled with merriment. "All the tongue waggers are going to be in for a surprise when they meet you. They were all quite sure you were some wicked femme fatale."

"Because Charles is older than me, I suppose?"

"Everyone was convinced he would never marry . . . now he turns up with a lovely young lady like you. You've got them all guessing."

"I suppose they think I married him for his money?"

"I expect some of them do, but you didn't, did you?"

"No, I didn't," I said and smiled at her. She was a gossip, of course, but easy to get on with, and I sensed that I had found a friend.

"Well, I can't stand here all day talking. I'd best get on or we'll never get done."

Between us we turned out every room, making the spiders run as we cleaned and polished. By the time we had finished the faint aroma of damp and mustiness had been replaced by lavender and the transformation had begun. There was much, much more to be done, but Larkspur had started to come alive.

On the night of our party lights blazed from every window and the house was filled with flowers; vases of tall lilies and bowls of wonderful scented roses stood on little tables and in alcoves, their perfume wafting through every room.

I had worked very hard to make this first dinner party a memorable occasion. The table looked like something from a Victorian picture postcard album, festooned with garlands of flowers that weaved in and out of the shining silver, pure white china and crisp cut glass – all of which sparkled in the light of the row of single silver candlesticks I had placed down the middle of the long, highly-polished table.

"It all looks wonderful," Charles said when he saw the finished effect. He put his arm about my waist and kissed my cheek. "You are very clever, Annabel. I'm proud of you."

I glowed in the warmth of his praise, and this helped to carry me through the slightly awkward period when our guests began to arrive. They were all strangers to me, most of them long-standing friends of my husband and nearer his age than mine. I sensed that they were very curious about me, and I could see the speculation in their eyes as they weighed me up, trying to discover what was special about me . . . so special that Charles had decided to marry at last.

They were not all from the village. Some had travelled down from London, some from even further afield. The last couple arrived some twenty minutes after the others were all safely ensconced in the large drawing room with their drinks. I had begun to think that they were not coming when the doorbell rang.

Charles looked at me as I moved to leave the room. "You check on the dinner, darling," he said. "I'll let Rosemary and William in. Now that they are here we shall be ready to eat in a few minutes."

"Yes, of course," I replied and smiled as I went into the

kitchen to make sure that everything was going according to plan. I had prepared everything myself earlier, but Mrs Robson was in charge of dishing up and serving the meal.

Having satisfied myself that everything was as it should be I returned to the drawing room. The new arrivals were standing with Charles by the window and I had a moment to observe them before they were aware of me. The woman was pretty with soft, dark hair and brown eyes, but not particularly stylish or remarkable; her husband was a tall man and rather good-looking with black hair and strong features. They all turned as I walked towards them, and I fancied I saw a slightly nervous expression in the woman's eyes.

"Annabel, darling," Charles said. "This is my friend William Carr and his wife Rosemary. William and I were at school together."

"Pleased to meet you, Annabel," William Carr said, taking my hand in a cool, firm grasp. "I'm delighted that Charles has at last found himself a wife, and such a delightful one. It's about time he had someone to look after him. Doesn't take anywhere near enough care of himself."

"William!" his wife admonished with a faint shake of her head. She extended her hand to me, removing it before our fingers had barely touched. "Annabel will be thinking Charles is an invalid if you go on like that."

"Oh, she knows what's she's taken on, don't you, darling?" Charles glanced at me and then away. "Well, shall we go in, everyone? I think dinner is about ready."

It was odd but I had the feeling that he didn't want me to talk to these new arrivals too much.

The evening was a success; it was very late when the last of our guests departed and Charles came back into the sitting room, where I was gathering up some of the dirty glasses.

"Leave that to the morning," he said. "You've been working hard all week, Annabel. Mrs Robson will clear up tomorrow."

"I'll just take these to the kitchen—"

"I said leave them!"

I was surprised at the harsh note in his voice.

"Is there something wrong, Charles?"

He ran a hand over his hair, looking weary. "No, of course not.

I'm simply tired and I know you must be. I don't want you doing too much, that's all."

I went to put my arms about him, looking up into his face. "It's sweet of you to be concerned about me, Charles, but I'm fine. I shan't need to start putting my feet up for months yet."

"It's just that I couldn't bear to lose you or the baby now," he said and bent to kiss me very gently. "My life was pretty empty before you came along, Annabel. I don't want to be alone again."

"You won't be," I said and touched his cheek. "I'm coming back with you this week. The house is looking much better now and Mrs Robson will come in twice a week in future. I'm going to stay with you in London, at least until a few weeks before the baby is born."

"Are you sure you wouldn't rather be here? I know how much you love the house."

"I love you more," I said. "Besides, I want to shop for some special wallpapers and materials for new curtains. I can do that better in town. And I married you to be with you, Charles."

He smiled down at me. "You do know I care for you very much, don't you, Annabel? I'm very grateful for all you've done for me."

"You don't have to be grateful," I said. "I love you. All I want is for us to be happy together."

"You go on up now," he said, turning away from me. "I'll make sure everywhere is locked up and then I'll join you."

I was thoughtful as I went upstairs. Charles seemed a little strange tonight, and for the first time since we had made love I had seen that deep sadness in his eyes.

The next morning I thought I must have imagined Charles's mood; he was relaxed and cheerful as we spent some time in the garden together, planning what we would do over the coming months.

"I should like all this area cleared in front of the library," I said. "These shrubs are old, Charles. I would like to replace them with roses and lilies, lots and lots of beautiful lilies. I think all the flowers in this bed should be white, and over there we'll have pale pinks and blues . . ."

"I'll get someone in to do the clearing and digging," he said, "then you can plan where you want things – but you mustn't do too much. We don't want anything to happen to the baby."

He was so excited about the child. It meant so much to him that he was to be a father at last.

"I promise nothing will go wrong," I said. "I'll be very careful, Charles."

"Just as long as you're happy," he said, and took my hand. "Let's go and have lunch somewhere now, Annabel, then we'll drive back to London this afternoon."

I took a last lingering look around the garden, which had been more neglected than the house, trying to imagine what it had been like before everything had gone wild. Gardening had never particularly interested me until now, but then I had never felt about anywhere as I did this place.

I turned to Charles with a thrill of excitement. "It's all going to be so wonderful," I said. "We'll have Christmas here together and then in the spring we'll have our child . . ."

He took both my hands in his, lifting them to kiss my fingertips. "Yes, it's all going to be wonderful," he said, and then we turned and went into the house arm in arm.

At Christmas we had a huge tree in the drawing room and draped holly and mistletoe down the stairs and over the fireplace. On Christmas Eve we held a huge party, inviting Charles's friends and business acquaintances, together with people from the printing works. Mary and her husband came for the party, bringing their new baby with them and staying over for Christmas lunch. Charles liked them and said how pleased he was that I had her as a friend.

"You don't seem to have many friends of your own age," he said. "I sometimes worry that you must be lonely, Annabel."

"All I really want is to be with you," I told him. "I still see Jane for lunch occasionally and there's Edith Fisher."

Charles frowned. We had been down to visit Edith once since our marriage and he hadn't liked her very much.

"I've been thinking about her," he said. "It might be best if you were to sell that old house, Annabel. Perhaps you should buy a small bungalow for her . . . though she isn't really your responsibility at all. It isn't as if she were related."

"No, but I feel responsible for her," I said. "I have thought about selling the house. Maybe I'll go down and see her after the baby is born."

"Well, there's no hurry," he said. "But if you decide to sell I'll handle it for you."

"I'll think about in a few months' time," I promised.

For the time being all I wanted to think about was my husband and my child. Charles was so protective of me, so caring that I felt as if I were wrapped in a cocoon of love.

The days and weeks passed and my time came nearer. I was beginning to feel uncomfortable now and Charles suggested that it was time for me to live at Larkspur.

"I shall feel easier if you're there," he said. "There's a good maternity hospital in Cambridge, and Mrs Robson will come in every day just to make sure you're all right, Annabel. I'll come down as often as I can, definitely every weekend."

I agreed reluctantly. Although I loved the time I spent at Larkspur I didn't want to leave Charles. He was very good about doing his insulin these days and he usually remembered to eat when he should, but I enjoyed being with him.

"I'll go," I said. "But after the baby is born I shall come back here, Charles."

"Well, we'll see," he replied and kissed me. "Perhaps I could find another house nearer to town."

"You wouldn't think of selling Larkspur?"

"I'm not sure. Let's wait and see how we feel, shall we?"

I had been lying down when Mrs Robson called to tell me there was a telephone call and I felt slightly woozy as I got up and walked to the top of the stairs. Somehow I must have missed my step when I was about halfway down and I fell the rest of the way.

"Lady Cheshire!" Mrs Robson looked at me in horror. "Are you all right, madam?"

"I missed my step . . ." I got to my feet gingerly. "I don't think there are any bones broken."

I could feel some soreness in my back but that was all. I went to answer the phone, talking to the caller – who was from one of the charities Charles was interested in – for a few minutes, then replaced the receiver and turned back to Mrs Robson, who was still standing there in the hall, looking at me.

"You might have killed yourself. I don't know what Sir . . ."

She stopped mid-sentence as I gasped and clutched at myself. "What's wrong? Are you in pain?"

I nodded, unable to speak for a moment, then, "I think, I think it's the baby."

"But it's not due for another week or two." She was obviously dismayed. "It's the fall, that's what's done it. You just sit down, and leave everything to me. It's a good thing I'm here, that's all I can say."

I obeyed, letting her take over as I fought the pain. It was much worse than I had thought it would be and I was terrified. Supposing I had harmed the baby? Charles would never forgive me if I lost it now.

Thankfully, the doctor arrived within a quarter of an hour and I was soon in an ambulance and on my way to the hospital. Once there I was reassured by the efficiency of the doctors and nurses, and I forgot to be afraid as the pain took over. From then on I was aware only of the struggle to bring my child into the world; for a while I suffered an indescribable agony, but at last it was all over and I was able to hold my son in my arms.

I looked at his tiny, red screwed-up face and felt a wave of fierce, protective love sweep over me. He was mine, my baby, my son.

"Charles always said it would be a boy," I whispered, tears stinging my eyes. "Isn't he beautiful?"

"Gorgeous," the nurse agreed, "but he gave you a lot of pain and I think you should try to sleep now."

She took the child from me and laid him in a cot next to my bed. I was in my own private room, just as Charles had arranged. I lay looking at my son's face for a while, then I closed my eyes and drifted into a deep sleep.

When I opened my eyes again it was to see Charles bending over the cot to look at his son. I made a slight sound and he turned to me, his face clouding with concern.

"Thank goodness you're both all right," he said and kissed my cheek. "I came as soon as I could. I was afraid I might lose both of you."

"It just brought things on a bit sooner," I said and held his hand tightly. "I'm fine now. I was very tired, but I'm all right, and Anthony is perfect."

We had chosen the names together; Anthony for a boy, Caroline for a girl.

111

"I couldn't bear to lose you, or our son," he said and glanced back at the cot.

There was such pride in his face as he looked at the child.

"Don't you think he looks a lot like you?" I asked. "He has your colouring, Charles. His hair will be dark like yours."

"Yes, but he has your eyes, Annabel. I hope he will take after you rather than me."

"Oh no," I said. "I want him to be just like his father."

"As long as he doesn't have diabetes I'll be happy."

There were signs of tiredness in his face. I moved my hand across the bedcover and he took it in his own once more. "Are you all right, Charles? I wish I were at home to look after you."

"I've been very careful," he said. "I leave notes all over the place to remind me to do things. You needn't worry, darling, there won't be any accidents."

"You're important to me and Anthony needs his father. You must take care of yourself, for us."

"Dearest girl," he murmured. "Sometimes I think I don't deserve the happiness you've given me."

"Oh, Charles!" I laughed and shook my head at him. "What an odd thing to say. You're such a good, decent man. Of course you deserve to be happy."

He said no more but that strange sad expression was there in his eyes again. Charles had given me everything I could possibly want; we shared a full and exciting life, so what was he hiding from me? What could bring such a look to his eyes on the day his son was born? The day that should have been the happiest of his life.

Ten

Charles gave me a double string of pearls the day we returned to Larkspur with Anthony. They were large beads with a rich creamy colour and a pretty platinum and diamond clasp, and they must have cost a fortune.

"You spoil me," I said, reaching up to kiss him. "They are beautiful, Charles. I shall always treasure them."

"You deserve them," he said, "for giving me my son."

Charles took the child in his arms and I glowed as I saw the pride and love in his face. It meant so much to him to have a son. For a moment I was almost jealous of his love for Anthony, but then he smiled at me and the feeling faded.

"Are you sure you will be all right here alone?" he asked. "Perhaps we should get a nurse in to help you look after the boy, Annabel?"

"Not just yet," I said. "I want to look after him myself, besides, I've got Mrs Robson and . . . I'm thinking of asking Edith to come and live in, Charles." I saw his frown and went on quickly, "I know you didn't like her very much, but she is devoted to me, and it would be useful to have someone here all the time. I want to be with you at the flat and it would be better if Edith looked after this house for us while we were away. I could sell Grandmother's house then."

"I was meaning to speak to you about that," Charles said. "Your solicitor rang while you were in hospital. It seems that they want to tear all those old houses down and build a supermarket. You could get a good price for it, Annabel."

"Let me have Edith here for a while," I said. "If it doesn't work out we'll get her a cottage in the village so that I can visit her sometimes. Please, Charles . . . I've been a little worried about her living alone in that terrible old house."

"Well, if it's what you want—" he gave in reluctantly. "But don't stop Mrs Robson coming in. And if it doesn't work out

Edith goes. I mean it, Annabel. There's something about her I don't care for, but I know you're fond of her."

"It isn't exactly that . . ."

I couldn't explain to Charles what I meant, but he wasn't really listening anyway. He glanced at his watch and I knew he was waiting for his taxi to arrive. He kissed my cheek as we heard it outside.

"I'll phone in the morning," he said. "I may be late this evening so don't bother ringing the flat, Annabel."

"I'll ring the office at lunchtime, shall I?"

"It isn't necessary, Annabel. I've got my routine mapped out now and I'm so much better these days anyway. I told you that new dietician had relaxed my diet, didn't I?"

"Yes. Well, as long as you're sure."

"Quite sure. Don't fuss, Annabel. I'll telephone you tomorrow."

I watched as he picked up his briefcase and went out, wondering why he seemed so impatient to leave that morning.

I wrote to Edith explaining what was happening with the house and asking if she would like to come and live at Larkspur.

'I know you're happy where you are,' I wrote, 'but it looks as if the house will have to come down soon. I think it might be best if you came to me for a while. I'll arrange to have the house cleared; there's nothing I want because I took all Grandmother's personal bits and pieces to London when I moved there. We'll see how things work out, and I can always buy a nice, modernised cottage for you somewhere near me. Please consider it, Edith, and let me know your decision as soon as possible.'

Having posted the letter, I forgot about it. Edith was stubborn and I doubted it would be easy to persuade her to move. As for myself, I should never again live in that house of shadows and memories that were best forgotten. I wanted to live here at Larkspur, except when I stayed with Charles at the flat.

I was missing him already, but we had agreed I should stay on at Larkspur. He had promised to come down every weekend and there was so much I wanted to do in the house and garden.

Charles had had the old shrubs cleared away as he'd promised and the flowerbeds in front of the library were prepared ready for me to plant the bulbs and rosebushes I'd

114

ordered. Summer was coming on and I should be able to spend many happy hours in the garden with Anthony beside me in his pram.

Anthony was sleeping peacefully in his cot. It wasn't warm enough to take him outside yet, but I thought I would make a start by planting a few summer flowering bulbs.

"Wrap up warm," Mrs Robson advised as she saw me preparing to go out. "And don't do too much. A little at a time, that's best until you're feeling yourself again."

I thanked her and went out into the garden.

I was in the garden four days later when Mrs Robson came to fetch me. She looked puzzled and slightly bothered as she said, "There's someone to see you, Lady Cheshire. She says her name is Miss Fisher and that she has come to live here."

"Edith . . ." I got to my feet, stripping off the gloves I had worn for planting the bulbs. "Edith is here? I only wrote to her at the beginning of the week."

"Here and all her baggage with her," Mrs Robson said. "She came in a taxi a few minutes ago with half a dozen boxes and a couple of suitcases. I told her to wait in the kitchen. I didn't realise she was a friend of yours, madam."

"She isn't exactly a friend," I replied. "She used to look after my grandmother when I was at school. I've asked her to stay for a while because the old house is going to be pulled down soon to make way for a supermarket."

I walked quickly up to the house. Edith was sitting primly on the edge of a wooden chair in the kitchen, her mouth drawn into a tight, straight line and her gloved hands folded in her lap. Apart from the colour of her hair, which was almost white now, she looked much the same as she had when we first met. She got to her feet as I entered and gave me an uncertain look; I realised she was nervous and I smiled at her encouragingly.

"Edith, I'm so glad you came," I said and went to kiss her cheek. "I wasn't sure you would agree."

"I've known they were going to knock them houses down for months," she said. "That solicitor of yours told me I would have to move out. He said he could get me a place in one of those cottages where they have a warden to look after you, but I told him I didn't like the idea of being fussed over. I'm not in my dotage yet."

115

"No, of course you're not," I said. I knew that she must be at least sixty but she was wiry and strong and she looked surprisingly fit. "But it will be much nicer if you live near me so that we can see each other sometimes, Edith."

"Well, naturally I came when you asked me," she said, and a little smile caught the corner of her mouth, making her look sly. "You know I always do what you want, Annabel. You won't need her now that I'm here." She sniffed and jerked her head towards Mrs Robson, who had lingered in the hall and was within hearing. "I can look after you and the house."

"Mrs Robson comes in twice a week," I said, ignoring her sniff that showed disapproval of my helper. "She will continue to do so, Edith, but there's more than enough work to do in a big house like this. Besides, you will probably want your own cottage to retire to soon."

"I'm not thinking of retiring just yet," she said and stood up. "If you show me my room I'll take my coat off and get started,"

"Wouldn't you like a cup of tea first?"

"I'll make it myself when I've unpacked," she said and sniffed again. "I would rather start as I mean to go on,"

Charles was dismayed to find Edith installed in the house when he came down the next day. He was his usual polite, gentlemanly self as he greeted her, but he allowed his annoyance to show once we were alone.

"I didn't dream you intended to have her here immediately," he said. "I expected we would discuss it further, Annabel, make the final decision together." Which meant that he had hoped to talk me out of it.

"You agreed I could ask her," I reminded him. "I wrote at once, but I thought she would need persuading. I was very surprised when she turned up four days later."

"You knew I didn't care for her. There's something—" He stirred his teacup, the spoon clinking agitatedly against the side. "To be honest she seems a bit odd to me, Annabel. I wouldn't trust her too much if I were you."

"I know she can be strange sometimes," I agreed, "but she is devoted to me, Charles. And she adores Anthony."

"I don't want her touching my son!"

"You should have seen her face when I showed him to her.

116

She wouldn't hurt him, Charles. Anyway I don't let anyone touch him, not even Mrs Robson."

"I still think we should have a nurse. It would make things easier for you, Annabel."

"Perhaps in a few months," I said. "When I come up to town it would be a little cramped with a nurse – unless we bought a larger flat?"

"I've been thinking about that," he said. "We could find a larger flat, or perhaps buy a house in Hampstead or Richmond. It would be easier for me than travelling up from Cambridgeshire."

"Would we have to sell Larkspur?"

"Not necessarily . . ." Charles was thoughtful. "I suppose we could keep it for holidays if you like, though you may change your mind when we find the new house."

"Larkspur is special," I said. "And even if we only come here occasionally it would be useful having Edith here to look after it."

"I suppose it might," he conceded. "But I'm still not happy about her, Annabel. We'll leave things as they are for a while, but once you've sold your grandmother's house, I think you should seriously consider buying her a little cottage of her own."

"Yes, I will," I promised, wanting to please him. "Now don't be cross any more, darling. I've missed you. Tell me what you've been doing with yourself these past few days."

"Just the usual," he said. "Work and a business dinner . . . nothing special." He finished his tea and stood up. "I think I'll take a bath, Annabel. Then we might go out for dinner this evening. Mrs Robson would come in and sit with Anthony."

I was about to protest that it wasn't necessary, that Edith could keep an eye on the child, but stopped myself just in time.

"I'll have a word with Mrs Robson before she leaves."

Charles went out into the hall. I heard him speak to Edith and then she came into the sitting room.

"Shall I take the tray now?"

"Yes, thank you," I said. "Don't bother to prepare the vegetables this evening, Edith. We are going out."

"I'll be in my room if you want me." Her mouth was tight and there was a stony expression in her eyes.

She picked up the tray, the china rattling ominously as she went out.

I stared at the door after she had gone. I was almost sure that she had been listening to my conversation with Charles – just how much had she heard?

Edith kept to her own room for most of the weekend. She rose early and went quietly about her work, then disappeared for the rest of the day, leaving Charles and I alone together. I wasn't sure whether she was being tactful or sulking, but I was relieved that she hadn't given him cause to complain of her presence again.

After Charles had left for the station on Monday morning she came downstairs and began to polish the furniture in the library.

"I'm going into Cambridge to do some shopping," I said to her after lunch. "If my husband should ring tell him I will telephone him this evening."

"Are you taking the child with you?"

Her eyes had a curious brightness as she looked at me, and I knew she was testing me. Charles had told me not to trust her, but I had seen her face when I first showed her my son and I was sure she would not harm him.

"No, I don't think so," I said. "He should sleep until I get back, but if he does wake it will probably mean he's wet. Do you think you can change him, Edith?"

"Anyone can use those things," she said with a little sniff, but there was a pleased look in her eyes. "I can manage, Annabel."

"Yes, I'm sure you can."

Perhaps I was taking a risk in leaving my precious son in her charge, but I thought Charles was wrong to be suspicious. She had always taken good care of my grandmother, and despite her sharp tongue and her funny ways, I believed she was genuinely devoted to me. Anthony would be safe with her.

I shall not pretend that I was perfectly easy in my mind as I set out for Cambridge, but I doubt if any new mother can ever leave her child without some qualms. I was gone just over an hour and a half. When I let myself in through the conservatory there was no sign of Edith in the kitchen or the downstairs rooms.

"Edith . . ."

My heart thudded against my ribs as I went up to the nursery. If anything had happened Charles would never forgive me, nor I myself . . . Seeing Edith sitting in a chair by the window I stopped to watch and my pulses ceased their frantic racing. She had Anthony cradled in her arms, a look of such bliss and contentment on her face that tears stung my eyes. How could I have doubted her for a moment?

Becoming aware of me, she turned and smiled. "He cried for a while, but he's better now."

"Thank you for looking after him so well, Edith."

"He's our baby, Annabel. He'll always be safe while I'm here. I shall always take care of you both."

She put the child into my arms and went from the room, closing the door softly behind her.

I knew then how much it had cost her to give up her own child for adoption all those years ago.

The next three weeks or so passed without incident. Charles wasn't happy about having Edith in the house, but he didn't say a great deal on the subject. She stayed in her own room as much as possible while he was at home and I thought that maybe in time he would come to accept her. Anyway, I was feeling so much stronger now that I was becoming restless without Charles. I wanted to be with him all the time and not just at weekends.

He felt that I should remain in the country for a few more weeks while he explored the possibilities of a new home for us, but after six weeks of seeing him only at weekends I decided I would go up to town in the middle of the week and surprise him.

I caught an early train on the Wednesday morning and took a taxi to the flat, half hoping to find him there. Laying Anthony's carrycot on the sofa in the living room, I called out to my husband but there was no answer. I was slightly disappointed that I would have to wait until the evening to greet him, but at least I could have a meal prepared for him.

I went into the kitchen. His breakfast dishes were still in the sink so he had obviously left in a hurry. Since it was not one of the days that his cleaning woman came in I washed the crockery, smiling when I realised that there was more than one day's washing up: two plates, two cereal bowls, two coffee cups and saucers. Oh, Charles! I thought, amused. So this is what you do when I'm not here to look after you. It's about time I came back.

The dishes neatly dried and replaced in their spaces, I went into the bedroom. The bed had not been made and the pillows were rumpled, the sheets and covers thrown back in disarray, as though Charles had been in a rush.

I shook my head as I went to plump up the pillows. The strong smell of perfume struck me as I bent over the bed and I froze in disbelief. That was a woman's scent and it was not one I had ever used. I backed away from the bed, looking at it with new insight. Both pillows had been used, as if Charles had slept with someone – a woman – here in our bed.

I was filled with revulsion. It wasn't true; it couldn't be true. Charles wouldn't . . . he wouldn't do this to me. He loved me, he adored me; I was the mother of his son. This was a trick of my imagination.

Moving slowly, my mind still reeling from the shock, I reached to pick up the pillow. The smell of perfume was stronger as I held it close to my face and then I saw the tiny smear of lipstick on the corner. I dropped the pillow and fled to the bathroom, where I vomited into the toilet, retching again and again until I was sweating and faint. At last I took a flannel and held it under the cold tap, wiping my face and rinsing my mouth. As I reached for the towel I was aware of that same perfume again and I backed away. She had been here, too! She had been everywhere in our home. Charles had brought another woman here. He had betrayed me! The god I had wanted only to serve had feet of clay: he was not worthy of the love I had given him so freely.

Anthony was whimpering. I went back to the sitting room, looking around me with fresh eyes. This was not really my home; it was exactly as it had been when I first came to work for Charles. I had made no impression on it: they were his books, his porcelain figurines . . . his bed . . . his whore!

Suddenly I realised what a fool I had been to imagine that Charles loved me. It was I who had gone to him on my knees, begging for love; I who had invested him with the qualities of a deity. But I could not have imagined all the things he had said to me, the kindness and tenderness he had shown me, the gratitude – gratitude! The word was like a canker in my brain, festering and spilling its poison through my veins. How many times Charles had thanked me for giving him his son . . . *his son*! Blind, stupid fool that I was! Imagining that he loved me when all the time it was the child he wanted.

Anthony was screaming for his feed. I took him into my arms, rocking him as I opened my blouse and held him to my breast. As his mouth tugged on me and his tiny fist clutched at my finger, I could feel the anger building inside my head, and the same words kept repeating themselves over and over again.

Charles had betrayed me. He did not love me. He did not love me. It was Anthony he wanted.

Replacing Anthony in his cot, I fastened my blouse. There was no point in my staying here. I would never come to the flat again. If Charles wanted to see his son he must come to Larkspur. That was my home now, my retreat. Anthony and I would go back there at once, but first there was something I wanted to do here . . .

"Annabel! What on earth are you doing sitting in the dark?"

Charles' voice startled me. I blinked in the sudden light as he switched on the lamps and glanced round the room, feeling dazed. For a moment I had thought I was back in my grandmother's house, in that world of green darkness I had inhabited as a traumatised child, but as I stared up at my husband everything came flooding back and I felt the pain strike deep into my heart once more.

Charles had betrayed me with another woman. I got to my feet and stared at him.

"I didn't hear you come in. I had been reading and I must have fallen asleep." Glancing at the cot beside me, I saw that Anthony was resting peacefully. I could not have slept for very long.

Charles was obviously ill at ease, his expression one of bewilderment and guilt. He was still wearing his overcoat and I knew he had come straight to this room to find me.

"Did you go to the flat today?"

"Yes." I lifted my eyes defiantly to his. "Why?"

"Why? You ask me why, Annabel?" He was angry and his eyes had the glitter of a hoar frost. I had never seen him like this before and it sent a chill of fear down my spine. "Why didn't you wait until I got back? Why not discuss things sensibly instead of . . ."

"After what I discovered?" I asked. "You had a woman there, Charles. You slept with her last night. Don't try to deny it. I smelt her perfume and I saw her lipstick on the pillow. You had breakfast together, didn't you?"

"Yes." The blunt affirmative was like a knife thrust in my heart. "But it doesn't affect you, Annabel. It has nothing to do with our marriage."

"How can you say that?" I cried, wild with pain. I wanted to strike out at him, to hit him, hurt him as he was hurting me. "You took another woman to our home. You went to bed with her, and then you tell me it has nothing to do with our marriage. How could you? I thought you cared for me, loved me."

"I do care for you," he said and the anger in his face was replaced with sorrow. "I care for you very much and I'm grateful—"

"Don't say that!" I screamed. My nails dug into the palms of my hands as I fought for control. I had worshipped him and he had betrayed me. Just like my father! "I don't want your gratitude. I thought you loved me, really loved me."

Charles took off his coat, his face grim. "Let's talk about this in a rational way. I never meant to hurt you, Annabel. Believe me, that was the last thing I wanted. What happened last night was something that may never happen again. Rosemary was upset. Her husband was away and—"

"Rosemary?" I glared at him. "Who is she? Some whore you picked up off the street?"

"Shut up!" His eyes glinted with anger. "I won't have you say such things. It wasn't like that."

"How was it then?"

"If you'll give me a chance, I'll tell you." Charles went to the sideboard to pour himself a glass of whiskey. "I've had meetings all day, and I could do without this from you."

"Have you eaten?" I asked automatically. "You shouldn't drink unless you've had a meal."

"I had something on the train. I wasn't in the mood to drive down after I saw the flat . . ." His eyes stabbed at me accusingly. "Did you have to do that, Annabel? I was particularly fond of those figurines. Did you have to smash them all?"

"That's why I did it. I wanted to hurt you. Did it hurt, Charles?" I saw the answer in his face and smiled bitterly. "Good. I'm glad you can feel pain, too." My mouth tasted of ashes.

"Annabel, don't be like this. Please—" He sank down wearily into an armchair. "It doesn't have to be this way. Rosemary isn't a threat to you, she never was."

"What do you mean, she never was?"

Suddenly it struck me and I knew who she was. Charles flushed as he saw I had made the connection.

"It's her, William Carr's wife, you invited them here to our first party—"

I was remembering the way he had tried to keep me from talking to Rosemary that night. I had thought it strange he had not suggested asking them to the Christmas party and now I understood.

"Did she want to look me over? How long has this been going on, Charles?"

"Fifteen years," he said and the knife struck deeper into my heart. "Rosemary can never divorce William. She cares about him in her own way and they have two boys. We never meant to hurt anyone. You may not believe this but last night was the first time we had been to bed together for years. I hadn't planned to see her again after you and I were married but it just happened . . ."

A harsh laugh escaped me. "You're in love with her," I said and I could feel the anger building inside me again. The fierce colours were burning behind my eyes and there was a throbbing at my temples. "You've always loved her, even when you were with me it was her you wanted,

Charles passed a hand across his eyes. "I can't deny I love Rosemary. I won't do that even for you, Annabel. But I do care for you. Our marriage has brought me a great deal of happiness and I'm sorry that you had to see what you did." His eyes were sad as he looked at me. "Please try to understand. Last night was nothing to do with you, with what we have. I don't want to leave you. Please try to forgive me and accept that it was outside our marriage."

"And if I can't?"

He shrugged his shoulders helplessly. "I don't know what else I can say, Annabel. What do you want from me?"

"I shall never come back to that flat. If we stay together, I shall live here. You can come down at weekends to see Anthony."

"If those are your terms I accept them," he said, looking unhappy. "Perhaps in time you will be able to forgive me. I should like us to have a comfortable relationship, Annabel. For our son's sake if nothing else."

My anger had drained away as swiftly as it had flared into life. I felt empty and sad. Maybe I should have told Charles then that it was over, but I was too hurt, too devastated to think clearly.

"I don't know," I said at last. "Perhaps in time . . . I was very hurt, Charles, that's why I smashed those figurines. I'm sorry. I shouldn't have done that. Sometimes I have this rage inside me . . ."

"They were only material things," he said sombrely. "Figurines can be replaced but I destroyed something infinitely more precious, didn't I? I destroyed your trust and your love. You have no idea how much I wish I could turn the clock back." His eyes pleaded with me. "I would never willingly have hurt you, Annabel. Please believe me."

Anthony had begun to whimper. I picked him up, holding him close to my heart and whispering soothing noises until he quietened. Charles watched me, his eyes full of a tearing sadness. I kissed my son's forehead and put him back in his cot.

"I shan't try to stop you seeing Anthony," I said quietly. "I'm not sure that I can forgive you, Charles. But give me time and I shall try."

"Thank you," he said. "I'll sleep on the sofa in the dressing room tonight. Perhaps you could have my things moved next time?"

"You can have our room. It's easier for you with the bathroom en suite. I'll move into one of the others in the morning."

"As you wish." He watched as I picked up Anthony's carrycot. "I have some work to do. I shan't disturb you when I come up."

I did not answer. Walking up to the nursery, I was thinking about the future. Larkspur would be my home and Anthony's. I would devote myself to my son, the house and garden.

I was not sure that I could ever forgive my husband.

Eleven

The hurt went too deep for tears. It would have been better if I could have cried away my disappointment and humiliation, but I couldn't. For the next few months Charles and I met as strangers. We were polite but distant, each inhabiting our own part of the house. We were united only by our love for Anthony, and it was his sudden illness that eventually brought us to a closer understanding.

It was a few weeks before Christmas. I had planned so much for our son's first Christmas and I intended to go ahead with it despite the continuing coldness between Charles and I. Both Edith and Mrs Robson were in the house when I went into Cambridge to do some shopping, and it was Mrs Robson who came rushing out to me when I got home that afternoon.

"What is it?" I asked, feeling a chill of fear as I saw her expression. "Anthony—"

"He started fretting soon after you left," she said. "I think he has a fever, should I ring for the doctor?"

"Yes, at once if you think it necessary." I was already inside the house and about to rush upstairs. "You shouldn't have waited for me to come home."

"Miss Fisher said I was making too much fuss."

Her words followed me as I ran upstairs. If Anthony was really ill the doctor should have been called immediately. I was already beginning to fear the worst.

Anthony was crying as I walked into the nursery. Edith had him in her arms as she walked the floor, trying to soothe him.

"Give him to me," I said. "Why didn't you call the doctor straight away?"

"It's only a little fever. He's probably teething."

I touched Anthony's forehead; he was very hot and he had a little rash on his cheeks.

125

"It might not be. You should have let Mrs Robson telephone."

I was angry with her because I was frightened. If my son had meningitis a delay in treatment could be fatal.

Mrs Robson came into the nursery. She looked at Anthony anxiously as she said, "The doctor's on his way, madam. He shouldn't be too long."

"Go down and wait for him," I said without looking at her. "You too, Edith."

They left without a word. I paced the floor with Anthony in my arms. He was screaming again and I was terrified. Supposing he died! I could not bear to lose him; he was all I had left now.

It was unbearable waiting for the doctor to arrive. He was there within a quarter of an hour but it seemed much longer. After a brief examination he looked grave.

"I should like to have him in hospital, Lady Cheshire."

"Is it meningitis?"

"I don't know," he replied. "He certainly has a nasty fever that needs treatment. Hospital would be the best place for him; they have special units and if it does turn out to . . . well, let's not think about that just yet."

"I'll take him straight in myself," I said. "I can't wait for the ambulance."

"I'll telephone and make the arrangements. They will be ready for you when you arrive."

I put Anthony back in his carrycot and covered him with his blanket, then I went downstairs. Mrs Robson was waiting at the foot of the stairs, watched from the kitchen doorway by a sheepish-looking Edith.

"Please telephone Sir Charles at his office, Mrs Robson," I said. "Tell him that Anthony has had to go into hospital with suspected meningitis."

"Yes, of course," she said. "I'm so sorry . . ."

"I'll speak to you both later," I said with a sharpness that was alien to me. "Excuse me, I have to go."

Afterwards I could never remember the nightmare drive to the hospital. A part of my brain told me to drive carefully, but my insides were churning and I felt sick. If Anthony died . . . Why did I always lose all those I loved? My father, mother, grandmother, and now Charles and I were estranged

. . . Without my son I should be alone again . . . my poor, darling little boy who hadn't even had a chance to live.

"Please don't do this to me—" I whispered. "I've been punished enough, please don't let my son die."

At the hospital they were waiting for us and a nurse took Anthony from my arms. I made a cry of protest but she gave me a sympathetic look.

"Just wait in there, Lady Cheshire. Someone will come and talk to you soon."

I walked into the small waiting room and sat down, feeling close to despair. I wanted to be with my baby. Where was he? What were they doing with him?

"Please don't let my baby die."

The words kept going through my mind as I stared blankly ahead of me. There were magazines on a small plastic table in front of me but I couldn't relax enough to read. After what seemed like an age but was probably about an hour a nurse brought me a cup of tea.

I looked at her hopefully. "Any news?"

"Doctor will see you soon," she said. "Is there anyone I can call for you?"

"My husband has been informed," I replied. "He will come if he can."

I sipped the tea, then left half of it to get cold on the table in front of me. The next hour was the worst of my life, until I finally heard footsteps and glanced up.

"Annabel—"

"Charles!" I cried and rushed to him. He enfolded me in his arms and I wept into his shoulder. "Thank God you are here. I've been waiting ages but they won't tell me anything."

"It's all right." He stroked my hair. "I've just spoken to the doctor. It is meningitis, Annabel, but not the serious kind."

"What do you mean? How can it not be serious?"

"Apparently there are two strains," he said. "One is a killer as you feared, but this is much less virulent. They are confident that he will be fine in a few days. It's all right, he isn't going to die."

"Oh, Charles," I sobbed with relief. "I was so frightened."

"I came as soon as I could," he said. "I'm sorry, Annabel. You shouldn't have had to go through this alone; I ought to have been with you."

"You're here now," I said, taking the handkerchief he gave me to wipe my face. "I'm so glad, Charles. I'm so glad you're here."

"Annabel . . ." His voice cracked with emotion. "I'm so sorry for everything. I've missed you so much." I lifted my head and he kissed me gently on the mouth. "Please forgive me. I've been miserable without you."

"I have forgiven you," I said. "Can we see him, Charles? Can we see our baby?"

"In a little while. They will come and fetch us." Charles gripped my hand tightly. "It's going to be all right, Annabel. Everything will be better in future. I give you my word."

I nodded and blew my nose. "You will stay, Charles? You won't leave us until he's home again?"

"Of course I'll stay," he replied. "I love you both, Annabel. These past few months have taught me just how much I need and love you."

It was almost a week before we could take Anthony home, but we spent the time together, visiting our son and getting to know each other again. This time there were to be no secrets between us.

The day we finally took our son home, Charles tried to explain about Rosemary. I told him it didn't matter, but he said that it was important that I understood.

For years they had accepted that they could not be lovers, because she was not prepared to either leave or betray her husband. She had never expected Charles to marry and when he did she felt betrayed and jealous herself, perhaps because I was so much younger and prettier.

"When she saw you at that party she felt that she had lost me," Charles said. "She started to ring me at the office and come over to the flat. Then one night she had a quarrel with William and she broke down in tears, saying that she felt her life was empty and that she wished she had left him years before."

"And so she stayed the night with you?"

I dug my nails into the palms of my hands. It still hurt me so much that he could have done what he had.

"Don't look like that, Annabel. It shouldn't have happened. I had loved her for so many years and she was in distress, but it's over. It will never happen again. I promise you."

"But if you love her—"

"I shall always feel something for her," he said. "I won't pretend otherwise. But I've missed you so much, Annabel. Please let me try to make up for what happened."

"I can't come back to the flat, Charles."

"I wouldn't ask that of you. I'll find us a house nearer London. We'll keep Larkspur if you really want it but—"

"I love Larkspur, Charles, but I want us to be together."

"We'll buy Edith that cottage," he said. "I'm sorry, Annabel, but I couldn't put up with her in the house all the time."

I was silent for a moment, then I nodded. "I suppose you're right, Charles."

"I shan't stop you seeing her. I'm not unfeeling, Annabel, but she has to go."

"I'll talk to her when you go back to London," I said. "It won't be for a while anyway. You've got to find the house and decide what to do about Larkspur."

"Even if we keep it I still think she should have her own cottage."

"Yes," I agreed reluctantly. I knew it would upset Edith to be separated from Anthony, but Charles came first. If we were to have a new beginning it was best this way. "See if you can find her a nice little cottage somewhere near here and then I'll take her to view it. We needn't say anything to her until it is all settled."

"I have to catch the early train tomorrow."

"I wish you didn't have to go, Charles."

"So do I but I'm afraid I must."

"I shall miss you."

"It won't be for long. I've arranged to see a house I think we might like on Tuesday."

"You will telephone me and let me know?"

"If it's suitable I'll take you to see it at the weekend and you can decide."

I stood up and offered him my hand. "Shall we go to bed now?"

"Are you sure, Annabel?"

"Quite sure." I smiled up at him, then remembered something. "Oh, before I forget, Charles, your new batch of insulin arrived today. I noticed they have packaged it differently. It's much stronger. You need to take only half the usual dose."

"Why must they change these things?" he said. "I get used to a routine then they do this."

"Well, don't worry." I reached up and kissed his cheek. "You have one more box of the old kind. Take that with you tomorrow and we'll check the new one out at the weekend. If I mark the new bottles I'm sure you will remember."

"You see," he said with a smile. "I couldn't possibly manage without you, my darling."

Charles left the house before I was awake. Anthony had been a little fretful in the night, and this time I thought perhaps it was his teeth starting to come through. Charles had seen me crawl back into bed at about one o'clock and he had thoughtfully left me to sleep on when he got up himself.

I fed my son and laid him back in his cot, once I'd watched him settle down and fall asleep, I went back to the bathroom I was again sharing with my husband and took a shower. While I was under it I thought I heard the phone ring, but by the time I had grabbed a towel and reached it, it had stopped. I hesitated and then picked it up, just in time to hear Charles's voice say goodbye.

"Goodbye, sir."

That was Edith replacing the receiver. I wondered why she hadn't come up to let me know he had telephoned, and I dialled the flat immediately. There was no reply. I replaced the receiver and rang his office number.

"I'm sorry, Lady Cheshire," his secretary said. "He hasn't arrived yet. Shall I ask him to call you when he comes in?"

"It isn't urgent. Just tell him I rang, will you?"

"Yes, of course."

When I was dressed I went downstairs. Edith was in the kitchen baking, a tray of small buns fresh from the oven in her hand. She put it on the table and took off the padded glove she was wearing.

"Did I hear the phone ring, Edith?"

"It was Sir Charles," she replied. "You were in the bathroom so I answered it. He wanted to know if he had left some papers on the hall table but he hadn't. He said he must have left them in the car and was going out to check."

"I see . . . I just wondered."

The small mystery was explained. Charles hadn't heard me telephone because he had gone down to the garage, which was situated beneath the block of apartments. When he arrived at the office he would get my message and ring me back.

It was a lovely day, and I spent most of it in the garden, weeding my lily beds. Anthony was beside me in his pram. He was awake some of the time but seemed quite peaceful.

At three o'clock I took a quick bath and washed my hair, then I went downstairs. Edith had just put the kettle on. She looked up as I went into the kitchen.

"Have there been any calls, Edith?"

"One from Mrs Robson to say her daughter is ill and she can't get in for a few weeks."

"Oh, I'm sorry. What's wrong with her daughter?"

"She didn't say."

"Well, I'll ring her myself and ask."

"No need. She's gone away. Her daughter lives in Bournmouth."

"Did she say when she would be back?"

"No."

I felt a flicker of annoyance. "Why didn't you call me, Edith? I should have liked to talk to her myself."

"She was in a hurry – and you were busy."

It was useless to pursue the argument, but I was a little put out that Edith seemed to have taken it upon herself to answer my calls.

"You're sure my husband hasn't rung?"

"Quite sure." Something flickered in her eyes. "He said he was going to be busy all day."

"Yes, I know." I took the cup of tea she had poured, sipping it thoughtfully. Charles was right. I hadn't wanted to admit it but Edith did have her own ways. It would be much better for everyone if she had her own cottage. I might as well prepare her for what was coming. "Edith, Charles and I have been thinking that—"

The telephone shrilled in the hall and I jumped up to answer it. Perhaps it was Charles. I snatched it up, my heart beginning to beat faster.

"Annabel Cheshire speaking . . ."

131

There was a pause for a moment, then a woman's voice, breathless and choked with emotion, "Annabel, I don't know how to tell you—" I heard her catch a sob in her throat. "It's Charles, he's – he took an overdose of insulin this morning—"

"Charles took an overdose . . ." I clutched at the wall to steady myself as the room began to spin. "Where is he? How is he?"

She hesitated, then, "He died in hospital five minutes ago."

"Charles is dead?" I held the receiver away from my ear, feeling bewildered, disbelieving. This couldn't be true. I was having a nightmare. "But why didn't anyone call me . . . Who is this?"

"It – it's Rosemary," she whispered. "I–I found him at the flat about an hour ago. I called the ambulance and I was going to ring you but your phone was engaged and . . . it was all so sudden, Annabel. They rushed him into the hospital but he had a heart attack. You couldn't have got here in time."

"What were you doing at the flat?"

Something didn't make sense. I tried to think what was wrong but my head was spinning and I felt faint.

"I called his office and they couldn't understand why he hadn't come in so, I went round to the flat . . ."

"But why didn't they ring me?"

"Charles's secretary said your phone was off the hook. She tried calling several times."

"I've been out in the garden. My housekeeper said there hadn't been many calls. She must have left it off this morning . . ." I tried to picture the phone as it had been when I'd first come downstairs. "No, she couldn't have done. I used it myself."

Had I left it off the hook upstairs? Had it been off for most of the day, maybe when Charles was trying to call me? I pictured him going into a coma, panicking, reaching for the phone . . . But he would have tried to call a doctor.

"It was engaged when I tried an hour ago." Her voice came to me from a long way off. I struggled to remain calm, to think clearly.

"Which hospital was he taken to?" She gave me the details and I wrote them down. "Thank you for calling."

"Annabel, I'm so sorry, sorry for everything . . ."

132

"So am I," I said coldly and replaced the receiver.

As I turned around I saw Edith come into the hall. She was looking at me oddly, almost expectantly.

"Charles . . . Charles is . . ."

The words stuck in my throat and then I fainted.

At the inquest the coroner passed an open verdict, though why anyone should imagine it was anything other than an accident I could not think. Charles had no reason to take his own life. I told that to the police when they questioned me about it.

"No, it couldn't possibly have been suicide," I repeated firmly over and over again. "My husband had no reason to kill himself. It was the new insulin. I told him there was one last box of the old strength left, but he took one of the new ones by mistake. He must have taken double the dosage."

The autopsy showed that Charles had taken a massive overdose. He must have done one injection and absentmindedly done it again. His memory had always been unreliable and this particular day it had proved fatal.

If only I had been with him! I would have been with him if I had not refused to return to the flat because of what had happened there. I was torn with guilt and remorse, blaming myself for what I knew was an accident. If I had been awake when Charles left . . . I could have checked that he had done his insulin properly; I could have made sure he had taken the correct box.

I went through the inquest and the funeral in a daze of grief. How ironic it was that Charles should die just when we had found each other again. All those months of being estranged and now he was dead. I felt numbed and I moved through the days like a zombie, hardly aware of what I did except for the times when I held my child in my arms.

"Oh, Charles," I wept as I looked down at my son. "Charles, why did you leave me?"

Every day seemed the same as the one before. Grey, empty days and long, restless nights. I paced the floor, feeling the loneliness seep into my soul. How could I face the rest of my life alone?

It was Edith who made me see what I was doing to myself. I came downstairs one morning still wearing my dressing robe, my hair hanging in lank wisps about my face, my eyes red from another night spent weeping and pacing the floor of my bedroom.

"You'll kill yourself," Edith muttered. "And what will happen to the boy, Annabel?"

"Nothing will happen to me."

My head was aching and I felt dazed. Why was she making so much fuss? There was nothing wrong with me.

She grabbed my arm, her fingers digging hard into my flesh as she dragged me in front of the hall mirror. "Look at yourself," she said. "Go on, look!"

I glanced in the mirror and then away. The woman I saw appeared thin and ill, her eyes red-rimmed with tiredness, but what did it matter? There was no one to care how I looked anymore.

"It doesn't matter. Charles can't see me."

"Is that all you care about?" Edith demanded and gave me a vicious shake. "You would let your son become an orphan and all for the sake of a man who betrayed you!"

My head went up at that. "You don't know what you're talking about. We had made up our quarrel. We were happy again."

"So how was it she found him?" Edith demanded. "What was she doing phoning him at his office, and why did she have a key to his flat?"

It did not occur to me to wonder how she knew so much about Rosemary. I had buried the voice of suspicion deep inside my subconscious. My grief for Charles had made me push my doubts to one side, but now I was remembering. Charles had lied to me once: he could have lied to me when he said it was over with Rosemary. She must still have been seeing him or she would not have had a key to his flat.

"That's it." Edith nodded, her eyes very bright. "Think about it, Annabel. You should know what men are. You know they all betray you in the end."

"I shall never know for sure."

"Because you don't want to," she said, and her grasp tightened on my arm. "Forget him, Annabel. Think about your son, think about this house and the future. Your husband was going to take you away from here; he was going to get a nurse for the boy. Now you can stay here, you can keep your son for yourself."

134

It was true. Charles had wanted us to sell Larkspur. He had wanted to employ a nurse to take care of my son. He'd wanted Anthony, had he lied to me so that he could see more of his son? Had he still been seeing her, the woman he really loved?

"I still have Anthony," I said. "And Larkspur."

"And me." Edith gave me her queer, crooked smile. "You're not alone, Annabel. I'll look after you. I won't betray you the way he did. I shall always be here to look after you and Anthony."

"Yes." I lifted my head and looked at myself squarely in the mirror. It was time I washed my hair and lifted myself out of my misery. Edith was right. Charles had betrayed me. He was probably hoping to go on seeing Rosemary and have me, too. "Yes, you're right, Edith. Men are not to be trusted. All of them betray you in the end."

She nodded and let me go. "We'll be all right," she said. "You, me and Anthony together, all of us. I'll look after you both, Annabel. I'll always be here to take care of you."

"Yes," I said and smiled at her. "You'll always be here, Edith. I think I'll have a bath and wash my hair. Then I'll go out and clear up those leaves that have fallen all over the lawn. They should make a good bonfire."

Twelve

For the first year after Charles's death I hardly left the house. I was lost in a world of mists and grief, relieved only by throwing myself into restoring Larkspur to the glory it must once have had. About a year after my husband's death one of the charities he had always supported approached me and asked if I would take over from him and join their board. I thought about it for a few days before I wrote and said I would be pleased to help. It meant that I had to attend several meetings, and that forced me to leave the house, otherwise I might have sunk further into myself and become a recluse.

Keeping busy helped to fill the days that were sometimes unbearably lonely and, as the months passed, I began to make new friends through my charity work. Some time later I was asked to work on another committee, this time for a local project. I began to entertain; I enjoyed cooking and I wanted to show off my beautiful house.

When Anthony was four and I had been a widow for several years, Mary, her husband and two children came to stay. It was summer and we spent a lot of time in the garden.

"Your lilies are so wonderful, Annabel. You should see my garden, it looks as if a bomb hit it. Yours is a haven of peace."

"I think that's what a garden should be, don't you? I like to see swathes of soft colours that lead the eye on to something spectacular, like that rose bush. Isn't it a beauty?"

Mary bent her head to smell a particularly fine bloom. "And it's scented. When you come and stay with us I shall get you to plan my garden for me, Annabel."

"Of course, I'd love to," I said. "Perhaps next year . . ."

"That's what you always say." She squeezed my arm affectionately. "Sometimes I think it would take an earthquake to prise you from your beloved house, Annabel."

"Oh, I'm really not that bad. I took Anthony to Hunstanton for

136

a few days last year and I thought we might go down to Cornwall next month."

"Please promise you will come and stay soon."

"Yes, of course I will," I said. "Now let's go and have some tea, shall we?"

I always meant to accept Mary's invitations but there was usually some reason why it didn't work out. The next summer I promised I would go, then Anthony fell out of the apple tree and fractured his wrist; and then I wasn't well . . . in the end it was the incident with Anthony's pony that made me decide we needed to get away for a couple of weeks.

I bought Anthony the pony for his seventh birthday. He had wanted one for a long, long time but I had resisted his pleas. He was such a clever, bright child and so adventurous that I was frightened to give him the pony too soon, but when he was seven I decided that he was old enough to have his own. He was already riding quite well. Several of his friends had ponies and he had been having lessons for a while, so on his birthday I arranged for the pony to be brought up to the paddocks beyond the orchard.

He was so excited. As soon as he saw the pony he was scrambling over the gate and into the field.

"Be careful, Anthony," I called after him. "He doesn't know you. He might kick or bite until he gets used to you."

"He won't bite me," Anthony said confidently. "What's his name?"

"He doesn't have one yet," I said. "He's yours so you can name him, darling."

The pony was a lovely golden brown with a pale mane. I had been assured that he had a mild temperament and was a perfect ride for a child of seven.

"I'll call him Bramble," Anthony said, putting his face up against the pony's neck and kissing it. "Hello, Bramble. Do you like your name?"

The pony snickered and pawed the ground but seemed to accept Anthony's touch without resistance. They had obviously taken to each other and I looked at the farmer from whom I'd bought Bramble with relief.

"It looks as if they suit each other, Mr Briggs."

"I was sure they would, Lady Cheshire," he said. "I'll show

137

young Master Anthony how to saddle the animal and watch him for a bit, just to get him used to things if you like."

"Thank you," I said. "I'm sure Anthony would prefer it if I left."

"He'll be quite safe with me, Lady Cheshire."

I nodded and turned to walk back to the house. John Briggs was our neighbour and he had fields adjoining the paddock. He and Anthony were friends, and whenever my son disappeared I knew that I would usually find him with the farmer, sometimes being taken for a ride on the tractor or simply watching.

Anthony really needed the company of an older man, someone he could look up to as a father figure. It made me sad when I glanced back and saw John Briggs showing Anthony how to saddle his pony; that should have been Charles' job.

I still missed my husband and I knew Anthony missed having a father.

I had left Charles's study much as it was when he died, and I had found my son there several times, sitting in his father's chair and touching his things.

Edith said it was morbid to leave the room as it was. She wanted me to clear everything out, but she had not been allowed to have her way. Charles may have lied to me about his affair with Rosemary being over, but he had been my husband and he was Anthony's father. So the study was kept as Charles had liked it; it was still his room.

Edith was in the kitchen as I went in.

"Left him to it, have you?"

"Mr Briggs is with him. You know Anthony doesn't like me watching him very much."

"That's because you make too much fuss," Edith said. "You worry too much over him, Annabel."

"Yes, I know, but I can't help it."

She sniffed to show me that she disapproved and I went out into the conservatory to look at my orchids. The sun streamed in through the domed roof all the morning in the spring and summer, and I had to have shades that I could pull down to protect the more tender plants.

Some people found orchids rather unsettling. I knew Edith disapproved of my passion for them, but they held a special charm for me. They were such delicate yet exotic blooms and there were so many varieties, so many colours to choose from: gentle greens, pale creams and pinks, besides the more exotic colours.

I had several varieties, including the rare and beautiful cattleyas, the more common but rewarding cymbidiums – which was the species most often found on florists' shelves – and the spectacular dendrobiums, the spikes of which sometimes had as many as fifteen flowers. One of my favourite miniature cymbidiums was just coming into flower. I checked the growing medium; it was moist but not waterlogged, just right for this particular variety.

After spending a pleasant half an hour tending my orchids, I went into the small green sitting room to write up my diary. It had become a habit over the years and I recorded most of the events in my life. Anthony's pleasure in his pony was special and definitely deserved an entry.

It was almost an hour later that I heard Anthony come in. His excited voice reached me from the kitchen and I knew he was telling Edith about the pony.

I came downstairs on the following Monday morning. Edith was in the kitchen but there was no sign of my son.

"Isn't Anthony down yet? We have to leave for school in a few minutes."

"He had his breakfast an hour ago," Edith replied. "He'll be down at the paddock, I dare say."

"But he knows he has to go to school." I glanced at my watch. "I shall have to fetch him or we'll be late."

I left the house, walking quickly through the gardens and the orchard. Just as Edith had said, I found Anthony with the pony. I watched him for a moment with an indulgent smile, then all at once my heart jerked with fright as I saw that he had set up jumps all around the field with some old fencing posts and oil drums he must have got from one of the outbuildings.

It was much too soon for him to start jumping; he had only just got used to the pony. As I watched he set the pony at the highest of the jumps, urging it on with excited cries.

"No!" I called, my heart in my mouth. "It's too dangerous, Anthony. Don't do it!"

He glanced towards me and I could see by the mutinous line of his mouth that he had heard and understood me. His heels dug into the pony's flanks as boy and beast raced across the field.

There was a recklessness in the way he rode that made my heart thud against my ribs. Seconds before the jump was reached, the pony stopped abruptly and Anthony let go of the reins and went flying over its head.

I screamed in fear and began running towards his ominously still figure. His eyes were closed and I was terrified. He was dead! I was sure he was dead. His neck must have been broken in the fall; the pony had killed him.

"Anthony," I wept. "My baby . . . my baby . . ."

His dark lashes fluttered against the pale cream of his skin and he gave a little moan, as his eyes opened and he smiled at me in that roguish way of his which could twist my heart.

"It's all right, Mother. I'm not dead."

"You're not ready to jump the pony yet. It's too dangerous, Anthony. You could have been killed."

"Stop fussing," he muttered and tried to sit up, then he moaned again and fainted.

Running anxious hands over him I discovered that there was something wrong with his ankle; it looked as if he might have broken a small bone. I looked round frantically for help and at that moment I heard a shout from the neighbouring field. Mr Briggs came racing across it to help us.

"I saw the boy take a tumble," he said. "Can I help?"

"I think he may have broken his ankle," I replied. "Could you help me get him back to the house, please?"

Anthony was stirring as John Briggs knelt beside him and gently examined his ankle.

"In pain are you, lad?" he asked. "We'll soon have you home and then the doctors will put you right."

He lifted Anthony in his arms, carrying him with ease. Anthony looked pale and frightened but he didn't cry.

"This is very kind of you, Mr Briggs."

"No trouble at all, Lady Cheshire. He's a plucky boy, your lad. I've been watching him take the jumps all morning. He was clearing them easily. Funny how the pony refused that last time."

"It's obviously too strong for him," I said. "I shall sell it and buy Anthony another in a year or two's time."

"No, Mother," Anthony cried. "Please don't sell Bramble. It wasn't his fault, it was mine. I hesitated and he sensed it, that's why he refused."

"Well, we'll see," I said. "Don't upset yourself, darling."

"Don't sell him," Anthony begged, close to tears now. "I won't take him over the jumps again until I'm older. I promise."

"Your mother won't sell him, lad. She's just upset because you're hurt," Mr Briggs said and smiled at me in understanding.

When we were back at the house I rang the doctor. He came at once and examined Anthony's ankle.

"It's a minor fracture, Lady Cheshire, but I think we'll have him in hospital for a couple of days."

I drove Anthony to Addenbrookes Hospital myself, staying with him until they were ready for him, waiting until his ankle had been set and he was ensconced in the children's ward.

Anthony looked white and sheepish as I went to kiss him. "I'm sorry," he said. "You won't sell Bramble, will you? I promise I won't jump him until you say I can."

"I think he's too strong for you. Would you be happy if I exchanged him for a smaller pony?"

"No! I want Bramble."

His mouth was set in a mutinous line and I sighed as I gave way. He usually got his own way because I hated to deny him anything.

"All right. I shan't sell Bramble this time, but if I see you jumping him before you are eight I shall change my mind."

"I promise," he said and kissed my cheek. "This ankle means I shan't be able to go to school for a while, doesn't it?"

"You young devil," I said and laughed. "I almost believe you did it on purpose."

"You know I wouldn't do that," he replied with an air of angelic innocence.

"No, of course you wouldn't," I said. "The nurse is telling me it's time for me to go, but I'll come again this afternoon and bring you some comics, shall I?"

Edith looked at me as I walked in. She didn't say anything as she put the kettle on but there was a brooding disapproval about her. She had been against the pony from the start and I knew she believed she had been proved right.

"You should have waited another year," she said as I sighed and reached for the Aspirin bottle. "He could have broken his neck."

"It was just a little tumble." She was always telling *me* I fussed too much over Anthony! "He has promised me he won't jump it again."

"And we all know what Anthony thinks of promises, don't we? As far as that lad is concerned they were invented simply to be broken."

"If I see him jumping again I shall sell the pony."

"Sell it now, before he kills himself."

"I can't, Edith. It would break his heart. He loves Bramble so much."

"Better a broken heart than a broken neck."

I picked up the cup of tea she had poured for me. "I think I'll take this up to my room and have a lie down," I said. "I have one of my headaches coming on."

"And who's to wonder at that? You spoil that boy, Annabel."

"You spoil him, too," I said. "He always runs to you when I scold him and you know it."

She didn't answer as I went out, but we both knew it was the truth. Anthony had been thoroughly spoiled by both of us and he was clever enough to set one against the other when he saw it was to his advantage. What he really needed was a father's firm hand, and that was something I could never give him.

I'd had three unfortunate experiences with men, and I did not care to become involved again, though I had gone out to dinner occasionally with various men since Charles's death. No one had even made me consider changing my mind and I thought that I should never love again. Charles had broken my heart and I did not want to repeat the experience.

I drank my tea and lay down on the bed fully dressed, pulling the quilt over me. Perhaps if I slept for a while I should feel better by the time I went to visit Anthony.

I must have slept for nearly three hours before I was woken by the shrill of the telephone next to my bed. I reached out for it sleepily; my headache was still lingering and I felt exhausted, worse than when I had lain down.

"Yes," I said. "Annabel Cheshire speaking . . ."

"Lady Cheshire," the voice was that of John Briggs. "I'm sorry to disturb you but there's something the matter with Anthony's pony. I've telephoned the vet but I think you should come, too."

"Of course I will," I said, throwing off the coverlet. "What's the matter with the pony, Mr Briggs?"

"I think it must have eaten something," he replied. "It's stomach is distended and it's obviously in pain."

142

"But what could it possibly have eaten? We've only given Bramble the food you sold us. . . . Besides, it was fine this morning."

"Sometimes they pick up something in the field – a nail, piece of wire or a poisonous plant."

"I do hope it's nothing like that," I said. "Thank you for ringing me; I shall come at once."

The vet was already there when I arrived. He was bending over the pony and looking serious. As I walked towards them he glanced up and his expression was grave.

"This animal has picked up some kind of poisoning, Lady Cheshire. I'm afraid I'm going to have to put it down."

"Oh no!" I cried. "Can't you do anything? Give it an antidote or something?"

"It's too late," he replied. "I'm very sorry but I can't let the poor creature go on suffering."

I watched as he took a syringe from his case and injected the pony. It shuddered a few more times and then lay still.

"I'll arrange for the carcase to be taken away," he said. "I can do an autopsy for you if you wish, Lady Cheshire."

"How could it have been poisoned? Do you think someone did it deliberately?"

"I doubt it. You haven't had the pony long enough for the vandals to know it was here. I should imagine it picked up something in its food, a nail or piece of rusty wire. It could have been a couple of days ago."

"In which case it would be my responsibility," John Briggs said. "I think I should like an autopsy. If it was already ill when I sold it to you, Lady Cheshire, I shall refund the purchase price or find you another pony."

"I think you had better look for one anyway," I said. "Anthony is going to be heartbroken. I don't think he should know what happened. I shall tell him I sold Bramble and he can have a smaller one."

"Don't you think he ought to know the truth?"

"I don't want him upset. Please, find him another pony, and will you have one of your men check this field over for anything that might have caused this, please? I don't want it to happen again."

"I'll certainly do that for you," he agreed. "And if the pony was ill when you bought it I shall replace it."

143

"Thank you. I don't for one moment think it was your fault, but it would be as well to clear up the mystery."

"You sold Bramble!" Anthony cried, his eyes wild with pain. "How could you do that to me? You promised, you promised me I could keep him."

I could not meet his eyes. I had known it would hurt him, but it was better he should think that I had sold the pony than know it had had to be put down.

"I had to to it, Anthony," I said. "I will buy you another one. Mr Briggs is already looking for a suitable replacement."

"I don't want another pony. I want Bramble."

Anthony was staring at me as if he hated me.

"I'm doing this for your sake, darling. Believe me. It hurts me as much as it hurts you."

"No!" He backed away from me. "I'll never forgive you. Never! I hate you. I hate you."

"Oh, Anthony—" I cried. "Please don't look at me like that. I didn't want to hurt you."

"You don't care about me," he shouted. "You wouldn't have sold him if you did."

Suddenly, he flung himself at me, beating against me with his fists. He was sobbing and I tried to put my arms about him, but he kicked me and I cried out in pain.

"You just stop that!" Edith cried as she came out into the hall. "Your mother didn't sell the pony, it got ill and the vet came and put it down."

Anthony pulled away from me, looking at her with fierce, wild eyes. "Liar!" he shouted rudely. "You always stick up for her. You're both against me."

"Please, Edith—"

"Your mother was trying to save you pain," Edith said. "The pony got ill and the vet came and gave it an injection to put it out of its misery. If you don't believe me go and ask John Briggs. He'll tell you."

"No, Edith. The doctor said he should rest his foot as much as possible." Anthony had started to hobble towards the door. "Anthony, come back . . ."

He turned and gave me a mutinous look, then continued to hobble through the doorway. I started after him but Edith caught my arm.

"Let him go," she said. "He's got to learn, Annabel. Life hands out some hard knocks sometimes, but we all have to take them. You should have told him the truth in the first place."

"I didn't want him to be upset."

"Do you want him to hate you instead?"

"No, of course not."

"Then let him go."

I stared after my son, feeling helpless. Whatever I did he was going to suffer his first terrible loss.

Anthony was white-faced and quiet when he came back a few hours later, but he apologised to me and then went to his room. I followed him upstairs, knocking before I entered. He was lying on his bed, curled up into a ball of misery.

"I'm so sorry, darling," I said and went to put my arms around him. "I thought it would be better to pretend I had sold Bramble. I didn't want you to know he—"

He suddenly flung himself against me and began to sob. I stroked his hair, kissing the top of his head.

"I know how much it hurts to lose something you love," I said. "I wish I could make it go away, but I can't. It will get better in time. I promise you it won't hurt so much soon."

He looked up at me then. "Did you cry when you lost my father?"

"Yes, of course I did."

"Has the pain gone away?"

"It gets easier to accept it," I said. "I missed your father when he died, Anthony. But I had you and that gave me something to live for. Why don't you let me buy you another pony?"

"I don't want another pony. I want Bramble."

"I know that. I wish there was some way I could bring him back, darling, but I can't."

"Why did he get sick?"

"I don't know. The vet is trying to find out."

"He was all right when I left him."

"Yes, I know. I can't understand it either. Mr Briggs thinks he may have picked up a bit of wire in the field, but we shan't know for a little while."

I wiped his face with my handkerchief and he gave me a watery smile.

"My ankle hurts."

"I'll bring you a cup of drinking chocolate and one of the pills the doctor gave you. It will make you feel better and then you can sleep."

"I'm sorry I said I hate you. I don't."

"I know." I bent to kiss him. "Whatever you do or say I shall always love you, Anthony. Now read your comics and I'll bring you that drink."

As I walked downstairs I was thinking about what I could do to make for what had happened. Perhaps I should buy him some other kind of pet, but not for a few weeks, not until he had begun to get over his very natural grief.

Perhaps I would take him away somewhere. Give him a holiday to help him forget his disappointment. It was too cold for the seaside yet, but Mary had been asking us to stay with her for ages. It would be good for Anthony to have the company of other children, and Mary had three now. Yes, that was the answer. It would be good for both of us. I hadn't seen her for a while and I was feeling a little low myself.

I would telephone Mary as soon as I had taken Anthony his hot drink and the Junior Aspirin the doctor had given us.

I received a telephone call a few days later. It was from Mr Briggs, the man who had sold me Anthony's pony.

"I thought I should just let you know the results of the tests, Lady Cheshire. It seems that the pony ate something poisonous, probably a weed that grows wild in the fields."

"Something growing in our paddock?" I said, surprised. "But surely we checked for that before we put Bramble out, didn't we?"

"Yes," he replied, sounding bothered. "I did it myself, Lady Cheshire, and there was certainly nothing I recognised, but these things do happen. I'm sorry."

"It wasn't your fault," I said. "Thank you for letting me know."

I replaced the receiver. So it had been an accident; Bramble had eaten something poisonous that grew wild.

Well, at least it was nothing worse. One heard sometimes of people doing dreadful things to horses and ponies these days. Bramble had died through his own greed.

I could not tell Anthony that just yet, but before we bought another pony he would have to learn what plants were dangerous to his pets and where to look for them.

146

Thirteen

Paying Mary a visit was the best thing I could have done. Anthony was a little quiet for the first couple of days, but after that he began to cheer up and join in with the games the other children played. His ankle was still in plaster, which made him an object of interest to his contemporaries, although he was no longer in any real pain. They envied him because he did not have to go to school, but at the end of the first week they all broke up for the Whitsun holidays.

The weather decided to turn warmer over the weekend, and as we watched the children playing together in the garden, Mary told me that she was thinking of having a barbecue the next Friday evening.

"Just pray it stays fine long enough," she said, then cast an eye over her garden. "Doesn't it look a mess? I shall have to do something to it before Friday."

"Why don't you let me help?" I asked. "If Jonathan cleared those two beds near the patio windows I could plant them out for you before Friday."

"Would you, Annabel? It's no good me going to the garden centre. I buy all the wrong things and it turns out looking like that in a couple of years."

"That's because you don't plan it properly," I said and smiled. "Why don't you leave it all to me? Anthony can stay here tomorrow morning while I pop into the garden centre and buy what I need. It will be my treat to you for having us here."

"I don't need paying for that," she said. "But I'm not going to refuse your offer to choose and lay it out for me, Annabel. But we'll pay for the plants."

"If that's what you want."

"Yes, I do," she said. "Do you think Anthony could bear to go to the circus this afternoon? I mean, they will probably have dancing ponies there. I don't want to upset him—"

147

"Let's ask him," I suggested. "Anthony, come here a minute, darling."

Anthony had already been told about the trip to the circus by Susie, Tom and Bobby, and he was as eager as they were. When the ponies first came trotting into the ring he slipped his hand into mine and I held it tightly, but he was soon laughing at the antics of the clowns, and the next time the ponies came out he seemed to take it in his stride. There was no doubt that being with Mary's children was doing him good and I was pleased that I had made the decision to bring him.

The next morning I took my car to the garden centre a few miles down the road and ordered what I wanted.

"I need plenty of compost," I told the assistant. "The kind that doesn't use peat, please, and I want two dozen roses in pots. I've picked out the varieties and I want the best bushes."

"Yes, madam. Did you want the rhododendrons you picked out?"

"Yes. I think the soil here should be suitable, don't you?"

"We'll send you a special growing medium for them. These days you can buy things to help adjust the soil to the right acidity."

"I'm going to plant a lily bed, though of course that will not flower this year, but I want something to brighten it up for this summer. Bedding plants would be best, don't you think?"

"You could use some," he agreed, "but we do have some lilies in pots that will flower this summer."

"Will you show me, please?"

He did so, then we picked out the plants, adding some irises that were already in flower to make a nice show in time for Mary's barbecue.

"How soon can you deliver these?"

"This afternoon?"

"Thank you. I want to make a start as soon as possible."

I had been gone a couple of hours. When I got back to Mary's the children were playing in the garden and I could hear the sound of their laughter. I decided to go in through the back garden, but when I got to the gate I stopped in surprise as I saw the source of their merriment. A huge Alsatian dog was tearing up and down the garden, chasing a stick the children were throwing for him. Anthony picked up the stick, holding it raised above the dog's head and making him jump for it, drawing it back so that he barked madly.

"Anthony! Be careful!" I cried.

The dog looked round, then rushed towards me barking. I froze as it stood a few inches away, baring its teeth and snarling.

"Down, Sabre!"

At the command the dog laid down at my feet, its head on its front paws in an attitude of servile obedience. I turned as the owner of the dog came towards me.

"There's no need to be frightened," he said. "Sabre makes a lot of noise but he won't attack you, not unless he thinks you are attacking me. He was frightened when you yelled like that."

"I did not yell. I thought my son was in danger from your dog."

"They've been playing quite happily together for the past hour. Sabre loves kids."

I stared at him in annoyance. He was a tall, spare man with dark hair that curled at the ends and was a little longer than it should have been. In his casual slacks and light jacket he could have been taken for a country man, except that there was something different about the way he wore his clothes, an air of confidence, almost of arrogance in his stance that made me think he was very sure of himself. Something seemed familiar about him and yet I did not think we had ever met before."

"So you two have met," Mary said, coming out of her back door. "Annabel, this is Jonathan's cousin Lawrence – Laurie, this is Lady Cheshire."

"Lawrence Masters." He extended his hand. "Forgive me – but haven't we met somewhere?"

"No. No, I don't think so."

My fingertips barely touched his as I lied. The name conjured up instant memories and I knew him at once, though he had changed considerably since that day in the park. It was almost eleven years and they had left their mark on him; there was a tiny scar at his left temple and a certain hardness about his mouth. His eyes narrowed thoughtfully as he looked at me.

"At the risk of sounding importunate, I have to disagree. I'm sure I have seen you before, though it was years ago."

Mary was watching us in fascination. "Annabel does a lot

149

of charity work," she said. "You've probably seen her picture somewhere."

"Maybe that's it," Lawrence Masters agreed, though there was doubt in his face and I could tell he wasn't convinced. "Well, I should be going."

"You are coming on Friday?" Mary asked anxiously.

"Yes." He glanced at me. "It was nice meeting you, Lady Cheshire. Sabre, come!"

The dog followed him obediently. Mary waited until they went out of the gate and got into a large, black estate car parked a few yards down the road, then looked at me with a gleam of excitement in her eyes.

"Do you think you have met him, Annabel?"

"I shouldn't think so." I wasn't sure why I was lying but his name had sent little shock waves through me and I still hadn't recovered from the surprise.

"He's looking a lot better these days, that's one thing."

"Has he been ill?"

"Not exactly . . ." She glanced at the children, who had turned their attention to the swing and sandpit. "It was ages before we could persuade him to come to a party."

"Isn't he very sociable?" She was obviously dying to tell me all about him.

"Not very. Not since Vivien died."

"Was she his wife?"

"Yes." Mary looked at the children again, but they were absorbed in their own games. "Don't say anything but . . . we think she killed herself. They were on what was supposed to be a second honeymoon but things weren't working out too well."

"How did she die?"

"It was reported as a swimming accident by the Greek authorities, but—" Mary pulled a face. "She was a strong swimmer and she'd been warned about the dangerous currents in that particular area. It really knocked Lawrence for six. For a while we thought, well, I thought, he might take his own life. He drank a bit and didn't take care of himself, then he had pneumonia. Jonathan wouldn't have it that he wanted to die, but . . ."

"When did all this happen?"

"Oh, years ago. Just before we got married as a matter of fact."

"Is that why he didn't come to the wedding?"

"Yes. It was all pretty awful."

"It must have been."

I was remembering that Lawrence had had to leave me because he didn't want to keep his fiancée waiting. He could not have been married many years before his wife died. Now I knew what lay behind that rather wintry expression in his eyes.

Mary looked a bit guilty. "You won't let him know I told you? Only he's still rather touchy about it. We never talk about Vivien or what happened to her."

"No, of course I won't, Mary. I promise."

She smiled and took my arm as we turned and went into the house. "I told you because we've always shared our secrets. Lawrence is all right really. I like him now, though I didn't for years. Jonathan thinks he's wonderful, and these days he's a brilliant barrister. Very clever."

"Yes," I said, picturing his lean, intelligent face and those keen eyes that seemed to see right through to your soul. "I should imagine he is . . ."

For the next two days I worked hard in Mary's garden, and it began to look much better. The children helped out now and then, fetching and carrying. It was on the third morning when it was almost finished that it happened.

"Mum," Anthony said as he watched me planting some Busy Lizzies. "Could we have a dog, . . . one like Sabre?"

I glanced up at my son as he handed me another pot.

"Is that what you want, Anthony?"

"Could we, Mum?"

Mary's children had always called her Mum. Until now my son had called me Mother, perhaps because Edith always spoke of me as his mother, and I had noticed other small changes in Anthony's behaviour, changes I quite liked. I thought this visit was doing him good. He was learning to share and give in to others rather than expecting his own way all the time.

"Perhaps we could have a dog but I'm not sure it should be an Alsatian. Wouldn't you rather have a nice, friendly Labrador instead?"

"I want one like Laurie's." Anthony's eyes took on the mutinous expression I knew so well.

"We'll see," I said. "You can certainly have a puppy, but we'll think about what kind it should be for a while."

"I want one like Sabre or I don't want one at all."

"Anthony—"

"You never want me to have anything I want. You say you love me but you don't really care—"

"Please, Anthony . . ."

"I hate you. You lied to me about Bramble. I hate you!"

"Anthony! That's no way to speak to your mother. Apologise, please."

I glanced over my shoulder in surprise. Lawrence Masters was standing a few feet away, the dog sitting to attention at his side.

"Sabre!" Anthony cried, and went to stroke his head.

"Apologise to your mother, Anthony."

Anthony looked up at him, his eyes mutinous. "She won't let me have a puppy like Sabre."

"Alsatians have to be properly trained. They won't obey you if they don't respect you and Sabre wouldn't respect a rude boy like you. I don't think I like you very much at the moment myself."

Anthony's cheeks went red. He hung his head, his mouth setting obstinately, then he looked at me. "I'm sorry, Mum. I didn't mean it."

"Of course you didn't." I forgave him instantly as I always did. "I didn't say you couldn't have the puppy, only that I want to find out more about them first."

Anthony looked at Lawrence. "Can I play with Sabre now? I didn't mean to be rude."

"You did but we accept your apology." Lawrence's mouth relaxed into a smile. "Go on then, but do as your Mum says in future, do you hear me?"

"Yes, sir."

I got to my feet as Anthony and the others called to the dog, then began chasing up and down the garden together.

"You were a bit hard on him."

"Perhaps it's time someone was."

"What do you mean? He was just upset, that's all. You don't understand . . ." My hackles rose at his implied criticism of Anthony. "His pony had to be put down a couple of weeks ago. He hasn't got over it yet."

"That's very sad, but it doesn't excuse rudeness to his mother.

If you don't control him now, Annabel, you will have trouble when he's older. If you knew how many spoiled mummy's boys we get before the courts."

"He isn't spoiled—" I stared at him as his brows went up, then a reluctant smile tugged at the corners of my mouth. "Well, I suppose he is a bit, but I can't seem to help myself. Since his father died . . . well, he's all I have. Between Edith and I he gets most of his own way."

"It can't be easy bringing up a spirited boy alone," Lawrence said, responding with a smile of his own. "But it's a shame. There's nothing wrong with him a little discipline wouldn't put right."

"I know. I do try to control him, but he resents it from me."

Lawrence nodded, his eyes watching me thoughtfully. "I think I've remembered where we met," he said. "It was years ago . . . in a park. You had cut your hand. I've been trying to recall what your name was then but it eludes me."

"Wright," I said, realising that there was no point in going on with the pretence. "It's nearly eleven years so it's hardly surprising that you can't remember. You gave me your handkerchief and we had tea together."

"So you did remember me?"

"Yes. I didn't recognise you at once, but I remembered the name. I suppose I was embarrassed. I was a silly child at the time."

"Crying because your grandmother had died, I seem to remember."

"Yes . . ." There had been more to it than that, but I wasn't going to remind him. "You helped me a lot, Lawrence. I've always been grateful."

"It's a small world," he said. "I gather you've known Mary for years?"

"Yes. I was at school with her. I went to her wedding."

Something flickered in his eyes. "I didn't."

"No."

He looked round the garden. "Did you do all this?"

"Jonathan got rid of those old shrubs, but yes, I've done the replanting. I enjoy gardening."

"So do I, when I have the time."

"You must be very busy."

"Sometimes . . . unfortunately, this Friday is one of those

times. I just came to tell Mary that I won't be able to manage her barbecue."

"She will be disappointed."

He shrugged his shoulders. "It's one of those things, I'm afraid. Something came up and I couldn't get out of it."

I took off my gardening glove and held out my hand. "Well, it was nice meeting you again. I'm sorry you won't be coming to the party."

He smiled and took my hand for a moment, and this time I didn't draw it away so hastily. "I'm sorry, too," he said. "Well, I'd better face Mary, and then I have to go."

"Goodbye then," I said.

"Perhaps not." He turned and whistled to Sabre, then walked towards the back of the house.

I went on with my gardening, letting my fine, straight, fair hair fall forward over my face to hide my pink cheeks. Just what had he meant by that last remark?

Mary was disappointed that he was not coming to the barbecue, but she soon got over it when the evening turned out to be fine and warm. Everyone complimented her on how nice the garden was looking and she told them all it was due to me.

We had strung small coloured lights around the door and to the children's swing, giving it a festive air, and the children had been allowed to stay up late and join in the fun. Mary's guests were a friendly bunch and I enjoyed myself more than I had for a long time. They were planning an amateur musical show they wanted to put on later that year and there was a lot of laughter and teasing going on as they discussed the various parts and who should play them.

It was nearly eleven o'clock when I put a sleepy Anthony to bed, kissing his cheek as I tucked him up. He flung his arms around me and kissed me back.

"It was fun," he said. "Can we come and stay with Aunt Mary again soon?"

"Perhaps she will bring everyone to stay with us in the summer holidays," I said. "Or we might even go to the seaside in a caravan with them. Would you like that?" Mary had suggested that she and I might take the children away by ourselves.

"Could we, Mum?" Anthony's eyes shone. "I've never had so much fun as these last two weeks."

I kissed him again and told him it was time to go to sleep, promising that we would do something with Mary and her children in the summer.

As I left him to settle down I was thoughtful. I had never realised how lonely he was before. He had friends at school and I asked them to tea sometimes, and he went to their houses, but this was the first time he had been with other children every day, as a family.

What he really needed was brothers or sisters of his own.

We stayed at Mary's until after lunch the next day. Neither Anthony or I really wanted to leave, though I was a little concerned for my garden and the house. I had telephoned Edith a couple of times just to make sure everything was all right, but she was taciturn, answering me in words of one syllable whenever possible.

It was almost dusk when we drew up outside the house and I frowned as I saw there were no lights on anywhere. Had Edith gone to bed already? I unlocked the front door, switching on the hall lights as we went inside.

"You go upstairs and get ready for bed, Anthony," I said. "You were up late last night and school starts on Monday."

"All right, Mum. Can I just say good night to Edith and tell her what we've been doing?"

"Yes, once we know where she is," I said. "Edith, Edith, we're back. Are you there?"

I walked into the kitchen, switching on the lights as I went. There was no sign of her, or of any cooking.

"Edith! Edith, where are you?"

I felt a flutter of fright. It was three days since I'd spoken to her on the phone and she was well over sixty . . . supposing something had happened to her!

"Edith."

I started up the stairs, then I saw the flickering light coming along the landing from the direction of her room.

"Edith!"

I ran up the last of the stairs and saw her walking towards me, carrying a lighted candle in an old-fashioned chamber-stick. She was wearing her dressing gown and her hair looked as if it hadn't had a comb through it for days.

"Edith, what's wrong? Are you ill?"

155

She blew out the candle and looked at me. "Of course I'm not ill. I just had a little chill, that's all, so I went to bed early."

"What were you doing with a candle, Edith? I've told you before that I don't want you using them. This house is very old. If there was an accident . . . if you knocked it over—"

"I'm not stupid," she said and gave me a hard look. "I wouldn't do anything to harm you or the boy, Annabel."

"No, I know you wouldn't," I said, and took the chamber-stick from her. "But no more candles, please? Please promise me, Edith. I really don't like them. I'm very frightened of fire."

"Yes," she said and gave me a sly smile. "Yes, I hadn't forgotten, Annabel. You have good reason, don't you?"

"There was an accident when I was a child," I said and shivered as the memories passed over my mind like a grey cobweb. "I never want that to happen to me again, so no more candles at night, Edith. You must promise me."

"I like candlelight," she said, and then as I frowned. "All right, don't look at me like that. I promise. No candles."

There was a dream but the dream had changed.

The nursery was in darkness as the woman entered, a lighted candle in her hand. She walked very softly to the cot so as not to wake the sleeping baby, then she bent over it, holding the candle so that she could see his face clearly. The hot wax fell onto his face and made him scream and she dropped the candle into the cot, as it caught fire, she watched and began to laugh. Wild, hysterical, insane laughter . . .

I woke shivering and shaking with fright. The baby in the cot had been Anthony and the woman had been me.

Switching on my bedside light, I threw back the covers, grabbed my dressing robe and ran down the hall to Anthony's room. My heart was thudding with fear, but as I opened the door and looked in I saw that my son was sleeping peacefully in his bed, a toy Alsatian dog that had arrived for him as a present from Lawrence Masters just before we left Mary's clasped in his arms.

I shut the door and leaned against the jamb, closing my eyes as the relief swept over me. It was so long since I'd had the old dream that I'd thought it was all over, that I was at last free from the nightmare of grief and guilt which had haunted me for so many years. Of course it was seeing Edith with that candle that

156

had made me have the dream. But what a terrible dream! It was worse than the one I'd had as a child; in that I had never seen beyond what happened when I struck the match, but in this I had been a woman, a wild-eyed, insane creature intent on murder.

"No . . . Please no . . ." I whispered and covered my face with my hands. "I didn't do it, Daddy. Please let me go, please let me go now. Haven't I been punished enough? Please don't make me go through it all again."

"Annabel . . ." I glanced up and saw Edith coming down the hall towards me. "Is something wrong? Anthony isn't ill, is he?"

"No, there's nothing wrong," I said. "I had a bad dream, that's all. Go back to bed, Edith. I'm sorry if I woke you."

"I wasn't asleep," she said. "You don't need much sleep when you're my age. I was going down to make a cup of tea. Shall I make one for you, too?"

"No, thank you," I said. "I think I'll go back to bed, Edith. Good night."

"Good night, Annabel," she said.

I turned when I reached the door of my room. She was still standing there watching me.

Fourteen

The telephone was ringing when I came in from the garden one afternoon some three weeks later, my arms full of flowers I had cut for the house. Edith was about to answer it, but when she saw me she turned away and went back to the kitchen. I laid the flowers on a table and picked up the receiver.

"Hello, Annabel Cheshire here. Can I help you?"

"You're there at last," the deep male voice said, sending a tingle down my spine. "It's Lawrence. I've rung a couple of times, didn't you get my messages?"

"No, I didn't." I frowned, watching the petals fall from some deep blue delphiniums onto the lush, cream pile of the carpet. "Edith must have forgotten to write them down. She does that sometimes. I think she has a deep distrust of anyone who phones that she doesn't know."

"That must make it awkward for you."

"Yes, it does. I've just come in from the garden as it happens, and I almost missed you again."

"I wondered if you were coming up to town in the near future?"

"As a matter of fact I have a meeting on Tuesday, why?"

"Perhaps we could have dinner? I know you do a lot of charity work and I wanted to ask your advice."

"That sounds intriguing." I was thoughtful. If I had dinner with him it would mean staying overnight or returning very late, and I wasn't happy about leaving Anthony all night in the house with just Edith. "Could we make it lunch? Dinner makes it awkward for me leaving Anthony."

"Couldn't you get someone in to look after him?"

"It's difficult," I said. "Unless . . . no, I would rather do lunch if that's all right with you."

"If that's what you want." He hesitated for a moment, "One day you're going to have to let go a little, Annabel."

"It isn't like that."

"What is it like?"

"I'll explain on Tuesday, if I may." I could not discuss my household arrangements with him when Edith might be hovering near by.

"Just as you wish." He named a restaurant. "We'll meet at twelve forty-five in the reception. I'm afraid it will have to be a quick lunch because I have appointments in the afternoon. Dinner would have been better."

"Perhaps another time." I was regretful but I tried not to let him hear it in my voice.

"Perhaps. I'll see you on Tuesday then."

"Yes. Goodbye then."

I replaced the receiver and went into the kitchen. Edith was slicing potatoes with a sharp knife. She kept her head bent, seemingly intent on her work, but her ears were red and I knew she was well aware of who I had been talking to.

"Why didn't you tell me Lawrence Masters had telephoned twice, Edith?"

"I wrote it down somewhere." She still didn't look at me, but her mouth twisted in a sour line of disapproval.

"No, I don't think you did."

She glanced at me and then away. "I forgot then."

"Please try not to forget in future."

"Is he going to be ringing you again?"

"He might be," I replied. "I don't really think that is any of your business, do you, Edith?"

She chopped at a potato viciously and cut her finger.

"Edith!" I cried as the blood spurted. "Now look what you've done. Put it under the tap while I find a plaster for you."

She did as I said and I dried the wound on a towel, then stuck a waterproof plaster over it. She looked up at me an odd expression in her eyes.

"He'll break your heart. You know that, don't you?"

"Don't be silly. I'm simply going out to lunch with him, that's all. He wants to ask my advice about something."

She gave me a darkling glance, full of ridicule and resentment. "That's the way it always starts, but it won't end there, not with this one."

"What makes you say that? Why should Lawrence be different?"

Her eyes darted away and I saw that sly smile on her lips. "If you don't know, Annabel, I'm sure I don't."

What was she hinting at? She couldn't possibly know that Lawrence Masters was special to me, that I'd never quite forgotten our meeting in the park the day my grandmother died or that I'd believed at the time that I had fallen in love with him. Unless of course she had read my diaries . . . I watched her as she turned away to put the kettle on. I'd often wondered how Edith always seemed to know my thoughts almost as soon as I did. It seemed now that she must have been reading my diaries, even though I kept them locked away in my desk.

"Don't bother making tea for me yet," I said, my voice sharper than usual. "I'm going up to have a bath before I fetch Anthony from school."

I was angry as I walked upstairs. How dare Edith read my private diaries? And how had she managed to find the key to my desk? In future I would need to find a more secure hiding place for it.

The meeting at the charity headquarters was as usual hectic but worthwhile. This particular charity was primarily concerned with handicapped children and projects that helped them lead normal, healthy lives as far as was possible.

The meeting went on until past twelve and when I came out all the taxis seemed to have disappeared. I stood on the path waving frantically as they were snatched from beneath my nose; it was several minutes before I could get one and I was five minutes late arriving at the restaurant.

Lawrence was in the reception area. He was dressed in a dark grey suit with a pale blue shirt and dark tie, looking very professional and businesslike. He flicked back his cuff and studied his watch impatiently, then glanced towards the door. His expression didn't change much as he saw me. I went to meet him.

"I was beginning to think you weren't coming."

"I couldn't get a taxi and the traffic was heavy."

"Well, you're here now. I hope you like Italian food?"

"Yes, I do." I glanced around at the quiet elegance of the restaurant he had chosen, liking the intimate atmosphere and the soft decor. In the centre of the dining room there was a round table set with bowls of fruit and flowers, piles of crisp, white napkins and baskets of crusty bread that smelt delicious. The tables were set at a reasonable distance from each other, ensuring some privacy, and there was a pleasant ambience. "I've never been here before but it looks nice . . . restful."

"I like it, but I prefer it in the evening."

"I couldn't make dinner this time."

"So you said." There was still that shade of annoyance in his voice and I guessed he didn't get many refusals. "Shall we go in? I've ordered for both of us to save time."

"If you are in a hurry we could just have a drink. I don't want to make you late."

He gave me an appreciative glance, then chuckled deep in his throat. "All right, I deserved that. I hate to be kept waiting and I don't much like being turned down."

"If I'd known sooner I might have arranged for Anthony to stay with friends," I said. "I just don't like leaving him alone with Edith all night. She's nearly seventy and . . ." I shrugged. I didn't want to tell him about Edith's passion for candles or why it frightened me so much.

"I didn't realise," he said, looking thoughtful. "Isn't there anyone you could ask to sleep in overnight?"

"I used to have someone who came in to help with the house. She stopped coming when her daughter was ill, but she might . . . Edith wouldn't be too happy about it, of course, because she would feel I didn't trust her. No, I think it would be better if Anthony stayed with friends."

We had reached our table. The waiter held the chair for me and I sat down. Wine was waiting in an ice bucket; the waiter poured it for us and departed. I smiled across the table at Lawrence as I sipped my wine.

"This is very good."

"I'm glad you like it. I've ordered grilled sole and a salad. Is that all right?"

"Fine." I decided to be as businesslike as he was. "You wanted to ask me about my charity work, I think?"

"I wanted some advice."

"Of course. Anything I can do—"

"I've been asked to lend my name to a particular charity," he said. "They want me as a figurehead, I gather, a name to put on their list of celebrities. I'll probably be asked to sit in on a few meetings or give the occasional after dinner speech."

161

"And bully your richer friends into parting with their money. That's very much what I do myself."

"Yes, I thought so, but you've had a lot of experience at it." A faint smile quivered at the corners of his mouth. "I'm not much into this sort of thing. I should like to support them. I wondered if you might have heard the name *Action for World Life?*"

"I may have heard it," I said, considering. "So many of them sound similar, don't they?"

"I wouldn't want to be associated with anything that wasn't on the level."

"Of course not." I fiddled with the stem of my wineglass, watching the liquid roll around the sides. The restaurant was beginning to fill up now and there was a little buzz of conversation all round. "Would you like me to find out what I can for you? I could make a few discreet enquiries."

"If it wouldn't be too much trouble. I know it's a lot to ask."

"Not at all." I sipped my wine. "It was kind of you to send that toy dog for Anthony. He's very fond of it."

"You should get him a puppy."

"Do you think an Alsatian is suitable for a child? Wouldn't it be too much for him to control?"

"Not if it had the right temperament and was properly trained. It would need to be obedience trained by an expert and then handed over to you as a family for further training."

"I shall have to make enquiries."

"Leave that to me," he said. "A fair exchange, wouldn't you say?"

"Yes . . ." As I gazed across the table into his eyes my heart did an odd somersault. "Yes, very fair."

Lawrence paid for the meal then had to rush away. He glanced at his watch – a solid gold Rolex – looking annoyed again.

"I wish we'd had more time," he said. "Perhaps you'll ring me when you've made some enquiries about that charity?"

"Yes, certainly. Please don't worry about me. I'll finish my coffee alone. You don't want to be late for your appointment."

His eyes seemed to hold a faint regret. "No, I mustn't do that. Goodbye for now then. I'll be in touch."

I watched as he walked from the room. He had a certain presence about him and I saw that my eyes were not the

162

only ones that followed him as he left. Most of them were female. Lawrence was the kind of man many women would find attractive.

"More coffee, madam?" The waiter hovered attentively. "Mr Masters told me to ask if you would like a liqueur?"

"That was very kind of him," I said, "but no thank you. I will have another coffee though."

"As you wish."

I was thoughtful as he walked away. It had been obvious throughout the meal that he knew Lawrence well. He must come here quite often, though usually at night and probably not alone. But there was no reason why he *should* dine alone. He was an attractive man without any real ties, at least none that Mary had mentioned.

Why was I even thinking about the women in Lawrence's life? It would be foolish to imagine that he had lived like a monk since his wife's tragic accident. I preferred to think of Vivien's death as an accident, despite Mary's hints about it being suicide. No, Lawrence would always have women in his life. He probably had someone now; after all, this had only been a business lunch. It would be foolish to expect or hope for anything more than a casual friendship.

I wrote to Lawrence a few days later, telling him that as far as I could ascertain the charity he was interested in was perfectly above board. My tone was cool and impersonal. He had been on my mind rather a lot since our lunch and I'd had to remind myself that it would be much better if I didn't get too involved.

Two days after I posted the letter I returned from a shopping trip to find a large bouquet of roses, lilies and carnations on the front doorstep. They had been left in the sun and were beginning to wilt; I put them straight into water as soon as I got in.

"Didn't you hear the doorbell ring, Edith?" I asked as she came into the kitchen to watch me arranging them in a vase. "Aren't they beautiful? They're from Lawrence."

She said nothing but her expression shouted disapproval. She watched me for a moment, then went out without a word. I ignored her silent disapproval and continued to arrange my flowers.

I read the card Lawrence had sent again. The message was

very formal – just a brief thank you – and I was a little disappointed. I had hoped he might telephone and ask me out again – but perhaps this was best after all.

I carried the vase through to the small sitting room and stood them on my desk. They really were beautiful and their perfume pervaded the air, making me think of Lawrence every time I caught a faint whiff of their scent.

Two days passed during which I thought of little except for Lawrence Masters. On the third morning I had almost made up my mind to phone him. I picked up the receiver twice and then put it down again. What was I thinking of? Surely I had learned my lesson? Every man I had ever known had hurt me. It would be foolish to start something that would probably end in tears and yet I wanted to see Lawrence again. Meeting him had made me aware of how lonely I was. I had friends, Edith and my son but I wanted more than that. I was still a young woman. I wanted love and laughter, closeness with someone special.

It was silly but I just couldn't get Lawrence out of my mind. I had tried to tell myself that if he were really interested he would ring me, but he had sent me those flowers. Perhaps he was waiting for my reaction. It would only be polite to thank him personally.

My heart thudded against my ribs as I picked up the receiver again and dialled the number he had given me. I was nervous and I almost hung up again, but then he answered and I had to speak.

"It's Annabel," I said. "I just wanted to thank you for the flowers."

"My pleasure," he replied. "I was thinking of ringing you. I've made some enquiries about a dog for Anthony. There's a nice-tempered bitch at the kennels where I bought Sabre. She's nine months old, well trained and just about ready to go to a family."

"I think he has set his heart on a puppy."

"A nine month bitch properly trained might be a better idea."

"May I think about it?"

"Of course." He hesitated. "Are you coming up to town soon?"

"Yes, next Monday. I have to meet someone from the printing works. Charles left it in trust for Anthony; I don't have much to do with the business, but every now and then I have to sign a few papers on behalf of my son."

"We could go to the theatre if you like, and have a late supper, if you can fix something up for Anthony?"

"I've spoken to the mother of his friend James. Sheila says he's welcome to spend the night with them, if I need to stay over in town. Anthony is quite excited about the idea. He thinks it will be an adventure. They have a touring caravan and James sometimes sleeps in it during the summer."

"Good, that sounds as if he'll have fun. I'm glad you can manage to get up. I'll see you on Monday then. Ring my office and let me know where you'll be staying. I'll pick you up at seven at your hotel."

"Yes. Yes, I will. I shall look forward to it."

I replaced the receiver. Glancing into the hall mirror I saw that my eyes were a brilliant blue and I looked more alive than I had for ages. Then I saw Edith's face reflected in the mirror behind me; she had obviously been listening to a part of my conversation. I turned to meet her scowling gaze.

"Yes, Edith. Did you want something?"

"It will end in tears," she muttered and went back into the kitchen.

After my business lunch I spent some time looking for a new dress. I'd tried on everything in my wardrobe at home and decided I had nothing suitable. In the end I found a clinging black jersey sheath, which I teamed with a pale grey cashmere wrap. It wasn't often that I wore black, but I wanted something sophisticated – something sexy – something that would capture the attention of a man like Lawrence Masters.

I went back to my hotel for tea, then had my hair done by the resident stylist. By this time my stomach was tying itself in knots, so I ordered a martini to calm my nerves. Why on earth was I so on edge? It was simply a theatre engagement; there was no need for me to feel like an excited schoolgirl.

I had almost convinced myself by the time Lawrence arrived, looking very distinguished in a black dinner suit, sparklingly white dress shirt and a well tied bow. The moment he smiled at me in that lazy way of his my heart started racing and I could no longer pretend; I was falling in love with him all over again, but this time he didn't have to leave to meet his fiancée.

"You look wonderful," he said and kissed my cheek. "That perfume is something special."

"It's called Dune. I'm glad you like it; it's not my usual one."

"You use Elizabeth Arden's Blue Grass. That has a softer, flowery fragrance. This is more sophisticated, and I do like it."

"So you're a connoisseur," I teased with a lift of my eyebrows. "I suppose that's because you've known so many beautiful women?"

"Not all of them were beautiful. I don't know whether I've mentioned that you are, Annabel?"

My heart was beating very fast and I hardly dared to meet his eyes for fear of letting him see how I felt too soon. "No wonder you win all your cases. I should imagine the female jurors fall madly in love with you."

"We don't always win. We've just lost a rather important one, I'm afraid. My client was a hot-tempered young man accused of raping his lover. He has been given five years' imprisonment."

"And you think he was innocent?"

"He used his strength to subdue her during intercourse," Lawrence said. "However, there was considerable provocation – technically he was guilty, morally I think there was fault on both sides. I must admit that in this case my sympathy was with him. Some women can be very vindictive, you know."

"Yes, I suppose so . . ." I glanced at him as we entered the hotel lift. His expression gave nothing away and it was impossible to read his thoughts. "Do you always take the case, even if you believe your client is guilty?"

"I happen to believe that everyone is entitled to a fair trial, though as a matter of personal choice, I prefer civil fraud cases, which are better rewarded from a financial standpoint; but it takes money to run chambers and, even though criminal cases are the worst paid area of the law, there are times when I have to accept a brief I'm not exactly keen on taking. I can't expect to be given all the plums, none of us can."

"Supposing you knew your client was guilty of murder?"

"The same principles apply, though if I was certain of a client's guilt I might have to think very hard whether or not I was the right persontorepresenthim. Whateverthecircumstances, heisentitled to a vigorous and extensive defence of his case."

"You don't think a murderer deserves to be punished?"

"It depends on the facts of the case, whether or not there was a viable defence – like diminished responsibility. Sometimes, too, there are mitigating circumstances. The French have a good way of dealing with crimes of passion."

"So you would feel easy about defending a murderer who killed in anger but not someone who planned the crime with precision?"

"It takes a certain kind of mind to do that." Lawrence looked thoughtful. "There's something evil about premeditated murder, don't you agree?" He laughed as he opened the taxi door for me. "Not thinking of committing one, are you?"

For a moment I was enveloped by a strange silence despite the roar of the traffic all around us. My temples pounded and I couldn't breathe. What would he say if he knew that I had once been accused by my own father of the most terrible crime? And that I did not know whether I was innocent or guilty?

The noise of the traffic broke through and I became aware of lights and hooting horns. Lifting my eyes to his, I laughed. "Me? Heaven forbid! I should have nightmares for the rest of my life. I was just interested in your views, in what makes you tick, Lawrence."

"Ah! Now that's a very different subject . . ."

"So you played rugby at college," I said and sipped my wine, letting the cool, white liquid roll over my tongue and savouring its flavour. We had spent a pleasant evening at the theatre and I was feeling mellowed as I toyed with a light supper of fresh salmon. "You don't look like a rugby player. I would have seen you more as a cricket man."

Lawrence laughed and speared his chargrilled sirloin steak. "You shouldn't always judge by appearances, Annabel." His eyes were teasing me. "Take yourself for instance. I think you've been deceiving me."

"What do you mean?" I opened my eyes wide at him. "Has someone been telling you secrets about me?"

"Do you have secrets, Annabel?"

"Perhaps – what do you think?"

167

"I'm not sure, I would have doubted it before this evening, but perhaps I was deliberately misled . . ."

"I can't imagine why you would think that." I met his challenging gaze.

"Can't you?" His eyes were so intense in the soft, pinkish light of the restaurant that my heart caught and then raced on. "You're different tonight, Annabel. Warmer, more approachable . . . alluring."

"Alluring?" The tip of my tongue moved over my lips, moistening them and my throat caught, making my voice husky. "That sounds rather naughty, but nice."

"It's very nice, I assure you," he said. "So tell me about yourself, what do you do when you're not being Lady Cheshire and sitting on the boards of various charities?"

"Nothing very much," I replied. "I enjoy my home but my garden is my real passion. I have a wonderful collection of orchids in my conservatory."

"Exotic tastes, Annabel?" He leaned back, his eyes moving searchingly over my face. "You go much deeper than you let anyone see, don't you?"

"Doesn't everyone have their own secret places?"

"I find some people an open book. It's disappointing to read everything in the blurb and find there's nothing much between the covers." He refilled my wine glass. "You intrigue me, Annabel."

"Do I?" I sipped my wine, savouring the sensuous feeling as it trickled down my throat. "I'm a very private person, Lawrence. I think you are too. You've told me almost nothing about who you really are."

"That's what I mean about you, you answer a question with a question."

"There's so little to tell." My eyes lifted to his. "I've been a widow for several years. After Charles died I decided that all my energy had to go into raising my son and looking after my house. It needed quite a bit of restoration and I've done that gradually, as much of it as I could myself. There's my charity work, and I entertain at least twice a month. I can afford to indulge myself and I do. I enjoy the theatre, classical music and traditional art. I read a lot and—"

"That's the public Lady Cheshire," Lawrence said. "I met her at Mary's, now tell me about Annabel."

"The real Annabel?" I gazed steadily into his face for a moment, then smiled. "The real Annabel wants to go to bed with you. She wants it very much indeed."

"I was rather hoping she did," Lawrence said and summoned the waiter.

We were alone together in my hotel room at last. The atmosphere had been charged ever since I'd made that outrageous statement over supper. Gazing up into Lawrence's eyes, which were very intense and smoky grey, I found it difficult to breathe. I wanted him so much, wanted to feel the touch of his hands, to inhale the soft musk of his body scent and run my fingers through that thick, dark hair.

"Annabel . . ."

His mouth was softened by desire as we gazed at each other. For one terrible moment he hesitated and I was terrified that he was going to walk away, that he was going to tell me it was all a mistake, then he bent his head and kissed me. The touch of his lips on mine was shocking, like grasping a live wire and feeling the current run through you. I tingled with anticipation, my mouth opening to the invasion of his tongue.

It was such a long, long time since I had felt like this. My body was melting with desire and I would have been ready if he had taken me there and then, but Lawrence preferred to savour his pleasures. He began to undress me, his hand moving with a deliberate slowness to ease the long back zip of my clinging jersey sheath. Suddenly, I was breathless and as uncertain as a girl making love for the first time.

Nothing I had previously experienced had prepared me for the sheer sensuality of Lawrence's lovemaking. Even the way he loosened his tie and unbuttoned his shirt made my toes tingle; it was the look in his eyes, the way his mouth went loose and crooked with desire that twisted my insides and made me tremble. When his hand smoothed over my shoulder it was with the reverence of a connoisseur for a beautiful work of art.

We drifted towards the bed. I felt relaxed, treasured, appreciated as his tongue and lips teased and caressed every part of my body. The hot wetness of his mouth dragging at my swollen nipples caused a firework explosion in my lower abdomen and I gasped, my head beginning to move restlessly on the pillow.

169

The warm honey was running between my legs and I moaned as desire mounted to fever pitch.

"Oh yes," I muttered. "Lawrence, now, I can't stand it . . ."

"Have patience, darling," he murmured against my ear. "Don't be in such a hurry."

I clutched at his shoulders, my nails raking his flesh as he continued to lavish me with his tongue and lips. And then he was inside me, moving with that same deliberate slowness that drove me mad. For a while I tried to hold back, to match him for sensuality but then I lost control. I writhed frantically, crying his name and weeping for the sheer joy of it. My climax brought an answering response and Lawrence moaned as he withdrew before the hot volcano of sperm could errupt inside me.

"Why did you do that?" I asked as I felt its stickiness on my belly.

"I'm sorry," he said, rolling over to pull tissues from a box on the bedside table. "I wasn't sure if you were protected. My fault. I'll wipe up the mess."

"They say it's the best skin cream ever," I said and laughed as I spread the sticky fluid over my navel. "It isn't that I mind this, Lawrence. I just wanted you to finish inside me."

"Next time," he said and used the tissues to good effect. "Perhaps you should have a bath, Annabel?"

I lay looking at him as he got out of bed and went to dispose of the tissues in the toilet. His body was all lean muscle without an ounce of fat, his skin polished and smooth like a marble statue, with a slashing V of dark hair down his chest to his navel. He had the physique of an Olympian and I could feel the desire beginning to burn deep inside me all over again.

"Why don't we have a bath together?" I suggested.

He looked at me as I lay sprawled in the tumbled sheets and there was surprise and amusement in his eyes as he saw that I was aroused.

"Still hungry, Annabel?" he asked and as I nodded, "Why not? Let's take it a little slower this time, shall we?"

"Why not?"

Now that my first aching need for him had been eased I was prepared to do whatever he wanted. As I rose and went to him I felt gloriously, wonderfully alive for the first time since Charles died. It seemed that perhaps my years of loneliness were over.

Fifteen

It was early morning when Lawrence left me after promising to ring me soon. For a while I lay smiling dreamily to myself, breathing in the scent of his aftershave, which still lingered on the pillow beside me, and letting my mind go over what had happened between us that evening; it was too soon to start making plans for the future yet, but I felt relaxed and happy – happier than I had since the day I discovered that Charles was cheating on me – and towards dawn I drifted into a peaceful sleep.

I had a leisurely breakfast of croissants and honey in bed, then went shopping before I caught the train home, buying a small present for both Anthony and Edith. It wasn't that I felt guilty for enjoying myself; I just wanted them to share in my happiness.

Edith was at the kitchen sink shelling broad beans when I walked in that afternoon. She glanced at me and then away as I went to fill the kettle. Her silence spoke volumes.

"I brought you a present," I said, laying the green and gold bag on the scrubbed pine table in the middle of the room. "Some special chocolates from Harrods, I hope you'll like them."

"Guilty conscience, Annabel?"

"What do you mean?"

Her pale eyes were expressionless as she looked at me. "If you don't know I'm sure I don't."

I was stung into an angry response. "No, that won't do this time, Edith. Why should I feel guilty? I have every right to go out sometimes. Now what did you mean?"

"Nothing." There was a note of resentment in her voice. "You obviously don't trust me or you wouldn't have sent Anthony to stay somewhere else overnight."

"He's seven years old," I said. "You're not getting any younger, Edith. I just felt it might be better for everyone."

"You'll be wanting me to retire to that cottage soon."

I could see that I had hurt her feelings, but it couldn't be helped. After the last incident with the candle I wasn't prepared to leave my son alone with her at night.

"Don't be silly, Edith," I said. "You know I couldn't manage without you."

"That's as maybe. One day you may change your mind."

"Of course I shan't," I said. "Your home is here with Anthony and me. Now stop sulking, Edith, and open your chocolates." I was suddenly tired of her criticism. Sometimes she acted as if she owned me.

I left her to make the tea while I went upstairs to place Anthony's present on his bed. It was a book about Alsatians and it showed how they were trained to help with police work; there were lots of pictures and I knew he at least would be pleased with his gift.

That weekend I took Anthony to some kennels where they had several different breeds of dogs for sale. We spent an hour looking at the puppies and talking to the owner. She agreed with Lawrence that a nine month-old-properly trained Alsatian bitch would be more suitable for Anthony than an excitable puppy.

"We don't have any Alsatian pups for sale at the moment," she said. "But we should have a new litter ready in about two months time. If you would like to come back then I'll be glad to show you."

"We'll think about it," I said. "Thank you for showing us round."

"I still want a dog like Sabre," Anthony said as we went out to the car. "Please, Mum. I don't mind if it isn't a puppy. It's Sabre I like."

I looked down at his eager face and felt a pang around my heart. He was my son and I loved him so much. If he wanted a dog that badly he could have one.

"I'll telephone Lawrence when we get home," I promised. "If the bitch he told me about is still available I'll ask him to buy it for you."

Anthony threw his arms around me. "Thanks, Mum. I promise I'll look after her myself. She won't make extra work for you or Edith."

172

"It doesn't matter if she does." I glanced at his face. "Has Edith said something to you?"

"She doesn't like dogs. She said they make a lot of work, but I'll look after mine, really I will."

"We'll take care of her together," I said. "But you will have to learn how to make her behave, Anthony. She has to walk properly on a lead and not attack other people when you take her out. A dog like that is a big responsibility."

"Laurie said I could go to classes with my dog."

"Did Lawrence give you permission to call him that?"

"Aunt Mary does, so do Susie and the others." Anthony glanced up at me curiously. "Are you going to marry him?"

"Whatever put that into your head? We've only just met, Anthony. I like Lawrence very much but . . . well, he might not want to marry me even if I wanted to marry him."

"Edith says you'll marry him, then we'll have to leave Larkspur and go to live in London with him."

"If I married Lawrence – and at the moment it hasn't been thought of – but if it happened, we would all discuss where we wanted to live. We wouldn't have to sell Larkspur. We could keep it and then one day it would be yours."

"Laurie is great to be with," Anthony said, his face thoughtful. "Was my father like him?"

"In some ways. Charles was an intelligent man and generous, but they are very different in other ways. Your father had an unpleasant illness. Diabetes isn't very nice, darling. He was always a little unwell. Lawrence is much stronger."

"Then he won't die, will he? I hate it when people die and leave you."

I put my arm around his shoulders. "I know it hurt when you lost your pony, Anthony, but one day when you feel better about it, I'll get you another."

He looked up at me then and there was a flicker of fear in his eyes. "You won't die, will you? You won't leave me?"

"I'll try very hard not to, darling," I said and laughed to show him that it wasn't likely. "Now stop being so morbid! Shall we have fish and chips today as a treat?"

"Oh yes!" he cried, his face lighting up instantly. "Can we have them at that café where they have slides outside? I want a milkshake, too. Can I have ice cream afterwards?"

"You'll be sick," I warned, amused by his quick change of

173

mood. "You can have whatever you want – but don't blame me if you feel ill."

Anthony demolished fish and chips, a strawberry milkshake and a double portion of ice cream and showed no signs of feeling queasy, even after using the slide at least a dozen times.

It was nearly tea time when we got home. I felt the sense of peace I always had when returning to Larkspur, and stood for a moment looking at the gardens as they basked in the shimmering warmth of a perfect summer evening. Anthony went straight upstairs to play with his computer games, and I used the telephone in Charles's study to ring Lawrence at his home. I was disappointed to be answered by a machine.

I left my name and a message saying that I had decided to buy the Alsatian bitch he'd suggested if it was still available.

Just before I replaced the receiver I thought I heard a little click, as though someone had been listening in. Edith again! Her habit of eavesdropping on my telephone calls was becoming annoying. If it continued I would have to speak to her about it.

As I went upstairs to run a bath, I was thinking about Lawrence; all week I'd been hoping that he might ring me but he hadn't, and now I'd had to leave my message on an answerphone.

It had been foolish of me to become involved. If all Lawrence wanted from me was a casual affair I was going to end up being hurt again.

I had just come downstairs on the following Monday morning when the telephone rang. The sound of Lawrence's voice sent shivers winging down my spine and my hand trembled on the receiver.

"I got your message," he said. "I've been away for the weekend but I'll ring the kennels today and let you know."

"Anthony badly wants a dog like Sabre. I'm afraid I'm going to have to get him something soon, but I think the older dog would be best."

"Good. I'm glad you agree. Puppies are fun, but it might pick up bad habits and be more trouble than it was worth."

"Yes, I'm sure you're right." I hesitated, then, "Did you have a nice weekend?"

"It was just work," he said. "But next weekend I'm going down to my cottage in the Cotswolds. How do you feel about coming with me?"

"Just me? I'm not sure I could leave Anthony for a whole weekend."

"There's no reason why you should. We could drop him off with Mary on Friday evening and pick him up Sunday afternoon."

"Do you think she would mind?"

"I'm sure she would be happy to have him."

"All right then. Yes, I would like that, Lawrence."

"I'll pick you up at your house at about five on Friday. Tell Anthony I'm going to leave Sabre with Mary, that should keep him happy."

"Yes, he adores that dog. He likes you, too."

"Maybe we'll take him somewhere another weekend, but I'd like to get to know you a little better first, Annabel."

"Yes, yes, of course."

"I'll be in touch then."

"Bye—"

As Lawrence hung up I was breathless.

"You're a fool to care so much," I told my reflection. "It won't last and then what will you do?"

Yet why shouldn't it last? Just because I had experienced the pain of betrayal before it didn't have to happen again. I was letting Edith's warnings get to me and that was stupid. I was still young enough to find happiness for myself and my son.

The wind was a little cool when Lawrence picked us up but once we were in his car the evening sun warmed us through the glass. Sabre was shut into the back of the estate car behind a wire barrier, his nose pressed up against it and whining as Anthony talked to him in between pleas that the dog be allowed to sit on the back seat with him.

"Now that's exactly what you've got to learn to accept," Lawrence told him. "Sabre is safer where he is, and so are you. If he started jumping all over the seats when I was overtaking he might cause me to misjudge my distance. That's what I was talking about when I said you have to be sensible with these dogs, Anthony. You can play with him when you get to Aunt Mary's. You'll have him all weekend."

175

"Yes, Laurie."

"I've asked about the bitch," Lawrence went on. "She has been bought by someone else, but there is another dog of seven months almost ready to go to a family. Next weekend we'll go and see him together and if you like him they will finish training him for you. It might work out even better this way, because you can learn a few things before you take him home. You could stay at my house on Saturday night and go to training classes on the Sunday morning, if you like?"

"Yes please!"

I glanced at Lawrence, feeling amazed at the way he so effortlessly disciplined my son, without appearing either to scold or cajole.

"That was kind of you," I said. "To invite Anthony to stay next weekend."

"Perhaps I had an ulterior motive . . ." His eyes teased me and I felt my cheeks become warm. "Annabel, you're blushing!"

I turned away to glance out of the window, not wanting him to see too much. He had been kind to Anthony and he obviously wanted us to be together more often, but it was best not to make too much of it.

We stayed at Mary's overnight in separate rooms, then set out early in the morning. It was a lovely day; the cold wind had dropped and it was already beginning to get warm.

"You're very quiet," Lawrence said after we had been driving for an hour or so. "Worrying about Anthony?"

"No. He'll be fine with Mary, I know that. I was just thinking about Edith. She wasn't particularly happy when we left last night. I tried to ring her this morning but she didn't answer."

"The poor woman was probably asleep," he said. "Relax, Annabel. Close your eyes and sleep for a while yourself. We've at least another hour's drive."

He was right, of course. It had been early in the morning and Edith might have been asleep. There was no point in worrying every time I left her alone in the house.

I leaned back and closed my eyes as he suggested. I must have fallen asleep because when I woke it was to the beauty of the Cotswolds; limestones ridges and gently-rolling hills with majestic ash trees, their branches clothed in summer finery

176

against a bright blue sky. As each mile passed the scenery grew ever more beautiful and I was aware of a deepening sense of peace.

"We're nearly there," Lawrence said as I stretched and smothered a yawn. "You must have been tired."

"Yes, I suppose I was." I smiled at him. "The sun is so warm and it made me sleepy. But it's a shame to sleep when everything is so beautiful."

"Spring is my favourite time down here. The woods are filled with wildflowers and birdsong, but it can be nice even in winter – a fragrant ash log fire and mulled wine to keep out the chill."

"M'mm . . ." I murmured. "It sounds like heaven at any time. I can't wait to see your cottage, Lawrence."

"It's not particularly grand, not like your house."

"It's Anthony's house, really. Mine for my lifetime, of course. Charles made sure of that, because he knew I was so fond of the place."

"You have a right to be; it's beautiful, Annabel, and you've worked hard on it over the years."

"It never seemed like work to me."

"It never does if you enjoy it."

"No, I suppose not." I glanced out of the window. "Where are we going, Lawrence?"

"Have you ever been to Castle Coombe?"

"No, I haven't. I've heard about it, though. Wasn't that where *Doctor Dolittle* was filmed years ago?"

"Yes. They actually made it look like the seaside, even though we're seventeen miles from the coast. It's back to normal now I'm glad to say."

"I believe it's very pretty?"

"We'll go through the village so you'll be able to judge for yourself."

We approached Castle Coombe through a deep valley walled by tall trees leading down from the main road between Chipping Sodbury and Chippenham. Lawrence told me that in the summer visitors were asked to park their cars and walk down into the village in an effort to try and preserve the special character of the place.

"There isn't much parking space anyway," he said. "The locals don't want to spoil their outlook by catering for tourists."

177

As he drove through I understood exactly how the villagers must feel. It was so beautiful! All the buildings – houses, cottages and church – were of the same buttery Cotswold stone with porous, moss-grown tiled roofs that pitched into high gables. And everything had a sleepy, timeless air of serenity. The church nestled in a haze of trees, ridged behind and sweeping down to the curve of the rough cobbled street which ran beside a rippling brook, its water shining and silver in the sunlight.

"Oh, Lawrence," I cried. "This is lovely, quite lovely."

"I thought it might appeal to you," he murmured and smiled. Then a few minutes later, "Well, here we are, this is my cottage." Despite his earlier disclaimers, there was a note of pride in his voice.

I looked out of the window as he drew the car into a gateway and stopped. Like the others we had passed, his cottage was built of that wonderful honey-gold stone, and the roof was steeply pitched above dormer windows glazed with old, grey glass that was opaque in the sunshine. Roses and clematis straggled the walls adding a blaze of pinks and reds, and the garden was filled with old-fashioned flowers that spilled over the path leading up to the front door. It had a haphazard wildness about it that was very different from the peaceful order of my gardens at Larkspur but had its own appeal.

"This is gorgeous," I said. "How old is it?"

"A couple of hundred years I think." He got out of the car and began to unload the bags. "I bought it three years ago. It was in a pretty bad state then and I've done most of the renovation work myself."

"I like it very much," I said as I walked up the crazy paving to the front door. "Who looks after your garden when you're not here?"

"I come down most weekends in the spring and summer," he replied, dumping the cases on the step as he fished for his key in the pockets of his comfortable sports jacket. The jacket had leather patches on the elbows and he looked very different from the man I had met in London. "But there's an old boy down the road who does work for me now and then. He grows vegetables out the back and I buy him a drink in the pub when I see him there."

As I went inside I was struck by the faint, tantalising smell of perfume and I looked for the bowls of potpourri I knew must be there. They were scattered all over the place, on the shining oak hutch, a small wine table and the windowsills, giving the cottage a welcoming atmosphere.

Lawrence left the cases at the bottom of the stairs and opened the door into the sitting room. It was furnished in shades of peach, yellows and browns blending from a plain, dark chocolate carpet to the bright chintz of the curtains and loose covers for the big old sofas and chairs. There were oak tables, lots of gleaming brass and fresh flowers on the dresser, flanked by blue and white plates, an assortment of pewter and some Staffordshire figures. Everywhere was spotless. Obviously, Lawrence had someone who cleaned for him regularly.

"I'll put the kettle on," he said. "Sit down and make yourself comfortable while I take the cases upstairs. I'll show you your room later – unless you want the bathroom now?"

"Why don't I make the tea while you take up the bags?" I suggested, a little surprised that we were to have separate rooms. "I hope you're going to let me do my share of the chores?"

"You bet," he said and grinned, looking much younger and more relaxed than I had seen him. "I was hoping you could cook, otherwise it's something on toast I'm afraid."

"I enjoy cooking," I replied. "Why don't you point me in the right direction?"

"The kitchen is at the end of the hall and the fridge should be full of food."

"That sounds as if you're hungry?"

"It's the air down here," he said. "But don't worry about it yet. We'll go for a walk after we've had some tea and I'll show you around. I thought we might eat out this evening."

I felt happy as I moved towards the kitchen. Perhaps the separate rooms didn't matter. We were together and that must mean something.

I woke from the nightmare with a little cry. What had made me dream about things long past and forgotten? My mind was filled with vivid pictures I could not shut out even now that I was awake. It was the old dream again, the one that had haunted me during my childhood. I reached out to switch on the light, feeling annoyed as I discovered it was still only three in the morning.

The wind had risen overnight and a branch was tapping irritatingly against my window, keeping me awake. There was no point in trying to go back to sleep for a while. I threw back the covers and slipped on a thin dressing robe, then went quietly downstairs. I didn't want to wake Lawrence. It was so silly to let the old dream disturb me. I'd had a wonderful day with Lawrence exploring the countryside and having more fun that I had in years – so why the nightmare?

Going into the kitchen, I made myself a mug of instant hot chocolate, nursing it in my hands as I went into the sitting room. We had spent the afternoon walking, had dinner at a lovely pub later that evening, then sat up until midnight listening to Lawrence's CD player and his collection of records, which ranged interestingly from classical to country and western favourites.

Perhaps that's why I felt restless. I had waited for Lawrence to make some sort of a move, but he had simply kissed my cheek and wished me pleasant dreams. His nearness had aroused a deep need in me but he had shown no sign of wanting to make love to me and I was still too unsure of him to let him see that I wanted him badly.

I went to the window, looking out at trees, fields and the spire of the church, all bathed in silver by a benign moon. Lawrence was a very sensual man. My common sense told me that there must be other women in his life; I had to be careful not to ask too much – but I wanted all of him. I wanted to wake up and find him in my bed every morning . . .

"Is something wrong, Annabel?"

I glanced over my shoulder. Lawrence was standing in the doorway. He was wearing a short silk robe belted at the waist, his feet and legs bare. The dark hairs on his legs glistened with tiny drops of moisture as though he had just come straight from the shower.

"Did I wake you?"

"No. I couldn't sleep so I took a shower. What made you get up?"

"I had a nightmare. A silly dream I used to have as a child. I can't imagine why I should have it now."

"You're shivering," he said. "I'll switch the electric fire on."

"Thank you," I whispered, watching as he bent to flick a

switch. He poured brandy into two goblets and came to me. "Want to talk about it?"

"It was just something that happened when I was a little girl, nothing important." I sipped the brandy. "This is good."

"You still look pale. Come and sit in front of the fire with me. I'll keep you warm."

His voice was so tender that it made my insides melt with longing for him. He led me to the sofa, his fingers stroking the delicate bones of my wrists, soothing me.

"We all have our personal nightmares," he said. "You're not the only one, Annabel."

"Do you have them?"

"Yes. Sometimes . . ."

The sudden lost, lonely look in his eyes made me catch my breath. I knew then that whatever had happened to Vivien, it had hurt him badly.

"Lawrence," I whispered. "Hold me, please hold me."

He drew me to him, nestling my head against his shoulder and rocking me gently in his arms. I melted into his embrace as the sense of emptiness fled and I was aware only of him and the musky, enticing scent of his body. His mouth moved against my hair, his breath soft and warm as it played over my ear. I pressed closer to him, wanting to take away the aching need, the loneliness and the pain. Turning my face to his I heard him moan and his lips moved across my cheek to my mouth. His kiss was sweet and gentle; he stroked my hair, his lips feathering down the bridge of my nose, then he kissed my eyelids and smoothed his thumb over my jaw. He lifted my hair, his fingertips caressing the sensitive skin in the nape of my neck, and slid the material of my robe from one shoulder and traced the curve delicately with his tongue.

"Lawrence," I murmured. "Oh yes, please, Lawrence. I want you so much."

"I want you," he murmured, then drew back his head to look at me. "More than you know."

His eyes were smoky with desire. His mouth slid over mine, moving with teasing little caresses as he moulded my lips with his own, his tongue invading and retreating. At the same time, his hands soothed me with gentle stroking along my thigh. The kisses and stroking went on for a long time and I was lulled into a dreamy state of wellbeing. The heat from the fire was making

181

me drowsy and I sighed with content as Lawrence loosened the belt of my robe. I was naked beneath it. His lips moved from my throat to my breasts, and then trailed sensuously down to my navel, causing me to moan with pleasure as my hands worked in his thick hair.

His tongue was licking me, its light flicking arousing me to fever pitch as he began to nibble and suck at the most secret, intimate place of all. The hot wetness of his mouth made me arch and shudder as little explosions of pleasure shot through me. Sensation built on sensation and soon I was moaning and writhing wildly as the climaxes shook my whole body time and time again and I called his name over and over.

"Lawrence, Lawrence, Lawrence. I love you. I love you . . ."

In my ecstasy I had said the very thing I had promised myself I would never say aloud.

I cooked brunch at about eleven thirty the next morning. Lawrence was very partial to steak and I did a mixed grill of steaks, sausages, bacon, mushrooms and jacket potatoes done in the microwave. He demolished most of it with every sign of pleasure and pulled a face as he saw that I ate very little myself.

"Not hungry, Annabel?"

"Not this early," I replied. "I usually just have toast or something light first thing."

"We'll have to educate you to eat properly," he said and grinned. "I can't have you wasting away. You're slim enough now, Annabel."

"Lawrence . . . last night . . ." I looked away from his bright eyes. "I got carried away. You don't, I mean, I understand that you may not want to make a commitment."

His eyes narrowed thoughtfully. "Why don't we leave this for a while?" he asked. "It's pretty obvious that we're very attracted to each other physically, but we don't know much about one another. I'm not ready to make a commitment yet, and I thought you might feel much the same way. Why don't we take things slowly, get to know how we feel over a few months?"

"Yes, yes, of course," I said. "That's much the best, Lawrence. I just didn't want you to think . . . because of what I said . . ."

"We all get carried away sometimes. I like you a lot, Annabel – but love and marriage isn't on my immediate agenda. I've been burnt once. I would need to think about committing myself that far again."

His eyes had that wintry expression I'd seen once or twice before. I would have liked to ask him what had gone wrong in his marriage, but I was afraid to intrude. Some grief is too private. I had secrets I had never been able to share with anyone. Lawrence was entitled to his.

"So would I," I said. "I'm glad we've spoken, that we understand how we both feel."

"So am I." He got to his feet. "That was a delicious meal, Annabel. I'll give you a hand with the washing up and then we'll make a start back."

Anthony came flying out to greet us, throwing his arms around me as his excitement expressed itself in a jumble of words. I looked down at him with amused affection.

"I take it you had a good time then?"

"Smashing!" he said. "When can I do it again, Mum?"

"We'll see," I promised and glanced at Mary. "Has he been good?"

"Of course he has," she replied and her eyes went to Lawrence. "There was a phone call for you, Laurie, from Belinda Dane."

"Belinda?" His forehead wrinkled. "Did she say what she wanted?"

"No." Mary shook her head. "It seemed urgent. She asked if you would ring her as soon as you got back."

"I'll use the car phone," he said. "Excuse me a moment, Annabel."

It was obvious that he wanted some privacy. I went into the house with Mary. She looked at me curiously and I knew she was bursting to ask how Lawrence and I were getting on.

"It's just friendship," I said. "Don't buy a new dress for the wedding yet."

"But you really like him, don't you? And I know he fancies you like mad. I can see it every time he looks at you."

"We're friends," I said. "Don't make more of it than it is." I hesitated, then, "Who is Belinda Dane? Is she one of Lawrence's clients?"

183

"I don't know," Mary said, not quite meeting my eyes. "Well, I think they had a thing going some time ago, but I'm sure it was over last summer."

"Belinda Dane doesn't seem to think so."

Nor did Lawrence if his instant response to her phone call was anything to go by. I felt a sharp pang of jealousy, but I told myself not to be a fool. Lawrence had made it quite plain that morning that I didn't have territorial rights.

"We'll have to leave straight away," he said as he came back a few minutes later. Mary gave a cry of disappointment and he made a sign of apology. "Forgive me, Mary. I would have liked to stay for tea but I'm afraid I have to get back to London." He looked at me. "I'm sorry, Annabel, but something has come up."

"It doesn't matter," I said. "It was a lovely weekend, Lawrence. Thank you so much for taking me to your cottage."

There was a little flurry of goodbyes and we all piled into the car, Sabre adding to the confusion by barking and jumping excitably, then we were off. I glanced at Lawrence and saw a little nerve flicking in his throat. Whatever Belinda Dane had had to say to him it had obviously upset him.

Sixteen

It was past seven when Lawrence dropped us outside the house and drove straight off after vague promises to ring me. He was so obviously in a hurry that I didn't bother to ask him in. Besides, I was a little nervous about what I might find – would Edith appear wild-eyed and barefoot with her candle again? My apprehension faded as I went in and the delicious smell of cooking made me wrinkle my nostrils in appreciation.

Edith was in the kitchen, her cheeks flushed from baking and the evidence of her industry spread out on the table in a tempting array of tarts and cakes. Anthony fell on a plateful of his favourite almond tarts with a cry of delight.

"Two of those, then off to bed," I said. "Say good night to Edith, darling."

He deposited a rather sticky kiss on her cheek and ran off, after snatching a third tart. Because I was feeling relieved to find Edith looking so normal, I didn't remonstrate with him.

"How are you, Edith?"

"How should I be?" Her pale eyes darted at me resentfully. "I'm here when you want me, just as I've always been. You don't have to worry about me. I'm not senile yet."

Had I allowed my anxiety to show too plainly? I must be more careful in future. Edith would hate it if she knew I had begun to worry about her, to wonder if she was safe to be left on her own.

"Of course you're not," I said. "I was just asking. I will have a cup of tea, if you don't mind, then I'll take a bath."

"Has he asked you to marry him yet?" she asked suddenly.

"When he does, I'll tell you," I said. "At the moment we are simply friends. I would rather you didn't put ideas into Anthony's head, Edith. I don't want him getting too fond of Lawrence too soon."

In the ensuing silence I could hear the steady ticking of the

185

grandfather clock in the hall and the sudden roar of a jet plane overhead. Edith stared at me for several minutes, then sniffed loudly and turned away to fetch a jug of milk from the fridge.

Walking upstairs a little later I thought about my time with Lawrence at his cottage; it had been wonderful while it lasted, but it would be foolish to hope for too much. I regretted that it had come to such an abrupt end and I was curious about Belinda Dane. Who was she? And what did she mean to Lawrence? She obviously had the power to bring him running to her side with a snap of her fingers. Perhaps Edith had been right to warn me after all, perhaps it *was* destined to end in tears.

I telephoned Lawrence on Tuesday and again on Thursday, leaving messages on his answerphone. Neither of them brought a response until late on the Friday evening. I was sitting at my desk looking out at the garden and watching the light gradually fade from the sky when the phone shrilled in the hall, startling me.

"Annabel." Lawrence was apologetic. "I'm sorry I haven't returned your calls but I've been tied up with one thing and another all week."

"I was wondering about this weekend. Anthony was expecting to see that dog you told him about."

"Damn! I'd completely forgotten about that," he said, sounding annoyed. "Look, I'm going to have to cancel this weekend. Please tell Anthony I'm sorry."

I felt a sudden surge of anger on my son's behalf. "He will be very disappointed. He was looking forward to it so much. Can't you cancel your other appointments?"

"No, I can't. I'm sorry, Annabel. I regret breaking my promise, but I have to do this. I've given my word to someone."

"That's not good enough, Lawrence. I don't mind you breaking an appointment with me, but it isn't fair to a child. He's set his heart on seeing that dog."

"He's old enough to understand. You pamper him as if he were made of china, Annabel." Lawrence's voice crackled with annoyance and I could just imagine the look in his eyes. "If I promise for next week and have to cancel again that only makes things worse. I'm not trying to get out of it but the situation here is rather delicate just now."

"I see. Well, ring me when you have time."

I slammed the receiver down hard. I was very angry and not prepared to disguise my feelings. Lawrence might not be ready to make a commitment to me, but a promise to a child was something different. Anthony was going to be terribly upset. I felt that Lawrence had let us both down.

As I turned towards the stairs I had a prickling sensation at the back of my neck and I swung round to see Edith watching me with a little smirk on her lips. She was already beginning to gloat because her prophecy looked like coming true.

I jumped every time the telephone rang the next week, but it was never Lawrence and the disappointment turned in me like a knife blade over and over again. I wanted to ring him but my pride wouldn't let me. Perhaps I had been unreasonable, but he had cancelled our weekend and I was entitled to be a little annoyed.

I had not felt this lonely since that time after Charles died, when for a while I had let myself slide into a slough of self-pity and misery, but I was determined not to give in, perhaps because I knew that Edith was watching me with those sly looks of hers, watching and waiting.

On the Friday morning I met the postman as I came back from shopping. He had a parcel for Edith and a pile of letters for me. I left the parcel on the hall table for Edith, and went into the sitting room to open my mail. As always there were the usual requests from charities, a few bills and a pale pink envelope that smelt faintly of perfume. I slit it open with my paperkife and extracted the single sheet of paper, feeling curious. Then as I opened it, and saw the jumble of letters and words cut out of a magazine, I gave a cry of alarm.

'YOU ARE A DIRTY WHORE. IF THE PAPERS KNEW WHAT YOU REALLY ARE YOU WOULD BE SORRY. STOP SEEING HIM OR YOU WILL REGRET IT.'

I dropped the sheet of paper as if I had been stung, feeling a hot rush of vomit to my throat. Who would send me such a letter? Could Edith have done it to punish me for ignoring her warnings? I picked up the envelope and looked at the postmark; it was smudged but I thought it was a London mark and dated several days previously, which ruled out Edith who hadn't been further than the village in months.

Who else would want to send me something like this? Only

Mary and Edith knew I had been seeing Lawrence – except perhaps for Belinda Dane. She might have discovered that Lawrence had taken me down to his cottage and sent this out of jealousy and spite.

For a moment longer I stared at the poisonous words; they had upset me at first but now I was feeling stronger. I had three choices; to tell the police, show the letter to Lawrence, or throw it away. After a brief hesitation I treated it with the contempt it deserved and tossed it into my wastepaper basket.

I had no intention of being intimidated by anonymous letters. Besides, if Belinda Dane were upset enough to send it, then that must mean she was jealous of me, of my relationship with Lawrence.

Perhaps he was more interested in me than I had thought.

He rang me the following Monday. The sound of his voice made me go weak at the knees and I had difficulty in speaking at first because my throat felt tight.

"Annabel, are you still talking to me?"

"Yes, I think so." I took a deep breath to steady myself. "I was angry for a while. Anthony cried, and it wasn't just over the dog. I'm not sure that seeing you again would be the right thing."

"For you or Anthony?"

"He is becoming attached to you, Lawrence. Beginning to see you in the role of the father he wants so much."

"And you're not interested in furthering that idea?"

"I didn't say that. I – I've been hurt before, but I don't want him to get to love you and then discover you aren't going to be around anymore."

"You're angry because I cancelled our weekend. It was for a very good reason, Annabel. Believe me."

"And if I do?"

"I've missed you. I would very much like to see you again soon." He paused for a moment and I heard him draw in his breath. "Supposing we take Anthony down to the cottage this weekend? I'll bring Sabre along and let him practise giving commands to him."

"Are you sure you want to do this?" My heart was urging me to agree but my head still advised caution.

"Yes. As I said before, I've missed you. I know I told you I wasn't ready to commit myself, but I've had time to think since then and—"

"Lawrence." I stopped him as my heart started racing. "Please don't say anything you don't mean."

"We'll talk this weekend, if I'm forgiven?"

"Oh yes," I breathed as my longing swept away the last lingering doubts. "Yes, of course you are. I know I was a little unreasonable over this but I was thinking of Anthony."

"Do you think I enjoyed letting him down? Do you imagine I did it on purpose?"

"No, certainly not."

"Look, I'll be down on Friday evening. We can leave early on Saturday, if that's all right with you?"

"Yes." Emotion made my throat tight and I could feel the sting of tears. "I'll look forward to having you stay at Larkspur."

"Take care of yourself, Annabel."

"And you."

Replacing the receiver I blinked hard. For the past two weeks I had been telling myself over and over again that my brief affair with Lawrence was finished now it seemed as if it might just be beginning.

Lawrence sent me red roses every day for the next three days. Their heady scent filled the house, reminding me with every breath I took that he would soon be with us.

I shopped in Cambridge on Thursday, filling the fridge with masses of food, far more that we would need for one dinner and breakfast, but I wanted everything to be special for Lawrence's visit.

"Having a party?" Edith asked as she watched me unpack the bags. "You didn't tell me."

"No, I didn't," I smiled at her mysteriously. "You'll know soon enough, Edith."

"I suppose *he*'s coming?" Her expression left me in no doubt of her opinion about Lawrence's visit.

"Perhaps."

I wasn't going to say more. I hadn't even told Anthony yet. I was afraid to build up his hopes just in case it all fell through at the last minute.

After I'd taken him to school the next morning I spent the

rest of the day preparing dinner. An iced cucumber soup would be followed by pot roasted leg of lamb with jacket potatoes and a green salad, with a side dish of fresh asparagus. Afterwards, there would be a choice of pear meringues with hot, dark chocolate sauce or a light orange souffle. I had decided to let Anthony stay up for dinner this once.

Edith watched my preparations with an increasingly dour expression. At four o'clock she took a tray of tea and sandwiches to her room, her attitude making it clear that that was where she intended to stay for the rest of the evening.

Anthony arrived home at half past four. James's mother had picked them both up from school and they had been to the village shop to buy some sweets.

"Don't eat too many of those," I warned as he came into the kitchen chewing a toffee. "We're having a special dinner this evening."

"Is someone coming?"

"Perhaps." I ruffled his hair. "I've put some clean clothes on your bed, go and change now, darling."

"Do I have to?" His voice rose in protest. "I wanted to go out and play in my tree house."

"If you don't, you won't be able to sit up with us for dinner."

He stared at me, excitement dawning in his eyes. "Is Laurie coming?"

Lawrence would surely have rung by now if he couldn't make it. It must be safe to tell him now.

"Yes, he's coming to dinner," I said. "He's going to stay overnight and then we're all going to his cottage for the weekend."

"Is Sabre coming, too?"

"Yes, darling."

Anthony gave a yell of delight and dashed out of the kitchen. As I heard him charging upstairs I allowed myself a smile. And then the telephone rang.

"Oh no! Please don't cancel now, Lawrence," I begged as I went through to answer it, my heart plummeting. It really would be too bad if I had to tell Anthony it wasn't going to happen after all.

I picked up the receiver. "Annabel Cheshire speaking."

There was a slight pause, then, "Bitch! You think you're

so clever but you won't much longer. Ask him about Vivien, ask him how she died. And what the Greek police thought at the time."

"Who is this?" I felt sick and shaken as I heard the hatred in that female voice. "Who are you? You sent me that letter, didn't you? Why are you doing this."

I heard the click as the phone was replaced at the other end. For a moment I felt faint, my head whirling, then I took a deep breath and replaced the receiver. It was a vicious trick by someone who wanted to ruin my weekend, but I wasn't going to let her win – whoever she was.

I went back to the kitchen and looked round. Everything was ready. I just had to switch on the oven, take a quick shower and make myself presentable before Lawrence arrived.

Lawrence brought more roses, chocolates for Edith and a puzzle with a picture of four Alsatian puppies on the box for Anthony. My son fell on him like a long lost friend, and asked if he could take Sabre into the garden.

"Don't go away," I warned. "Dinner will be ready soon."

"I just want to show Sabre the garden, Mum."

"You can take him for five minutes," Lawrence said.

"He adores that dog," I remarked as they disappeared through the conservatory door together.

"Sabre seems to have taken to him, too. Maybe we should hold fire on the new dog for Anthony."

"Why?" I stared at him and my pulses raced. "Lawrence . . ."

He came towards me, reaching out to draw me against him. His hands cupped my face as he kissed me tenderly on the lips.

"I'm not making any promises, Annabel, but I care about you more than I expected to at the start." He placed a finger against my mouth as I would have spoken. "After Vivien's death, I decided I would never get that involved with a woman again. It seemed the best way for me, but I hadn't reckoned with meeting you."

"I didn't think I could love again after Charles died."

"Were you very much in love with him?" Lawrence looked down into my face, his expression serious.

"I – I don't know. He was much older, of course. I was fond of him. When we met I was lonely; he made a fuss

191

of me and I enjoyed that but then . . . then things started to go wrong."

Lawrence tipped my chin with his fingers. "What happened. Did he hurt you?"

"I discovered there was someone else, someone he had loved for years. They had been sleeping together and I saw her lipstick on the pillow . . ." My voice shook as for a moment I felt again all the pain of my husband's betrayal.

"But you didn't divorce him?"

"I had Anthony to think of. Charles begged me to forgive him. We were going to try again – and then he died." I turned away to pour us both a glass of wine, my hand shaking so much that I spilled a few drops on the sideboard. "He was a diabetic and he took an accidental overdose of insulin, collapsed and died of a heartattack on his way to hospital. She found him . . ."

"You think he was still seeing her?"

"I've never been sure. It seems likely, don't you think? She still had the key to his flat."

"It hurts when someone lies to you, doesn't it?" The wintry look was back in his eyes. "Vivien lied and cheated with other men almost from the beginning. She couldn't help herself, affairs just seemed to happen to her. She promised me over and over again that it wouldn't happen any more, then it would all start, and she would phone to say she had to work late again. We went to Greece for a second honeymoon; it was to be a new beginning but she couldn't keep her eyes from the other men. When I found her in a passionate embrace with a very young and handsome waiter I asked her for a divorce. That was the day she died."

"I'm sorry." I could see the pain in his eyes.

"Don't be. It was over a long time ago."

"But it still hurts you, doesn't it?"

He was silent and I sensed there was something he hadn't told me, something that still haunted him. I remembered the vicious telephone caller had told me to ask him about Vivien's death – had implied that there was some mystery behind it.

"Do you want to tell me?"

"It's just that—"

Lawrence broke off and Anthony came in, followed by a panting Sabre. By the look of my son's hands – which were dirtier than before he washed – they had been having a wonderful time in the garden.

"Mum, there's a pan boiling over in the kitchen."

"The asparagus! I forgot to turn it down. Wash your hands, Anthony. We'll have dinner now."

Anthony began chattering to Lawrence as I made a dash for the kitchen. I had the feeling that Lawrence had been on the verge of telling me something important, but the mood was broken now. It didn't matter, we had the whole of the weekend before us.

I had never been as happy as I was that weekend at Lawrence's cottage. Lawrence assumed the role of a father figure as easily as he would shrug on a pair of comfortable shoes. He was firm but considerate as he began to teach Anthony how to walk Sabre on the lead, how to give clear commands, and how to reward good behaviour.

"It's all a matter of being kind but firm," he said. "Sabre respects that. He has been obedience trained. He won a cup for it at Crufts three years ago."

"He's so clever," Anthony said admiringly. "Can I teach him to do tricks, like they do on television?"

Lawrence smiled. "He knows them all, Anthony. You're the one who has to learn how to give him the correct commands."

I watched them through the kitchen window as I prepared and cooked lunch. They looked enough alike to be taken for father and son by anyone who didn't know them.

It was all so perfect! If it could only go on this way for the rest of our lives . . . I felt the coldness start at the nape of my neck and creep slowly down my spine. It was too good to last. I didn't deserve to be this happy. Before long, I would be punished for daring to forget.

For a moment I closed my eyes, trying to shut out the awful sensation of fear. Why did I feel this way every time something went well for me? Why was I haunted by guilt? Surely I was entitled to be happy at last? I had been punished so many times – but this time it was going to be all right.

"Stop feeling guilty because you're happy," I told myself sternly. "You were a child. It wasn't your fault. You couldn't have known. Even if . . ."

I had to stop this! It was because of that hate letter and

the threatening phone call; they had unsettled me, making me uneasy. Nothing was going to happen. Why should it?

Perhaps I ought to have told Lawrence about the letter and the call but we were having such a good time that I didn't want to spoil things. It was only my guilty conscience upsetting me, the fear that had overshadowed my life all these years.

I made an effort to put that fear to a small corner of my mind and went out to call Anthony and Lawrence in for their meal.

Lawrence did not mention his wife's death again that weekend. Maybe like me he wanted to keep things light and carefree. He and Anthony had certainly hit it off and we were all reluctant to leave the cottage. Besides, if Lawrence wanted to tell me anything he would do so when he was ready. I had my secrets; he was entitled to his.

It was quite late when we got back to Larkspur on Sunday evening. Lawrence couldn't stay overnight because he had an early appointment the next morning, but he agreed to break his journey for long enough to have a cup of tea.

The house was in darkness when we arrived and there was no sign of Edith as we went in. Anthony kissed me and mumbled something about going to bed. I kissed him back but I was thinking about Edith. I called to her but there was no answer so I assumed she was sulking.

"Could I wash my hands?" Lawrence asked. "Do you have a downstairs cloakroom?"

"It's down the hall, opposite the study."

Lawrence went off in the right direction and I filled the kettle. The kitchen looked just as it had when we left, as though Edith hadn't bothered to make herself a cup of tea. I was preparing the tea tray when Lawrence returned; his expression was so odd that I was alarmed.

"What's wrong? Has something happened?"

"I think you had better come and look for yourself."

I followed him down the hall, my heart jerking with fright. Had he found Edith unconscious or something? As we approached the study I saw that the door was partially open and there was a strange, flickering light coming from inside.

"What is it?" I looked at Lawrence and my blood ran cold as I suddenly began to guess. "Edith—"

I pushed open the door and froze. At first all I could see was

194

a blaze of light coming from the candles, at least a hundred or more arranged so that they formed a halo of golden fire around a photograph of Charles. It was like a holy shrine – a shrine to his memory – and its message was clear. Edith had taken it upon herself to remind me of the way I had gone to pieces after his death.

"How dare she!" I cried and rushed past Lawrence to start blowing out the flickering flames. The smell of hot wax mingled with the acrid odour of burnt wicks. "How dare she do this?"

Lawrence helped me to blow them all out, his eyes narrowed as he looked at me afterwards. "Why would she do this, Annabel? Do you normally light candles in here at night? It looked like some kind of a shrine." His expression was so odd that I thought he suspected me of an unhealthy fetish.

"It was Edith. I've left Charles's things much as they were for Anthony's sake, so that he has something left of his father – but I never bother to come in here."

"Has she done it before?"

"I've forbidden her to have candles," I said. "She knows I'm terrified of a fire, she knows how dangerous it could be!" I was shaking and I had to sit down suddenly as I felt faint.

"Calm down," Lawrence said. "It was a bit of a shock for me too when I first saw it but it isn't the end of the world."

"It's why I won't leave Anthony alone with her," I said, breathing deeply. "I came home after we'd been to stay with Mary the first time and found her looking vague and walking about with a lighted candle."

Lawrence's expression was thoughtful. "Perhaps you should talk to a doctor. You said she's getting on a bit, maybe she isn't quite, well, up to it."

"I've been worried about her for a while now," I confessed. "This house is so old, Lawrence. If there was an accident . . ."

"Come on," he said. "The candles are out now, the danger is over. Let's go back to the kitchen and talk about this."

"Where is Anthony? Have you seen him?" I looked up in sudden alarm.

"He went up to his room when we got in. He kissed you good night, Annabel. You must remember?" Lawrence pulled me to my feet and took me by the shoulders, giving me a little shake. "What is this all about? Why are you so frightened of a fire?"

"I can't talk about it." I was trembling all over, my teeth chattering as though I were cold. "It happened when I was a child—"

I moved away, turning my back to him.

"What happened, Annabel?" His arms went round me and I felt his mouth against the back of my neck. "Can't you tell me?"

The warmth of his body against mine was soothing and I found that the words just came tumbling out as if a dam had been released inside me.

"There was a terrible fire when I was five years old . . ." Suddenly the tears were pouring down my cheeks and I turned to face him, gazing up into his eyes, needing to see his reaction. "My mother and baby brother were burned to death and – and my father blamed me. I was outside the nursery; he carried me away to safety and then went back to get them but it was too late. He – he thought that I might have started the fire with a box of matches. I don't know whether I did or not. I was traumatised and I couldn't speak for a long time. I've never been able to remember what happened."

"My God!" Lawrence's jaw dropped as if he were stunned. "What a hell of a burden for you to carry all these years. You think you might be guilty, don't you?"

There was understanding in his eyes, and I could see he was remembering things I had said – the nightmare I'd had that first time at his cottage – and my interest in his feelings about murder.

"You poor kid," he said and drew me against him. "Even if you struck that bloody match you couldn't have known what you were doing. You were five years old, for heaven's sake! What kind of a man was your father to lay that on you?"

"I was jealous of the baby," I said slowly. "I remember thinking that no one loved me and I was alone in the nursery. My father had left a box of cigarettes and matches on the table. In my dream I took out a match and struck it—"

"And then what?"

"I always wake up at that point."

Lawrence was silent as he drew me from the study and walked me into the kitchen. The kettle was boiling and he made the tea, pouring for both of us.

"I've been haunted by the fear that I might have done it," I said. "All my life I've expected punishment because of what I may have done."

"It's a wonder you haven't had a nervous breakdown," he said with a little frown. "I'm surprised that you've managed to remain so normal."

"Am I normal, Lawrence? Sometimes I think I must be evil. I must have been wicked if I set fire to that cot."

"That's ridiculous! I don't want to hear you say that again. You can't blame yourself for what happened so long ago. Whatever happened, you've more than paid the price."

"I try to tell myself that," I said as I drank my tea. I was beginning to feel better now. "Don't worry about it, Lawrence. It was just the shock of finding those candles like that."

"You'll have to do something about her, Annabel."

"Yes, I suppose I shall. But what?"

"Can't you get her a place of her own? Or perhaps arrange for her to go to a residential home where someone can keep an eye on her."

"You don't know Edith." I laughed shakily. "She would never agree."

"She isn't a relation, is she?"

"No, none at all. She looked after my grandmother when she was dying, and she was good to me when I was ill after Charles died. I don't want to hurt her, Lawrence."

He glanced at his watch. "Pop upstairs and take a look at Anthony. I can't stop much longer, but I won't go until you're sure in your mind that everything is all right."

"Thank you." I smiled at him and went out, running up the stairs.

Anthony was in bed and already asleep, his arm curled around the toy dog Lawrence had given him. I felt relief wash over me. Of course Edith wouldn't deliberately harm him; she thought of him as her own.

I closed Anthony's door softly, hesitating before walking down the hallway to Edith's room. I knocked but there was no answer, then I tried the handle. Her door was locked.

"I know you're not asleep," I said. "We found the candles, Edith. That was a very silly thing to do. I shall talk to you about it in the morning."

She still didn't answer so I turned away and went back downstairs. Lawrence had been outside and was standing in the hall.

"I was just checking on Sabre," he said. "Is everything all right?"

"Anthony is asleep. I tried to talk to Edith but she wouldn't answer."

"I wish I could stay over," he said, and came to take me in his arms, his hands stroking the back of my neck. "I don't like leaving you after this, Annabel. I have to be in court early tomorrow or . . ."

"Please don't worry about me," I begged him. "I was upset or I wouldn't have told you. Edith wouldn't hurt either me or Anthony. I promise you there's no need to be concerned."

He bent his head and kissed me, his mouth caressing mine with a softness that made me want to cling to him and beg him not to leave me but I held back the words, knowing that I had to let him go.

"I still feel uneasy about all this. I wish I didn't have to leave you but I'm afraid I have no choice."

"I'm fine now, believe me."

He touched my cheek. "It's not you I'm worried about, Annabel. You're one of the sanest people I know and I don't for a minute believe you started that fire."

"Oh, Lawrence . . ." I was between tears and laughter. "How can you know? It was so long ago. I don't even know the truth myself." I drew a shaky breath. "I would never have told you if I hadn't been so upset. I never told Charles."

He kissed me then, very tenderly on the mouth. "I'm glad you did tell me, my darling. I'll be in touch very soon, I promise. And now I really do have to leave."

I went to the door and waved as he started the car and reversed, then watched as his tail-lights disappeared down the drive and out of sight. As I locked the door, walking back through the hall and up the stairs I was feeling much better. It was strange, but telling Lawrence about the past seemed to have lifted some of the guilt from my mind at last.

Seventeen

When I came downstairs the next morning the candles had all disappeared from the study, and if Lawrence had not been with me when I saw them the previous evening I might have doubted my own memory.

"Edith," I said as I went into the kitchen and found her busily cleaning a brass pot. "About last night—"

"I was in bed when you came home," she said. "I didn't hear you arrive."

"The candles in the study. I asked you not to light candles, Edith. I've told you before how dangerous it is in this house when you're here alone."

"I don't know what you mean," she replied, her eyes sliding away from mine. "What candles in the study?"

"They were there last night, a hundred of them or more set around that photograph of Charles as if it were a shrine. What made you do it? Was it to punish me for going away with Lawrence again?"

"He'll hurt you," she said, and now there was an angry glint in her eyes. "You've forgotten that men are betrayers. You think this one will be different, but you'll see – you'll see."

"I'm going to lock the study," I said. "I don't want you to go in there again, Edith, and I'm going to ask for your promise that you won't do anything like that again."

"I like candlelight," she said, an odd, sly expression in her eyes. "It helps me see into the shadows. Don't you want to look into the shadows, Annabel?"

"What do you mean?"

"You can see things, things from the past." She looked at me. "Sometimes I see *him*, staring at me from the shadows . . ."

A chill ran down my spine. Lawrence may just have been right when he said her mind could have begun to wander.

"Who do you see, Edith?"

She blinked and then glanced away. "No one. I put the candles there because I wanted to warn you, that's all. That man will hurt you – just as *he* did."

"What did you do with those candles, Edith? I want them out of this house today."

"I've thrown them away," she said. "Look in the dustbin if you don't believe me."

"I'm going to look," I said, stopping as the phone rang. I saw her eyes dart towards the hall. "I'll answer it, and I should be grateful if you will just get on with your work. I know you listen to my private calls, Edith, and I would prefer it if you didn't in future."

She didn't answer as I went out into the hall, but I could hear her banging the pot on the table as she cleaned it. For a moment, as I reached for the phone, I wondered if it would be another of those threatening calls, but Lawrence's deep tones reassured me.

"How are you this morning, darling?"

"I'm fine, thank you," I replied. "The candles have gone and I've spoken to Edith. I think you may be right. I can't say any more at the moment and it would be best if you didn't, but I believe you gave me some good advice last night."

"We'll talk about it at the weekend," he said. "This is going to be a busy week for me, Annabel. I doubt if I'll have time to ring you, unless it's late at night."

"I don't mind that," I said. "Don't worry, there's no immediate panic, but I think I'm going to have to do something along the lines you mentioned."

"Don't worry too much just yet," he said. "We'll sort it out together. You won't be alone in future, Annabel. You've got me to turn to when you need help."

"Lawrence, you don't know how much that means to me."

"I must go now, darling. Take care of yourself." He paused for a moment, then, "I love you."

I closed my eyes as a wave of emotion hit me. "I love you too, Lawrence. Very much."

I was near to tears as I replaced the receiver. After he had left me the previous evening I had suffered agonies of doubt, wondering whether he would change his mind about us when he'd had time to think things over. He had accepted my innocence so easily that I'd wondered if he'd really taken

200

in what I'd been saying, if he might start doubting me when he'd had time to consider the facts. Even my grandmother had been unsure whether or not I'd started that fire out of childish jealousy. She had tried to hide her doubts, and I knew that she had loved me very much, but she had never been certain. Doctor Mills had wanted to hypnotise me to discover the truth, but Lawrence had been convinced I was innocent. That made me feel good; for the first time in my life someone was completely on my side, even after they knew my terrible secret.

I was smiling as I went back into the kitchen. Edith came in at the back door, carrying a plastic dustbin bag. She opened it to show me the candles inside.

"Satisfied?"

"Yes, I'm satisfied," I said. I felt upset. She had been my housekeeper and friend for a long time, and I was dreading the moment when I would have to tell her that she must go. "Don't let's fall out, Edith," I said in a cajoling tone. "It's just that I'm so frightened of an accident."

"It won't happen again," she promised. "I – I'm sorry, Annabel."

She had never apologised to me before. As I looked at her in surprise, I saw the fear in her eyes and I knew she was frightened that she had gone too far this time.

I took the candles out to the dustbin and put them in myself, then I went back into the house just as Anthony came down for his breakfast. Watching the way Edith fussed over him, I felt a pang of regret. It would break her heart if I sent her away.

The second letter came the next day. It was in a pink envelope just as before and smelt of the same perfume; this time the postmark was clearly from London and posted a day earlier. I stared at it for several minutes before I could bring myself to open it. When I did so I saw that once again there was a jumble of letters and words cut from a magazine.

'IF YOU WANT TO KNOW THE TRUTH ABOUT LAWRENCE MASTERS ASK HIM WHY HIS WIFE DIED. ASK HIM WHO KILLED HER.'

I was sickened by the implication behind this message. Someone was obviously trying to make trouble for Lawrence. I decided that this time I had no choice. I was going to have to show it to him. I placed it in the top drawer of my desk with my current diary, replacing the key in the tiny, silver rose vase, in which I had chosen to hide it from Edith's prying eyes.

Perhaps I ought to telephone Lawrence and tell him about the letters and the phone call? I picked up the receiver and dialled his number, but he was out and I was answered by a machine.

"It's Annabel," I said. "Ring me if you have time. I love you."

I spent the rest of the morning working in my garden. It was very warm and the roses were in full bloom, their heavy, musky perfume wafting pleasantly on the gentle breeze. At lunch time I asked Edith if there had been any phone messages."

"It hasn't rung," she said. "Not that I've heard."

"Are you sure, Edith?"

"I've been polishing the hall and dining room all morning. I would have heard."

I had already seen evidence of her industry and the house smelt faintly of lavender. She had been subdued since the episode of the candles, and I was inclined to believe her. Edith was being careful for the moment. I only hoped it would last until I could sort something out for her.

"I'm going into Cambridge to do some shopping this afternoon. Is there anything you want, Edith?"

She shook her head and I knew she did most of her own shopping through magazines or catalogues; there was quite often a parcel for Edith on the step in the mornings.

"If Lawrence does ring, please tell him I will be here all evening."

"If that's what you want."

"Don't look like that, Edith. I know you mean well, that you're only trying to protect me, but you're wrong about Lawrence. He loves me and I love him."

It was out in the open now and I was glad.

Edith shot me a look of disbelief but said nothing. I decided to let her mull it over and went upstairs to take a quick shower.

Cambridge town centre was crowded with tourists. I drove by the wide, spacious greens of Midsummer Common and parked in King Street, walked through Rose Crescent, past the bookshop and Woolworths, then crossed the street, went down a narrow path past a beautiful old church and into Marks & Spencers. It took me ages to get served at the busy store, which fronted onto the market square with its stalls, modern shops and glimpses of elegant buildings that belonged to a more gentle age.

I was in a hurry when I left and in my haste I neglected to look where I was going. My shopping bags knocked into a woman, causing her to cry out in alarm.

"I'm dreadfully sorry. It was all my fault, Mrs Robson!" I stared at her in surprise. It was years since I'd seen her. We'd almost met once at the village shop but she had deliberately turned away as if she did not wish to speak to me. "How are you?"

"I'm very well, Lady Cheshire."

"And your daughter – the one who lives in Bournemouth – how is she these days?"

"I don't have a daughter in Bournemouth."

"But surely . . . I was certain it was Bournemouth. She was ill, that's why you stopped coming in to help me."

She stared at me and her eyes went cold. "You asked me not to come in," she said. "I was told that I wasn't needed anymore."

"Not needed?" I was stunned. "But who told you that, not Charles?"

"Your housekeeper informed me on the telephone."

"Edith? But I never gave her permission. She told me that you had gone to Bournemouth to look after your daughter, who was ill. Why didn't you speak to me about this?"

"You were never available, and then I had your letter and the money I was owed."

"I remember sending you a cheque, but I asked how your daughter was and said that I would be glad to have you back when you were ready."

"That wasn't the message I received."

"But this is terrible, Mrs Robson. I had no idea. I can't understand how it could have happened."

She gave me a frosty, disbelieving stare. "If you will excuse me, I have to catch my bus."

"Please, won't you let me drive you home?"

"I'll catch the bus if you don't mind."

I watched as she walked away, feeling as if I'd just been punched hard in the stomach. If what she had just told me were true Edith had lied to me – more than that she had replaced the letter to Mrs Robson with one of her own. It had been during that dreadful time after Charles died; I had been feeling too ill to go out, and had asked Edith to post the letter for me.

Why had she done such a dishonest and mean-spirited thing? The only possible answer was of course that she had been jealous of Mrs Robson, and had wanted to get rid of someone she saw as a rival.

I was thoughtful as I drove home. Listening to my phone calls was one thing, but this was serious interference in my life. She'd had no right to do it and it made me very angry. I wished now that I had taken more notice at the time, but Charles's death had overtaken Mrs Robson's departure. Immersed in my grief and self doubt, I had not bothered to enquire or even wonder why she had decided to give up her job. It had not seemed important and I had accepted Edith's explanation as the truth.

There was no need or reason for Mrs Robson to lie to me. She had obviously been very put out over the whole affair and was still smarting from it even after all this time. Now that I was aware of Edith's deceit, I too was angry.

My first reaction was to demand the truth from my house-keeper, but somewhere in the deeper regions of my mind a small voice was telling me to wait. After the bother over the candles I was afraid that Edith might feel that I was getting onto her unfairly; at the moment she was being careful not to annoy me, but if I quarrelled with her again it might make things unpleasant.

I wanted to wait until the right moment to tell her that I thought the time had come for her to retire.

When I got home I found a bouquet from Lawrence waiting for me in the kitchen. This time Edith had taken the flowers in and put the stems in a bowl of water in the sink. I read the card and smiled.

'Counting the days. Love Lawrence.'

I too was counting the days. The weekend could not come soon enough for me. I was aware of a growing silence between myself and Edith. It was not helped by what I had just learned from Mrs Robson. Although I'd decided not to say anything for the moment I was annoyed with her, and it showed in my manner towards her.

I had always tolerated Edith's little ways and her disapproval, which some people might see as rudeness, because I felt sympathy for her. Life had not been kind to Edith before she came to my grandmother's house. Besides, she was a part of my childhood, of memories good and bad. Even now I was reluctant to take the steps that I knew were necessary.

I would discuss it all with Lawrence at the weekend.

Lawrence arrived on Friday afternoon. I had just returned from fetching Anthony from school when his car drew in behind us. I glanced in the wing mirror, my heart leaping with relief and pleasure as I saw him get out with Sabre at his heels.

Anthony was out of the car in a trice and flying to meet him. He caught him up, swinging him off his feet and whirling him round while the dog jumped around them both, barking excitedly. I locked my car, turning to watch as Lawrence ruffled the boy's hair and gave him a bar of chocolate from his pocket, then our eyes met above his head and we smiled.

"Take Sabre down to the paddock and give him a good run," he told Anthony. "See if you can remember how to make him obey you."

As they disappeared round the side of the house together, Lawrence came to meet me. We kissed briefly, joining hands to walk into the house together.

"I managed to get away early for once. I'm sorry I haven't been able to ring you but there's been a bit of a crisis one way and another. Was your call important?"

"It might be. I'm not sure yet," I said. "There's something I think you should see."

"This sounds serious. Has Edith been misbehaving again?"

"Yes and no." I grimaced. "Edith isn't my main worry at the moment. I ought to have told you last weekend, but I didn't want to spoil things."

I led the way through the conservatory. In the kitchen the kettle was boiling, but there was no sign of Edith. I wasn't sure whether she was sulking in her room again or just keeping out of the way for a while. I would worry about that later, for the moment I was more concerned about the letters.

Unlocking my desk I handed the latest one to Lawrence. "That came this week. I had another which I threw away and a rather unpleasant phone call last week."

Lawrence glanced at the letter, screwed it into a ball and tossed it into the wastepaper basket.

"I'm sorry you've been subjected to this, Annabel."

"Don't you think you should show it to the police?"

"No. I know who sent it. I can deal with this myself." He was quite positive, and that confirmed my own suspicions about the sender.

"Have you had one, too?"

"No. She wouldn't attempt to send them to me. She was hoping to cause trouble between us, Annabel. It was just a rather silly trick."

"Belinda Dane?"

"Yes. I might have known you would work it out for yourself." He sighed and went over to the sideboard, lifting the whiskey decanter to show me. "May I?"

"Of course. Help yourself."

"Would you care for anything?"

"It's too early for me."

"I could do with something. It has been a hell of a week, Annabel, and now this . . ." He gave a sigh of frustration and poured the drink.

"I'm sorry. Perhaps I shouldn't have shown you the letter. I threw the other one away. That was about me and not important, but I felt I had to let you see this. It – it implies that your wife's death was—"

"Not an accident?" His brows rose. "Do you believe this filth, Annabel?"

"No, certainly not. I don't know anything about Vivien or how she died."

"I was going to tell you." He sipped his drink, a weariness about him as he loosened his tie. "When Anthony came in last week . . ."

"Yes, I remember. You don't have to tell me anything, Lawrence. I showed you the letter so that you could protect yourself from vicious lies and innuendo, not because I wanted an explanation."

"I'm glad you did show it to me" He turned and that bleak expression I had seen before was in his eyes. "Some time ago I made the mistake of telling Belinda that I felt responsible for Vivien's death." He hesitated, finished his whiskey and went on, "Viv and I quarrelled violently over that waiter she was making up to, and I asked her for a divorce. She swore she would never give me one. I said that our marriage was over whatever she did and she stormed off – that was the last time I saw her. You must believe me, Annabel. I had nothing to do with her death."

"Of course I believe you."

His mouth twisted in a rueful smile. "The Greek police didn't, not at first. They questioned me for three days before they finally let me go."

"You mean . . ." I stared at him. "You were accused of murdering her?"

"Not quite. They carefully avoided saying that, but Stavros Constantine – he was their chief officer – believed I was guilty. I could see it in his eyes, hear it in his voice. He couldn't prove anything but he was convinced I had contrived her death."

"Oh, Lawrence, how awful for you. It must have been terrible. Vivien was dead and you were being treated like a criminal."

"It was an unpleasant experience," he said. "Something I never ever want to go through again."

"Yes, I know exactly how you feel." My eyes opened in recognition as I thought of something. "So that's why you believed in me instantly."

"That was a part of it." He smiled at me with a deep tenderness that warmed me. "Most of it was sheer instinct. You develop a sixth sense about people in my work, Annabel. My judgement of you would be that you don't have the killer instinct, that love of self at all costs, that most murderers have. You might be able to kill in self-defence, but it wouldn't come easily to you."

"You've made me feel so much better about myself. I haven't had the dream once since last weekend, but go on, you were telling me about Vivien, and Belinda Dane."

He poured himself another drink and sat down, stretching his long legs out in front of him as he closed his eyes for a moment. I curled up on the settee and waited; this was obviously going to be a long story.

"I said some pretty rotten things to Viv that day." Lawrence's voice was muffled by pain, and I guessed it was costing him dearly to talk about all this. "I called her a whore and worse! It was the most terrible row we had ever had. I only just stopped short of hitting her. When she went storming off she said she was going to kill herself. I didn't believe her. I said she could go to hell with my blessing. She said I was a cold bastard and that I'd driven her to other men—"

"Oh, Lawrence, I'm so sorry." I understood how he must have felt when she was drowned. He had ignored Vivien's threats thinking she was just talking wildly and would calm down after a while. "You must have felt so guilty when she died, and understandably you blamed yourself."

No one understood his feelings better than I!

"For a while I was almost suicidal myself. I wouldn't have put a gun to my head, but I was doing a pretty good job of drinking myself into an early grave. I came close to losing the trust of my partners and finishing myself as a barrister, but then I managed to pull out of it – largely due to Jonathan and Mary, I think. They stood by me, supported me, believed in me, and eventually I cut back on the drinking and began to feel better."

"But the guilt didn't go away?"

"No." He gave me a rueful look. "I don't suppose it ever will completely, but it's under control now. I can cope with it."

"And Belinda, where does she fit into all this?"

"In between bouts of heavy drinking there were women. I'm afraid I was a bit of a bastard, Annabel. Whether I wanted revenge on womankind as a whole or whether I was just trying to get Viv out of my head, I don't know, but I used the other women for sex and dropped them as soon as they bored me, which was usually in a matter of weeks."

"Nothing between the covers?" I suggested. "I believe that's what you told me once. You hated to read the whole story in the blurb, isn't that what you said?"

He pulled a wry face. "I can't lie to you, Annabel. You were going to be just one of the crowd. But then I discovered that this time I cared. You mattered and I couldn't just walk away."

"Did you care about Belinda?"

"Belinda was different . . ." His eyes narrowed. "She was Viv's best friend. I'd known her for years. We were friends before we became lovers."

It hurt to hear him talk like this of his lovers, but I knew I had to listen. I had to let him get it all out of his system, and I had to accept him as he was with all his faults.

208

"Belinda has been married three times. She's had a rough time, Annabel. The first marriage was when she was seventeen; he was killed in a car crash, and her baby with him; the second cleaned out their joint bank account and left her for someone else – the third one knocked her around. She turned to me for comfort. One thing led to another . . ."

"And now she doesn't want to let go?"

"I've been trying to break it off for months." He sighed and ran his fingers through his hair. "Belinda drinks. I mean, she *really* drinks, far more than I ever did even at my worst moments. She's lonely and scared and she doesn't have anyone else she can talk to. We haven't slept together in over a year, but she still rings me all the time."

"And you go running when she calls?"

He looked annoyed. "Not always. The other week when she phoned Mary she was suicidal, Annabel. Her mother died and Belinda couldn't cope. I had to give her some support visiting the hospital and arranging the funeral, that's why I had to cancel that weekend."

"What about the letters and the phone call, are you going to let her get away with them, Lawrence?"

"I'll talk to her. It isn't a matter of getting away with anything, Annabel. She needs help – proper professional help. I've been trying to persuade her, but it isn't easy."

"I don't suppose it is. It's you she wants, Lawrence, not a cure. You know that you'll never be free of her while you dance to her tune, don't you?"

"That's a bit harsh, Annabel. Belinda has been through hell."

I understood that, much more than he realised. I knew what it was like to go to the bottom of the pit, but Belinda was taking advantage of his Achilles heel. Because of the way Vivien had died he was susceptible to Belinda's blackmail and threats of suicide; he couldn't ignore her cries for help in case she really meant it. But even though I understood, I was fearful that she would manage to come between us.

"Yes, I know. I didn't mean to criticise. You must do whatever you think best, Lawrence. Just don't let her ruin what we have."

"She couldn't do that," he said and his smile made me go weak. "I love you. I think I always shall."

209

"I love you," I said. "Shall we try and forget all this for a while? Make the most of the time we have together?"

"We'll have the rest of our lives," he promised and stood up. "I could do with a shower, Annabel. And then we'll take Anthony for a burger and chips, if you like?"

"He would love that," I said. "I'll call him in and get changed myself."

At the door Lawrence turned to look at me. "Was there something you wanted to tell me about Edith?"

"It will do another time," I said. "Let's just think of ourselves for this weekend, shall we?"

"Suits me," he murmured and went out.

I was thoughtful as I went to fetch Anthony in from the garden. After what Lawrence had told me, my little problems with Edith seemed petty and insignificant. I couldn't worry him with them when he had so many of his own.

Eighteen

The dream had changed. Always before it had been vague, shadowed in mists and a strange green darkness that seemed to suck me in like a pool of murky water, down, down until I was choking and I woke in terror. Now it was crystal clear, like a big screen movie with all the words and pictures sharp and focused.

The child was playing with her bricks on the floor of the nursery, and that child was me. It was warm and cosy despite the snowflakes that drifted past the window, settling on the roofs of the houses and making it all look like a Christmas card. It would not be long to Christmas now and I was looking forward to it; I had helped my mother dress the tree with a pretty fairy doll and we had laughed together, sharing a mutual excitement. My mother was such a beautiful, fair-haired, gentle woman and I loved her so much.

But now I was in the nursery. A huge log fire was burning safely behind the wire grate, and as I looked around me, I could see the rocking horse I loved to ride, my teddy bears and dolls ranged on the old, green sofa with its sagging frame and lumpy seat. I could see the cot too, fancy and pretty with its white, nylon frills and pale blue coverlet.

I got up from the floor and wandered over to look down at my baby brother sleeping in his cot. He looked warm and soft when he wasn't crying and I wanted to touch him, but my father had told me I mustn't. I could smell the rather sickly sweetness of the powder my mother used when she changed his nappies, and also the lingering odour of my father's cigarettes.

I glanced at the ashtray and saw the matches lying there. My father had warned me not to play with them, but I was cross with him. He was always smacking me these days. He had hit me hard across the face when I pinched the baby.

I knew I ought not to have done it. I wasn't sure why I had, except that I had been feeling jealous and neglected. I didn't really hate my brother; sometimes when he was sleeping instead of screaming, I quite liked him, and when my mother snuggled us both up together in her arms I felt safe and loved – but my father had turned against me since the baby arrived. I didn't understand why, but I knew it made me miserable.

"Don't take any notice of Daddy," my mother had said when she saw me crying after I'd been scolded. "He's just worried and tired."

But he hadn't been like this before the baby came.

I picked up the box of matches, took one out and struck it deliberately; the orange flame surprised and fascinated me as I watched it run up the thin sliver of wood. As it reached my fingers it burnt me and I dropped it . . . into the ashtray.

"Annabel – what are you doing?"

I looked up fearfully as my father came into the nursery and I saw the anger in his eyes as he noticed the match dying harmlessly in the metal tray.

"I've warned you, Annabel," he cried, pouncing on me in a sudden fury. "You wicked, wicked girl! You could have set fire to your brother's cot."

"No, Daddy, no," I whimpered as he started to hit me again and again. 'Please, Daddy. I didn't mean to do it. I didn't mean to be wicked. Don't hit me again, please—"

"Annabel! Annabel, wake up!"

I came out of the dream with a start. The bedside light was on and Lawrence was bending over me, a look of concern in his eyes. He stroked my hair back from my forehead as I gazed up at him in bewilderment.

"You were having a bad dream," he said. "It's all right, darling. I'm here."

I pushed myself up against the pillows. For a moment I couldn't focus, the dream was still with me and all at once I knew that it wasn't a dream, it was what had actually happened that day in the nursery when I was a child of five.

"No," I said slowly. "It wasn't bad dream, not this time." I caught his arm. "I saw beyond the match, Lawrence. For the first time I saw beyond the match. I didn't start the fire with that match. It burnt my fingers and I dropped it into the ashtray, and then my father came in and hit me."

"You were crying in your sleep," Lawrence said and wiped

the tears from my cheeks with his fingertips. "Your father was hurting you, you begged him to stop."

My throat was dry and the words came out as a harsh whisper. "He kept on and on hitting me. I remember my mother heard me screaming and she made him stop."

"You remember? So it wasn't just a dream?"

"Not this time. I remember my mother coming into the room. She shouted at him and tried to stop him physically, they struggled and then he hit her and she cried. He was sorry then and he begged her to forgive him."

"Are you sure, Annabel?"

"Yes, I'm sure." I looked into his eyes as I spoke and the relief was sweeping over me. "I know that's what happened. I know I didn't start the fire."

"Can you remember how it did start?"

"No." My euphoria faded. I had remembered what happened when I struck that match, but I could have done it again at some other time. I might still be guilty. "No, that's all I can remember, but it was the dream I've always had, the dream that made me think I might have done it."

"It's good that you're beginning to remember," Lawrence said. "Don't you see, Annabel? You've begun to feel better about yourself, you told me so earlier this evening, and that new self-confidence is starting to release the block in your mind. You've kept it in place all these years, because you were afraid to let it down, afraid of what you might discover if you did."

He was right. As a small, bewildered child in my grand-mother's old house I had listened to all the whispers, and stories about myself and the fire, and I had retreated further and further from reality into my safe world of vague mists and half-remembered dreams. The dream I'd had for so many years was based on what I'd heard those old, dry women saying about me, and my father's accusations. Even as I grew up and the mists retreated, I was still afraid to see beyond the match, because I was terrified that I might just be guilty – that I had killed the mother I adored and my brother out of a childish jealousy.

"Why can't I remember the fire? I want to know the truth, Lawrence. Whatever it is, I want to know." I caught back a sob. "I want to know if I'm a murderer? Why can't I remember?"

Lawrence pulled me to him so that I nestled against his bare shoulder. He nuzzled my neck with his lips, his hands

213

stroking the fine, pale silk of my hair as it fell across his face.

"Because it was too horrific," he said soothing me with little kisses. "You've shut the memory out, Annabel, because it frightens you. Perhaps it's better that way. Now that you know you didn't start the fire you don't need to remember the rest of it. If you saw what happened, it's no wonder it affected you so badly. Just forget it, my darling, and be happy. Remember I love you. I would still love you even if you did drop that damned match into the cot."

"Oh, Lawrence," I whispered chokily, somewhere between tears and laughter as I felt an overwhelming surge of gratitude and love. "Where have you been all my life? How have I managed all these years without you?"

"I've no idea," he murmured as his mouth slid over mine, his tongue probing and teasing as we kissed. "You might like to show how much you appreciate me . . ."

A tiny pulse was beating at the base of his throat. I flicked at it with my tongue and he groaned; his skin was slightly moist and warm and he tasted of shrimp as I kissed and lavished him with my lips and tongue, wanting him, needing him so desperately.

"I love you so much," I whispered, working my way down his lean torso to his navel and beyond with little darting kisses, then taking him into my mouth to tease and tantalise, to give him a deep, sensual pleasure that made him gasp and tangle his hands in my hair. "So much . . ."

He shuddered several times, then rolled me over onto my back. We moved together urgently, our bodies surging with a fierce, panting desire. I moaned as Lawrence's mouth sucked at my nipples and I arched into him as I felt the hot, pulsating hardness of him thrusting at me, the rising tide lifting, carrying us both to a tumultuous climax that left us both shattered and satiated.

Afterwards, we lay entwined as one, legs curled over each other's body as we drifted into a deep, dreamless sleep.

"Mum! Laurie! Wake up!" I woke to see my son's anxious face as he shook Lawrence's shoulder. "Laurie! Wake up. Sabre is sick. You've got to come."

Lawrence was awake and alert instantly. He sat up and reached for the black, silk dressing gown that lay across the chair

214

next to the bed, pulling it over his nakedness before pushing back the covers.

"What's wrong with Sabre?"

"I don't know. He's ill. I went down to the kitchen and he was whining and he's made a mess. You've got to come, Laurie. I don't want him to die." Anthony looked wild-eyed and was obviously close to tears.

"Calm down, Anthony," Lawrence said as he pushed his feet into leather mules. "He was fine last night. It's probably just a tummy upset, nothing to worry about."

"I'll be down in a minute," I said, but neither of them gave any sign of having heard me.

I was thoughtful as I went into the bathroom and turned on the shower, stepping under the steaming water and covering myself in a creamy perfumed gell. It was refreshing and it drove the cobwebs from my mind. I suddenly wondered how Anthony had known that Lawrence would be in my room. He had shown no surprise at finding us clasped naked in each other's arms, but of course his immediate concern had been for the dog; it might be different when he'd had time to think it over. I would face that problem when it came to it; at least he liked Lawrence.

Lawrence was in the bedroom pulling on a pair of faded blue jeans when I came out of the bathroom wrapped in my towel. The expression on his face told me that he was very concerned for his dog.

"What's wrong with Sabre?"

"I don't know. He has been very sick and he seems to be in pain. I'm taking him straight round to the vet. Anthony is coming with me to show me the way." He dragged on a baggy sweater. "I'm afraid I haven't got round to clearing up."

"Don't worry about it, I'll do it. Just look after yourselves and Sabre." He nodded and walked to the door. "I hope Sabre is all right."

"So do I, for all our sakes."

I knew what he meant. We were going to have trouble with Anthony if anything happened to that dog; it was too soon after he had lost the pony. I could hardly believe that it could happen again. It was almost as if there was some kind of a jinx on my son.

I dressed in casual slacks and an old shirt and went downstairs. There was an unpleasant odour coming from the kitchen and a

215

sticky brown mess on the floor. I grimaced and pulled a great wodge of kitchen paper from the roll, using it to wipe up the sick and taking it straight out to the dustbin. As I was about to dump it inside I saw a piece of half-chewed raw beef lying on top of the other rubbish.

I stared at it for a moment, then picked it out. There were definitely teeth marks on the meat and it looked very much as if Sabre might have eaten a piece of it. I knew that Lawrence never gave him raw meat; he had told me that he used only a special brand of tinned food because the dog had a delicate digestion, and he had brought a supply of the tins with him. Could Anthony had given Sabre the meat thinking it would be a treat for him? Lawrence would be very angry if he had.

I threw the beef back into the bin and went in to finish washing the kitchen floor with hot water and a strong disinfectant, which took away the unpleasant smell of the vomit. It was as I was rinsing my hands afterwards that Edith came in. She stared at the wet floor in surprise.

"I washed that yesterday morning."

"Sabre was sick." I began to smooth some cream into my hands.

"Dogs." She gave a sniff of disapproval. "Nasty, smelly things. I never did like them."

"Anthony and Lawrence are both very fond of Sabre and I am too. He's good company for all of us."

"Will you be wanting me to cook breakfast?" She was deliberately avoiding my eyes.

"I'll get it later, when Lawrence and Anthony come back. They've taken Sabre straight round to the vet."

"Lot of fuss for a tummy upset."

"What do you know about it, Edith?" I stared at her in sudden suspicion. There was something about her, a sly, secret smile on her lips that made me think she might know a great deal.

"Dogs are always making a mess, being sick and having diarrhoea."

"Sabre certainly hasn't before. He always asked to go out at the cottage and Lawrence is very careful about his diet. Lawrence was concerned enough to rush him straight to the vet. I hope nothing happens to Sabre: Anthony adores him, and I suspect he means a lot to Lawrence, too."

Edith shrugged and turned away, but not before I'd seen an

expression of satisfaction in her eyes. I watched her slicing bread and scrambling eggs for herself. She was certainly in a good mood this morning; she usually disappeared to her own room when Lawrence was around, just as she had after Charles had told me she would have to leave all those years ago . . .

"Do you want me to do the vegetables for lunch, Annabel?"

"You can scrub the potatoes; I'm going to jacket them. Or perhaps I'd better wait and see what happens first. They might not feel like eating if the news is bad. Leave it to me, Edith."

"If you don't need me I might catch the bus into Cambridge this morning."

I was stunned, hardly believing my ears. It was years since Edith had gone anywhere unless I took her with me in the car.

"Of course, if you want to. There's nothing wrong, is there?"

"Why should there be? I can go out if I want, can't I?"

"Whenever you like. I'm glad you want to, Edith. I was just surprised, that's all." I hesitated, thinking that now might be a good time to start preparing her for what I had in mind. "I've been thinking that this house is getting too much for you, Edith. Perhaps you might like to have your own little cott—" I broke off as I heard a car outside. "That must be Lawrence—"

I ran outside to greet them as they got out of the car. Anthony had been crying; his face was streaked with tears and Lawrence was looking serious.

"Where's Sabre?" I felt a chill at the nape of my neck. "He isn't—he isn't . . ."

"We've left him with the vet," Lawrence said. "He seems a decent sort, Annabel, knows what he's talking about."

"Yes, he's very good. But what about Sabre? How is he?"

"The vet thinks he ate something that disagreed with him."

"He hasn't been poisoned?"

"No, I doubt that it's that serious. He was already picking up a bit by the time we got there." Lawrence frowned and looked at Anthony. "Sabre has always had a delicate digestion, that's why I'm so particular about his food. You didn't give him anything yesterday, Anthony?"

Anthony looked guilty. "I gave him a chocolate digestive last night. Did that make him ill, Laurie? Was it my fault he was sick?"

"No, that wouldn't do it. I give him them sometimes myself,"

Lawrence said. "Are you sure you didn't give him anything else? No meat of any kind?"

"I wouldn't do that. You made me promise not to."

"Anthony wouldn't give Sabre raw meat," I said and looked at him hard. "Would you?"

"No, Mum. Honest, Laurie, I only gave him the biscuit." Tears filled his eyes. "I don't want him to die."

"He won't die." Lawrence relented and gripped his shoulder. "He was like this once before, but he'd been eating raw meat. I can't understand it . . ." He glanced at me. "You didn't leave any about on the table that he could have stolen, Annabel?"

"No . . ." I gave Anthony a little push towards the house. "Edith will get you some breakfast, darling. We'll be in in a minute."

Anthony looked at Lawrence, then walked off, a picture of dejection. He was breaking his heart over the dog, just as he had over Bramble, but the pony had died.

"I think Edith may have given Sabre the meat," I said when my son was safely out of hearing.

"What!" Lawrence's eyes snapped with sudden temper. "Damn her! Why do you say that?"

"I found a piece of half chewed, raw beef in the dustbin. I was afraid that Anthony might have given it to him, but he wouldn't lie to you, he respects you too much. He told you about the biscuit so it must have been Edith."

"But why would—" His gaze narrowed in suspicion. "Is that why you asked if Sabre had been poisoned?"

"I was afraid she might have done it out of spite."

"Surely not! She isn't that vindictive, is she?"

"I don't know . . ." I faltered unhappily. "I don't want to believe it of her but . . . Anthony's pony died soon after he fell off it and hurt himself. It was fine a few hours earlier. Mr Briggs told me it had eaten a poisonous plant and we assumed Bramble must have found it for himself; supposing Edith fed it to him?"

"Would she have known what to give it?"

"Yes, I think she might. She once warned me about a plant I was pulling up, told me the sap could cause me harm if it got in my eyes."

"You should have done something before. If she poisoned that pony it could be you or Anthony next."

"No. No, you're wrong. She wouldn't harm us. She's devoted

to us both. If she made Sabre sick it was to force you to leave, because she is afraid of you, afraid of the changes you may bring. She loves Anthony."

"It sounds like it!" He was furious, his voice rising ominously. "If I thought she had deliberately tried to poison Sabre I would have her committed." Ice crackled in his eyes. "You have to get rid of her, Annabel. She isn't safe to have around you. She ought to be in a secure hospital."

"Please don't lose your temper, Lawrence. I know she ought not to have done it, but I have to be careful about this. I can't just turn her out of the house, and I don't want her upset."

"You don't want her upset!" He glared at me. "What about the rest of us? Are you prepared to risk all our lives for the sake of some crazy old woman?"

"Lawrence, it isn't like that. Please be reasonable. I'm going to tell her she has to—"

"Annabel, telephone!"

Edith had come to the front door. Neither of us had noticed her; it was possible that she had heard every word we were saying.

"I'm going to take a bath," Lawrence muttered.

He strode past me and into the house, giving Edith a murderous glance as he passed her. She waited for me, her face very pale. She might defy me but she was afraid of Lawrence.

"It's Mrs Robson," she said. "I told her you were busy, but she insisted on speaking to you."

"Thank you, Edith."

I went into the hall and picked up the receiver. Obviously Mrs Robson had learned not to be put off by Edith's excuses. I wondered what she had said to ensure that she got through to me this time.

"Annabel Cheshire speaking, may I help you?"

"I'm sorry to disturb you, Lady Cheshire, but you told me I should have insisted on speaking to you the last time . . ." I heard the uncertainty in her voice and smiled grimly to myself.

"It's quite all right. You haven't disturbed me. I wish you had insisted the last time, now what can I do for you?"

"I was wondering if we could talk one day. There's something I think you should know; it's been on my mind for a long time.

Not on the phone, though. I should like to say my piece face to face."

"Would you like to come here?"

"I would rather not. Would you mind coming to me? It's . . . well, it's confidential."

"Yes, I can come to you, on Monday morning. Would that be convenient?"

"Yes." She paused, "I'm sorry if I was rude the other day but you took me by surprise."

"I was surprised, too," I said. "In fact I was shocked. I still haven't decided what to do about what you told me."

"You might after we've spoken, though it's only a thought, or more of a suspicion, really, but it played on my mind and then when you told me you hadn't wanted me to leave, I got to thinking it through. It's best I tell you in person, Lady Cheshire, then you can decide whether or not to take it further."

"This sounds serious. You don't want to tell me now?"

"Not on the phone. Someone might be listening. As I said, this is private, and I don't have any proof, just my own thoughts."

"We'll meet on Monday morning at eleven then. Goodbye and thank you for phoning."

What could she have to tell me after all this time that was suddenly so important to her? I was frowning as I replaced the receiver and turned round to find Edith watching me. She had obviously been listening to every word. As her eyes met mine I saw apprehension in her, and I knew she was afraid that her misdeeds were about to be discovered. It was on the tip of my tongue to tell her that I already knew what she had done, but Anthony came into the hall looking for me and I decided to let it go. It wouldn't be for much longer. I was going to have to talk to Edith very soon.

"Mum," he said, his expression anxious. "Was that the vet? Did he say Sabre was going to be all right?"

"No, darling, it wasn't the vet, but I'm sure Sabre is fine. He was just a bit sick, that's all."

Edith had told me it was just a stomach disorder. I believed she had given Sabre something in the meat to make him sick in the hope of causing trouble between Lawrence and I – or perhaps just to punish us – but I didn't think she had tried to poison the dog. She knew that Lawrence wouldn't just let it go as I had when Bramble died.

Bramble's sudden death had always disturbed me. Edith had wanted me to get rid of the pony because she was afraid that Anthony might be killed falling off it; at the time I had not even considered the possibility that she might have poisoned it, it had just been a tragic accident. Now I was beginning to wonder.

If she was capable of sending a letter of dismissal to Mrs Robson in my name, if she could make a dog sick out of spite – she might be capable of administering a fatal dose of poison to a pony she considered a danger to Anthony.

It was a horrible thought. I was aware of feeling sick in my stomach. If Edith had done these things then she wasn't the woman I thought I knew, she was a stranger, and dangerous.

"You don't mind if I go then?" she asked as I was silent. "To Cambridge, on the bus."

"No, of course not," I said. "Please do, Edith."

As she turned, and went into the kitchen, I suppressed a shudder. The way I was feeling at that moment I would be glad to have her out of the house!

Anthony came and slipped his hand in mine. I looked down into his anxious face and squeezed his hand.

"What's the matter, Mum? Why are you looking like that? Have I done something wrong? Is Laurie cross because I gave Sabre the biscuit?"

"No, he's not cross with you, darling. He thinks, we think, that Edith may have given Sabre a piece of raw meat."

"But she knew he wasn't to have it. I told her so." Anthony's face darkened with anger. "She did it on purpose. I know she did. She hates dogs. She wanted him to die. I hate her! If he dies I'll kick her."

"Stop that!" I said sternly. "I won't have you say such things. You will not kick Edith. She is very fond of you, Anthony, you know how she always spoils you. Now please behave and stop all this nonsense or I shall be very cross."

"I'm sorry, Mum." He looked surprised and chastened by my unusually sharp tone. "But she was wicked to do it to poor Sabre."

"I think perhaps Edith isn't very well," I said. "She may have to go and live somewhere else, somewhere she can be looked after."

"I'm glad she's going." He was subdued but defiant. "She was

221

cruel to make Sabre sick. If she really loved me she wouldn't have done it."

"She does love you," I said, "but she's getting old. I think perhaps she doesn't always know what she is doing."

"Of course she knew what she was doing," Lawrence said as he helped me stack the dishes in the washer after a late brunch. "You're making excuses for her, Annabel."

I knew he was right, but I was defensive. Edith had been a part of my life for a long time.

"As you do for Belinda Dane?"

"That's different."

"I don't see that, Lawrence. Edith hasn't exactly had a wonderful life either."

"She seems to have done well enough these past few years, the run of this place, your friendship and a decent wage, besides her living. That sounds pretty good to me. Most women in her situation would kill for a place like this."

A frightening silence fell between us at his words. I was glad that Anthony had gone to play in the garden.

"She didn't poison Sabre, Lawrence. She only made him sick."

"Don't you think that was bad enough?"

As his accusing eyes met mine I sat down suddenly, feeling sick and dizzy. "Yes, yes, I do. I think it's horrible, Lawrence, and I'm very sorry it happened. I wouldn't have had it happen for anything. I didn't think she was this bad. I knew about the candles and the eavesdropping, but I didn't think she could . . ."

Lawrence knelt down in front of me and took my hands in his. "You are going to have to do something about her, you do know that, don't you?"

"Yes, I do." I closed my eyes for a moment, then opened them again and looked straight at him. "But not today, not this minute. Let's take Anthony out, Lawrence. I don't want to think about any of this for a few hours."

"Let me telephone the vet, and then we'll go. Where do you suggest?"

"It's only a short run to Heacham or Hunstanton, why don't we go to the seaside for the afternoon?"

"That sounds good." He smiled and I was relieved that we had reached an understanding. "I'll just check on Sabre. It will set Anthony's mind at rest, as well as mine."

222

Fortunately, the news was good. Sabre was almost back to his old self, but the vet had decided to keep him until Sunday morning.

"He just wants to make sure there are no ill effects," Lawrence told us as we went out to the car. "So you can stop looking so miserable, Anthony. We're going to the sea and we're all going to enjoy ourselves. And that's an order!"

We all laughed from sheer relief.

Once we were at Hunstanton there was no need to order my son to enjoy himself. It was a perfect June day and the sun was hot despite the breeze blowing in from the sea.

The small town was crowded with visitors, but we managed to find a parking space on the headland near the lighthouse. We walked back along the wide greens overlooking the cliffs and the sea, down towards the main beach area where the shops and ice cream booths were. Lawrence bought us all large cones of soft, whirly ice cream with chocolate flakes stuck in the top, getting a dab of ice cream on his nose in the process. We laughed and found our way down onto the sand, sinking into some convenient deckchairs that someone else had abandoned.

I lay back in my chair, watching the holidaymakers having fun and relaxing. How good it felt to be free and happy.

Lawrence and Anthony had come prepared with various spades and moulds, and they soon embarked on the building of a splendid fort, complete with towers and battlements. There were to be no petty bucket castles for them, but a well planned and executed structure that attracted a crowd of interested onlookers; as the magnificent edifice grew so did the audience; it wasn't long before we had half the children on the beach begging to be allowed to help. I watched my son directing the excavation of a large moat with amusement. He had changed so much recently and it was all for the better.

I lay back, closing my eyes as I enjoyed the warmth of the sun on my face and the relaxing swish of the waves rushing endlessly against the wooden breakwaters. How peaceful I felt despite the children's laughter and the eerie scream of the gulls circling overhead, away from Larkspur, and the dark shadow that had lain over our lives in recent weeks.

It was strange that I should have lived with Edith's brooding presence for so many years and not realised what she was doing to us. I had allowed her to contradict me in front of my son,

223

to colour my thoughts and dictate many of the small everyday decisions I made. Because of her I had nursed a grief that should have faded long ago. I had become used to her; I had not noticed her strange ways or the changes, which had come so gradually that I accepted them without knowing I did so.

Edith had always had a vindictive streak in her nature, but I had convinced myself that she cared for Anthony and I – yet as he had so innocently said, she would not have harmed the dog he loved if she really loved him.

It was herself Edith cared for. Lawrence had opened my eyes at last. She had tried to persuade me against seeing him because she was afraid he would brings changes into my life, changes that *she* feared. I had ignored her, so she had deliberately made the dog ill to spite us. I was very much afraid she had also poisoned poor Bramble. She might have done it out of her fear for Anthony, but it had been a wicked, cruel act, and she had caused my son so much pain.

Lawrence was right. Here on this crowded beach surrounded by normality, by ordinary people enjoying their commonplace lives, I was able to make the decision I had found so hard at Larkspur. When we got home I would give Edith a choice, she could have a cottage of her own or I would pay for her to move into sheltered accomodation, but she could no longer share our home. It was time to leave the past behind, to forget the shadows and the nightmares that had haunted me for so long. I wanted to live in the sunshine Lawrence had brought into my life.

"Mum! Mum, can I go on the donkeys with Dave and Gill?"

Anthony was on his knees in the sand beside me, tugging at my arm, his new friends waiting on my decision.

"Of course you can, darling." I reached for my purse but Lawrence already had a note in his hand. "Do you want me to come with you?"

"It's only a donkey," my son said, full of his new authority. "When I get my new pony, Laurie is going to teach me to go over the jumps without falling off."

Tears stung my eyes as I watched him race across the beach, shouting and laughing with the others. He had become a different child in the past few weeks. I knew then that whatever happened in the future between Lawrence and I, the lives of my son and I had changed irrevocably.

Nineteen

The house was in darkness when we got back late that night. Anthony had fallen asleep in the back of the car and he moaned as Lawrence carried him into the hall. I went ahead of them, switching on the lights.

"I'll take him straight up," Lawrence said, smiling at me. "He's exhausted."

"I'm not surprised after the day he's had. You must be, too."

I watched as he walked upstairs carrying Anthony carefully, thinking how lucky I was that he had come into my life, then I went through to the kitchen and filled the kettle. Everything was as just as it had been, with the dishes we had used still in the washer, and as far as I could tell Edith had not been in since we left.

I decided to look in her room. Something felt different about the house; it was odd but it was as if it had lost the oppressive atmosphere of the last few days, or perhaps it was me who had changed.

I knocked at Edith's door. There was no response so I called softly, not wanting to wake her if she were asleep; again there was no answer. I was about to turn away but something made me stop and try the door handle; it was unlocked so I opened it and switched on the light. The bed had not been slept in and there was no sign of Edith.

Lawrence had come out of Anthony's room as I started back down and we met on the landing.

"I took off Anthony's shoes and trousers, but left the rest on," he told me with an amused expression in his eyes. "He's out for the count."

"Good." I hesitated and Lawrence sensed something. He raised his brows at me. "Edith isn't in her room. I don't think she has been back to the house since we left."

"Does she often stay out late?"

"Never. It's years since she went anywhere on her own. I was surprised when she said she was going."

"I'll have a look round, shall I?"

"Yes, please do. I can't imagine what she's up to. She doesn't have any friends that I know of, so where can she have gone?"

Lawrence and I searched every room in the house, looking in every room she might have shut herself into; he even went up into the attic, though no one had for years and I didn't think Edith could manage the funny little ladder that had to be pulled down to allow access. We spent nearly an hour looking for her, but she wasn't in the house.

We ended up in the kitchen drinking tea. Lawrence frowned as he noticed my abstraction.

"I shouldn't worry about her, Annabel. It's probably just another of her tricks to upset you. She'll come back when she's ready."

I gazed at him across the table, thinking how strong and serious his features were, and how much I loved and needed him.

"You don't think I should ring the police?"

"To say what, that your housekeeper has decided to go off on her own somewhere? Have you any idea of how many missing person cases they have to deal with? They wouldn't even think she qualified yet. After all, she has a perfect right to stay out all night if she wants."

"Yes, I know." I sighed, stood up and put the cups on the drainer. "I'm tired. Let's go to bed. Edith will just have to ring the bell if she wants to get in after we've gone to bed."

"Does she have a key?"

"To the kitchen door? Yes, I'm sure she does."

"She can get in at any time then if she wants."

"Yes, I suppose she can."

I wasn't sure why I suddenly found that disturbing. For years Edith had slept a few doors away from me, but all of a sudden I would have liked to lock her out of my house.

The night passed without incident, and in the morning sunshine I could laugh at myself. Edith was just Edith, with all her annoying little ways and her sulks.

She still wasn't in her room and I had started to feel uneasy. She did have a perfect right to go when she liked and return when she wished – at least until I had arranged for her to live somewhere else – but I was anxious just the same.

"She must be about seventy," I said to Lawrence as we lingered over breakfast. "It's possible she had a stroke or something while she was out."

He glanced up from his paper. I could tell that he was not in the least interested in Edith's whereabouts, but he was concerned for my peace of mind.

"If it will make you feel better phone the hospital, the police, too, if you wish. She will probably turn up this afternoon wondering what the fuss was about, but it's up to you."

"I think I will make a few calls, just in case."

Lawrence nodded and returned to his paper. Obviously he thought it would be an undisguised blessing if Edith had just walked out of our lives for good, but it made me uncomfortable. Whatever she might or might not have done, she was an elderly woman with no relatives. As her employer, I had a duty to at least try to discover where she was.

I made several calls but there were no reports of her being found ill in the street, or of an elderly, unknown woman having been taken to hospital.

"I told you she was just trying to upset you," Lawrence said. "Forget her, Annabel. What shall we do today?"

"We could spend some time in the garden, or go to the Botanical Gardens in Cambridge."

"I noticed your back lawn needs trimming. Supposing I take care of that, then after lunch we'll go into Cambridge."

"You don't have to work for your lunch, Lawrence."

"It will give me an appetite," he said and went out whistling.

I heard Anthony call to him and I smiled as I stacked the dishes, then I went into my conservatory and pottered amongst my orchids, spraying a fine mist of water over one or two that looked as if they were suffering in this warm spell. Orchids were not the easiest of plants to grow; they needed just the right amount of humidity and light, and they hated to be disturbed. Repotting them was a hazardous enterprise as they were inclined to sulk if their pot was too large and then they refused to flower.

I cooked a traditional roast beef lunch with light, fluffy Yorkshire puddings, baked potatoes and fresh vegetables, but decided to serve only fruit or ice cream for a sweet course.

As it happened, neither Lawrence or Anthony wanted anything more.

Anthony was eager to leave so that we could pick up Sabre on our way into Cambridge.

"You can't take him into the gardens, darling," I warned. "But we'll give him a walk later."

"I would rather not leave him in the car. We'll fetch him when we come back," Lawrence said.

Anthony pulled a face, but Lawrence's word was law, and he soon got over his sulks. He cheered up as we set off in the car. The University Botanical Gardens was one of our favourite places. I'd taken Anthony before and we had fed the squirrels under the trees.

That afternoon we parked in Trumpington Road and entered through the attractive ironwork gates. Here, where the sweeping branches of magnificent specimen trees reached down to caress the earth, there was so much to interest and delight the eyes; ducks swam on a pool surrounded by a rockery which was bright with the colour of delicate alpines. There were acres of beautiful parkland to explore and glasshouses filled with exotic plants.

I had learned a great deal about plants from wandering round these gardens looking at the amazing variety of shrubs and flowers from all over the world. It was here I had first learned to appreciate orchids, and to discover how many there were to collect.

We spent an hour or so in the gardens. Lawrence offered to take us for tea afterwards, but Anthony was impatient to be reunited with Sabre so we decided to go straight to the vet's house.

The dog came bounding towards us as soon as it was let out of its kennel, lavishing a great deal of affection on both Lawrence and my son, and obviously none the worse for its ordeal. I received a few licks, but it was clear that the dog had attached itself to Anthony. They were inseparable for the rest of the afternoon, and it was a pleasure to watch them as we all went for a long walk over the common.

"It's just as well I didn't buy another dog," I was saying to Lawrence as we got back into the house. "Sabre might have—" I broke off as the telephone shrilled and went to answer it. I thought it might be about Edith and my heart jerked a little. "Annabel . . . Mary! This is a nice surprise. We've just got in. Yes, yes, Lawrence is here. I'll put you through to him." I handed him the receiver.

"Yes, Mary?" Lawrence was smiling as he took the phone but his smile faded after a few seconds. "When did this happen? I see. We were out. Yes, I will. Thank you for calling. I'm sorry you were troubled. Bye. Yes, I'll give Annabel your love."

"What's wrong?" I asked as he replaced the receiver. "Something has happened . . ."

"Belinda slashed her wrists this afternoon. Her neighbour found her a couple of hours ago and they've taken her to hospital."

"Oh, Lawrence, that's awful," I said, staring at him in horror. "Is she going to be all right?"

"She's in a pretty bad way and asking for me." He sighed and ran his hand over his hair, looking shocked and pale. "I'm sorry, Annabel. I have to go to her."

"Yes, of course," I said. "You were afraid of this, but you couldn't be with her all the time. You mustn't blame yourself."

"I don't," he said. "I've tried to talk to her. I spent a lot of time comforting her after her mother died, but she wouldn't listen. She needs professional help."

"Perhaps she will get it now."

"If she lives." He looked grim. "I don't want to rush off, Annabel – but I have to."

"I'll pack your things."

"Leave them," he said and reached out to take me into his arms. "I'll be back as soon as I can. We have some serious talking to do. I want to get this thing with Edith sorted out."

"Yes, that's my first priority. I shan't feel settled in my mind until I know where she is." I kissed him. "Drive carefully, darling, and don't worry about us. We'll be fine."

"I'll ring you as soon as I can, and I'll be down again before the weekend."

He called to Sabre, who came running, and went back out to his car. I put my arm about Anthony's shoulders and we went to the door to wave them off.

"I wish Laurie and Sabre didn't have to leave, Mum."

"So do I, darling." I drew him inside, locking and bolting the door after us. "We might go and live with them one day. How would you feel about that?"

229

"Great," he said and looked around. "It seems a bit empty here without them, doesn't it?"

"Yes," I replied. "It does."

The house became increasingly lonely and empty as darkness fell. Anthony had pleaded to stay up, but I insisted on his going to bed at his usual time.

"You were late last night and there's school tomorrow."

"Only another week, then it's the holidays. Can we go somewhere this year, Mum?"

"Yes, I think so. We'll go with Aunty Mary, unless Lawrence can make time to come with us."

"That would be the best of all," Anthony said sleepily. "'Night, Mum."

"Goodnight, darling."

I kissed his cheek, pulled the covers up around him, then went downstairs.

I had never found Larkspur lonely before, but now I was listening for Sabre's paws pit-a-pattering in the hall. I wished desperately that the dog and his master were both still here.

I went round the house checking the doors and windows. They were all securely locked; the study door was locked too. I had kept it that way since the incident of the candles.

Perhaps Charles had been right all those years ago. He had wanted me to get rid of Edith then, warned me that she was a little strange. I might have had to ask her to leave then if he hadn't died, but after that I had been so ill and unhappy that I had come to rely on her.

A little breeze blew through the hall and I glanced round, startled. All the windows were closed or had I missed one? I checked again, trying the handles and making sure; they were all secure. Old houses were prone to mysterious draughts, creaking and groaning at night, and there were always strange little scurryings in the roof. Larkspur had always had its noises but they had never bothered me before. I had felt so welcome in this house, but I had never been here with just my son before . . .

The telephone made me jump. I rushed to answer it.

"Lawrence—"

"Lady Cheshire?"

The deep tones of a stranger unnerved me. "Yes. Who is this please?"

"Sergeant Ross, madam. You telephoned us this morning about an elderly lady you were concerned about I believe?"

"Yes, that's right. Have you found Edith?"

"That would be Miss Edith Fisher?"

"Yes. I gave your desk sergeant her name earlier."

"No, madam. We haven't found Miss Fisher. It was another little matter . . ."

"I don't understand," I said, feeling confused. "You asked if I rang, and my call was about Edith."

"Yes, madam. It was the coincidence, the two matters are probably not related. I happened to notice the phone number was the same—"

"Please will you explain? I'm not following you at all."

"Your telephone number was on her – that's Mrs Robson – pad, not Miss Fisher. Would you know Mrs Robson, by any chance? She lives in the village just—"

"Yes, I know where Mrs Robson lives," I replied impatiently. "She used to work for me years ago. She telephoned me yesterday morning and asked to see me. I have an appointment with her tomorrow morning." An icy finger trailed down my spine. "What is this all about, Sergeant Ross?"

He hesitated for a moment, "There has been an unpleasant incident, Lady Cheshire. We were called to Mrs Robson's house this afternoon. She – we have reason to believe that her death may not have been accidental."

"Mrs Robson is dead?" I felt as if he had thrown a bucket of cold water in my face and I started to shiver. "How did she die?"

"She received a nasty blow to the head, madam. We think it happened sometime during last evening, but that hasn't been confirmed. It could have been a fall, though the injuries are more consistent with her having been struck a blow from behind. What is rather strange is that there was no sign of a forced entry. If Mrs Robson was killed it seems likely that she knew her attacker, that she let whoever it was into the house herself."

"That's horrible," I said and my hand trembled on the receiver. "Have you any idea what happened or who might have done it?"

"Not at this time. We are following a few leads, one of which was your phone number. May I ask why Mrs Robson phoned you?"

231

"She had something to tell me. I don't really know what it was about. Perhaps she wanted to come back to work for me? I was to have gone to her house tomorrow."

"You weren't there by any chance yesterday afternoon or evening?"

"I was in Hunstanton with my son and a friend until late last night."

"And your friend will confirm that?"

"Certainly he will. Are you accusing me of something?"

"No, madam, simply eliminating you. Someone told us that Mrs Robson had a woman visitor either in the afternoon or early evening, they weren't positive of the time, and with your phone number being on the pad I thought I would pursue the inquiry a little further."

"We didn't get back to Larkspur until quite late, probably past ten in the evening."

"May I send someone to take a statement tomorrow?"

"Yes, yes, of course. I'll be here after I've taken my son to school."

I replaced the receiver feeling shocked and shaken. Surely the police could not really imagine that I might have killed Mrs Robson . . . poor, poor Mrs Robson. I drew a deep breath as it began to sink in. It was awful, unbelievable! If she had been deliberately struck over the head . . . A murder in our own little village!

My knees felt as if they were giving way and I had to sit down quickly. I was struggling to take in what Sergeant Ross had just told me. It was likely that Mrs Robson had been murdered and by a woman she had invited into her house.

Edith had gone out alone for the first time in years yesterday and she hadn't come back.

No, it wasn't possible! Edith might listen to my phone calls and read my private diaries but she wouldn't . . . I felt sick as I remembered that I had recorded my meeting with Mrs Robson and my feelings about what had happened over her dismissal. Had Edith found the key to my desk again? If she had read that I was thinking of asking her to move out of Larkspur . . . No, she wouldn't have killed Mrs Robson just for that. She might walk about with lighted candles, she might have made Sabre sick, she might even have poisoned poor Bramble, but she wouldn't, she couldn't possibly have killed Mrs Robson!

Surely she wasn't that evil? She couldn't be, not Edith!

I got up and went into the kitchen. The silence of the house seemed suddenly oppressive and I had to stop myself running wildly all over the place to check the doors and windows for a third time.

Edith had a key to the kitchen door! I rushed to push a chair beneath the handle. Would that hold it? Perhaps I should put a table across it. Even if she managed to get in then I would be woken by the noise.

"Stop panicking," I told myself. "This is nonsense. Mrs Robson probably fell and hit her head; the police were just following up leads. Besides, Edith wouldn't hurt us."

Even if Mrs Robson had been killed it didn't have to mean that Edith was her murderer – and yet it was strange that it had happened now.

I filled the kettle and switched it on. Edith surely didn't have the strength to murder anyone. She was over seventy! Yet I knew that she did have a wiry strength that was amazing for her age. She could lift heavy objects and open jars that were beyond me. A blow with a heavy instrument to the back of the head, this was ridiculous! Edith wasn't a murderer. How could she be? Ordinary, plain Edith who I had known for so many years.

Why had Mrs Robson wanted to see me? What could she possibly have had to tell me that might have cost her her life? If only I had gone to her house straight away! She might still have been alive.

No, I had to stop this. I was assuming in my own mind that Edith had been her mysterious visitor, if there really was a mystery. Perhaps it had been a friend or Mrs Robson's daughter, but not the one who had never lived in Bournmouth.

Edith had lied to me about that. Why? I tried to think back to that time, to remember just what had happened. I'd had all the worry of Anthony's illness and I'd been annoyed with both Mrs Robson and Edith for not calling the doctor sooner, but the trauma had brought Charles and I together again. We had decided to buy a new house nearer London, and that Edith should have her own cottage.

We had been talking about it that last night before he died. I remembered telling him something important . . . that his new batch of insulin had arrived and that he should be careful because it was much stronger . . . And yet there was something else that I just couldn't remember. Charles had died and my overwhelming sense of grief and sorrow had swept everything else away, but that evening was the last time Mrs Robson was in the house.

What had she seen or heard that had stuck in her mind for all these years? What was it that she felt I ought to know?

It was no good, I had no idea. And yet something was hovering in my subconscious, something that might give me the clue to the reason for Mrs Robson's murder. If it was a murder. Perhaps I was getting myself all worked up for nothing.

I went through into the hall and rang Lawrence's home number. His answerphone was on so he probably hadn't got back from the hospital yet. Why did everything always go wrong at once? If only he was here so that I could talk it over with him.

"I've had some disturbing news," I said into the receiver. "It might have a bearing on Edith's disappearance. I think she may have done something terrible, Lawrence, but I can't be sure. I hate to bother you at the moment but this may be important. Please ring me tomorrow if you can. I'm very worried. I hope Belinda is recovering. I love you. Bye."

It was almost midnight. There was no point in waiting up for Lawrence's call any longer. I was tired so I might as well go to bed, though I doubted I should sleep with so much on my mind, but at least I would be resting.

Twenty

I'm not sure what woke me but something must have done, for I lay in the darkness with my heart beating faster than normal and a horrid sense of something being wrong. My skin prickled and my ears strained to pick up whatever it was that had disturbed me, but there was only the faint, far away whine of a car engine and the usual creaking noises in the eaves.

Yet I was sure there was someone in the house. I sat up and switched on the lamp beside my bed, throwing back the covers and pulling on my thin, silk dressing gown as I slipped my feet into soft-soled mules. It was no good, I had to investigate.

My first instinct was to check Anthony's room and I hurried down the landing, my heart racing as the silence of the house closed around me. I was afraid but I didn't know why. Pushing open his door, I peeped inside. The faint glow of the outside security lights showed me that he was still fast asleep, his arm curled around his precious toy dog; I drew a breath of relief and pulled the door to after me.

Perhaps there was no one in the house; it was probably all a figment of my imagination because of what I had been thinking about before I went to bed. I hadn't expected to get any sleep, but obviously I had dozed off. Could I have had a nightmare? Was that what had woken me so suddenly?

Turning away from Anthony's room I hesitated, and went to look in Edith's own bedroom. Her bed was untouched and the relief washed over me: she wasn't back. I was alarming myself for nothing. I was about to return to my own room when I heard a slight sound from downstairs and stiffened, a chill running down my spine. There was someone else here! My instinct had been right.

It had to be Edith! Deep down inside me, I knew it was her; I had been expecting her to come even though I had hoped she wouldn't. I had no idea how she had managed to get in, but there was no doubt in my mind that she was here. The oppressive feeling I had experienced earlier had returned but it was much stronger now; it was in the air, thick and fetid, almost like smoke. I could smell something burning – wax! Candle wax. But it was so strong! What was she up to?

"Edith! Where are you?"

I ran to the head of the stairs and then I stopped and caught my breath: the hall was a blaze of light . . . the flickering, eerie glow of innumerable candles of all shapes and sizes and colours. As I walked slowly down the stairs I could see that she had stood them everywhere, on tables, on chairs, on the floor, on the windowsills. It gave the house a strangely hypnotic atmosphere that drew me on and on and on, following the trail of fire.

"Annabel . . . Annabel . . ." The whispering voice came to me from the darkness beyond that blaze of light.

I turned towards the study, sensing that she would be there. I had locked the door but if I could not keep her out of my house what was the use of locking doors inside it?

"Annabel, come to me . . ."

I felt as if I were in a walking nightmare. It was almost like the time of the green darkness when the whispers had followed me, flitting across my mind like ghostly shadows, and everything seemed unreal. This was unreal; it was not, could not be happening, and yet I knew that it was and that Edith would be waiting for me in the study.

The door was wide open and the room was blazing with the flickering light of so many candles that I blinked as the brightness hurt my eyes and at first I could not see her. I put up my hand to shield my eyes.

"Edith, where are you?"

"Over here, Annabel. In the shadows, look into the shadows."

I glanced towards the sound and saw her in the corner of the room well away from the window. She was wearing a black dress and it was hard to pick her out, impossible to see her face.

"What are you doing, Edith? You promised me you wouldn't do this anymore. You know I don't like you to have candles in the house."

"You break your promises, too. You promised me I would

236

always have a home with you, but you don't want me anymore. You tell lies, Annabel, but I know the secrets of your heart. I know all about you. What you do, where you go and what you think—"

"Is that what all this has been about? Why you stayed out all night? Did you do it to punish me, Edith, because you read my diary and you were afraid? But you know I wouldn't desert you. I'll buy you a cottage of your own and I'll look after you."

"I can't trust you anymore. You want to send me away, away from you and my child, you want to take him away from me."

There was something odd about her voice. I peered into the shadows trying to see her face, but I could see only the dark, shapeless mass of her body and the white of her hair.

"You can still see Anthony sometimes. I promise, Edith. We'll come and visit you, we won't forget you." I would have promised anything at that moment to buy time. The fear was creeping over me and turning my blood to ice water.

"You tell lies, Annabel. You're just like all the others. You're going to betray me, after all I've done for you." She sounded so accusing as if I had somehow let her down.

"What do you mean, Edith? What have you done for me? I know you've looked after my house, but I gave you a home and I paid you – now I'm going to make you a present of your own cottage. Why do you say I betrayed you?"

"You were going to let *him* send me away."

"Lawrence has nothing to do with this."

"I mean *him*, the *other one*, the one in the shadows. He's always there watching me, watching and waiting, but he won't get me. I'm too clever for him. I always was."

"Who are you talking about, Edith?"

I was chilled right through. She was talking so strangely and her voice was odd; it was Edith but it didn't sound like her, she was almost childish, petulant.

"He was cheating on you, Annabel. He was still seeing her even though he promised he wouldn't. He would have hurt you again if . . ."

"Are you talking about Charles?"

She had to be! It was Charles she saw in the shadows; she lit the candles to keep him away from her: she was afraid of him.

"Why are you afraid of him, Edith? Why is Charles always watching you? Why does he wait for you in the shadows?" I was beginning to feel an ominous dread and there was a pounding at my temples.

"He wants to take me with him. He's waiting in the dark, like the devil; the devil frightens me, Annabel. I know he's after my soul, he wants to carry me off to hell."

"Why are you afraid of Charles? What did you do that he should want to punish you?"

All of a sudden I knew the answer. I had picked up the telephone at the end of their conversation that morning, the morning of the day Charles had taken his fatal overdose. Edith had told me he had telephoned to ask about some papers, but I was sure now that he had actually rung to ask me if he had done his insulin before he left that morning. I was as certain of it as if I had been there.

"What did you do, Edith? Did you tell Charles he hadn't done his insulin . . ." My blood froze as I realised what else she had done – what Mrs Robson had seen her do! "You changed the bottles in the old box for some from the new one, didn't you? You heard me tell him to use the old box up first. You knew the new bottles contained a much stronger dosage. You killed Charles. You murdered my husband just as surely as if you had plunged a knife into his heart!"

It suddenly all slotted into place and I knew exactly how it must have happened. Edith had heard us talking that night, and she had been afraid that Charles was going to send her away. He had gone to talk to Mrs Robson and Edith had decided to seize her chance to swop the insulin bottles, hoping that Charles in his usual absentminded way would not realise what had happened and take an overdose. She couldn't have known that I would oversleep the next day and that fate would give her the chance to make sure that he took far more than he needed . . . how she must have laughed when he accepted her word that he had not used his insulin that morning! Poor, poor Charles, who had warned me not to trust her, had fallen into her trap.

Mrs Robson must have seen Edith doing something to the insulin bottles but not quite understood the significance. That was the reason Edith had told her not to come in again. She had hoped that no one would ever guess what she had done and it had worked. Her crime had been more successful that she could have dreamed. No one even suspected it was anything other than an accident. She had got away with it for years, until I bumped into Mrs Robson that afternoon in Cambridge.

That was the turning point: once she'd realised that Mrs Robson was going to tell me of her suspicions, she had known it was all over, so she had killed her.

"You killed Charles," I said in a choked voice. "And now you've killed Mrs Robson because you thought she was going to tell me what she saw that last evening."

"I did it for you, Annabel," she said and moved towards me out of the shadows. "He would only have hurt you – you wanted him to die. You hated him. You hated him because he had betrayed you with that woman."

She looked so odd, so unlike herself. The candlelight turned her skin to the colour of old parchment and her eyes had an unnatural shine that made my blood run cold.

"I didn't hate Charles," I said. "He hurt me and made me unhappy but I still cared for him. We were going to try again. You knew that, Edith. You heard us talking that night."

"All men betray you in the end, don't you know that yet, Annabel? You've been hurt by them as I was hurt . . ." She moved towards me, her hands outstretched like skinny claws. "We're alike, you and I. We always were, that's why I knew I could trust you, you had secrets just as I . . ." She stopped and stared at me, seeming bewildered. "But you don't want me anymore, you're sending me away, away from my baby,

"Anthony is my baby. You gave your son away, Edith."

Her eyes stared at me blankly. "No, you're wrong. They took him away from me, said I wasn't fit to be a mother. I begged them to let me keep him." She caught herself up, seeming to come back from wherever she had been in the past. "You shouldn't have said those things about me in your diary, Annabel. I thought you were my friend. I don't like you anymore."

Suddenly I saw that she had a carving knife in her hand; she must have concealed it about her, but now she was gripping the handle, and holding it poised to strike. The blade gleamed wickedly silver in the light of the candles as she drew her arm back and then lunged towards me.

"No, Edith!" I screamed and dodged away from her. "I'm still your friend. I'll help you. I promise I'll help you."

"Liar! You want me locked away," she cried. "You tried to

lock me out of your house, but you couldn't keep me out any more than you could keep your secrets hidden from me. I was always too clever for you."

I backed away from her, my mind seeking some way of escape. It wouldn't be enough just to run from her: my son was asleep upstairs in his bed and she was dangerous – insane! She had always been a little odd, I realised that now, but something had pushed her right over the edge.

"Please listen to me, Edith," I pleaded. "You're frightened by what you've done, but I understand. I know why you did all those terrible things. You don't have to kill me. I won't betray you. You know I'm your friend. I always have been."

She stared at me uncertainly. There was a flicker of fear in her eyes and I believed that perhaps somewhere inside her there was just enough of the old Edith left to reason with. I had to try and reach her.

"Don't be frightened, Edith. I'll tell everyone it wasn't your fault; they will understand. You won't be punished. You're just not very well. You need to be looked after for a while . . ." I walked towards her very steadily and slowly, my hand reaching for the knife. "Give it to me, Edith. Stop all this silliness. We'll go into the kitchen and have a nice cup of tea."

"A cup of tea, Annabel?" She blinked at me. "Yes, a cup of tea would be nice."

"Give me the knife then."

I reached out to take it. For a moment she stared at me and I thought she was going to let me have the knife, but then the look of bewilderment faded. It was replaced by one of such cunning and evil that I gasped and drew back.

"You don't think I'm stupid enough to fall for that one, Annabel?" The tone of her voice had changed again, becoming cold, confident and cocky. She gave a high-pitched laugh. "Once you've got me in the kitchen making tea you'll phone the police and let them take me away. You don't want me here. You want to be with your lover." Her mouth curved in a sly smile. "I know all about your lovers and your dreams, you've told me everything in those diaries. You thought you killed your mother in that fire. I could have told you the truth—"

"What do you mean?" She was lying. What could she know about the fire? It had happened long before she came to my grandmother's old house.

240

"She did it – your mother. She took the guard away from the fire, then she went out when he called to her. It was his fault for telling her to hurry and making her flustered, but he blamed you, Annabel. He blamed you because he knew it was his fault."

"How do you know all this?" Why should I believe her? Yet her words carried the ring of truth.

"Your grandmother confided in me. She always sensed it but he told her in the end. It was the reason he drove himself off the road because he could not bear to live with his own guilt any longer."

"And you knew . . . you knew but you never told me."

"You didn't ask me." She began to laugh wildly, her eyes brilliant in the candlelight. "I liked reading your secrets, Annabel. I liked knowing about your dreams and your guilt; it gave me power over you and you never suspected—"

"You wicked, evil old woman! I want you out of my house now. Do you hear me? You get out tonight!" In my anger I had lost all caution.

"Not until I've done what I came to do!"

She lunged at me again with the knife. This time I didn't back away. Her taunts about my past had made me angry. All those years of feeling guilty and she had known the true cause of the fire! She could have saved me so much pain but she had preferred to use her knowledge against me. As her arm went back to strike I caught her wrist. Somehow I was no longer afraid of her; my fingers tightened, digging into her skinny flesh, twisting, hurting her, forcing her to drop the knife. She was strong and she fought me desperately, but I was fighting for my life.

Her fingers uncurled and the knife dropped to the floor. I tried to kick it under the settee but she pushed me off balance and I stumbled against a small wine table, sending it flying with all its bits and pieces. In that instant Edith grabbed the knife and came at me again. We struggled and I felt the blade score my left arm, making me cry out with pain. For some reason that gave me renewed strength and I hit out at her, punching her in the stomach and then slapping her across the face. The knife flew from her hand and went sliding across the floor, disappearing into the shadows. She looked towards the corner of the room, seemed startled, then gave a cry of terror and backed away from

241

me, holding up her arm to shield her face as if she had seen something so horrible that she could not bear to look at it.

"No!" she screamed. "Get away from me . . . get away from me."

"Edith?"

I glanced towards the corner of the room but there was nothing there, nothing I could see.

"Get away, make him get away, ahhh—"

Suddenly I could smell burning and I swung round. When I had knocked into the wine table a candle had fallen onto the chair and a cushion was on fire. I looked around in desperation, then I pounced on a pair of long brass tongs from the fireplace and picked up the flaming cushion, holding it at arm's length as I deposited it in the empty grate where it burnt fiercely, filling the room with an acrid smoke. The candle had rolled onto the floor and was scorching the polished wood parquetry. I snatched it up and blew out the flame. When I turned back Edith had gone.

"Edith! Edith! Where are you?"

A draught was making the candles flicker, one of them ominously near the curtains. I switched on the electric lights and began blowing out the candles, all the while aware that Edith was somewhere in the house and that she was mad – completely insane. I wanted to follow her, to telephone for help, but the candles were too dangerous to leave.

The cushion was safe enough now and the last candle was out. I picked up the brass poker. Edith was quite likely to attack me again. Going out into the hall I saw the candles were still burning there but I couldn't waste more time, though I blew out those I passed on my way to the bottom of the stairs; the others would do later. I had the lights on now and that strange eerie atmosphere had gone. I was sharply aware of the danger to myself and my son.

"Edith," I called as I went upstairs. "Edith, where are you? Don't be frightened. I only want to talk to you. No one is going to hurt you. I won't let them."

My arm was smarting where she had stabbed me and I could feel blood trickling from the wound, but I had no time to waste. Where was Edith? What was she doing? She had wanted to kill me but something in the study had frightened her so much that she had fled in terror. A scream from upstairs made my blood curdle. That was my son! I raced up the stairs and tore along the landing to his room.

Edith was standing over his bed, a lighted candle in her hand. The curtains at the window were on fire, so was what looked like a pile of his comics in the middle of the room. She was obviously intending to set his room on fire while he slept but fortunately he had woken.

"What are you doing?" Fear made my voice a hoarse whisper. "You love Anthony. He's your baby, Edith. You love him . . . you can't do this to him."

She was staring at me in that terrifyingly blank way and I knew she was no longer capable of rational thought; it was useless to try and reach her.

"Mum." Anthony was wide awake and frightened. "Mum, she's going to kill me."

"Don't worry, darling. She won't hurt you. I promise." I was moving very slowly towards them. "Edith, he's your baby. You can't hurt your own baby."

She blinked at me, her pale eyes owlish and fixed. "My baby . . ."

I was close enough now.

"Anthony! Run!" I cried and threw myself at her. "Run downstairs! Now! Go quickly!"

He scrambled across the bed as I began to wrestle with Edith. She gave a scream of rage and dropped the candle onto the bed as we fought like two tigresses, clawing, biting, scratching and spitting. In the study I had been fighting for my own life, now I was fighting for my child. My precious, beloved son was in danger from this monster and I no longer saw her as a woman I had known half my life.

I hit her with my poker but she caught it and pulled hard, almost wrenching it from me; I hung on and managed to strike her right wrist hard. She gave a howl of pain like a demented animal, then backed away from me, her teeth bared in a snarl like a cornered beast, her eyes swivelling from side to side in fear.

"Get away from me!" I shouted. "Get out of my house now. If you try to touch Anthony again I'll kill you. I'll kill you."

I was screaming my threats at her, all control gone as I advanced purposefully. There was so much rage in me. In that one terrible moment I could have killed. I *would* have killed to save the life of my son!

Edith stared at me, beginning to whimper like a mindless idiot, her eyes rolling and the saliva dribbling from her slack mouth, then she turned and fled from the room as if all the devils in hell were after her. In that same instant I became aware of the thick, choking atmosphere and I glanced back – Anthony's bed was blazing and the whole room seemed to be on fire. Flames were shooting up the walls and smoke was billowing towards me in great clouds.

"Mum! Mum! Where are you?"

Anthony's cry galvanised me into action. I pulled the door of his room shut behind me and ran along the landing and down the stairs. My son was watching anxiously from the hall and I saw that one of the candles had fallen over and had set fire to the bottom of some long curtains. We had to get out! We had to get out now before the whole house went up in flames.

I grabbed my son's hand, snatched my car keys from the hall table and ran to the front door, dragging Anthony with me. The door was bolted and locked. I was shaking with fright as I wrestled with the bolts that seemed to have stuck, swearing and cursing in my panic, fearing that we were trapped – and then they suddenly shot back and the door was open, swinging wide on its hinges.

A breeze blew in as I pulled Anthony outside into the blessedly fresh air of the night, and then a sudden blaze of light blinded me as a car swept into the drive. I dragged my son away from the house. The car screeched to a halt and someone jumped out.

"Annabel!" Lawrence's voice came to me from out of the darkness. "I drove straight down when I got you message. What's happened? Why are you out here in your nightclothes?"

"It's Edith," I gasped. "She tried to kill me with a carving knife, then she set fire to Anthony's bedroom."

"My God!" he cried. "I tried telephoning on my way down, but I couldn't get through."

"She must have taken the receiver off," I gasped. "I didn't notice it because of the candles . . ."

Lawrence's face was deathly pale. "Where is she?"

I glanced back towards the house. "I think she's still in there—" He started forward but I caught his arm, trying to hold him back. "She's gone mad, Lawrence. Be careful."

"Use my car phone to ring the fire brigade," he said. "I'll have to try to get her out, Annabel, before it's too late."

I led Anthony towards Lawrence's car. He was shaking so I wrapped him in a tartan rug from the back seat and settled him in.

"Are you all right, darling? She didn't hurt you?"

"No . . ." He looked at me, his eyes wide and scared. "She just frightened me. Lawrence won't get hurt, will he?"

"No, of course not. He'll be back in a few minutes."

I tried to sound confident but I was far from being sure of anything. I still had that sense of being in a nightmare and my hands were shaking as I dialled the emergency numbers: my teeth chattered as if I were cold but it was a mild night.

"What service please?"

"F-fire, police and ambulance," I said. "M-my house is on fire and my housekeeper has gone mad. She tried to kill me and she's still in the house. Lawrence has gone in to get her but—" I was gibbering like an idiot."

"Steady, madam," the female operator said. "Try to calm down. Give me your name and your address slowly and clearly."

"A-annabel Cheshire. Larkspur House—"

I heard a sudden whooshing sound and looked towards the house, feeling startled. Flames were shooting through the roof and smoke was billowing into the air: Larkspur had become an inferno. I dropped the phone as I remembered that Lawrence was inside it.

"Mum!" Anthony cried in alarm.

"Stay here!" I yelled and starting running towards the house. "Lawrence! Lawrence! Where are you?"

The stink of burning wood and old plaster was strong as I went in and looked up at the landing; black smoke was pouring down the stairs and it was impossible to see more than halfway up. Lawrence was up there. What had Edith done to him? Was he hurt? I started up the stairs, calling to him to get out before it was too late, then I saw him coming through the smoke towards me; he had a handkerchief over his mouth and he was coughing and spluttering.

"Get out," he cried as he saw me, then caught my arm and

propelled me towards the door. There was a fearful spitting and cracking sound from above us and a part of the ceiling crashed onto the upper landing, sending showers of burning wood and plaster raining all around us.

We ran out of the front door, gasping and choking as the acrid smoke followed us out. I glanced back and saw that the fire had raced along the dry wooden beams of the house and was shooting up into the sky. As I had always feared, Larkspur had been a tinder box, and the fire had spread through the attics within minutes, becoming a death trap.

For a few seconds neither of us could speak; the smoke had made us cough and we had trouble getting our breath.

"Edith?" I asked when I could breathe again.

"She locked herself into her room. I tried to break down the door but it was too solid, it wouldn't give. There's nothing we can do, Annabel. It's probably already too late."

We had reached the car now. Anthony was hugging the rug around himself and crying. I got in the back with him and put my arms about him, hugging him to me and kissing the top of his head as I whispered to him that it was all right now. He was quite safe, we were all safe. He clung to me and wept as Lawrence started the car and backed out of the drive. We parked a few yards down the road in a layby and looked back towards the house.

"Give me the keys to your car, Annabel. I'll fetch it. We might as well save what—" Lawrence's words were drowned by the huge explosion that rocked the car on its wheels. We jumped out of the car and stared at the house as a fireball shot into the sky. "Bloody hell! What was that?"

The night sky was red as the whole house went up in flames. We all watched fascinated and awestruck as the sirens began to wail and screech and suddenly it was all noise and confusion.

Then I was no longer aware of the emergency services rushing to our aid or of Larkspur itself. The lights were flashing behind my eyes: red, gold and orange, so bright that they hurt and the screaming had begun . . . such terrible, agonised, inhuman screams that they filled my head, making me dizzy.

"Mummy! Mummy, come quick," I whispered. "The baby's on fire, come quick!"

The pictures played in front of my eyes like an old movie in slow motion. Once again I was a child – a very frightened child. Then my mother came and I tried to tell her that the baby's cot was on fire, but I could only point frantically and cry.

She was wearing a frilly blouse and floating skirt. She screamed as she saw the fire had started from a log that had fallen onto the mat and caught a newspaper she had left lying there; it had spread rapidly to the cot, catching the nylon frills and engulfing the baby in its flames. She reached into the cot to grab the child and her clothes caught at once.

"Daddy! Daddy! Come quickly. Mummy's on fire." I put my hands over my ears as I heard my mother start to scream. "Mummy! Mummy! She's burning, she's burning."

"Annabel! Annabel, wake up! It's your dream, it's only your dream." Lawrence shook me, his hands digging into the soft flesh of my upper arms. "Annabel, it's all right. I'm here. You're safe. Anthony is safe. It's all over, darling. It's all over."

I became aware that I was crying. I was a woman, not a child: Larkspur was on fire and fire engines were screaming up to the house, people were everywhere. Two police cars had arrived and an ambulance.

"Is the lady hurt, sir?" A police officer came over to us.

"She's in shock," Lawrence said. "And she's been bleeding. Someone tried to stab her with a carving knife."

"Would that be the housekeeper, sir?"

"Yes. Edith Fisher. She went berserk and set the house on fire after she attempted to kill Annabel. I tried to get her out when I arrived but she locked herself in and I couldn't break the door down. The smoke was so thick by then that we had to leave her."

"If she's still in there she's dead by now. No one is going to get out of that. Anyone else in there? Any pets?"

"No, thank goodness," Lawrence said. "There was just us and the housekeeper."

"Right, sir. Leave it to us now. Best get the lady to hospital. What did you say her name was again?"

"It's Annabel," I whispered. "Annabel Cheshire. Thank you for your concern, officer, but I'm perfectly all right." I took a step forward and then the darkness came rushing in like a great wind and I felt myself falling, falling, falling into the black void.

*　　　*　　　*

247

I opened my eyes to see Lawrence standing beside the hospital bed. He was carrying an armful of wonderful red roses, their perfume a welcome change from the antiseptic which seemed to hang over the wards. I knew that he had brought me flowers every day since I was admitted, but until now I had not really appreciated them. He smiled as he saw I was awake.

"Feeling better, darling?"

"Yes, much better, thank you," I said and stretched out my hand to him. "Where is Anthony? Is he all right?"

"He's in the car with Sabre and he's fine, Annabel. They kept him in one night just to make sure he hadn't inhaled too much smoke — me too — then they let us out. You're the one we've all been been worried about. You were delirious for a couple of days and you had a bit of an infection in your arm, but you're fine now."

"Yes, the pain has gone at last and I feel really well. The doctor visited earlier and he says I can go home tomorrow." I caught my breath as for a moment I saw the night sky turned crimson and smelt the acrid smoke. "Larkspur . . ."

Lawrence held my hand tighter. "I'm sorry, darling; there's very little left of it. What there is will have to come down."

"I suppose so." I took a deep, shaky breath. "Will you take care of things for me, Lawrence? I don't know whether the insurance company will pay out because in a way it wasn't accidental."

"But it wasn't your fault either. Don't worry, darling. I know how to handle that side of it for you, but I can't give you Larkspur back as it was, I'm afraid."

"In a strange way I'm — I'm glad. It's as if I've closed a door on the past once and for all. I don't think I would ever have wanted to live there again after—"

"You remembered, didn't you?" he asked gently. "Just before that police officer came over and you fainted. The shock brought it back. You remembered what happened to your mother."

"Yes." My eyes moistened with tears as the years between slid back like silken curtains and I remembered that day as if had been only yesterday. "My mother took down the fireguard to poke the logs, then my father shouted to her that he couldn't find his clean shirt and she went out in a fluster to look for it. In her hurry she forgot to replace the guard. I was at the window watching the snow – the flakes were so pretty as they floated against the glass – I was thinking that it would soon be Christmas, then I smelt something burning. I turned around and saw that a log had fallen out onto the mat and set fire to a newspaper. Before I realised what was happening the flames licked across the carpet and caught the nylon frills on the cot. I rushed to the door and screamed for my mother. She came running and snatched at the baby, but it was too late. His clothes were on fire. He – he was burning and her clothes caught . . ." I had to stop because I was crying too hard to continue.

"You saw the whole thing. You poor little devil," Lawrence said in a voice roughened by compassion. "You were five years old and you did your best to save your brother, then you were blamed for his death. It was so unfair, no wonder you were traumatised. It could have ruined your whole life."

"It almost did," I said. "My grandmother knew how it started but she never told me. I've just discovered that Edith knew – she taunted me with it just before she tried to kill me – but I wasn't told. All these years I've thought that I might have . . ." I caught back a sob.

If only my grandmother had talked to me about the fire, told me just how it had started and why my father had turned against me. Perhaps then I might have remembered for myself long ago; I might never have been haunted by that dream of the match, never have felt so guilty, and my life might have been different in so many ways.

"I suppose she did what she thought was best," Lawrence said. "Out of a mistaken desire to protect you, I expect." He wiped the tears from my face with his fingertips, then bent to kiss me, his thick hair falling across his brow in the way I loved. "It's all over now, my darling. The past is a closed door. You – we – have the future before us, and it's going to be wonderful."

"Yes." I smiled up at him as the last lingering shadows retreated and the bright colours faded, disappearing with the mists that had overshadowed my life for so long, and I knew that I would never be haunted by my memories again. "Yes, it's going to be wonderful."

I would be Lawrence's wife – a woman absolved of guilt – normal, happy and free.

AFTERWORD

My diaries were lost in the fire and perhaps that was just as well, but I have set everything down exactly as I remember it, and this is the last time I shall write in my journal.

Lawrence and I went back to Larkspur one last time. As he had told me, there was very little left to see, only ashes and the blackened remains of some walls. I understand that they could find nothing of Edith, but I have had some ashes from the fire buried at the crematorium and prayers have been said for her soul; I hope with all my heart that she is at peace.

We have decided to have the remains of Larkspur cleared and the ground planted with trees. The land belongs to Anthony and one day he may wish to sell it or build again, but that will not be for many years, when the memories have long faded.

I shall never go there again. For me the past is buried and, if not forgotten, at least laid to rest.

I am happy now as Lawrence's wife and soon I shall have his child. I have no need or wish to look back.